VANISHED

ALSO BY DR. DAVID JEREMIAH

VANISHED

A NOVEL

DR. DAVID JEREMIAH

WITH SAM O'NEAL

THOMAS NELSON
Since 1798

Vanished

Published in Nashville, Tennessee, by Thomas Nelson. Thomas Nelson is a registered trademark of HarperCollins Christian Publishing, Inc.

Published in association with Yates & Yates, www.yates2.com.

Thomas Nelson titles may be purchased in bulk for educational, business, fundraising, or sales promotional use. For information, please email SpecialMarkets@ThomasNelson.com.

Scripture quotations are taken from the King James Version unless marked otherwise. Public domain.

Scripture quotations marked NIV are taken from The Holy Bible, New International Version®, NIV®. Copyright © 1973, 1978, 1984, 2011 by Biblica, Inc.® Used by permission of Zondervan. All rights reserved worldwide. www.Zondervan.com. The "NIV" and "New International Version" are trademarks registered in the United States Patent and Trademark Office by Biblica, Inc.®

Scripture quotations marked TLB are taken from The Living Bible. Copyright © 1971. Used by permission of Tyndale House Publishers, a Division of Tyndale House Ministries, Carol Stream, Illinois 60188. All rights reserved.

Scripture quotations marked NLT are taken from the Holy Bible, New Living Translation. © 1996, 2004, 2015 by Tyndale House Foundation. Used by permission of Tyndale House Publishers, Inc., Carol Stream, Illinois 60188. All rights reserved.

Publisher's Note: This novel is a work of fiction. Names, characters, places, and incidents are either products of the author's imagination or used fictitiously. All characters are fictional, and any similarity to people living or dead is purely coincidental.

Any internet addresses (websites, blogs, etc.) in this book are offered as a resource. They are not intended in any way to be or imply an endorsement by Thomas Nelson, nor does Thomas Nelson vouch for the content of these sites for the life of this book.

Library of Congress Cataloging-in-Publication Data

Names: Jeremiah, David, 1941- author | O'Neal, Sam, 1981- author
Title: Vanished : a novel / David Jeremiah with Sam O' Neal.
Description: Nashville : Thomas Nelson, [2025] | Summary: "As leader of a special
   military unit charged with stopping potential pandemics before they spread, John
   "Haggs" Haggerty has a front-row seat to the sharp increase in natural disasters
   that precede the Rapture—including plagues, earthquakes, famines, wars, and
   rumors of war. And each crisis is becoming more intense"—Provided by publisher.
Identifiers: LCCN 2025013952 (print) | LCCN 2025013953 (ebook) |
   ISBN 9781400351541 paperback | ISBN 9781400350735 hardcover |
   ISBN 9781400350759 epub | ISBN 9781400350766
Subjects: LCGFT: Christian fiction | Novels
Classification: LCC PS3610.E684 V36 2025 (print) | LCC PS3610.E684 (ebook) |
   DDC 813/.6—dc23/eng/20250410
LC record available at https://lccn.loc.gov/2025013952
LC ebook record available at https://lccn.loc.gov/2025013953

Printed in the United States of America

25 26 27 28 29 LBC 5 4 3 2 1

PART 1

CHAPTER 1

I t's gotta be here somewhere."

John Haggerty shifted his perch atop a small, cramped desk in the middle of a small, cramped office at the edge of the small, cramped city of Heraklion on the island of Crete. He dug his left hand blindly through an open drawer at the front of the desk. His right hand wiped another drop of sweat off his forehead. "You see anything?"

Leaning against the opposite corner of the room, a tall Black man wearing US Army fatigues shook his head. "What are you going to say when she finally gets here and finds you rooting around in her desk?"

"*If* she comes in, I'll muster all my available charm to apologize profusely," said Haggerty. "Then I'll ask her very politely to please turn on the air-conditioning because it's way too— Hold on . . ." He had slipped his hand into a second drawer, and he pulled it out to reveal a white rectangular remote control. "Bingo."

The other man smiled, then shook his head again. "I doubt it works."

Haggerty said nothing. He pointed the remote at a larger white rectangle bolted to the wall above the desk—an independent HVAC unit. The European kind, designed for a single room. He pushed a button. When the unit emitted a soft beep and rattled to life, Haggerty looked over at his friend and tilted his head slightly to the left. He raised one eyebrow. *Told you.*

The other man shook his head a third time. Still smiling. *No chance.*

Haggerty reached up and placed his hand in front of the small plastic flap now oscillating up and down at the base of the AC unit. The stream of air flowing out from the machine was warm—warmer than room temperature.

Frowning, he pressed a different button several times. *Beep. Beep. Beep. Beep.*

He kept his hand in the still-warm flow of air as he looked back toward his friend. He raised his eyebrow another quarter of an inch, then shrugged. *Maybe it'll kick in?*

The tall man in the corner pointed his chin at the remote, then toward the second drawer at the front of the desk, which was still open. *May as well put it back. Not happening.*

After another thirty seconds of waiting, Haggerty lowered his hand. He tossed the remote to the top of the desk in a rare gesture of defeat.

No gloating came from Caleb Johnson, wordless or otherwise. He stood still and quiet for several moments. A tower in uniform. A living plumb line. With his slender legs, frame, and neck and large bald head, he looked a bit like an upside-down exclamation point. When he did speak, his voice was deep and resonant and clear. It was a professor's voice. Or a preacher's voice.

He pointed to the manila folder squashed under Haggerty's leg. "You've got about twenty different items on those pieces of paper, and each one would make today her worst day ever." He glanced at the empty chair behind the desk. "She's going to fight the whole thing. And she could make things difficult."

Haggerty snorted. "It's difficult no matter what she does."

"You know what I mean, Haggs."

Haggerty nodded.

"You're sure it's necessary."

Not a question, but Haggerty nodded again in answer. "I'm sure it's necessary."

They heard voices coming down the hall through the open office door. A man and a woman, both speaking Greek.

Elena Kazantis, the secretary-general of the Decentralized Administration of Crete, was a dynamo. She stomped her way into the room, hands swinging wildly in mid-conversation, her voice low and nasal—and continued forward for several more stomps until she was confronted by the sight of a strange man balanced on the corner of her desk. She had a sharp face with large, liquid eyes and a shock of black hair that tumbled over her shoulders and down the back of her blue and white dress.

Her colleague was a little taller, a little thinner, and much less observant. He almost bumped into her shoulder when she stopped short and was only able to avoid a collision by one-foot-hopping himself to the side and resting a hand on the nearest wall.

"What is this?" The secretary-general's eyes flashed at the intrusion. "Who are you?"

Haggerty remained seated on the desk. "Major General John Haggerty. United States Army. I'm afraid I've come with some bad news." He pulled out the manila folder from under his leg and handed it to the woman. "Official communication from the United States government, which includes my orders."

She opened the folder and glanced at the page, then looked back at Haggerty. "What it says? You tell me."

"It says the island of Crete is under quarantine by order of the US Army."

"Quarantine?"

Haggerty nodded. "It says all aspects of the quarantine will be managed by the Potential Pandemic Task Force, of which I am the commander."

"No, no, no." The Greek man spoke up for the first time, his voice a reedy tenor. "No pandemic on Creta."

Haggerty ignored him, keeping his eyes on the secretary-general. "It says our task force will take control of all airports on the island, including the international airports in Chania and here in Heraklion. All outgoing flights will be grounded, and all incoming flights will be denied access. It says all ports will be closed, and that ships from the Hellenic Coast Guard already docked in Crete will be used to patrol local waters and maintain the quarantine. It says—"

"Enough." She had a strong voice and a thick accent. Authoritative and confident. She didn't look angry yet, but Haggerty could tell she was starting to steam. "This is for the sickness in Rethymno. The virus. Yes?"

"Yes," said Haggerty. "But it's moved beyond Rethymno."

In the previous three weeks, more than a thousand people had been hospitalized in and around the city of Rethymno, which was centrally located on the island. Other cases had been identified in Chania to the west and Heraklion to the east. When cases were discovered on the nearby island of Rhodes, the Army sent Haggerty and his team to assess the situation.

Haggerty gestured toward the tall man still leaning against the corner. "This is Caleb Johnson, my executive officer."

Caleb stepped forward. "We're calling it SARS-CoV-12. It's a new type of coronavirus, and it's very serious."

The Greek man piped up again. "Coronavirus? It is like COVID?"

Caleb and Haggerty exchanged a glance, each raising an eyebrow. Several epidemics and pandemics had cut their way through the global population during the years since COVID-19, but most people still thought of 2020 as the baseline for worldwide disease.

You never forget your first, Haggerty reminded himself.

"It's worse than COVID," Caleb told the man. "Much worse."

"We're still running tests." Haggerty gestured to the manila folder in the woman's hand. "But what we know is in those files. And what we know is bad."

So far, most of the patients who had contracted this new version of SARS-CoV were relatively young. Twenties, thirties, and forties. Most developed a pronounced rattle in the chest because of overstimulated mucous glands in the lungs. After several days of worsening symptoms, most patients began coughing up blood. Then coughing up alarming amounts of blood. Then worse.

In the past five days, Haggerty's team had linked a total of 112 deaths to SARS-CoV-12 across the island of Crete.

The secretary-general looked at the manila folder as if it were a cobra coiled around her wrist. "What you are saying, a quarantine of the island—it is impossible. We have ten thousand tourists on Creta even this day. At least ten thousand."

Haggerty nodded. "They will not be allowed to leave for three weeks at the minimum. Probably longer. They'll need places to stay."

The woman sniffed, then scowled. "Tens of thousands more tourists booked for July and August. The ferries come and go between all the islands in Greece every day. The cruise ships come and go every day. This is life in Creta."

"Not anymore. Anyone not currently on the island will be denied access. Again, for at least three weeks but probably longer."

She shook her head, not worried about showing her disgust. "All of Greece lock down for COVID-19, and it was terrible for tourist season. Terrible for our people who have only four months to earn their living. We lock down again for monkeypox, and many Cretans cannot afford their homes. They cannot afford enough food." Her nostrils flared as she spoke. "When they tell us to lock down for the children's disease ... the ..."

"The RSV mutation," Haggerty said.

"Yes." She waved a hand. "That one. Greek government said we must lock down again, but the people refused. Cretans refused. We are tired of lockdown. Then came the bird virus, and the Greek government did not lock down. The people are finished with lockdown."

"I remember," he told her. "That's one of the reasons I'm here." Which was true. Each time a new pandemic locked a vise around the world, people became more resistant to lockdowns and other draconian protective measures. Many refused to participate even in the face of jail.

The Potential Pandemic Task Force had been formed as a solution to those issues. Its job—Haggerty's job—was to identify regional epidemics and nip them in the bud before they made the jump to global pandemics. He had been tasked with demonstrating brutal efficiency in a small space, such as Crete, because the global population as a whole was no longer willing to do what was necessary.

"The United States will help as much as we can," he said, trying to project compassion, "but hard times are coming for the people here. They will need to find a way to survive."

Elena's brows furrowed. Her voice rose. "No! You have no authority on Creta. You have no authority in Greece. How dare you come into this office and demand these things?"

Haggerty pointed again at the manila folder. "My orders are signed by the commander in chief of the United States Armed Forces. The president. By her authority, I am empowered to take whatever actions I deem necessary to evaluate epidemics and other medical emergencies, both foreign and domestic, that pose a potential threat to citizens of the United States. I am also empowered to take whatever actions I deem necessary to eliminate those threats in a manner that protects the lives of United States citizens."

"Your citizens," said Elena Kazantis. "Typical arrogance of America." She held up the manila folder. "These things you say"— she threw it down on the desk near Haggerty's leg, papers spilling out like a deck of cards—"these things will not happen. Please go!"

She turned away from Haggerty and Caleb and began speaking rapidly to her colleague in Greek.

"Madame Secretary." Haggerty's voice was calm.

She ignored him. Her hands swung back and forth as she continued giving what seemed like commands to the other man. He had taken out his phone and responded to whatever she was saying with short phrases and quick nods.

"Madame Secretary . . ."

Nothing.

"Elena." There was a slight elevation in Haggerty's tone. A hint of irritation. Of command.

She whirled around to face him. "This my desk you are sitting on. Get off. Move away from my chair. Go!"

Haggerty stood. He was two inches shorter than his XO but much broader in the chest and shoulders. Between them, they made an intimidating duo in the small office. The Greek man stepped back involuntarily, but Elena stood her ground. She continued to glare up at Haggerty, nostrils flaring.

Good, he thought. He would need tough people to make it through the next several weeks. Crete would need tough people.

"You take these." Elena swept up the folder and the papers from the top of the desk. "I say again, these things will not happen. Therefore, go!"

"These things are already happening." Haggerty spoke quietly, but he kept his eyes locked on hers. "Troops were deployed from the US Army base in Souda early this morning. My orders were set for zero eight hundred, which means"—he looked down at his watch, which read 8:09—"both airports have been grounded for nine minutes now. Same with the seaports. Same with the coast guard."

For the first time, Elena appeared visibly shaken. She placed a steadying hand on the desk Haggerty had just vacated. "You . . ." She took a moment to breathe. "You have done this?"

"Yes." Haggerty felt a little shaken himself, but he tried not to show even a hint of his uncertainty. This was the first time he'd invoked his authority to essentially commandeer the local government of a sovereign nation—an authority that had never been accepted or acknowledged by any nation outside the United States. This was a watershed moment, and he felt the weight of it.

The secretary-general seemed unable to believe what she was hearing. "Soldiers in the airports," she said, her voice low. "Soldiers in the cities?"

"Yes."

"No authority on Creta," she repeated, although with much less assurance. "The international community accept this?"

She seemed to be asking a genuine question, so he answered honestly. "Yes, we think they will. We've already spoken to the relevant NATO reps, and they understand the stakes. The secretary of state will be in Athens this afternoon to work with your prime minister. They're probably on the phone together right now."

Haggerty knew the U.S. would catch a lot of flak for this decision—for *his* decision. There would be official proclamations and condemnations from other governments, including some in Europe. There would be hyperbolic headlines in the press. *America*

Imposes Its Will Once Again—that kind of thing. And, of course, the United Nations would kick up a fuss, but it had been a long time since anybody had given any real credence to what the UN said or did.

In the end, Haggerty believed the quarantine would save millions of lives, not just in America but around the world. Which made his decision clear. Even so, he regarded the woman in front of him with considerable compassion and admiration. He'd do everything he could to carry the consequences of this moment, both now and in the future. But he was setting a heavy burden on her shoulders as well.

"I cannot allow this." She whispered the words at first, then spoke more firmly. "I will not allow you to do this."

"It's already done. The island is quarantined." Haggerty placed a hand on her shoulder. Lightly. The tips of his fingers barely touching the fabric of her dress. "Now I need your help."

Like most things about Crete, the helicopter flight from Heraklion back to the US base in Souda was striking. And colorful. And baked by the sun.

As the helicopter flew low along the Mediterranean coast, Haggerty's gaze followed the shifting shades of cobalt and sapphire where the deep sea merged into shallows and bays and beaches. His eyes were drawn most often to the wide swaths of silvery green and mossy green and forest green that seemed to cover every meter between the shoreline and the gray, rocky mountains at the center of the island. Olive groves. Mostly olives but also citrus and star pine and many vineyards.

Something about the precision of those groves resonated with Haggerty in a profound way. He responded to the planning involved. The dedication. Generations of Cretans had carefully cultivated each tree among the millions of trees dotting the coastlands, covering the hills, and even spreading like ranks of stationary soldiers across the chalky crags. Seen from above, the island was lovely in its vitality and its regimented order.

Once on the ground, Haggerty and Caleb ducked unconsciously away from the helicopter's whirling blades, then walked toward a group of staffers and soldiers waiting like expectant vultures for their turn to pounce. He and Caleb read papers. Checked screens. Heard reports. Answered questions. Issued orders. Then they both walked with long strides toward the hastily but efficiently expanded medical facilities now sprawling along the outskirts of the base.

"I'll be at the hospital for a bit," Haggerty said. "Quarantine center."

Caleb raised his eyebrows. "The girl?"

Haggerty nodded. He was trying to figure out how to explain his motives when his friend cut in.

"I'll get started on the paperwork." He took the folders out of Haggerty's hand. "And I'll put together some press releases. You take care of your patient."

"Thanks, Cay." Haggerty offered a grateful salute, then strode toward the on-base hospital. Once inside, he had himself washed and prepped. Sanitized and disinfected. Dressed in level A hazmat gear, which always made him feel like something out of a B movie filled with nuke-mutated monsters. As soon as he was cleared, he stepped into one of the small patient rooms near the center of the quarantine zone.

The room itself was sterile and relatively quiet. Neutral walls. No windows. Soft lights and softly whirring machines that occasionally offered a muted beep. There was a bed in the middle of the room, set close to the wall. There was a girl in the middle of the bed. Blue gown. White sheet. She lay on her side, facing away from the door. Knees tucked up toward her chest. Arms wrapped around her knees. A ball of humanity in the middle of an antiseptic collection of tubes and plastic sheets.

Haggerty walked around the side of the bed to see her face. He knew she was nineteen, but what he could see of her exposed skin looked much older. She was desiccated, her lips pulled down in a grimace of pain.

She smiled when she recognized him. "Dr. America."

"That's me," said Haggerty, though he didn't feel like a doctor. Not anymore. It had been decades since he graduated from Uniformed Services University. Then residency, several deployments as a combat surgeon, and three years at Walter Reed. That's when he'd transitioned over to administration. It was a better choice for the family, with more stability and better opportunities for advancement. But it hadn't been long before he missed the simplicity of working with specific patients and healing specific wounds—of dealing with solvable problems.

Administrative traumas were often much harder to handle.

Two years ago, he'd been offered command of a new unit—a special task force focused on the wave of epidemics and pandemics sweeping across the world. The Potential Pandemic Task Force had been formed after the hybridized avian influenza (called the duck flu because the first cases were in Oregon) infected billions and killed millions. That was after a novel version of RSV infected millions of children and killed tens of thousands. Which was after COVID-19 infected billions and killed millions. There were other pandemics, but those were the biggest.

Something had to be done. Too many lives had been lost and too much money spent (with far too little results). People were afraid of a world in which wars, natural disasters, and food shortages had become increasingly common—and nobody seemed to understand why. The United States Army still had budget resources (unlike the rest of the government) and was attempting to plug the gaps.

Haggerty had jumped at the promotion to commander because it felt like a chance to be a doctor again—to solve problems in the real world rather than keep wading through the shifting quagmire of political nonsense within the Army Medical Department. In practice, his life had become the worst of both worlds. He felt the weight of global bureaucracy pressing down on his head and the weight of billions of lives pressing down on his heart.

"Dr. America," said the girl, her voice raspy, "I thirsty."

He handed her a large thermos of ice water from a nearby tray table, the straw sticking out through the lid. His hazmat gloves were clunky but functional.

As she drank, he took a quick peek at her chart. Blood pressure and heart rate remained normal, but oxygen was down to 86 percent saturation, which was a big drop from yesterday. She'd started coughing up blood. Haggerty glanced over at the red stains on the front of her smock, then up at her face.

She was looking at him. Her gray eyes strained to penetrate the plastic visor, searching for his own. "My mother die?"

"Yes," said Haggerty. The mother had died several days ago. The girl already knew, but she kept asking whenever he came to see her. Maybe she was trying to wake up from a nightmare.

"My sister die?"

"Yes."

Her family was from Rethymno and had been caught up in the earliest wave of the disease. The mother owned a café downtown. The patient and her sister were two of the servers. The other three servers had caught the same illness. Two had recovered quickly, but the third died shortly after starting to cough up blood.

"Family die," said the girl. "But yesterday you say I be okay?"

"I said you were looking strong." He took a few seconds to ponder the difference between *were* and *are*. "I said I expect you to be okay—and I do."

"Dr. America . . . you good doctor?"

"Yes," he answered after a slight pause, offering what he hoped was a reassuring smile. "Good doctor."

"Good. Because you are bad liar."

Haggerty was struck by a moment of gaping surprise, then a guffaw erupted from inside his protective headwear. Then he laughed without reserve, bending over and resting one hand on his knee to regain his breath. He felt a little embarrassed to be carrying on this way in such a sterile environment, but he was also pleased. He'd forgotten how good it felt to laugh like this.

The girl watched as his laughter died down. Her face wore a triumphant grin that temporarily overshadowed her usual grimace of pain.

"Thank you, Sonia." The sound of her name made Haggerty wince in spite of his recent mirth. It was the same name he'd given his own daughter not too many years before this one was born.

"Thank you," he said again. "I needed that."

She nodded tiredly. Still smiling.

He reached over to touch the top of her hand with his gloved fingers but didn't quite make contact. The gesture carried him back across time and time zones to another set of slender fingers reaching out toward his own. Reaching for his chin. Reaching for a ball. Reaching for his keys.

"Sonia, we're learning new things every day. We're making progress toward treatments every day. And I'm going to do everything I can to get you back home soon."

He realized too late that *home* would be a painful word rather than a comforting one, but she showed no reaction.

"I need you to help me by staying strong," he said. "When you beat this thing, you'll help us figure out how to treat other people here on Crete and other people in different parts of Greece. You'll be a hero, like Hercules. Like Athena. You just have to hold on while we figure things out. Okay?"

She nodded as the last traces of her smile drained away. She was drifting toward sleep. "Good doctor." Her head sank a little lower into her pillow, and her eyes closed.

Haggerty stayed in the room a long time as she slept. He stood by the bed, the tips of his gloves still resting two inches from the tips of her fingers. He looked from her face to the chart still open at the bottom of the bed. Looked from her face to the machines as they whirred and beeped, whirred and beeped. Unceasing. Untiring. Looked from her face to the clock as the seconds ticked, ticked, ticked their relentless march toward afternoon.

CHAPTER 2

J ones!" Caleb held up his hand to shield his eyes against the early morning sun. "Jones! Come over here."

Caleb was standing in the middle of the base's airfield outside Chania, and he was doing his best to work through a thick stack of paperwork while also supervising two dozen soldiers on loading duty. Four large helicopters were lined up in the middle of the airfield—each one a CH-53E Super Stallion that could comfortably hold up to ten tons of supplies.

In this case the supplies were pallets of food, water, and other emergency items. Northern Africa was in the middle of another food crisis caused mainly by famine and super-swarms of locusts straight out of the Old Testament. Whole regions were starving and desperate for help. The president and her cabinet knew the decision to enforce a mandatory quarantine of Crete would be unpopular on the world stage, so the secretary of state had arranged for the Potential Pandemic Task Force to make a very public aid delivery to Benghazi, Libya, as a way of appeasing other NATO members and regaining a measure of goodwill. It was a peace offering on a grand scale.

Caleb hoped it would work, and he was glad the people of Benghazi would receive some much-needed help. He just wished he wasn't the one required to manage everything.

Private First Class Jones jogged over to Caleb's position in front of the lead helicopter.

"Sir?" He was young, tall, and splashed with freckles across his arms and forehead.

"Are you wearing sunscreen, Jones?"

"Yes, sir." The young man met his eyes for a moment, then looked away. "No, sir."

Caleb crossed his arms and sighed. The Cretan sun was notoriously intense, even in the early morning. Especially for twenty-two-year-old Alabama boys with freckles.

Jones hung his head in acknowledgment of Caleb's unspoken order. "Yes, sir."

Caleb pointed to the helicopter in front of him. "I'm riding this bird today, and I do not want to be crushed by any loose cargo. When you get back, hand-check every hook, strap, and pallet. Everything secure. Understood?"

"Yes, sir." Jones offered a salute, then slunk off in search of sunscreen.

Caleb turned back toward the helicopter and glared at it for a moment. As a former officer in the Transportation Corps, he had traveled to many places in the world using many different vehicles—and he enjoyed almost all of them. He liked cars, trucks, trains, airplanes, cargo planes, and boats. He even liked the new electric scooters that had started springing up on bases.

He did not like helicopters. Maybe it was the lack of wings, but Caleb wasn't thrilled at the idea of being squeezed in with tons of supplies and then choppity-choppity-choppered several hundred feet above the open ocean with just a few whirling sticks keeping him in the air.

Not thrilled a bit.

Sighing, he walked over to the cockpit and knocked loudly on a metal panel. "How are things coming along, Ms. Peterson?"

A young woman poked her head through the open window. "Fine, sir. I'm almost through with the preflight. Everything is green."

"Very good." Caleb started to walk away but stopped when she called after him.

"Sergeant Major? Some of the other pilots said you know a lot about spiritual things. Bible things, I mean. And since you'll be on the flight, too, I was thinking . . ." She scrunched her face together in an effort to find the right words. "I mean, I was wondering . . ."

Caleb thought he understood. "Would it be okay with you if I prayed over this flight, soldier?"

She relaxed. "Yes, sir. Please, sir. There've been reports of anti-air on the Libyan side, and I like all the help I can get."

I wish I hadn't heard that. "Antiair" meant missiles or other artillery designed to destroy aircraft in flight, and four big, fat choppers would be especially juicy targets for any bad guys looking to make a statement. *Oh, Lord, You know this is why I hate helicopters.*

Caleb closed his eyes and raised a hand toward the cockpit. "Heavenly Father, You said in Your Word that they who wait upon the Lord shall renew their strength; they shall mount up with wings as eagles; they shall run and not be weary; and they shall walk and not faint. Bless our mission with those wings. Renew the strength of our pilots. And bring us home safe. In Jesus' name, amen."

When Caleb opened his eyes, he was surprised to see Haggerty standing close by. For such a big man, he'd always been able to move quietly when he wanted to.

"Got a minute, Sergeant Major?"

He didn't have a minute. Not really. But there was very little Caleb wouldn't do to accommodate this man who was both his commander and his oldest friend.

As they walked toward the perimeter of the airfield, Caleb studied his boss. The man was huge by any measure, with a broad chest and wide shoulders. His most noticeable feature was a dime-sized chunk of flesh missing from his right ear. The rest of his face was a collection of planes—as if a sculptor had started with a cinder block but forgotten to round out the flesh. He had a flat forehead, dark brown eyes, and a thick, well-trimmed hedge of a mustache atop thin lips and a strong, square jaw. The cleft in the middle of his chin was deep enough to hold a pencil.

It wasn't a handsome face, but it was one Caleb had known and appreciated for close to forty years.

When did those wrinkles get so deep? He was looking at Haggerty's eyes and at the sides of his mouth. *And since when is there gray in your mustache, Haggs? Was it there in Spain? Was it there last month?*

"You're gonna see something new today, Cay." As always, Haggerty dropped the formality when they were away from other soldiers. "When you get to the delivery site, watch for the rich man's army in black uniforms. They'll be handling security in addition to unloading the choppers and managing distribution, so you can't miss 'em."

Caleb grunted. A rich man's army was a private military organization. Such groups had been part of the world stage for decades, from Blackwater to the infamous Wagner Group and many others. But the recent increase in pandemics, famines, and other natural disasters had produced high levels of chaos and unrest around the globe, which in turn created a palpable need for private security on a mega-scale. Billionaires and multinational corporations had invested huge amounts of money in acquiring, equipping, and merging private armies in recent years—many of them quite large—and found them to be hugely profitable.

"Why will that be new?"

"Because these guys don't use any electronics."

"What?" Caleb stopped walking and tilted his head to the side.

Haggerty nodded, a grin on his face. "You heard me. There's no electronic equipment for the entire private army. No comms. No computers. No drones. No battery-powered scopes—no batteries for anything."

Caleb was flabbergasted. He'd never heard of such a thing—had a hard time even imagining it. "What about the vehicles? They've all got computers running things now."

"Not these guys. Everything from the trucks to the choppers are basically big versions of gas-powered lawn mowers. No onboard equipment or circuit boards or anything like that."

"Why?" Caleb felt professionally offended. "For what possible reason?"

Haggerty shrugged. "I'm hoping you can tell me when you get back. See if you can connect with the officer in charge and get some answers."

I'll definitely do that. Caleb looked over at his friend, who was fidgeting with the sleeves of his uniform. He seemed a little out of sorts. Or nervous. Or something. "Is that what you wanted to talk about, Haggs?"

The smiled vanished from Haggerty's face. "No, there's something else." He rubbed a hand across the back of his neck. "You and the pilots and the other volunteers—they've all been medically cleared in regards to the Dirty Dozen, right?" That was the nickname many on the team had given the new virus because of the twelve in SARS-CoV-12. "No possibility of infection?"

"That's correct. We've done full workups and checks against all known markers. Blood tests confirm we've never had the virus in our system."

"Then how about a little company?" Haggerty tried to renew

the grin, but his face revealed a curious mixture of apprehension and anticipation. "What would you say if I went through the same protocols and joined you?"

Caleb frowned. *I would say it's a terrible idea to leave an island you just forced into quarantine. And you should know that.* Actually, from the pained expression on Haggerty's face, it seemed like he did know that. So why was he trying to make this happen? Caleb let the silence stretch for several seconds while he looked around to make sure nobody else was in hearing range.

"Is this about the girl, Haggs?"

Sonia had died early that morning. Acute overproduction of the mucous glands in the lungs and severe hemorrhaging from the capillaries within the lungs, according to the report—which Haggerty himself had signed. She'd drowned without regaining consciousness.

Haggerty was fiddling with his sleeves again but said nothing.

"Did you get any sleep last night, Haggs?"

"No."

"Did you try?"

"No."

"And all this is because of the girl? Because she died?"

"No." There was a pause. "Yes. She didn't just die, Cay. I failed her."

This again. Lord, help me. Caleb knew Haggerty would be affected by the young woman's death, but he'd hoped it wouldn't be this bad. He hadn't guessed the commander would deal with it by trying to do something stupid.

"Remind me, Haggs, how long have you been a doctor now?"

"Thirty years, give or take."

"And how many patients have you lost?"

"Thousands."

"So help me understand the connection to this one patient."

Caleb intentionally avoided the word *obsession*. "I know she had your daughter's name and they're about the same age. I can see why you'd feel responsible because of what happened with Ry—"

"No." Haggerty spoke sharply, raising a finger. "Don't." His face was a mask of stern intensity, but Caleb could see the wounded animal underneath.

Okay. Now we're getting warmer. Caleb decided to take a different approach.

"Look, Haggs. For the first time in United States history, we just forced another country to accept a medical quarantine within its borders. An ally. *You* just did that to one of our European allies, and the world is watching. Do you really think this is an acceptable time for you to go out joyriding? Do you think that's appropriate?"

"I'm part of the team, Cay. I'd be on an official mission. That's all."

Caleb shook his head. "You're not part of the team. You're the commander, and you just made the decision to quarantine a whole lot of people."

Haggerty nodded. "I know. I just . . . The pressure keeps building. I think I could handle it if I could get away for a day. Or even a few hours."

It was the same old story. John Haggerty was so talented and so dedicated that he could solve almost any problem and right almost any wrong. Almost. But in those rare moments when he failed, Haggerty had a tendency to run away—to find an escape hatch rather than resolve the issue.

Caleb wanted to say, "You can't run away from this one, Haggs." He wanted to say, "Leaving this island won't make you feel any better." Instead, he asked the only question that mattered in that moment.

"What are your orders, Commander?"

Haggerty met Caleb's eyes. His gaze was steady. "Same as before,

Sergeant. Take a bunch of food to a bunch of hungry people and do some good on behalf of the US Army. Then get back here safe."

"Yes, sir." Caleb snapped off a salute.

"Also," added Haggerty, "don't break any of my choppers."

"Ha!" Caleb turned to resume his inspection, but he was called back for the second time that morning.

"One more thing, Cay. There's something I've wanted to ask you for a little while, but it's about Tess. Do you mind?"

That got Caleb's attention. Haggerty rarely talked about family these days—especially when he was on duty in any official capacity. "No, I don't mind. What's up?"

"How long has it been since she passed? Two years?"

Caleb glanced down at his watch. "Two years, two months, and thirteen days."

"And how long were you married before . . . before it happened?"

Caleb smiled. An easy calculation. "Thirty years."

"That's right." Haggerty lifted one corner of his mouth. "You went to Fiji. You came back with those crazy war clubs."

Caleb recalled the moment he'd surprised her with the tickets. *"I want to give you a week in paradise because you've already given me thirty years."* He did not voice that memory to Haggerty.

"I know it hit you hard when she . . . when it happened. I know you were torn up. The whole thing was terrible. I know that." Haggerty rubbed his eyes with his palms, then squared his shoulders and looked up. "But how are you doing so well, Cay?" He pointed a hand at his friend and moved it up and down. Indicating, Caleb assumed, his physical and emotional self. His life. "She's gone and you're still here. How are you handling it so well?"

Am I handling it well? Am I doing okay?

His mind wandered again back to those days. To that season and those memories. Less than two months after they returned from

Fiji, the duck flu swept across North America, then swept across the globe, then fizzled into memory.

Tess fizzled with it.

Caleb had been there for every moment. Each appointment. Each conversation with the doctors—and there were many doctors. Each evening as the lights dimmed and the hospital equipment *beep beeped* its regular rhythm. Each time a nurse banged through the door to check on things during the night. Each time they woke her up in the morning to point at a row of facial expressions and ask, "What's your pain level?"

The last few moments were precious. And painful. She'd been in and out of consciousness for several hours, but she swam back to the surface for a final conversation, her eyes moist and her lips cracked but smiling. Her hands felt insubstantial when pressed between his own.

"Going home, Cay," she'd told him, still smiling. "Going home today."

"'In my Father's house are many mansions,'" he answered. He was weeping but also smiling. Neither of them could stop smiling in that long, strange, somehow familiar moment. "'If it were not so, I would have told you. I go to prepare a place for you.'"

"Yes, Lord," she said. "Yes, Lord." There was a long pause, and then her eyes widened. She was focusing not on him but something behind him. Something beyond him. A renewed strength energized her hand as she squeezed him. "Oh, Cay. Oh, Cay. Going home."

And she did. Her eyes met his as she stepped through whatever door had opened in front of her. Briefly they saw each other one last time—then her eyes were empty. His eyes were too filled with tears to see much of anything.

Is all that in the past? Caleb wondered. *Is it something I went through, or is it something I'm going through still?*

He didn't know. But he saw Haggerty watching him. Waiting patiently in the midst of memory.

"You know how I'm handling it," Caleb told him. "You know what gets me through."

Haggerty grunted. He raised his hand to touch the missing chunk from his ear. "'They that wait upon the Lord shall renew their strength,' and so on and so forth. Right?"

"Right."

Haggerty shook his head. "But what is it that . . . ? How can . . . ?" He moved his head up and down. Frustrated. Trying to find a way to say what he wanted to say. "I'm talking about something practical. Something real."

Caleb put his hand on his friend's shoulder. "Faith is practical. It is real. For both the dead and the living."

Haggerty's face clouded. "What does that mean?"

Caleb didn't answer right away. *It's been a while since the two of us have gone down this road*, he thought. *Can you handle what I want to say? What you need to hear?*

"Death has taken people from both of us, Haggs. That's a tragedy. But you've also been separated from people who are still alive. I can't help thinking that must be just as hard to carry."

Haggerty was quiet, but he stayed still. He didn't crack a joke or pretend he had some urgent duty to carry out. So Caleb kept pushing.

"How long since the divorce?" They both already knew the answer, but Caleb wanted his friend to say it out loud.

"A long time. Sixteen years." Haggerty glanced back toward the helicopters, and Caleb was certain the conversation was over. He fully expected his friend to turn on his heel and stride back toward the gathered soldiers, barking orders the whole way.

But he was wrong.

"It's not just that I lost Sonya and Marianna, Cay. It's that I'm *still* losing them. I've been losing them in slow motion. It doesn't stop."

Caleb put a hand on his shoulder. "So why not try something different? Why not do everything you can to get them back?"

They looked at each other for several seconds, the moment heavy with questions and memories and questions about memories. Then one of the Super Stallions fired its engines and roared to life. Then another. And another.

"Time to go." Just like that, John was gone. Commander Haggerty was back, large and in charge.

Caleb took his hand off his friend's shoulder. "Time to go." As they walked back toward the choppers, he once again considered the questions Haggerty had asked of him—once again peeked behind the curtain of memories as sharp and penetrating as knives.

Am I really doing well? Could that be true? He smiled and shook his head. *What a wonder that would be.*

CHAPTER 3

JULY 1
THE PENTAGON

Gotta win this one, John. Gotta win this one right now.

Major John Haggerty of the United States Army was in the middle of a battle. Familiar territory. He'd been in and out of fights all his life. He expected to be in and out of fights for the rest of his life, and he always expected to win.

Including now.

Win this, John. Win this fight!

The theater for this particular battle was a large, crowded conference room deep in the bowels of the Pentagon. The room was dominated by an expansive oval mahogany table, polished and gleaming under buzzing fluorescent tubes. Two dozen leather chairs surrounded the table. Two dozen women and men wearing dress uniforms occupied the chairs. Several more staffers, executive officers, associates, and admins had tucked themselves behind the table, some leaning against walls and others perched on metal folding chairs. The odor of lemon-scented cleaning agents permeated the room. A few of the table-sitters were munching on stale donuts or sipping coffee from ceramic mugs.

The enemy in this particular battle was sleep. More particularly, lack of sleep. Even more particularly, the crushing, overpowering desire for sleep caused by the refusal to rest across several days in combination with heavy jet lag from multiple international flights the day before.

No quarter, John. Haggerty willed himself to remain awake. *No retreat.*

The women and men gathered around the conference table were important and influential. They held critical offices within the Army and the federal government. Many were Haggerty's peers and many others were his superiors—people he respected and admired.

". . . Many of these algorithms display promise as predictive models for seismic activity. The challenge is that it is currently impossible to predict the geographical locations of seismic anomalies before they occur—which, of course, is why we require these new algorithms and other machine-learning solutions in the first place."

The man delivering the presentation was standing in front of a small lectern a few feet away from the head of the conference table. Henry Wilson was the executive officer on the Seismic Anomalies Task Force, which—like Haggerty's own task force—had been launched a little more than two years ago.

Altogether, the Army (in cooperation with several federal agencies) had put together five special task forces designed to evaluate, support, and ultimately resolve five critical crises threatening humanity on a global scale. Haggerty's team was chartered to address the sharp rise in infectious diseases that had taken place in recent decades—SARS, swine flu, MERS, Zika, Ebola, COVID, mpox, duck flu, RSV, and so on. More recently, the increases had become exponential with novel variants of those diseases, plus entirely new diseases, wreaking havoc on global health.

The stated purpose of the Seismic Anomalies Task Force was to provide quick, efficient support for local governments dealing with devastating earthquakes, which was why SATF rapid-response squads were stationed all over the world. Its implied mission was to uncover whatever geological anomalies were causing a sharp increase in the number of devastating earthquakes around the world—and, if possible, to develop technologies that would predict the location of future earthquakes before they struck.

If Haggerty understood the gist of Wilson's presentation so far, there had been little progress on either of those implied goals.

". . . rather surprising results, which Commander Fan will explain in greater detail in just a few moments. But I want to zero in on a few of the more technical aspects of our evaluation process, which I believe have fascinating implications for . . ."

Wilson was a pinched, nasally type of man with a pinched, nasally voice that was easy to hear but difficult to follow. Haggerty struggled once more against the desire to close his eyes just for a moment, but he felt the inevitability of defeat circling him like a shark. Deciding drastic action was necessary, he removed the top of his pen and quietly snapped off the little plastic clip attached there. Then he placed both hands in his lap and pressed the broken edge of the plastic clip against the tip of his left forefinger. Not hard enough to pierce the skin but enough pressure to cause real pain. Which, he hoped, would result in a shot of much-needed adrenaline and cortisol somewhere beneath the surface.

When Wilson finished his presentation, he received a smattering of applause from his colleagues around the table, Haggerty included. He liked Henry. The man was a pointy head, but he was doing his part to try to help the world. Haggerty respected that.

As Henry sat down, all eyes in the room rested on General Melissa Burgess, who stood near the head of the table. She was

Haggerty's superior officer. In fact, General Burgess was the immediate supervisor for each of the five task forces represented at this meeting. The entire operation was her brainchild, which made her one of the most powerful individuals in the world.

With broad shoulders and a thick waist, Burgess seemed built to wield that power. She wasn't a tall woman, but she rarely sat in public, which meant her face remained slightly elevated above her audience. She had a low forehead, prominent cheekbones, and wide-set eyes that complemented her ready smile and straight gray-black hair.

She was a confident commander. A competent leader.

"Thank you, Henry," she said in a warm alto. "As always, we appreciate your attention to detail." Some around the table grinned or coughed into their hands.

Henry beamed.

"Dr. Fan, I believe you're next."

Haggerty looked down at the printed agenda on the table in front of him. There were at least nine more presentations to be delivered by the various task forces before Haggerty's own turn to speak. A long day, and still a long way from finished.

Clapping broke out again as Dr. Li Fan stood and walked to the lectern. Haggerty lifted his mug and found it empty. He picked up the nearest donut box and gave it a shake—rattle of crumbs. With a sigh, he settled back in his chair and positioned the pen clip against the tip of his finger. Ready when needed.

"Thank you, General Burgess," said Li Fan in a high, soft voice. "Welcome, Secretary Williams." She nodded to the secretary of state who sat at the opposite end of the table from Burgess. "I will do my best to keep these remarks brief, since I know many of us are tired from long days and long travel."

Was that a wink? Haggerty thought. *Did she wink at me?*

"Let me begin with something each of you may find surprising." Dr. Fan flipped through her phone for a few seconds before she sent an image to the TV screen. She was small and slender with pale skin and coal-black hair, but she was a force to be reckoned with. A tornado in a teapot.

"This graph shows the number of significant earthquakes that have taken place throughout the world over the past century. This was calculated using data tabulated more than a year ago, and some of you may remember seeing this same chart at our combined task force conference last year."

Heads nodded around the room. Haggerty remembered the chart. It showed that the number of significant earthquakes had remained relatively stable for a period of fifty or so years before beginning a steady climb upward. The last three years on the graph were noticeably higher. The final year showed a total of thirty-seven "significant" earthquakes—meaning quakes that registered at 7 or higher on the Richter scale.

"Just last week," said Dr. Fan, "our team was able to update the chart based on more recent data. Here is the newest version."

Audible gasps ricocheted around the room as a new chart replaced the old. Then a moment of undignified chatter as people asked one another if what they were seeing could be real.

Dr. Fan had highlighted the most recent year in yellow, but there was no need. The final bar rose high above all other data points. According to the chart, there had been 104 significant earthquakes over the past twelve months. Almost triple the year before.

"All right." General Burgess addressed those still talking loudly around the table. Several attendees now seemed to be arguing with various members of the Seismic Anomalies Task Force. "All right, everyone. Let's move forward. Dr. Fan." She turned to the slender woman waiting patiently behind the lectern. "What does this data mean practically? What can you tell us?"

"The official answer is that we are not certain." Dr. Fan's face remained poised and confident, yet a gravity underscored her voice. Perhaps even fear, although Haggerty found that difficult to believe.

"What's causing it?" The question came from one of the staffers on the Global Hunger Task Force. "What could possibly create such a huge increase?"

"We don't know. The simple truth is that we have never seen an increase of seismological activity on this scale. We are in uncharted waters."

"Uncharted waters." Hardeep Singh scoffed as he rose to his feet. He was commander of the Task Force Tackling Climate Change—a name he had workshopped himself and refused to relinquish. A zealot in both personality and appearance, Hardeep believed in the righteous efficacy of his chosen cause with an unmatched fervor that tended to grate on his colleagues (and his immediate subordinates). He encouraged a similar fervor in as many of his underlings as possible, which had resulted in his task force functioning almost as a faith-based organization for more than two years. Climate change was the primary dogma. Singh was the self-appointed messiah.

"We *do* know what's causing these anomalies," he said. "There is a clear connection between seismological activity and climate change!"

Many around the room lowered their eyes or softly shook their heads. Haggerty heard a lot of grumbling and more than a few groans. He gave himself a good poke in the finger—more of an angry gesture than an effort to stay awake.

"When will we stop ignoring the evidence?" demanded Singh. "Climate scientists have predicted for decades that rising sea levels will create greater pressure on the earth's crust in general and at fault lines specifically. We have foreseen this!"

Henry Wilson spoke up. "Actually, Commander Singh, I'm aware of the hypothetical models you are referencing, but I'm not sure the data is suggestive of any definitive correlation between climate change and seismic phenomena."

"You are not sure," jeered Singh, swiveling his whole body to face the older man. "What are you ever sure about, Henry? How can you say there is no correlation? No connection?"

"Well, I didn't say *no* correlation. It's certainly possible for some form of . . ."

"Don't patronize me," snapped Singh. He was a tall, thin man with sharp shoulders, narrow cheeks, and penetrating eyes. Those eyes burned with fervor as he hunched forward toward his prey. "What evidence do you have to suggest that climate change is not the primary factor here? Can you show me a single data point that would prove—?"

"He's just saying it doesn't make sense." Haggerty was surprised to hear himself speak the words out loud. "Seismology and climatology are separate fields. It doesn't make sense to jam them together."

Still standing, Singh shifted his shoulders until they pointed directly at Haggerty. Eyes narrowing and lips pinching.

Out of the corner of his eye, Haggerty saw Caleb lean back and cross his arms while exhaling a long, slow sigh. *Here we go.*

"They certainly are not separate fields." Singh spoke softly, but his eyes continued to blaze. "Climatology, as you call it, has long been recognized as an interdisciplinary system of—"

"No." Haggerty pushed down his annoyance, making sure to keep his voice calm. "I've had to deal with this nonsense for years now on the epidemiological side. People keep telling me how climate change is at the root of pandemics. Well, it's not." He gestured toward Caleb, representing the PPTF. "We've done the research. We've done the studies . . ."

"You have no idea what you're talking about, John! You—"

". . . We've assessed the data from all angles, and we've come to the proper conclusions. Climate change has not been a contributing factor to pandemics. There's no connection . . ."

"This is completely irresponsible!" Singh was shouting again, which was what Haggerty had been hoping for. Pushing for. "We are dealing with an existential threat to the human race, and you have the gall to—"

". . . And the more you try to make a connection between climate change and every other problem the world is facing," Haggerty continued, refusing to be interrupted, "the more you damage your own credibility. Which is exactly why so many people are so tired of hearing about climate change."

"Are you hearing this?" Singh, shivering with rage, turned toward Burgess. "We have climate deniers spewing their ignorance right here at this critical meeting, and you just stand there?"

"That's enough, Hardeep." The general's voice had lost much of its warmth.

"This is exactly what I was telling you about earlier," he went on. "Our task forces are siloed and compartmentalized because their leaders can't see beyond their own petty specialties, which is exactly why so little gets done."

"Commander Singh."

"No, General, I have said this to you many times, and it must be spoken here as well." He gestured around the conference table. "Our resources are spread far too thin to make a difference. The only answer is to pool what we have in an effort to achieve one singular goal—to solve our planet's most critical problem. And I feel strongly . . . I feel very strongly . . ."

Burgess was no longer trying to speak over Hardeep Singh. Instead, she walked around the conference room toward him, moving slowly but implacably.

"I feel quite strongly that climate change . . ." Singh was slowing down like a child's toy with a dying battery. He watched as General Burgess approached, head up and hands behind her back, like she was about to ask a question across the fence from her neighbor. But her eyes locked with Singh's eyes. Matched his intensity. Broke it.

"Let's be finished with this conversation for now, Commander Singh. Shall we?"

He nodded, then sat down, glowering.

Burgess looked back at Li Fan, who was still standing behind the lectern, looking bemused. "Dr. Fan, do you have any concluding thoughts before we hear from the Global Hunger Task Force?"

"Yes, one final thought. I feel compelled to emphasize that the data points our team has presented are not an anomaly. They are not flukes. Instead, we seem to be at the beginning of some new epoch—perhaps a new phase of geological history."

The room was silent now. Haggerty could hear the whir of air handlers and little else.

"I understand the urgency communicated by Commander Singh. I feel it as well. More specifically, I feel uncertain . . ." Li Fan paused for a moment. She looked down at her hands, then over at Henry and the other members of her team, then fixed her eyes on General Burgess. "I feel afraid. Afraid for our future. Every significant earthquake represents a region destroyed and hundreds of lives taken—often thousands of lives. So I am afraid of what this new development could mean, both for our planet and for humanity, if we don't figure out how to get things under control."

"The official name is SARS-CoV-12, although our team is calling it the Dirty Dozen." Haggerty paused a beat before adding, "Honestly, I hope that doesn't stick."

Several people around the table chuckled, which was gratifying this late in the day.

Haggerty spent the next five minutes outlining what the Potential Pandemic Task Force had learned about SARS-CoV-12, which wasn't a whole lot in terms of an epidemiological profile. As with most coronaviruses, the primary danger was respiratory infection, including the often-fatal possibility of acute respiratory distress. Similar to COVID-19, the Dirty Dozen carried the risk of cardiac inflammation and extreme levels of clotting within blood vessels. A dangerous combination.

"I'm most concerned about the demographics of this particular virus." His throat ached with every word, and his eyelids scratched with every blink, but he kept going. "The overall infection fatality rate is about point one percent, which is significant. That means we could expect one person to die from every thousand patients who contract the disease. For some comparison, the IFR of the original COVID-19 pandemic ended up somewhere in the neighborhood of two hundredths of a percent. So, much less.

"What I don't like about the Dirty Dozen, though, is that the fatality rate is much higher among younger people—say, ages twenty to fifty. That's concerning." He paused. "Beyond those basic facts—"

Haggerty stopped again as someone near the back of the table raised his hand. Benjamin Abramowitz, commander of the Refugee Relocation Task Force. "Yes, Ben?"

"Why does that concern you?" Abramowitz asked. "The demographics, I mean."

"Well, it's the inverse of what we saw with COVID-19, which

posed almost no danger to patients under fifty unless they were degraded by other serious health conditions. This one seems to be more dangerous for younger people. At least so far."

"So if someone has to die from these constant pandemics, better it should be us old dinosaurs. Is that what you're saying, my good doctor?" Abramowitz smiled, his eyes sparkling in the middle of thick, black-framed glasses. He ran a hand through his silvery hair and then scratched his white beard, as if emphasizing his own advanced age.

Abramowitz had helped launch the refugee task force less than a year ago, which made him a relative newcomer in the room. Even so, he was highly respected—largely because he'd willingly taken leadership of a task force whose mission was impossible to achieve on any practical level. Put simply, the chaos currently boiling throughout the world stage had created more refugees than at any other point in human history. Yet the urgency generated by that chaos made it impossible—even unthinkable—for most governments to allow those refugees legal entry across their borders, or even significant aid on the outside.

Faced with few options, the RRTF had spent the last year creating several refugee camps in an effort to stop the bleeding. In theory, these camps were meant to offer temporary, humane, and healthy sanctuary for any person impacted by global catastrophes. In practice, they had already become fetid, festering swamps filled with disease, deprivation, devastation, exploitation, violence, and greed.

"What I'm saying, Ben," Haggerty continued, "is that I get nervous about any virus able to overwhelm otherwise young and healthy immune systems. That's rare—or at least it used to be. And I don't like it." He paused. "Any other questions?"

"What about containment?" Ivo Marcello spoke up from the

other side of the table. "How confident do you feel that the virus can be pinned down in Greece?"

Not confident at all, Haggerty thought. He'd read several alarming emails just thirty minutes ago, and he was still trying to parse the implications.

"There's reason for confidence," he said out loud. "We were able to initiate the quarantine around Crete after being on the island for less than a week, and we are highly confident in our systems and personnel. But"—he scratched the back of his neck—"because coronaviruses are so communicable, fully containing the Dirty Dozen at this point would be like hitting a home run on the very first pitch of a baseball game."

"It's tourist season in Greece," chimed in one of the staffers from the Seismic Anomalies Task Force. "How do you account for travelers?"

"It's a good question," said Haggerty, "and we are certainly monitoring each of the high-traffic zones that house returning visitors from Crete. But we don't believe the virus was widespread on the island even a week ago, which means the chances of multiple tourists encountering multiple infected Cretans are relatively low. And in order for the virus to spread to new regions, multiple people from those areas would need to be infected, and then those infected individuals would need to be part of what they used to call 'superspreader events'—church services or concerts or large markets. That kind of thing.

"Bottom line," said Haggerty, "if we caught things early enough, we could be okay. If not, the virus will spread, and we'll have to be both vigilant and nimble in extinguishing whatever little fires of infectious activity appear."

Which will be incredibly difficult in Europe. Especially in the summer.

"Is there a treatment?" Ivo Marcello spoke again. He was a large man, and the brass buttons of his service uniform bulged at odd angles as he leaned back in his chair. The mop of silver hair on top of Ivo's head was, like the rest of his physique, pushing the boundaries of Army regulations.

"No." Haggerty felt the weight of reality as he answered the question. "We're experimenting with different antivirals to see which are most effective, but as with all coronaviruses, there is no actual cure. No vaccine, either. Not at this stage."

"Please keep us up to date on developments," said Ivo. "I have several teams in the Mediterranean region, and I want to know what dangers they may face."

Haggerty nodded. The Global Hunger Task Force had been formed a year ago as part of an effort to counterbalance several severe food shortages around the world—especially throughout Africa and parts of Asia. South America was also experiencing significant food insecurity. The causes of those shortages were generally known: rising costs, poor harvests, supply chain breakdowns, corruption, war, and the continued rise of infectious diseases. It was not generally known (or generally agreed upon) how to handle those problems. But the GHTF used Army resources to act as a global middleman in moving supplies from areas of surplus to areas of need. The recent mission to Benghazi had been spearheaded by Commander Marcello's team, and Haggerty believed it had gone well. Ivo was making an impact.

There were a few other minor questions, most of them technical. When Haggerty returned to his seat, he took a drink of water, relishing the coolness against the back of his throat. Then he looked over at Caleb, eyebrows raised.

His friend briefly popped up a long, slender thumb. *Good job.*

"All right, everyone, that's a wrap." Somehow, General Burgess was still standing, though even she sounded worn out. "I know we had some individual meetings scheduled for this evening, but I'm canceling them all. We need some rest. But first, please allow me one more minute to summarize what we've experienced today."

The general was silent for a few seconds, staring down at the table. When she spoke, Haggerty heard the gravity and the sincerity in her tone.

"I don't think it's possible for anyone to hear what we've heard today without coming to the conclusion that our world is in trouble. I don't mean our culture. I don't mean our way of life. I mean our civilization. We are currently experiencing something unprecedented not only in our lifetimes but seemingly in human history. An extraordinary rise in seismic activity, catastrophic storms, and flooding. An extraordinary increase in regional epidemics and global pandemics. An extraordinary surge in famines and food insecurity across multiple continents. And an extraordinary flood of refugees seeking shelter and finding none.

"There is no doubt that many of these crises can be seen as the avoidable consequences of our own actions as a civilization." She glanced over at Singh, then away. "But there is also little doubt in my mind that we are facing calamity at a scale we have never before considered. Ladies and gentlemen . . ." She paused as she scanned the room. "I am not exaggerating when I say the world is in danger. Humanity is in danger. But I am also not exaggerating when I declare that those of us in this room are equipped to meet that calamity head-on—and to steer our world to victory.

"We're at a tipping point, and I believe the actions taken by our five task forces *over the next twelve months* will determine whether humanity advances to our destiny—or retreats into oblivion. So, let's go save the world."

Several cheers and shouts of appreciation rang out, followed by a long round of applause. Most of the attendees remained in their chairs, savoring a few moments of having nothing to say and nothing to hear before heading back to hotel rooms and emails and text messages and phone calls.

Haggerty swiveled his chair toward Caleb. Somehow, he now felt almost too tired to sleep. "Well?"

"I think she did a great job."

"Well, yeah." Haggerty waved his hand. "Of course *she* did. How did I do?"

Caleb offered a golf clap. "Very good. Almost made it seem like we know what we're doing."

Haggerty grunted.

"I didn't like what Ivo said during his presentation." Caleb sounded somber. "Not at all."

Haggerty didn't like it either. Each presentation from the Global Hunger Task Force had focused on rising food insecurity around the world. According to their information, a little more than half the global population now qualified as moderately or severely food insecure—meaning they did not have adequate access to food within their household, or they were regularly forced to reduce the amount of food they consumed because of a lack of resources. Four billion people. Close to 1.5 billion within that group were severely food insecure, which meant they often went more than a day without eating.

Ivo had spoken less on the current issues with global hunger and more on the future. Specifically, he offered new intelligence suggesting China was about to make it illegal for any individual or corporation within its borders to export foodstuffs of any kind. That included raw ingredients such as rice, buckwheat, soybeans, and tea. It also included packaged and processed foods.

Meaning one of the largest food suppliers in the world was about to turn off the pipe. On everyone. Worse, Ivo's sources had confirmed that other nations were considering taking the same approach. If that happened—if multiple nations decided that food and other edible goods produced within their borders could only be consumed within their borders—what was presently tragic would turn appalling very quickly.

"You think they'll do it?" Caleb asked. "China, I mean?"

"I could see it. I could see others following suit. It would be like they had permission."

He thought of Elena Kazantis and the people of Crete. An island whose entire economy was built on tourism and olives. He himself had taken away the former. How would they function without enough grain? Without rice?

He heard Elena's voice once more in his mind. *"You . . . You have done this?"*

Caleb tapped him on the leg, then pointed his chin off to the side. Haggerty turned to see General Burgess standing beside his chair.

"You're thinking about Crete, aren't you?" she said. "About exports."

Haggerty nodded.

"These are the decisions we have to make, John. The hard decisions. You made the right one."

Haggerty inclined his head. "I guess we'll see."

She sighed. "I know you need to get some rest, but I wanted to talk something through with you before you go." She glanced at Caleb. "Both of you. We may have a problem."

Haggerty gestured to the empty chair on his left, but she shook her head. Eight hours of meetings and still standing.

"I think I know what this is about," said Haggerty. "I received some messages today from WHO contacts in Italy about a new virus showing up in the interior. Seems to target young people. Difficulty breathing. Coughing up blood."

Burgess's face softened, and she put a hand on the back of Haggerty's chair, leaning slightly forward. "So I'm not the bearer of bad news."

"Not the first, anyway. What have you got?"

She sighed. "One of my contacts in the Italian Ministry of Health says what you just said. Right now, most of the cases seem to be clustered around a little town called Spoleto in Umbria. About four hours north of Rome."

Haggerty felt another set of weights settle on his shoulders. Another load of responsibility. He'd leveraged himself quite a bit to enforce the quarantine on Crete, not to mention the reputation of his task force and even the Army at large. So far the results were encouraging. They'd managed to stem the rising caseload from the Dirty Dozen, and they were making progress on treatments. There was reason for optimism.

But if the virus has escaped . . . if it's already on the mainland, then all that work will have to be done again. And done on a much larger scale.

A ball of ice began to roll around the pit of his stomach. Flashes of those headlines pressed against his mind: *Pandemic Task Force Helpless as Millions Perish.*

It took an effort not to hang his head or strike the table in frustration. Instead, Haggerty looked at Caleb. "I guess we're going to Italy."

Caleb stretched his arms above his head and yawned. "How many of us? The operation in Greece is still in full swing."

"I think just a few. We'll bring our tests. The first thing we have to do is confirm it's the same virus." He looked over at the general, who nodded. "Then we go from there."

Burgess put her hand on Haggerty's shoulder. "What do you need, John? From me?"

Haggerty's mind was churning sluggishly, trying to force itself into gear. Trying to complete the thought that had just begun to occur. "Do we have any translators who can speak Italian?"

The general stepped back. "Is that necessary? Most of the officials there will speak some English."

"I'm not worried about the officials. I'm worried about locals. Especially seniors. I'm worried about possible quarantines and communicating to large groups of people at once."

Burgess inclined her head. "Okay. I can check with Intel, but resources on the ground are pretty limited. Especially short term."

"I may have a better idea." Haggerty swiveled back to his XO. "Cay, if you get there half a day ahead of me, can you get the ball rolling?"

Caleb nodded. "Shouldn't be a problem. I'll have Smith and Martinez meet me in Rome. They know the drill. I can radio ahead to have the tests ready." He squinted at his commanding officer. "Why? What have you got in mind?"

"Quick stop in Ohio." Haggerty raised one eyebrow toward his oldest friend. *Just go with me on this.*

"Ohio." Caleb was unable to stop the slight smile at the corners of his lips. "Okay."

Burgess looked between them. "Whatever you're cooking up, John, I don't care—as long as you do it quickly. If this Dirty Dozen is already threatening to become a regional epidemic, then we're in very dangerous waters. All of us."

"Yeah." Haggerty glanced between Caleb and Burgess. All three of them were weighing the word *pandemic* in their minds. None of them spoke it out loud.

"Right now you have the chance to preemptively save hundreds of thousands of lives, just like you did in Brazil. Maybe more. Your team has done amazing work, John, and now we need you to do it again. So get to Spoleto and tell me what kind of problem we're dealing with—then solve it. Yes?"

"Yes, General. Right away."

When she left, Haggerty saw Caleb still squinting at him. He knew his friend was thinking about Ohio. "Don't look at me like that. It'll be fine."

"You think she'll want to go?"

Haggerty shrugged. "I hope so. I think I can convince her."

"You think *you* want her to go?"

Haggerty smiled. "'Course I do, Cay. You asked why I'm not doing everything I can to get my family back. This is an opportunity to actually do something—to be proactive."

"I'm talking about her health, Haggs." Caleb was serious. "You'd be taking her into an active quarantine situation with a potentially lethal virus."

"She'd be with us. We can teach her all the protocols, no problem. Besides"—Haggerty winked—"good translators are hard to find."

CHAPTER 4

Haggerty took a sip of gas station coffee, then winced. It tasted like cigarettes.

You gotta get out of this thing. It was the third time he'd given himself the same command.

He was in the driver's seat of a Honda Accord that, despite being only a few years old, had already succumbed to its ultimate fate of being beaten to death. Both the inside and outside of the windshield were crusted with grime. The steering wheel was sticky, and the upholstered seats had threads poking out at all angles like whiskers. A faded No Smoking sign was glued to the dash, but the car still exuded the unmistakable and inescapable odor of cigarette smoke infused with perspiration.

Haggerty felt saturated by the stench, but he stayed in the driver's seat.

"It feels like things are spinning out of control. I thought we had it pinned down in Crete, but . . . maybe not. Maybe it got loose."

He was talking to the phone propped on his leg. More accurately, he was talking to the contact photo displayed on the phone, which showed the face of the woman he'd married more than thirty years ago. She'd been smiling at the camera when he took the picture. Laughing. Her eyes were open wide and sparkling with some hidden delight—some secret joke. She had a wide mouth with a flash of white teeth. Her small nose, round cheeks, and strong chin were framed by long black hair.

"Now I'm off to Italy, and I'm afraid of what I'll find." He took a deep breath, then confessed the truth out loud. "I'm afraid to mess this up. I don't want to make a mistake when so many lives are at stake. Not while the whole world is watching."

In his mind, he saw the headlines that had been prominent online and on TV after the Potential Pandemic Task Force's recent victory in Spain. *Haggerty Shows New Way Forward in Fight Against Pandemics. Pandemic Task Force Offers Hope for Humanity. John Haggerty: A Hero for Our Time.*

The press hadn't turned him into a celebrity or anything. There were no invitations to the big podcasts or comfortable chairs in front of late-night TV hosts. Still, Haggerty had been recognized. His team had been recognized. Which had felt good.

But things could have worked out differently.

New headlines popped up in his mind. *John Haggerty: From Hero to Zero. Pandemic Task Force Helpless as Millions Perish.* He thought about the potential for congressional subpoenas, hostile interviews, and angry phone calls. He worried about the possibility of his legacy turned to ashes because of a virus that refused to be contained.

It could happen. Actually, it *would* happen sooner or later. He couldn't maintain a perfect record against nature, especially if new viruses kept popping up at these increased rates. What would he do then?

"Lots of people are gonna die if this gets out," he told the photo. "That's the main thing. That's what I have to keep at the front of my mind."

His finger touched his wife's picture on the phone, then traced downward, following the line of her hair, inching closer until it stopped just above the button marked *Message*. The same finger reached back up and touched the top of the picture again, then traced down the opposite side until it stopped just above another button marked *Mail*.

His eyes flicked to the name beneath the photo: "Marianna Haggerty." He frowned.

Marianna Rodriguez. That's what she calls herself now.

"I could just walk up the driveway," he told the picture. "Open the screen and yell, 'Mary, Mary, quite contrary, how does your garden grow?'"

He looked through the windshield and studied the well-manicured garden off the side of a three-bedroom brick house about a hundred feet down the street. It was bursting with flowers. Big hydrangea bushes arranged in alternating patterns of creamy white and sky blue. Purple coneflowers and blazing star. Patches of peonies nestled among green circles of hostas and elephant's ear. Knock Out roses standing tall and proud and red as blood.

"I could pluck some of those roses on the way up." Haggerty smiled at the idea—at the double consequences of such a provocation. "I could—"

His eyes opened wide and he hissed in a breath as the screen suddenly brightened under his unmoved finger. He felt panic tightening his chest. It took him a moment to register the sound of his own ringtone—a standard, chipper tune. It took him another moment to realize Marianna's picture was gone, replaced by a younger woman with short hair and dark-framed glasses. His daughter.

Finally, his brain clicked into place and he accepted the call.

"Sonya?"

"Yep, it's me. Whatcha up to these days, Dad?" She spoke in a silly, singsong voice dripping with sarcasm.

Haggerty said nothing.

"Are ya out there fightin' the good fight in France? Are ya slingin' vaccines in Slingapore—I mean Singapore? Are ya changing the world, Pop?"

"Sonya, I—"

"I mean, I assume you *are* out there saving the world in some exotic locale, right? I keep telling myself that's the reason you hardly ever call me. One thing I know for sure is if my father were back in the good ol' USA, *of course* he would let me know. Right? If he were in Ohio, definitely he would tell me about it. Right? And there's no possible way that my own father would show up in my own town without letting me know he was coming. Isn't that right, Dad?"

Haggerty squinted at the house in front of him. It was a standard three-bedroom with red bricks and a large bay window. Looking at the window, he could almost make out a face looking back at him.

"Don't squint like that," said Sonya. "Your forehead might freeze."

He kept squinting. "How are you seeing me?"

There was a motion in the window, as if she was waving an object back and forth over her head. "Binoculars. Me and Mom took up bird-watching last year."

Haggerty grunted. "It's good to see you, Sonya."

"Yeah, I'm guessing you mean that in more of a metaphorical kind of way, 'cause I don't think you can see much of anything through the windshield of that car." He could hear the smile on her face, even if her voice still carried an edge.

"Listen, Dad, I think it's wonderful that you've chosen to set up a stakeout in our neighborhood and keep an eye on our house from your nasty little car. There's something weirdly romantic about it, with an emphasis on *weird*."

"Sonya—"

"But I'll have to be the bearer of bad news on this one, because Mom isn't here. She's taking food to Aunt Rita. Won't be back until tomorrow."

Haggerty smiled. For once in what seemed like a very long time, he enjoyed the sensation of being one step ahead of his lightning-quick daughter—of knowing something she didn't know.

"Just in case you forgot, Rita is Mom's oldest sister. She lives by herself in Dayton, which is a city in Ohio, which is the state you are currently—"

"Actually, I'm not here to see your mom. I'm here to see you."

A pause of several seconds followed, and then her voice came back on the line—though it sounded smaller. "Me?"

Haggerty winced. The genuine surprise in her tone—surprise that her own father was here and wanted to spend time with her—squeezed his heart like a vise. That single syllable was a slap across his face.

It hurt. Quite a bit.

"Yeah," he said, trying to sound casual. Trying to prevent any of the pain from leaking through the phone. "Yes, of course. I've got something I want to talk through with you. An opportunity."

"What opportunity?" She was suspicious now. "What's up?"

"How about we go somewhere? Can I get you a coffee and a donut from Mac's?"

"Well, well, Mr. Moneybags." Another pause. "Yeah. Okay. But I'll meet you there in five. I'm not riding in that thing."

———

Mike MacIntosh's Magnificent Café was a Millersville staple. It had been around for decades, although the original Mike had passed the business down to his oldest son, Michael. The outside of the building featured yellowish bricks stacked around tall windows. Lots of flags. Several flower boxes with half-hearted roses and marigolds. The inside boasted rows of square tables on scuffed linoleum. The original Mike had been fond of tacky posters with catchphrases such as "Donut Worry, Be Happy" and "Hot Dog This Is Good Food!" They still held court on the main walls with weary, weathered cheerfulness.

Haggerty sat across from Sonya at a corner table. Both were enjoying one of Mac's huge handmade donuts. Sonya's was a confectioner's dream topped with chocolate chunks and toasted coconut and caramel drizzle. Haggerty's was a plain glazed. Both sipped coffee from ceramic mugs.

"When you called me Moneybags, I thought you were being sarcastic." He held up his receipt. "How can two donuts and two coffees cost twenty-three dollars?"

Sonya was sawing at her donut with a plastic knife and fork. "Well, these are *luxury* donuts. Or they're supposed to be." She looked with pity at her father's plate. "Besides, I don't know what it's like at Army cafés or grocery stores or however else you buy stuff from Uncle Sam, but prices have been out of control around here for a while now."

He nodded. "The Army does help. But I've been to grocery stores in"—he took a moment to count on his fingers—"seven different countries in the past year. Prices are high in all of them. And getting higher."

Actually, Haggerty had made a point to visit grocery stores, supermarkets, farmers markets, roadside vegetable stands, and lots of restaurants throughout his travels. He was a strong believer in the connection between good nutrition and good health, and what he found in those countries continued to alarm him. Anything organic was difficult to track down no matter the price—meat, fruits, vegetables, eggs. There had been riots in Spain and France over the cost of bread. The sticker prices for rice and flour hadn't risen tremendously, but the bags had become smaller and smaller.

If Ivo's right about China banning all exports of food . . . Haggerty shook his head, contemplating possible consequences.

Sonya coughed to regain his attention. "Penny for your thoughts, Pop?"

"Sorry. People are struggling, that's all." He tilted his head to look at her. "What about you? Are you doing okay? Financially?"

Sonya chewed thoughtfully for a long moment, then stared out the window as she answered. "Me and Mom help each other. And I know she gets a lot of her income from you, so . . ." She looked him in the eyes. "Thank you."

Haggerty waved it away. "You know if you ever need anything, all you have to—"

"Yeah, Dad. I know." After a pause, she said, "Mom knows too. We talk about it."

Haggerty cleared his throat again. He felt the questions shape themselves at the tip of his tongue—*How is your mom?* Or *How's Marianna?* Or even *How is she doing, honestly?* But the words did not emerge.

He crumpled the receipt in his palm. "Well, I'll be good for a donut whenever I'm in town." He felt the stupidity of the statement as soon as the words left his lips. The hurtfulness.

Oh, you idiot, he thought.

Sonya just stirred her coffee. She was a lovely young woman and filled with promise—filled with potential. But somehow she'd gotten stuck in this dying town and didn't seem eager to leave.

"So, you mentioned some kind of opportunity. Are you marrying me off to the mysterious progeny of a Saudi Arabian prince?"

Haggerty leaned forward. Conspiratorial. "That could be arranged."

She laughed, which was good. He loved that sound.

"Actually, it's a short-term job opportunity." He held up his hands to forestall the argument she was already prepping to launch across the table. "*Very* short term. I'm talking six or eight weeks at the most. And to be honest, it's more of a favor to me than an opportunity for you."

Sonya had leaned forward in her chair when Haggerty said "job opportunity," weight on her elbows and eyebrows pushing toward her scalp. Now she settled back down, seemingly pacified. "Okay, I'm listening."

"There's a situation brewing in Italy." He noted the way her eyes opened a little wider. "I think I'm gonna be there awhile. Little town in Umbria called Spoleto. Did you ever . . . ?"

She shook her head. "No, I don't think so. I got to see a few places in Umbria, but I was mostly in Rome."

He nodded. *Don't overshoot this, John. Play it right.*

"I need a translator. There's a medical situation that could be . . . Well, I think it could be serious. I think it *will* be serious. So I need someone to help me communicate effectively and efficiently with local officials and with regular citizens and with whoever else needs to hear what I have to say."

"Translate?" She was surprised. "Dad, I took Italian for a few years in college and I spent nine months in Rome studying art history. That hardly qualifies me as a translator."

"I don't need you to create legal contracts or lecture a classroom. I just need someone who can help me talk to people. Especially those in rural areas who might not know much English."

Sonya sipped her coffee. He could tell she was processing. "Doesn't the Army have translators lined up for this kind of thing? Like, can't you just requisition one or something? Oh, come on, Dad."

Haggerty sat back. "What?"

"I saw your little frown, and I know what it means. I say *like* sometimes, okay? It's, like, something my generation, like, does when we're, like, having a conversation."

He raised his hands in surrender. "Okay, you got me. I'm sorry." Then he grinned. "Remember what I used to say when you were in high school?"

She answered in a rough, growling impression of his voice: "I don't like the *like*."

He had probably said that phrase two hundred times over the course of her freshman year in an effort to stamp out the offensive word—which apparently hadn't worked.

Was that ten years ago?

"But seriously, why not use a regular Army translator? Why me?"

"I *could* get someone else," Haggerty admitted. "Eventually. But this whole situation feels like it's turning into a mess. I need someone who knows me as much as the language. I need someone I can trust."

She ate the last bite of her donut. Took another sip of coffee. Removed her glasses and cleaned them on a napkin, working slowly and methodically.

Thinking.

Haggerty got the impression she had planned to say no to whatever opportunity he put in front of her, but now she was genuinely chewing on the possibility. Part of that was Italy, he knew. She'd always been fascinated by classical artists, and she'd loved her time in Rome. He wasn't surprised she was interested in going back, even if only for a few weeks.

But part of it might be me, he thought. *Part of it might be spending time with me.*

Haggerty hoped that was the case. She'd always teased him

about his constant travel and his poor record on phone calls. But there was truth behind it. There was hurt behind it. She felt unimportant to him. Unvalued. Maybe even unloved.

He wanted to change that. He had come here to change that. He just didn't know if she would let him.

Sonya looked back at his face, her expression a strange mix of challenge and apprehension. "I'm trying to remember, how old was Ryan when we visited you at that base in Germany? Was he eight?"

Haggerty never saw it coming. The muscles in his abdomen clenched, then loosened, then clenched again. It was like he'd been punched in the gut. Punched hard by someone who knew what they were doing. Heat flushed his cheeks and the back of his neck. He blinked several times, then coughed weakly into his elbow.

"Ryan . . ." Oh, the pain of saying that name. Haggerty tried again. "I don't think he . . . I don't think you guys made it to Germany, did you?"

"Yeah, we did. You bought us all those gummy bears because they were so cheap, and me and Ryan ran around the outside of your barracks until he threw up. Remember, Dad?"

He did remember. But he didn't want to talk about it. He didn't even want to think about it. Not about Ryan.

Haggerty's heartbeat accelerated. He shifted in the chair, seeking relief from the sudden pulsing in his chest. In his neck. In his fingers.

When Sonya spoke again, her voice remained casual. But her eyes stayed fixed on him. Her gaze weighed every ounce of him. "What kind of donut would Ryan get if he were here with us? Something more than plain glazed, I hope."

Haggerty massaged his forehead. "Why are you doing this? Why are you talking about this?"

"About Ryan? He's my brother. He's your son. Why wouldn't we talk about him?"

Maybe this isn't a good idea, thought Haggerty. *Maybe I should just go. Catch the plane to Italy and try this again another time.*

"You know why."

"Yeah, I know why. But I also know it's not good. It's not healthy, Dad." Moving slowly, Sonya reached across the table and set her hand on top of his. The touch startled him. It also felt nice. Haggerty heard Caleb's voice in his head. *Why not try something different? Why not do everything you can to get them back?*

Haggerty looked down at his daughter. Met her eyes and refused to look away. "You want me to talk about Ryan." Not a question.

"I'd like to hear you talk about him, yes. Honestly, Dad, I'd like to see you be *able* to talk about him. It's been a long time."

Haggerty understood what she was saying. For once, he even thought he understood what she chose not to say. *It's been a long time for a lot of things.*

"Tell you what," he said. "You come with me to Italy, and we'll talk about Ryan."

She kept looking at him, her head tilted to one side.

Haggerty closed his eyes for a moment. Concentrating. *She wants you to open up, John. She wants you to be vulnerable, just like the therapist kept saying. So give her what she needs!*

He opened his eyes. She was still holding his hand. "Look, Sonya Pie . . ." She smiled at the old nickname. "There's a lot of stuff I'd like to talk with you about. I know there are quite a few things you'd like to hear from me—things you need to hear from me." He placed his free hand on top of hers. "That's what I'm here for. That's why I'd like you to come to Italy. I'd like to spend some time with you."

He hoped her face would brighten at the words or show some kind of excitement. Instead, she kept looking at him. She seemed to be waiting for something else. Something more.

"I'm not asking you to volunteer, either," he said. "You'd get paid. Five hundred."

She narrowed her eyes. "Five hundred dollars for six or eight weeks?"

Haggerty laughed. "No, no, no. Five hundred a day."

"A day!" Her face didn't brighten so much as electrify—eyes open wide, nostrils flared, and eyebrows touching her scalp. She pulled her hands free and popped out of her chair with a squeal. "I'm in! Let's do this."

"Yeah? You'll be able to figure out something with work?"

She put a hand on her hip. "Dad, Dr. Keen pays me twenty bucks an hour. If he wants to replace me, he's welcome to it."

"Ah." He frowned. He knew she'd been working as an office assistant for the past year or so, but he had no idea the pay was so low. It was another reminder of how privileged he was in the Army. Privileged to manage a significant budget and spend his time doing something worthwhile—or trying to.

"When do we go?" she asked.

Haggerty offered a sheepish grin, then rubbed his right hand on the back of his neck. "Well, that's part of the fun." He checked his watch. "We're wheels up in just under five hours. How quickly can you pack a bag?"

She studied him a moment, hand still on her hip. "You're not kidding."

"Nope. We're saving the world, Sonya Pie, and the world doesn't wait."

"Yeah. I remember when you used to tell me that. Listen." She looked out the window toward her house. Marianna's house. "I'm gonna go pack what I can and make some calls. Can you pick me up in an hour? Does that work?"

He nodded, then watched her carry the empty mug to the counter and walk through the door. He noticed again how very much she looked like her mother, and he wondered what she would tell her mother about the trip. What would Marianna say about it? What would she think about? Feel about it?

Haggerty stayed in his chair. He pressed his palms to his face and took a deep breath, waiting for the pain in his heart to pass. Or at least to ease.

He waited a long time.

CHAPTER 5

JULY 10
SPOLETO, ITALY

E ighty-four. Eighty-five. Eighty-six."

Sonya counted under her breath as she walked up the narrow street with slow, measured strides. *Up* being the operative word. As with most cities and villages in Northern Italy, Spoleto was constructed on the side of a hill, which meant everything she did was up or down. The roads were carved up and down. The buildings were stacked up and down. Even the stray cats seemed to stretch themselves vertically rather than horizontally on stone steps and stone walls and stone-colored branches.

"Ninety-seven. Ninety-eight. Ninety-nine. Thirteen hundred."

This was the third day in a row she'd tried to count the number of steps from the parking lot in the central square at the bottom of the old city to the Army's de facto headquarters on the lower level of an abandoned hotel near the top. So far she'd been unsuccessful.

The main reason she had trouble keeping count was that there was *so much to see!* Every street was lined with shops and cafés and apartments and parks. The balconies of the upper floor were bursting with flower boxes and potted plants and sheets and towels and clothes in all manner of colors hanging on lines and over railings. Everywhere she looked was a riot of colors and textures and shapes.

This was what Sonya had loved about Italy for years. Except . . . something was different this time. The people were different.

Normally Sonya would expect to see vast multitudes of people out and about on a glorious day like this. People walking together in the streets, talking enthusiastically while waving hands up and down, left and right. People walking alone and speaking loudly into unseen phones. People sitting and smoking and sipping and chatting at little tables in front of sidewalk cafés or watching from their balconies. Normally this city would be humming with life in a way she almost never experienced back in the States.

But not today. Not this week. There were people on the streets, of course, and she did see several Italians and tourists eating and shopping and talking. But the energy was missing. The vitality.

She remembered what her father had said back in Millersville: *"People are struggling, that's all."*

What have you seen out here in the world, Pop? How did it change you? How will it change me?

As she walked, Sonya gazed out across the countryside to a neighboring hill. Centuries ago, it had been cropped and pruned and arranged into a vast olive grove with ordered rows of green-and-silver trees covering the entire expanse, which was lush, verdant, and vital.

Oh, if I could paint that! she thought. *If I could somehow capture the luxuriousness of those trees and that sky and those clouds. I would never—*

She'd lost count of her steps. Again. Shaking a raised fist toward the neighboring hillside, she mock-yelled in a muted voice, "Curse you, Spoleto!"

Then she moved on. Or, more accurately, she moved up. And up. And up. Finally, she reached her destination: Il Complesso del Duomo di Spoleto. A marvelous plaza nestled near the top of the town and crowned at the center by the Cathedral of Santa Maria Assunta.

Sonya found her usual spot off to the side of a brick-and-stone-paved ramp leading down to the bricked courtyard in front of the cathedral. Then she leaned back and gazed with wonder at the vista spread out beneath her: sand-colored stone buildings to the left topped with red-tiled roofs and a crest of hillside to the right, overflowing with the branches of evergreens. In the center, the cathedral. Its façade featured more sand-and-gravel-colored stones stacked atop elegant archways. Several ornate rose windows were spaced throughout the second and third levels. The focal point at the top was an arched mosaic showing Christ flanked by two women. All three figures were enveloped in a golden backdrop that shone wonderfully in the morning light.

Oh. Sonya drank in the scene. *Oh, this is so, so lovely.*

She'd stood in this same spot every morning for the past five mornings. Completely captivated. Awestruck. Worshipful. She believed she could plant herself here every morning for the rest of her life and feel this same gratitude—this same deep well of appreciation—every single time.

Many locals milled about in the courtyard and on the ramp. A few, like Sonya, seemed to be transfixed by the loveliness of the cathedral in the golden light. Most simply went about their morning.

She loved that about Italy. If this cathedral had been built anywhere in America, it would be a national treasure. But here in a country where every town and village was laced with beauty and bursting with art, this wonderful courtyard and all it contained were just another stunning part of a standard day.

She felt a tap on her shoulder. "Thought I'd find you here."

She sighed and took one final look at the plaza, then turned to greet her father. "Morning, Dad. My, you're dressed sharp today." She brushed at the sleeves and shoulders of his combat uniform, then glanced down at his feet. "I love the way you're using those boots as accent pieces. Very stylish."

He smiled and lifted a foot. "Shined 'em myself." He held up a small spiral notebook. "Plans and assignments for the day. You ready?"

"Let me guess. I'll start out with some contact tracing. Then I'll move to contact tracing. Then, just to shake things up a little bit, I'll jump over to a little something I like to call contact tracing. That about right?"

He smiled again. "That's about right."

Sonya wasn't sure why she kept tapping the seemingly in-exhaustible well of sarcasm that rose inside her whenever she was around her father. But he never seemed to mind. He didn't even roll his eyes. *Mom would have whacked me with a stick by now.*

So far, Major General John Haggerty had been true to his promise back at the café in Millersville. He'd made it a point to spend time with her. The flight over to Italy had been interesting—especially the second half on an Army transport, which had been a little scary. But he'd stayed with her every step. They ate dinner together each evening and often took a walk through the streets of Spoleto, which she loved. When they first arrived, he'd kept her close during conversations with local officials and meetings with other task force leaders. He'd asked for her ideas and basically made her part of the team. Which was nice.

Still, it felt like a barrier of formality stood between them. He didn't treat her like one of his subordinates. But he didn't really treat her like his daughter, either. Not in some of the ways she'd hoped when she said yes to the whole crazy plan.

In recent days, her initial work as her father's primary translator and sometimes adviser had given way to the necessity of contact tracing. She'd become part of the small team that ventured out in search of anyone who potentially could have been in contact with current patients before they were placed under quarantine.

"Can I ask a question, Commander?" She was trying to use the title respectfully, even submissively, but she saw from her dad's amused expression that she was still coming across as sarcastic. "A serious question, I mean. Is that allowed?"

He tilted his head to the side. "What's up?"

"I'm trying to wrap my mind around the big picture of everything we're doing. I get the idea of testing and contact tracing and all this stuff, but . . . what's the endgame?"

"Oh." He put his little notebook in his pocket. "That's a great question. It's important for team members to understand the broader reasons for *why* they're doing what they're doing."

She felt a little glow of warmth at hearing herself described as a *team member* but kept quiet.

"The big picture is that we've identified a new virus that is both dangerous and transmissible through human-to-human contact. A vaccine is months away at best. So our biggest priority right now is to stop it from spreading."

"But it already spread from Crete to here," she said.

"Yeah." She could see the disappointment on her father's face, and she remembered how devastated he'd been when the first tests confirmed that the mystery virus popping up around Spoleto was in fact the Dirty Dozen. "We hoped we had it nailed down there. But the virus had been active for a couple weeks before our team even arrived, so . . . it slipped through the cracks and came here."

He did a half turn and stared up at the crest of an adjacent hill, which housed a magnificent castle-like structure. Sonya followed his eyes to the old fortress, complete with towers and thick walls and even an ancient aqueduct running down across the valley. Hundreds of years old. Spectacular. It used to be open to the public but had been closed several years ago because of damage sustained during a particularly violent earthquake.

She looked back at her dad. "Is there any chance the virus spread to other places? Other than here, I mean?"

He nodded. "A chance, yes. Probably a good chance. We're searching for any signs, but so far there's been nothing else. Thankfully." He pulled his notebook back out from his pocket. "At this point, the biggest weapons we have in this fight are testing, contact tracing, and isolation. We test anyone who has symptoms that mirror the Dirty Dozen. When someone does test positive, we keep them isolated, and then we find anyone who might have been exposed to the virus through that person—then test them. On it goes."

"And you think that can stop it?" She held up her fingers as air quotes: "Stop the spread?"

"I think it can," he said. "It has before. In Spain. We should have our quarantine facility up and running tomorrow. If we can isolate the majority of the people who've contracted the virus, it won't gain enough momentum to grow exponentially. Nipped in the bud."

"What if you don't?"

He lowered his head. "Then we move to regional quarantines—shutting down whole provinces and keeping everyone in isolation for a minimum of three weeks. Like we did in Brazil. And Crete."

"And if that doesn't work?"

"Then we've got a pandemic. Which, given the characteristics of this particular virus, means hundreds of thousands of people will die. Maybe millions."

Sonya swallowed involuntarily. She'd known these things on a general level. Known the stakes and what it all could mean. But hearing the stark reality was sobering. She felt the weight of responsibility settle on her shoulders—and found it heavy.

You carry this all the time, don't you, Dad? How can you stand it?

Another moment of silence continued before he said, "Listen, Smith and Martinez are gonna do another round at the local hospitals to prep the quarantine center. So Caleb will be leading the CT team today. We've got local folks on loan from hospitals for talking with locals in their homes—same team you worked with yesterday, I think. But I'd like you to stick with Caleb in case he needs to make himself heard in a big way. Sound okay?"

She snapped off a salute. "Aye aye, Cap'n."

With business seemingly taken care of for the moment, he put his notebook away and turned a slow circle, looking at the square and its surroundings. Then he stopped and gazed at the cathedral.

Sonya took the opportunity to examine her father's profile. He'd reached his mid-fifties but was still larger than life. He seemed to be in good shape. She peered more closely at the side of his face. Everything about him was solid and square and formidable. Standing there in uniform, he looked like another sculpture chiseled from the marble of a long-ago age.

Except for his ear. That missing chunk. That forever mystery.

Spontaneously she said, "Dad, will you tell me what happened there?"

He turned toward her. "Where?"

"Right th—" She was reaching up to touch the missing part of his ear, but he jerked back. Instinctively. Violently.

She raised her eyebrows, surprised but not surprised. He'd always been sensitive about that spot.

"This?" He reached a hand to the side of his head. He forced a smile. "I've already told you what happened. Lots of times."

Sonya rolled her eyes. "Oh yeah, let me see if I can remember."

She held up a hand to count out the different wild explanations he'd offered when she was younger. "You invented the world's first firecracker earring. You were attacked by a baby great white shark while scuba diving. And you were stranded on an island for three nights and got really, really hungry."

"Don't forget about my boxing match with Mike Tyson."

She sighed. She had no idea why he refused to talk about such an interesting injury. But even Mom said he'd never told her about it, so . . .

He was looking at the cathedral again. "It's beautiful. Your mom would love it here."

Change the subject much, Dad? But he was right. "Yeah," she said. "Mom could spend an hour here with her camera."

"Have you been inside?"

She nodded. "Several times. There's . . ." She held her hands out wide to express the huge amount of artistic treasure housed in that one structure. "There's so much to see." Which was an understatement. The inside of the cathedral was decorated with glorious frescoes, sculptures, and stained glass images. The whole thing was a work of art in its own right.

"The apse has a series of frescoes depicting the Virgin Mary that are . . ." She spent several seconds reaching for the right word before settling on ". . . breathtaking."

"Filippo Lippi," he said. "I hear he was buried within the cathedral so his body would never be separated from his work."

Her mouth gaped open as she stared at him.

He smiled and held up his phone. "I did a little research when I realized you liked this place. Thought I'd try to impress you."

"Well, color me impressed. Well done, Major General!"

"Hey, that reminds me." His face turned serious again as he looked down at her intently. "There's something I wanted to talk with you about. I wasn't sure how you would adapt to this type of life. Army stuff and protocols and all that. I mean, I knew you could handle it, but . . ."

Sonya could tell he was thinking about how to say what he wanted to say. Inwardly, she braced herself for a moment of correction or critique. Prepared herself to face the twin monsters of disappointment and disapproval. *Don't respond,* she reminded herself. *Don't get angry or say something stupid. Be like these other soldiers and just take it.*

"I want to tell you that everything I've seen from you since we arrived in Italy has been exceptional," he continued. "You've jumped into the work with both feet, and I haven't heard you voice a single complaint. You've made yourself part of the team, and you've made yourself *useful* to the team—to me especially."

He was smiling down at her. Beaming at her.

"I'm so glad you agreed to come here with me, Sonya." He didn't say Sonya Pie or Sonya Bear or any other pet name from her childhood. Just Sonya. Just her. "I'm so proud of you."

She felt something spark in her chest. A warm radiance that spread slowly outward to her shoulders and her fingers and her belly and her toes. She had to swallow several times before she felt safe to speak.

"That's kind of you, Dad." She felt the urge to lunge forward and wrap her arms around him—to see if he would pick her up and squeeze her like he'd once done so often. But she resisted, choosing instead to smile. And offer another snappy salute. "Happy to be of service."

He reached out to squeeze her shoulder. "I'm happy too. I'm grateful." He looked up the hill. "Same place for dinner tonight?" They had a favorite restaurant up there near the very top. Actually it was the basement of an old hotel, but the strangozzi was incredible.

"Yeah." She nodded again. Then watched as he walked away,

moving up toward the task force headquarters. The others in the plaza and the street noticed him in a way they would never notice her—backed away unconsciously or cleared a path for this giant of a man in military fatigues. He seemed to notice none of it. Just kept walking with his hands swinging wide and his feet conquering the ground in long, straight strides.

"Love you, Dad," she whispered, still watching him go. For the first time on that spot, the cathedral and all its beauty seemed unimportant and far away.

———————

"All right, team, I'm going to go over this one more time." Caleb spoke with calm authority as he turned the Škoda SUV down a half-paved, half-gravel lane about twenty minutes from the center of Spoleto. "Today's mission is fact-finding only. We are gathering information and only information. There will be no need for security measures outside of standard protocol, and there will be no hint of aggression or intimidation toward the people of this village. Am I clear?"

"Yes, sir." All three soldiers in the back seat answered in unison.

"Yes, sir!" Sonya piped in from the passenger seat.

Caleb turned to look at her and smiled, then brought his gaze back to the road. "I wasn't including you in those orders."

"Well, that could be a problem, sir," she answered. "I am feeling especially aggressive and intimidating this morning."

A few chuckles rolled out from the back seat. Caleb smiled again, then continued his briefing. "Our main point of inquiry for this village is Lorenzo Ricci. Twenty-four years old. Male. Six feet or six-one and approximately a hundred and sixty pounds. Black hair. No current facial hair. Often wears a red baseball cap. Mr. Ricci's girlfriend, Maria Rocha, is believed to have contracted

SARS-CoV-12, pending further tests. Mr. Ricci is a close contact as of yesterday. We would like to speak with him and anyone else who may be a close contact of his or of Ms. Rocha. Our local friends will be the primary points of contact and questioning, and we will record all information obtained."

Sonya looked ahead at the second SUV driving in front of them. The four Italian doctors and nurses had ridden together.

As Caleb continued to lay out the various plans and priorities for this particular trip, Sonya's attention drifted out the windows and into the luscious countryside around her. Yellow wildflowers were in bloom everywhere—in the fields and on the hillsides and even growing up in little clusters through the cracked pavement of the road. It was like God had spilled blotches of Cadmium Yellow No. 2 while painting the sunrise and decided not to clean them up.

She saw various lanes and trails leading off the road but few houses. No shops or businesses. Not close to the road, anyway. She did see one large sign advertising a resort of some kind, with pictures of four-wheelers and horses and bottles of wine surrounding what appeared to be a refurbished convent. The place was called Il Borgo Incantato."

The enchanted village, Sonya thought. *Sounds fun.*

Could she convince her father to spend a day with her out there for a little rest and relaxation? He worked such long hours every day and seemingly never took a break. But no, she had a different plan in mind for Commander Haggerty—a more realistic plan.

Hopping out of the car a few minutes later, Sonya sighed with disappointment as she looked up at the little hamlet of Pompagno. Once again, *up* was the operative word. It was only nine thirty, but the sun was already beating down the back of her neck with an aggressive intensity.

Aggressive and intimidating, she thought. Then she scooped her wide-brimmed hat out of the car, snapped a mask over her nose and mouth, and prepared to start climbing with the rest of the team.

The next hour proceeded according to established routine. The four volunteers from Italian hospitals spread out to knock on the doors of different homes and speak with the occupants inside. Each volunteer was accompanied by a PPTF escort, who recorded the necessary information. Caleb worked through Sonya to offer instructions or suggestions to the volunteers, and the volunteers worked through Sonya to ask him questions or offer suggestions of their own.

Several of the villagers wanted to speak with Caleb. Most of their questions were the same. "Why is the Army here?" "What has Lorenzo done?" "Where is Maria Rocha?"

Caleb always maintained eye contact with the villagers who wanted to see him, even when Sonya began translating his answers. He smiled often and generally made every effort to show that he was not a threat.

For Sonya's part, she continued to feel a creeping sense of disquiet about the state of the villagers. She'd spent the better part of a year in Rome during her undergraduate studies, but she'd also visited the Italian countryside on several occasions. What she experienced on those outings were lovely people filled with warmth and hospitality—not just among individuals, but in the towns and hamlets as a whole.

This was different. It *felt* different. Hunger ran rampant in Pompagno, that much was clear. She saw few gardens and almost no chickens scratching around in the yards. The people she talked with were too thin, their faces too gaunt, and their eyes too sallow.

But the overall feel of the village was wrong. The vibe. She didn't hear laughter. She didn't see children out kicking soccer balls or chasing one another. Instead of warmth and hospitality, the people regarded her with suspicion—sometimes even with something close to hostility.

"You've been quiet today."

Caleb's voice pulled her out of her thoughts, and she glanced around. The Italian volunteers and the task force soldiers were sitting together under a shady tree, their backs against a stone wall. She must have missed Caleb's call for a water break.

"Me, quiet?"

He grinned. "Quieter than usual. Something on your mind?"

She took a moment to put her hands on her hips and stretch her back, which was starting to get sore. She felt the sweat on her shoulders and at the bottom of her shirt. The day was still getting hotter.

"I'm trying to process what I've been seeing in these towns the past few days. The people . . ." She struggled for a way to express what was bothering her. "It's not what I remember. It's not what it should be."

Caleb nodded as if he understood. "People are hurting all over. The system has been under tremendous strain for years now, and things are getting worse."

"What system?"

He shrugged. "I don't know what to call it exactly. The West. Our modern way of life. There's always been a tug between corporations and governments in that system—both seeking control. Both seeking to take advantage when the other was struggling. Now both are struggling at the same time."

"Because of the horrors?"

He tilted his head sideways, a wry smile on his lips. People had started using that phrase on social media to blow off steam about all the bad headlines that kept piling up. *Another hurricane batters the Southeast—the horror! Your children are at risk from the duck flu pandemic. #TheHorror.*

It had started as a quirky way to deal with something overwhelming. Hurricanes on the rise. Earthquakes on the rise. Flooding on the rise. New diseases popping up all over the place. Food shortages and supply chain problems. They all became "the horrors," and the name seemed to strike a nerve somehow. It stuck.

"Everything is connected," Caleb continued. "Natural disasters put a strain on the insurance market, and prices go up. Energy costs too. Pandemics put a strain on the health industry, and prices go up. Governments try to step in by throwing money at everything and building more bureaucracy, which means taxes go up. People don't have money to buy what they need, which hits retailers, and they start cutting jobs and dropping salaries."

He shook his head. Spent a moment looking up and down the road zigzagging through Pompagno. "Rural places like this usually get hit first and hardest. It's happening all over."

"But this isn't some third-world nation." Sonya didn't buy the cool efficiency of Caleb's calculations. "This is Italy. This is Europe! There are supposed to be safeguards in place. How can things be this bad?"

Caleb raised an eyebrow. "Things are better back in Millersville? Is it any different there?"

She lowered her eyes and crossed her arms over her chest. No, things weren't different back in Millersville. Not really. She had friends who'd sold their cars to keep food on the table or who rode their bikes or walked to work. Lots of people were in the process of losing their homes to the bank. Several small businesses had shut down. Truth be told, even though Sonya and her mom worked hard at multiple jobs, they wouldn't be making it without the money they received from her dad every month.

It was time to change the subject. "Hey, I wanted to ask you something. I know you've been talking with Mom about spiritual stuff. Like, the Bible and other things."

Caleb lifted his head, his eyes wide. He gazed at her with interest and surprise, but also with a good deal of caution.

He doesn't feel comfortable sharing anything about Mom, she realized.

"I know that's all personal." She held up her hands. "But Mom and I have talked about it a lot. I've been thinking about a lot of . . . well, a lot of those types of things."

Jeepers, talk about spinning your wheels. Move on, girl!

Should she share with Caleb about the group she'd become part of on Wednesday nights, or about some of the questions she'd been chewing on? No, something more pressing was on her mind.

"Anyway, Mom's had a lot of good things to say about your conversations, and I guess I was wondering . . . I guess I'm wondering if you've had any of those conversations with Dad?"

Caleb still hadn't said anything. He leaned back against a stone wall and scratched the top of his head for a few moments. Somehow, he didn't seem to be sweating in the still-rising heat. "You'd like to know if I've had spiritual conversations with your father?"

Sonya met his eyes. "Yeah, I'd like to know that."

"Okay." He thought for several moments, head down. Then he met her eyes once more. "First, you need to know that my faith isn't something I just talk about. It's part of who I am. It's actually the most important part of who I am."

She nodded, forcing herself to say nothing and wait for him to continue.

"What that means is that everything I do, I do as a person of faith. Every conversation I have—including conversations with your dad—are spiritual conversations for me. They have spiritual implications . . . spiritual weight."

She waited.

"So . . . if you're asking whether I've had direct conversations with your dad about God and what it means to have a relationship

with Him—the same topics your mom and I have spoken about—
the answer is yes. Lots of times."

What does he say? How does he respond? What does he believe?
The questions swarmed into her mind, but once again she held
them back—once again clamped her lips closed and kept them
closed.

Now it was Caleb's turn to be silent. Perhaps he was playing a
vocal game of chicken. Sonya was right on the verge of letting one
of those questions slip through when he said, "If you'd like to hear
my opinion, I think the biggest obstacle between your father and
God is the issue of control. You've heard about his history? His
relationship with your grandfather?"

She nodded. In truth, she'd heard very little from her father
about Grandpa Steve, who died when she was only four or five.
But her mother had filled in a few of the details.

"At least partly because of that history, your dad places a high
value on control. I think in some ways he *needs* to be in control of
himself and in control of what's happening around him. But the
first thing a person has to do in order to accept a relationship with
God is give up control of their lives. I have to say, 'God is God, and
I am not.' I have to let go of my will and my plans and then submit
to God's will and God's plans."

"I don't think I've ever seen my dad submit to anything."

He smiled. Sadly, she thought. His face was shadowed by grief.
"What about you?"

Me? The new direction caught her off guard. *Is he asking if I
can submit or if I have submitted? Does he want to know what I
believe?* The questions whizzed through her brain, but no answers
whizzed along behind them. There was so much she still needed
to understand and to process.

"I . . ." She started to stammer out some kind of answer, but then
Caleb finished his question.

"Do you have someone you can talk with about these kinds of things?"

Oh, thank God. She didn't recognize the irony of that particular thought—that phrasing. She just enjoyed the moment of relief, then nodded.

"Yeah." She was thinking of her Wednesday night group and of Pastor Burrows and his kindness. "A few people, actually."

"That's good." He was smiling now. "If you ever need another, I'm here."

"Thanks."

"Well, we'd best get this show back on the road." Turning toward the shade tree, he called out, "Gentlemen!" The three men from the task force pulled themselves up to their feet, and the Italians followed a few seconds later.

Sonya turned away to gaze back across the fields. She still felt a flush of adrenaline working through her system. Her heart was beating rapidly. *What about me? What do I believe about all this? What would it mean for me to—*

Something red flashed across the corner of her eye. Turning slightly, she saw a man working his way through a tree line in the middle of the field, doing his best to keep the trees between himself and the village. He wore jeans and a generic-looking white T-shirt, but he carried a bright red baseball hat in his hand. Sonya guessed he was six feet tall and about 160 pounds.

"Caleb!" she hissed. "I mean, Sergeant. I think I see Lorenzo Ricci in the field behind you. I think he's running away."

To his credit, Caleb didn't turn around and crane his neck. He didn't cry out, "Where?" Instead, he remained still and calmly called out to his men, "Murphy. Yang. Come here." When they complied, he bent his head and quickly gave them a series of instructions, speaking too softly for Sonya to make out the words.

Both soldiers said, "Yes, sir." Then, as if by some invisible command, both men turned around, hopped over the low wall they'd just been leaning against, and sprinted into the field. The man with the red hat yelped in surprise, then turned and dashed away. He was fast, but both soldiers seemed to be gaining on him quickly.

Sonya looked over at Caleb and raised her eyebrows.

"They won't hurt him," he said. "They won't even touch him. But they will make it clear through gestures or whatever means they can that they want him to come back to the village and that they're not going to leave his side until he does return. Until then"—he sighed and looked up at the sun now almost directly above him— "we get back to it."

Which they did. Sonya went back to walking and talking and translating, mostly remaining by Caleb's side. But she couldn't help glancing back at the field every few minutes to see what might turn up.

Sure enough, about twenty minutes later, she saw the man with the red cap—flanked by Murphy and Yang—trudge around the corner of a nearby stone house. He slouched forward toward Caleb, who had just turned around to meet him.

"Good eyes back there," he told her.

"Thanks. I—"

With a sudden burst of speed, the man with the red cap darted forward and skidded to a stop directly in front of Sonya.

"Where Maria?" he cried out. "Where Maria?"

Caleb was there in an instant, knifing his body between hers and the man's. His shoulder brushed against her face, pulling her mask off to the side. "Don't touch him!" said Caleb, and Sonya realized he was talking to the soldiers, not to her. "Don't touch him!"

She felt Caleb's weight moving away from her, but there was still one more moment when Ricci's face pushed toward her own. "Maria!" he screamed. "Maria!"

Then it was over. Caleb somehow moved the man away without grabbing him, and then Murphy stepped in front of her, shielding her.

Standard security protocols, she thought. She felt shaken as she replaced the mask. She was breathing rapidly, her hand nestled protectively near the base of her throat—as if by instinct she'd believed Ricci would go for the jugular. She was also uncertain whether she'd done anything wrong.

Murphy was looking down at her. "You okay?"

"I'm fine. Go help Caleb—er, go help Sergeant Johnson."

"Never a dull moment," said Murphy. Then he left.

Sonya took another breath. She considered sitting down but decided staying on her feet was best. Not for the first time she wondered, *Oh, Commander Haggerty, what have you gotten me into?*

CHAPTER 6

So we're talking about two separate leaks?"

Haggerty was trying hard to keep the frustration and anger from seeping into his conversation with Corporal Yang, but the heat made it difficult. They were seated in their headquarters near the top of Spoleto. It was about one in the afternoon, which meant the sun was blazing through the thin curtains hung above the windows and turning the little plastered office area into what felt like a miniature oven.

"Yes, sir," answered Yang. "Two separate leaks. One yesterday evening and another this morning."

Haggerty wiped his hand across his forehead and through his hair, then spent a moment rubbing the back of his neck. "That would be two separate shifts, correct?"

"Yes, sir. Two shifts."

Haggerty sighed, then looked toward the other side of the room where Caleb leaned against a wall. "Make it make sense, Cay."

His friend shrugged. "Quarantine protocols have been in place for three days now. Same protocols we used in Spain and in Crete— but not the same security personnel. We don't have our own guys, so we've requisitioned the equivalent of the local national guard. But..."

"The locals are leaky," Haggerty finished.

Caleb nodded.

This was a problem they'd dealt with before. One of the key aspects of maintaining any kind of quarantine zone was the ability to enforce that quarantine. Even when people knew they'd been infected with a dangerous and contagious disease, they rarely volunteered to be isolated for days or weeks at a time. They had to be confined and monitored by security personnel, which took training and constant vigilance.

The Potential Pandemic Task Force had its own security force for maintaining a quarantine, but the majority of those soldiers were still in Crete. Here in Umbria, they'd been relying on local forces to provide security for their initial operations—administering tests, contact tracing, and more. But as of three days ago, Haggerty's team had officially established a new quarantine center at a local hospital and had begun enforcing isolation for those who tested positive for the Dirty Dozen. So far only a few dozen people had officially tested positive, but Haggerty expected that number to grow as they continued to broaden their efforts in testing and contact tracing.

Now he had to deal with leaks, which were people who had tested positive for the disease and been assigned to the quarantine facility for a minimum of two weeks—yet had somehow slipped through the cracks and left that facility. More than likely, they had been allowed to leave by local security forces who either knew them personally or were persuaded that they posed no threat.

Which was a problem whenever communicable diseases were part of the picture. A big problem.

Haggerty rubbed the bridge of his nose between his thumb and forefinger, trying to relieve the pressure building there.

We didn't stop the virus in Crete, he thought. *We let it out. Now it's leaking through security in Italy, and if we can't stop it . . . if I can't stop it . . .*

"Okay, guys." Haggerty glanced from Caleb to Yang and back to Caleb. "Options?"

The three of them bounced around a few half-hearted suggestions—more training for the local security officers, wiring up more video-surveillance systems, finding a new quarantine facility that offered fewer points of exit, and so on. They were picking at the symptoms of the problem without addressing the root.

Finally, Caleb voiced the only option with any real chance of success. "When it comes to it, the only way to ensure proper containment is to bring in a lot more soldiers. Our soldiers."

Haggerty nodded wearily. This was the approach that had worked in Brazil. And Spain. And Crete. It would mean once again leveraging General Burgess's authority in order to essentially occupy a large area of a foreign country. It would mean using the United States Army to force the compliance not only of government officials within a sovereign nation, but of a huge percentage of that nation's population as well.

"I've heard from Burgess on this," said Haggerty. "Our actions in Crete seem to have worn out our welcome for much of the European Union. If we try to assert that authority again, she's not sure it will hold just because we're asking nicely."

"What does that mean?" Caleb asked. "Nicely?"

Haggerty rubbed his face with his palms. "It means we are running out of carrot, but we still have plenty of stick. If we want to enforce another rigid quarantine within the borders of a sovereign nation, we may have to do it by force."

"You mean a declaration of war." Caleb's voice was grave.

"Yes. That's what it may take to force the Italians to accept a full quarantine in Umbria."

"A full quarantine is our best shot at containing the Dirty Dozen before it moves into more of Europe." Caleb and Haggerty were mainly talking to each other now, with Yang listening politely. "It may be our only shot."

Out of the corner of his eye, Haggerty saw movement in the lobby of the old hotel they were using as a temporary HQ. The contact-tracing team had returned for the day. Sonya pushed through the outer doors, appearing more haggard than usual—much more tired. She was limping slightly.

"Listen," Haggerty told Caleb and Yang, "I need a little time to think this through. In the meantime, Yang, I'd like you to visit the hospital again and raise a little hell in there. See if you can put the fear of God into the admins and anyone who's overseeing security. Let's get the current leaks plugged, and then we'll figure out next steps."

"Will do, sir."

As Yang left, Haggerty followed him through the office door. "Hey," he called out to Sonya, waving his hand. "How'd it go?"

She walked over to him—or, more accurately, trudged over to him, still with a limp. "Hey, Dad. Bit of a long one today, to be honest."

He didn't like the sound of her voice, which was raspy and too soft. He also didn't like the way she was carrying herself. Shoulders slumped, movements stiff and jerky. Her face seemed pale and flushed, and her eyelids were fluttering—as if she was trying hard to keep them open.

"You look shot."

She flashed a wry smile. "Glad I can always count on you for that fatherly encouragement." Even her attempts at humor seemed worn out.

"Okay, you need the rest of the day off. I want you to punch out and get some sleep."

She rolled her eyes. "Don't go into dad-mode now. We have plenty of contacts that still need tracing. I just came in for some coffee or . . ." She looked around the room, as if trying to remember a previous train of thought. "Or something."

"Nope." Haggerty spoke with authority. "This isn't a dad thing. This is a commander thing. Bad stuff happens when overly tired personnel try to push through the fog, so I'm ordering you to get some rest."

"If I had AC in my hotel room, I might take you up on that." She fluffed the front of her shirt back and forth to generate a little air. Haggerty noticed the sweat stains on her shirt. He examined again the flush of her cheeks and forehead. It was their hottest day yet in Italy, which was saying something.

"There's gotta be somewhere you could go that would be cooler. What about a movie?"

She shook her head. "Not interested. Although . . ."

"What?"

"Nah," she said. "It's nothing."

"No, really." Haggerty touched the top of her arm. "What is it?"

"Well, the Frasassi Caves are about an hour from here. I went there a couple times when things were too hot in Rome. The walk through the caves is just gorgeous—I mean, it's *so* beautiful." Her face brightened for a moment, charged by memory. "*And*, because it's underground, everything stays seventy degrees all the time. It's deliciously cool."

"Okay," said Haggerty. "That's what you need. We'll arrange a driver to make sure you get there and back without any issues."

"Actually, Dad, I—"

"No, no," he broke in. "No excuses and no insubordination. This is an order."

She watched him in silence for several seconds. A strange half grin lit her face that Haggerty didn't understand. Not at first.

"What I was saying is that I already know who's going to drive me to the caves." She waggled her eyebrows up and down several times in rapid succession. The half grin became a full-on smirk. "Remember: You promised two days ago we could do something together outside Spoleto."

"What do you mean I prom—? Oh." He started to shake his head. "Sonya, I really would love to go with you, but I just can't. There's too much going on."

"Really?" She put a hand on her hip and lifted her chin. "Because I've been keeping track, and I'm pretty sure you haven't taken *any* time off since we got here. You're here early in the morning and you come back here after dinner every evening. I'm not even sure you're actually sleeping at night."

"Look, Sonya, it's—"

"*And*," she continued, "I've heard with my own ears that the commander of this task force doesn't want team members pushing themselves that hard. 'Bad stuff happens when overly tired personnel try to push through the fog.'"

Haggerty sighed. He'd always resented it when Marianna tossed his own words back at him. He liked it even less coming from his daughter. "I understand what you're doing, and I will take you up on that promise soon. But not now. Not today. There's . . . there's too much going on."

"Actually, sir . . ."

Haggerty jerked his head to the left. He hadn't realized Caleb had followed him out of the office.

"You did mention you needed some time to think about recent developments," Caleb finished. "This might be a good chance for you to get away from all the distractions of the office."

Haggerty stared at Caleb for several seconds. Stared at him closely. Then spent the same amount of time examining his daughter's face. Neither of them smiled or winked at each other.

In fact, both seemed to be making an effort *not* to acknowledge the other.

Et tu, Cay?

Sonya was still smiling. "Sounds like this would be a win-win for everybody." Her shoulders were no longer so slumped. She'd regained her usual posture and her face looked less haggard. He guessed if he asked her to take a walk with him down the street, her limp would be gone as well.

"I'm not asking you to take the whole day off." Sonya was staring at him intensely. "I can see you really are dealing with something big today. All I'm asking for is three hours—an hour drive to the caves, an hour in the caves, and an hour back. Just a little break. You can still take your evening shift and clean up whatever messes are left over from the afternoon."

He said nothing. In all honesty, he was impressed at how efficiently she had maneuvered him exactly where she wanted him to go without leaving him any real options for refusal. *Marianna would be proud.*

"And," she said with a flourish of her hands, "you can make phone calls on the ride there and back if you really need to. So it's really only an hour. *And* you did promise we would spend some time together."

Check and mate. And I didn't even realize we were playing.

"Sergeant Major." He looked over at Caleb. "Please spread the word among senior staff that my phone will be limited to actual the-base-is-exploding emergencies for the next four hours. I'm going to spend some time with my daughter."

"Really? Yay! Yay! Yay!" Sonya squealed as she jumped up and down, clapping her hands. Ecstatic that her plan had worked.

Watching her, Haggerty was transported twenty years back in time to the living room of their modest apartment in the suburbs of Washington, D.C. He saw a little girl dressed in rumpled pajamas and clutching a plastic doll, shreds of wrapping paper scattered at her feet. He heard the same squeals and the same "Yay! Yay! Yay!" Saw the same jumps and the same claps. The same unfiltered joy.

The memory was sweet and poignant.

And painful.

Still, in that moment, as he watched his daughter's face and drank in her delight, he felt like a father again for the first time in a long time. A real father.

This is what I've been missing all these years. This is what I've chosen to miss because I couldn't handle Ryan's ... because I couldn't handle my own failure. But no more. He took her hand in his own and opened himself to the happiness it represented. And the grief. And the fullness. And the loss. He opened himself to the possibility of what might be.

No more, he told himself. *I won't lose this again.*

Ninety minutes later, Haggerty was walking next to his daughter in the middle of the largest cave he'd ever seen. They were part of a tour group of about forty people, but the group had spread out after only a few minutes. He and Sonya were walking alone. She'd taken hold of his arm when they descended a set of metal stairs near the middle of the tour, and she still held it, her fingers wrapped softly around his forearm. He enjoyed the feeling of closeness as they walked. He relished again the sensation of giving and receiving affection.

My little girl. He looked down at her face as she gazed outward into the cave. *My little Sonya Pie all grown up.*

She smiled up at him. "Well, well, Commander Haggerty. If I

had to judge based solely on the expression on your face right now, I'd say you're having a pretty good time."

He heard a hint of smugness in her voice, but something else simmered under the surface. Uncertainty, or maybe even anxiety. *She wants to know if I'm mad at her because she tricked me into coming here,* he realized. *She wants to know if she did the right thing.*

He saw the confirmation in her eyes. "I would tell any inquiring minds that my daughter is a wise young woman who is filled with good ideas. Including this one."

She grinned up at him. "Which would be another way of saying . . . ?"

"That you were right."

"Ahh." She indulged herself in a long, luxurious sigh. "'Make the upcoming hour overflow with joy, and let pleasure drown the brim.'"

"Is that Shakespeare?"

She nodded. "Yep. I like to break out the Bard when I'm in lovely places."

"Well, there's another thing you're right about." He took a moment to examine their surroundings once more. "This is a lovely place."

The cave was huge. Actually, it was more than a single cave. It was a massive series of mammoth, river-carved chambers set deep in the heart of a mountain. This particular chamber was several hundred feet wide—longer than a football field, at least— and perhaps a hundred feet high from floor to ceiling. The entire space was enclosed in limestone, with no visible access to the outside world.

Standing there, craning his neck to gaze upward and outward, Haggerty felt the slow drag of eons across the face of the world.

At some unconscious level, he could sense the power of time in this place—the muscular contractions of ages piled upon ages and forces clashing with other forces outside his active comprehension. It made him feel tiny and exposed, as if he were lurking in the long-abandoned lair of some colossal beast.

But the caves themselves were not the main attraction Sonya had brought him to see. That honor belonged to the Seussian stalactites and stalagmites that filled each chamber with crazy formations of every size and shape, both imaginable and un-imaginable. Dripped into existence out of the limestone, most of the formations ranged from brilliant white to eggshell white to pinkish white, with each color highlighted by well-placed lighting.

The entire experience was weird and wonderful and beautiful and strange.

It was also cold. Sonya had been right about that as well. The two of them were walking along a metal pathway made up of textured grating and sturdy railings, which allowed a steady breeze to play across their arms and legs. Haggerty was glad he'd allowed Sonya to talk him into wearing a jacket. He felt delight-fully chilly for the first time in weeks.

They were nearing the end of the tour, walking a second time through chambers they'd already seen. As they rounded a corner of the pathway, he reached out to touch a mushroom-shaped protrusion branching off an especially large stalagmite. He expected the stone to be wet because of the way it gleamed in the light, but it was dry. And hard. And very smooth. It felt exactly like what Haggerty imagined ice might feel like if it were somehow trans-formed into stone.

"Huh." He turned toward Sonya and started to say, "Feel this," when a sharp male voice called out from behind him.

"No, no! *Fermare!*"

Haggerty turned his head to look behind him. A man scowled up at him, speaking rapidly and angrily in Italian. He wore plain clothes—jeans and a T-shirt—with a bright red baseball cap. He was pointing his index finger directly at Haggerty.

Instinctively, Haggerty turned and stepped slightly backward, placing himself between this angry young man and his daughter—and also placing his chin directly in front of the smaller man's face. "Is there a problem?"

The man continued his flow of words, still pointing at Haggerty's chest.

Haggerty was starting to feel annoyed. *"Non parlo Italiano."* He felt Sonya shift behind him as he spoke, probably leaning to the side so she could get a look at whomever he was talking to. Then he felt her stiffen. Her fingers clenched more tightly against his arm.

The man stood still for a moment in silent rage. Then he yelled in a thick accent, "No touch! No touch! No for America. No touch!"

Haggerty crossed his arms in front of his chest, looked down at the man, and waited.

With a final angry exhalation—"Chuh!"—the unknown man stepped past Haggerty and hurtled down the path. Four or five others followed him, heads down to avoid making eye contact with the large American soldier.

When they'd all moved on, Haggerty turned to Sonya. "What was that about? Could you understand?"

She nodded but seemed shaken. "He didn't want you to touch any of the limestone. Something about Americans ruining everything. But, Dad." She lowered her voice. "That was Lorenzo Ricci!"

Haggerty looked ahead at the retreating group, then back at Sonya. "Who?"

"Lorenzo Ricci. We found him on one of our contact-tracing assignments. His girlfriend tested positive for the Dirty Dozen, and Caleb's team quarantined him. How can he be out here instead?"

Haggerty grunted. He took her hand in his and smiled regretfully. "It's been a wonderful break, but we'll need to catch up with him and make sure he's detained—him and the group he's with."

"You're going to arrest him in the caves?" Her voice was half hopeful and half incredulous.

Haggerty shook his head. "We'll stay close to him on the tour, and we'll catch the same shuttle back to the parking lot. Then we can call for backup." He flexed his shoulders and rubbed his hands together. "I may have to physically prevent him from driving away. You okay with that?"

Sonya grinned. "If he's got one of those tiny European cars, you can probably just lift the back wheels off the ground. I'll lay on the hood or something. Let's go!"

They went, hurrying for a minute or more until they caught up within a hundred feet of the red hat and his friends, then maintained that gap. Haggerty estimated they were about five minutes from the long, tunneled ramp at the entrance of the tour.

"I don't understand how this happened," said Sonya. "I thought this guy was quarantined—like, he was in the facility. So how did he get out?"

"We're dealing with a leak in our security." Haggerty tried to temper his anger at the thought.

"You mean Ricci was a friend of the guard's or something? Oh, or maybe he bribed the guard! Does that happen?"

"It *shouldn't* happen. Not when the guards understand how serious . . ."

Haggerty's voice trailed off. Then he slowed down. Then he stopped. He looked back across the cavernous chamber, head tilted to one side. Something was wrong. He could sense it somewhere in his subconscious—maybe all the way down in the brain stem where the instincts of his ancient ancestors still lurked.

Sonya had continued walking for a few paces, but now she turned and stared back at her father. "What is it?"

"I don't know." His words seemed to come from far away. "I feel like—"

The metal walkway shifted. It was a subtle movement. Haggerty sensed it through his boots more than his eyes. Then the walkway jolted sharply upward, then down again. Then it began to shake.

Haggerty flexed his knees instinctively, looking over at Sonya. She was holding the nearest railing, and she gaped at him with wide, terrified eyes.

"Earthquake . . ." He said the word softly at first, speaking only to Sonya. Then he turned and shouted at the tourists making their way through the chamber in various groups and clumps. "Earthquake! Everyone get down! Stay close to the—"

The sound struck at the same time as the massive vibrations. Haggerty was overwhelmed by a deep, resonant rumbling mixed with a tremendous cacophony of cracks and snaps. In between the raw power of those sounds, he also heard the cries and shrieks of terrified tourists. And Sonya's voice as well. She was screaming.

He managed to take one step toward his daughter before the walkway shifted crazily beneath his feet, sending him sprawling backward. His lower back struck the textured metal, sending up flares of pain, but he managed to tuck himself into a roll and wrap his arms over his head.

He came to rest against the railing, his eyes searching frantically for Sonya in the shifting light. He saw her crouched against her own section of the railing, squatting like a catcher ready to take a pitch. One of her arms was wrapped around the metal bar of the railing.

"Stay down!" he called to her. "Stay—"

A tremendous series of crashes overrode the end of his command. Huge chunks of rock and stalactite were falling from the ceiling. Most of them smashed into the bottom of the cave or crashed against shaking stalagmites rising from the floor.

Some of the projectiles struck the metal railing, each time making a terrible *clang*.

Haggerty heard yells and screams in between each colossal impact.

How long has it been? His mind whirled with insane speed, trying to capture and catalog every moment. *Two seconds? Four?*

He tucked his feet beneath his waist and began edging his way forward, holding on to the railing for support. Making his way toward Sonya slowly. And implacably.

She's okay, he told himself. He could see the fear radiating from her face but also the grim determination. The will to survive. *She's okay. She's—*

An enormous *crack!* rang out very close by. The sound of it alone almost knocked Haggerty rolling backward again. Looking up, he saw one of the larger stalagmites break free from the ground. It swayed lazily to the right, then back to the left—toward the walkway. Toward Sonya.

She saw it too. Or sensed it. She raised herself to a crouch and began shambling toward the mouth of the chamber, which was away from the falling column of rock—and away from Haggerty.

"Go! Go! Go!" Haggerty cried, unable to reach her but willing her forward.

He watched, rooted to the spot, as the stalagmite tipped over in slow motion. The limestone pillar was a glimmering white streak with patches of dull pink. Several rounded joints and bumps protruded from the vertical shaft, as if different pieces had been welded together over the millennia. Several larger nubs and knobs jutted out from the sides of the shaft like weathered spikes on a war club. Like everything else in the caves, the whole column was encased in an unforgiving frosting.

It's like Ghostbusters II, Haggerty thought. He was still watching Sonya—still willing her to run. To escape. But his mind kept zagging off in wild directions and making crazy connections. *The scene where they cover the inside of the Statue of Liberty with slime and it looks like a pink cupcake exploded all over everything. That's what this whole cave looks like.*

The broken stalagmite kept falling. Sonya kept shuffling away, although slowly. Oh, so slowly.

Jump! Haggerty screamed in his mind. But she didn't jump. She kept moving forward as the column of rock slammed into the metal walkway behind her. There was a screech of metal and a scream from Haggerty's throat. Both impossibly loud.

Sonya stumbled forward, seemingly untouched. She caught hold of the railing even as the walkway twisted and groaned behind her. Then the top of the stalagmite struck the rock wall behind the walkway. It exploded, sending chunks of rock in every direction.

One of the chunks struck Sonya just above the waist. Haggerty saw it. Reached out. Could do nothing.

"No!"

The piece of rock was about the size of a carry-on suitcase. It hit Sonya at an angle, spinning her body farther forward—farther away from Haggerty.

The sound of the rock striking her body was a hideous, horrible *thump*. A golf club striking an overripe pumpkin at full speed. He knew even in that instant that he would hear the same sound in his nightmares over and over again.

"Sonya!" The room was still shaking, but Haggerty rose to his feet and ran. He sprinted forward. He vaulted over the still-settling column of rock where it had crashed into the metal walkway, skimming and scrambling over stone that still felt unnaturally cool and disturbingly dry. Then he ran again several more steps until he slid to his knees and lifted her head in his hands.

Gently, he reminded himself. *So, so gentle now.*

"Sonya!" he called to her. Looked desperately at her face. At her eyes. At her hair spilling darkly over his arm.

She opened her eyes. Blinked once. Twice. Then looked at him.

"Oh, thank goodness. You're okay. You're okay." He wasn't sure if he was talking to her or to himself, but he kept repeating those same words. "You're okay."

"Dad." Her voice was weak. Raspy. "Dad, I . . ."

The majority of the shaking had stopped several seconds ago, and now the last vestiges of the quake dwindled into stillness. But not silence. Haggerty still heard the roll and rumble of rock throughout the cavern. Heard the cries and wails of people nearby. But his attention was on Sonya. Only Sonya.

"Dad, I think I—"

The lights had flickered several times during the peak of the earthquake. Now they went out completely. Haggerty, Sonya, the rest of the tourists, the cave—everything plunged into a deep and uncaring darkness.

CHAPTER 7

Hey! Sir!" Caleb was half walking, half jogging along the edge of a narrow road, moving toward a group of Italian men in workman uniforms. He called out to the man at the front of the group who, based on earlier observation, Caleb understood to be in charge. "Hello, sir? Sir!"

The man heard him and turned around. When he recognized Caleb, he sighed and rolled his eyes.

That makes two of us, friend.

It was nearly six in the morning, and Caleb had been hovering outside the entrance to the cave system for several hours. He'd already attempted to have two separate conversations with this particular gentleman—first by speaking in English and hoping someone on the man's team would be able to translate, and second by trying to lead the man in an increasingly complex game of charades. Both attempts had been colossal failures.

Caleb was ready for round three, but he had a new approach. He held up a finger toward the man to say, "One second." Then he opened the translation app on Corporal Yang's phone.

"Have you heard anything from the victims trapped inside the cave?" Caleb spoke loudly into the phone, making sure to enunciate each word. He looked down at the screen.

Nothing happened.

He held up another finger toward the man. *One moment. I'll get this.* He pushed a button in the shape of a microphone on the screen, then spoke again. "Have you heard anything from the people trapped in the cave?"

The microphone button dissolved into a spinning wheel for two seconds, and then his own words appeared in English on the screen. *Okay. Progress.* He made sure *Italian* was selected as the target language, then pressed the button marked *Translate.* There was another spinning wheel, this time much longer, then an error message. "No connection detected. Please reconnect and try again."

"Oh, for crying out . . ." Caleb glanced around. The place where he stood was surrounded by mountains and sheer rock faces on several sides. Not a good spot for cellular reception.

The Italian man was tapping his foot, his face plastered with impatience. With a parting phrase in Italian, he turned and walked back to the other members of his crew. They resumed their conversation, which included a lot of pointing and gesturing toward the main tourist entrance for the cave.

Oh, Haggs, you would love seeing me like this. You would laugh and laugh and laugh.

He looked up at the mountain directly atop the entrance to the cave, trying not to imagine the weight of something so immense crashing down on top of his friend. On top of Sonya.

Once again, the questions began cramming themselves into his brain like roaches squirming toward some rotting prize. Were the caves intact, or did they collapse? How many collapsed? How many people were inside? Did the authorities have any evidence of survivors? Had there been any sort of communication at all with the people still inside? What kind of secondary access tunnels were available for the rescue teams?

So many questions. Yet after several hours of phone conversations and in-person contacts and countless trips walking up and down the taped-off perimeter of the cave's main access, Caleb had very few answers to connect with those questions. Very little information at all, really.

The uncertainty gnawed at him, making him feel hot and flushed even in the brisk early morning mountain air.

Is my friend alive? That was the biggest question of all. The heaviest and the hardest to leave unanswered.

Thankfully, Caleb knew how to keep the roaches at bay. At least for a little while. Stepping off the road, he leaned his shoulder against a rock face and closed his eyes. He breathed in deeply through his nose, then let the air out through his mouth—a long and measured exhalation. Then he did it again. And a third time. He allowed his shoulders to relax, feeling the tension leave his knees.

"Heavenly Father, You are on Your throne." He spoke softly and calmly, his voice not quite a whisper. "Heavenly Father, You are in charge of all this mess. I confess I feel afraid. I am afraid for my friend. I am afraid for Sonya. So I am relying on You who protected Daniel in the midst of the lions' den. I am relying on You who kept Jonah safe in the belly of the whale. I am asking You to protect every life in that cave and to bring them out safely. And soon."

He prayed for several minutes. Sometimes talking. Sometimes listening. Sometimes opening himself to new thoughts and new feelings. Eventually he became aware that someone was standing close by. He opened his eyes and saw Yang standing a few feet away, looking uncomfortable.

"Corporal." Caleb handed back the borrowed phone.

Yang's usually clean-shaven face was lined with stubble. He put the phone in his pocket. "Did it work?"

Caleb shook his head. "No signal."

"Yeah." Yang scratched the back of his neck. "I should have downloaded the file for Italian, but Sonya was so helpful . . ."

"Irony," Caleb said. He mused in silence for a moment, then asked, "Did you have any luck? Find anything?"

Yang shrugged. "Not much. I got one seismologist on the phone. She said the earthquake struck at 3:27 p.m. local time. So if anyone sur . . ." He trailed off after seeing a warning look from Caleb, then started again. "So they've been in there for"—a glance at his watch—"almost fifteen hours."

Caleb nodded. "A long time." He glanced up at the eastern sky, where a thin line of pale light had appeared. It would be a while before the sun actually peeked up over the mountains in front of him, but he took comfort in that light all the same. The sun was there. A new day had come.

"'Weeping may endure for a night, but joy cometh in the morning.'" He whispered the long-familiar words. Yang nodded without saying anything.

Caleb was about to walk around the security perimeter for the fourth time—not for any particular reason but simply to be moving rather than standing still—when his phone rang. An unfamiliar ringtone. He took the device out of his pocket, but the screen was blank. He heard the ringtone again, but it wasn't coming from the phone in his hand.

With a start, he pulled out a second phone from his jacket pocket. A satellite phone—one to be used only in case of emergencies.

"Caleb." He was surprised to hear General Burgess on the other end of the line, mainly because it was 1:00 a.m. back in D.C.

"What's the latest on Commander Haggerty?"

"No news, General. We are still at the mercy of local rescue teams."

"Well, I'm sorry to hear it." Her voice, typically a smooth alto, sounded hurried and harassed. "There's a lot of news happening here, Sergeant, and it's forcing me to be blunt. Because you are currently the PPTF's senior officer, I am going to spend the next two minutes updating you on recent events that will be hitting social media in about three minutes. Then I will relay a series of orders I need you to execute without hesitation. Are you ready?"

Caleb felt an uneasy sensation in his stomach—more like a badger rummaging around in there than butterflies. *You're supposed to take these phone calls, Haggs. You're supposed to carry the weight of whatever she's about to tell me.*

After a quick breath and a quick look at Yang, he said, "I'm ready."

The general began to talk. While Caleb listened, he rubbed his hand gently over his midsection. As if he were feeling sick. As if he were about to vomit. After a minute, he lowered himself on creaking knees to sit down on the road, his free hand now cradling the back of his head. When the general asked a question, he said, "Yes, ma'am. I understand." Then he listened once more.

When the general finished speaking, Caleb remained silent for several seconds. His hand now covered his eyes, his long fingers massaging his temples in a rhythmic back and forth, back and forth.

"Caleb?" Burgess was still on the line. "Can I count on you?"

"Yes, ma'am. Except . . ." He spoke with a sense of hollowness that was foreign to him. "Except you can't expect me to leave Haggs trapped in a cave."

"No." Her voice was understanding but also firm. "But I do expect you to relocate somewhere with reliable cell service so you can coordinate everything that needs to be done—both in Italy and in Crete. And if Haggs is ali—" She paused. "When Commander Haggerty is freed from the cave-in, I expect you to make sure he complies with every order I have given you this morning. And I do mean *every* order."

Caleb sighed, then looked again at the cave entrance. There was no jumble of rocks that he could see. The collapse had apparently occurred somewhere deeper in the various tunnels or chambers.

You'd better be in there, Haggs. And you'd better get out here soon.

To the phone he simply said, "Understood." Then he ended the call and rose to his feet.

Yang looked up at him, curious but patient.

"We're relocating to Spoleto, Corporal. I'll explain on the way, but . . ." He gazed up at the mountains surrounding them, then down again at the mouth of the cave. "But right now I very much wish I was in there and Haggs was out here."

As they walked toward the car, Caleb thought of Nehemiah sending up little prayers like arrows before speaking to the king of Persia. *Dear God, give me favor. You protected Daniel. You protected Jonah. Please protect my friend. But oh, my Father, please protect all of us down here on earth. Please protect us from what's about to come. Please have mercy.*

CHAPTER 8

C'mon, gimme something."

Haggerty leaned his forehead against a smooth chunk of limestone, then rotated his head so his left ear rested gently against the rock. He listened. Trying not to breathe. Trying not to think. He willed himself to hear something—the distant rumble of machinery, maybe. Or the echoing shouts of rescuers working frantically to clear away a section of rubble.

Nothing.

He pressed his palm against a different rock, trying to sense if there were any vibrations coming through the tangled pile in front of him. He felt stupid. He felt like one of those guys from old cowboy movies who lay on the ground to feel the vibrations of enemy horses miles off in the distance. But he palmed the rock anyway. Waiting.

Gimme something. He wasn't certain to whom he was addressing his request, but he was fervent in his desire for an answer. *Give. Me. Something. Please.*

He felt nothing. Sensed nothing.

He sighed and stepped back. He was standing in front of a huge pile of rocks, dwarfed by massive chunks of dull gray stone that had collapsed from the ceiling, with similarly massive chunks of pearly stalactites mixed into the mound.

Several hours after the earthquake, Haggerty had led a team of volunteers to try to "dig" their way through this pile of debris. Six men and three women who were relatively unharmed. They'd managed to lift or tumble several loose rocks at the front of the pile, which had given them hope. But after about thirty minutes, it became clear that the majority of the stones were immovable. Their combined efforts hadn't even made a dent in the pile.

In that half hour, though, they had discovered several bodies within the heap of rock. They'd been able to remove three, now laid out as respectfully as possible on the ground near the pile. At least three others remained trapped in the rocks, pinned down by boulders that would not budge. Haggerty could see a woman's shoe sticking out in one place, still strapped to her foot. Others had seen pieces of colored clothing deeper in the mound, and in one spot several strands of black hair.

Haggerty stepped carefully backward, away from the pile. The metal walkway was bent and warped in several places where larger pieces of rock had struck, but overall it seemed relatively stable. He looked at the three bodies lying side by side at the edge of the walkway. One of them was Lorenzo Ricci. His red hat, now matted with dust, covered his face. His neck was broken, which meant he likely didn't suffer. *Small comfort to him now. Small comfort to anyone.*

Farther down the walkway, about twenty feet from the rock pile's edge, was a sturdy map of the cave system that had been mounted to the railing. It was still intact. After moving over to look at it, Haggerty set his finger on top of a big red dot. *You Are Here* written in Italian and English. According to the map, Haggerty was currently in the second chamber of the system. The next chamber—the one currently blocked by the immovable pile of rocks—was the main vault, which Haggerty remembered as being especially huge and especially grand. Then there was a long tunnel carved into the rocks, and at the end, the exit to the outer world.

He traced the tunnel on the map. It was a long, square shaft. He'd noticed on the way in that it was heavily braced, which meant it probably survived the earthquake without collapsing. If Haggerty could somehow make it to the main chamber and it was still clear, and if the tunnel really was still passable—then he could make it back to the world. Make it back and find some help.

A lot of ifs.

Haggerty pulled his phone out of his pocket and turned it on. He checked the signal strength—nothing. Which wasn't a surprise given the fact he was encased in a mountain's worth of rock. But still vaguely disappointing. His battery was at 37 percent.

It was 6:27. A little after sunrise. He thought of Caleb, who was notorious as an early riser. Had he heard about the earthquake? Had he felt it? Had he figured out why Haggerty and Sonya didn't make it back to Spoleto?

Haggerty felt pretty confident the answer to all those questions was yes.

You gotta help me, Cay. You gotta get in here so we can help my Sonya.

He thought about the moment immediately after the earthquake when the decorative lights had flickered, then failed. For several seconds he'd been buried by a darkness unlike anything he'd experienced before. The kind of darkness that carried a suffocating weight—a malicious intensity. Then the emergency lights had kicked in, bathing the entire chamber in a harsh, blue-white glare.

The glare remained, throwing mischievous shadows along the shelves of rock as Haggerty carefully made his way toward the rear of the chamber. Every now and again he encountered a person or a group of people huddled on the metal grating. Sleeping or trying to sleep. Many were wounded, and Haggerty stopped to check on several patients he had treated the night before. An American woman with a broken arm. (*Not compound but likely displaced. She'll need surgery.*) An older man with a nasty gash on his forehead. (*The bleeding stopped. Keep checking for infection. Possible concussion.*) Several people who seemed to be suffering withdrawal symptoms from drugs or medication. (*Got to stay hydrated if possible.*) Several with scratches and cuts of varying severity.

Haggerty reached a place where the metal walkway expanded into a large, semicircular observation deck. Sonya was lying at the back of the observation area near one of the places where the walkway was bolted directly into the cave wall. He'd set her up as comfortably as he could with his uniform jacket as a makeshift pallet. She'd carried a backpack on the tour, which was now tucked under her head as a pillow. She'd been sleeping when he left to check the rockslide. She was awake now, looking at him.

"Welcome back." She spoke in a strained half whisper, heavy with pain.

"I was glad to see you sleeping. You need it." He knelt to study her face, which was difficult to do in the blue-shadow glare. Sweat beaded on her forehead. Pain lines showed around her eyes. She was breathing in harsh little sips, and he heard a rattle in her chest before each exhalation. Her arms were cradled protectively over her abdomen.

Haggerty gestured toward her waist. "May I?"

She moved her arms. Slowly. Carefully. "Knock yourself out, Doc."

Very gently, Haggerty moved aside the unzipped sections of her sweatshirt, then lifted the edge of her blouse. With practiced care, he did not wince or frown at what he saw. Her stomach was a mass of bruises, especially on the right side. Vivid purple splotches surrounded patches of dull, mottled green. She had several broken ribs, at least two of them badly displaced. Haggerty was certain she was bleeding internally—as certain as he could be without a FAST exam. His main concern was whether any of her organs or major blood vessels had been punctured. Not her lungs, thankfully, based on her breathing. But her kidneys or spleen could be damaged. He leaned forward to examine her more closely.

"Please don't touch anything," Sonya croaked.

"No," he answered, speaking gently. "No more of that." His physical examination last night had been necessary but quite painful. For both of them.

He replaced the blouse, then rested a hand gently on top of her foot. "I want you to drink some more water in a little bit." Thankfully she'd brought a couple of bottles in her backpack, but what was left wouldn't last long.

"Have you had any?"

He smiled. "Not yet. I will when I need some."

"Promise?"

He nodded. "I promise. In the meantime, what do you need right now? What can I do?"

She was quiet for a moment. Watching him. "I could really use one of those stories. About before."

Haggerty knew what she meant. He closed his eyes and steeled himself to open that particular box of memories—the one marked *Ryan* in his mind. More than memories resided in that box. There were land mines—explosives filled with shrapnel that would tear his mind apart if he pressed on them too firmly or too often.

After about a minute, he opened his eyes and smiled. "Do you remember Doodle Bear?"

She shook her head. One slight movement to the left, then an even smaller movement back to the right.

"Okay," Haggerty said, still smiling. "He was a stuffie. This was back when you were two or three years old. Which means Ryan was six or seven."

"My stuffie?"

He shook his head. "No, it was Ryan's. But you *thought* it was yours. Or that it should be yours. It was pretty much a regular teddy bear, except it came with special markers you could use to draw on it, and whatever you drew stayed. You could even throw it in the washing machine and the drawings stayed."

She nodded. Slightly.

"You remember it?"

"No. But I get the idea."

"Okay," said Haggerty. "Anyway, Ryan got the Doodle Bear for Christmas, and he liked it okay. He drew on it and played with it sometimes. But you were fascinated with it. You were like a pudgy little cat perched on a tree limb, and whenever he let his guard down or put the Doodle Bear somewhere you could reach it, you pounced."

She grinned. "Pudgy?"

"Yeah. A pudgy little toddler kitten. Anyway, you were still learning to talk—I think you must have been two. So you couldn't really say 'Doodle Bear.' Instead, you said 'Doo Doo Bah.'"

"Oh, nice." Her smile touched her eyes now, adding a sparkle there. Which meant she might be a little distracted from the pain. Which meant he should keep going.

"One night before bed I heard a big commotion out in the hall between the living room and our bedroom. I think I was brushing my teeth. I peeked out, and I saw you running toward me with the Doodle Bear clutched against your chest. You were squeezing it for all you were worth, and you were chugging forward as fast as your little legs could go."

He smiled at the memory, allowing the image to wash over him.

"Ryan was right behind you. He kept trying to reach over your head and grab the bear. But you were squeezing it so tight, and you were kind of wobbling left and right as you ran. He couldn't get it."

She was still smiling. Waiting for the payoff.

"You saw me, and you ran right toward me, and the whole time you were running you were shouting, 'Doo Doo Bah! Doo Doo Bah!'"

He was laughing now. "I don't know why I did it. I mean, it *was* Ryan's bear. I guess you just looked so cute. So I scooped you up in my arms, and I bent down toward Ryan, and I roared like a Tyrannosaurus Rex. I mean, I gave him a full bellow. Crazy eyes and mouth open and everything."

"You roared at him?"

"I roared at him." Haggerty slapped his leg. "And Ryan ran back down the hall like his pants were on fire. Then—" He met Sonya's eyes. "Then you looked up at me, and you held the stuffie up above your head like you were a chief returning from a hunt, and you shouted, 'Doo Doo Bah!' And then I shouted the same thing: 'Doo Doo Bah!' And then I carried you through the living room and around the couch, and both of us kept yelling it like a victory chant. 'Doo Doo Bah! Doo Doo Bah! Doo Doo Bah!'"

Sonya barked a laugh, then clutched protectively at her side. "Nnnnnnnn. Ouch."

"Okay, sorry." Haggerty squeezed her foot gently. "Sorry. No more laughing."

She was still looking at him, and he saw the wetness in her eyes. Tears of pain? Tears of sadness? Tears of laughter? Probably a mix.

"What happened to the stuffie?" she asked.

"Nothing officially, but Ryan pretty much let you have it from that point on. Which, of course, meant you pretty much lost all interest in having it."

"Pretty much." She closed her eyes for a moment. Her lips worked upward into a sly grin. "Doo Doo Bah," she whispered.

He laughed again.

When she spoke next, her voice was once more strained. Once again heavy with pain. "Dad, please tell me what's wrong."

Haggerty stopped grinning. He looked at her for several moments, then shrugged. "Broken ribs for certain. I'm worried about internal bleeding, so . . ."

She was shaking her head. "Not that. We talked about that. What's making you feel afraid?"

He looked up at the chamber around them. Felt the pressure of so many tons bearing down on top of him. On top of his daughter. He scanned the different groups of survivors huddled here and there along the metal walkway, many nursing injuries as serious as Sonya's. He looked down at the backpack under her head, which held two half-used bottles of water and a few crumbled granola bars.

He tried to think of what to say. How to answer her question.

In the middle of those thoughts, he heard the voice of another young woman—another Sonia. *"Dr. America . . . you good doctor?"* She'd looked at him with trust in that moment. Looked at him the same way his own Sonya was looking at him now.

What do you need to be? he asked himself. *A good doctor? A good father? Can you be both?*

Haggerty pulled in a deep breath of air, then let it out. He leaned back against the railing behind him, then winced. He had his own bruises from his tumbles and rolls during the earthquake. After a few more seconds had passed, he looked his daughter in the eyes and told her the truth.

"The day Caleb went out with your team for contact tracing, the day you found Lorenzo Ricci . . ." He saw a brief moment of confusion in her eyes, then resolution. She remembered. "Were you wearing a mask?"

"Yes. N95. Snugged up tight."

"Good girl. Did you have any close contact with Ricci? Did he touch you?"

She started shaking her head, then stopped. "How close?"

"Anything. What's the closest he came near you?"

"He yelled at me. He tried to get in my face, but Caleb got between us. Then he pulled him away."

Haggerty nodded. Feeling hopeful. "Your mask was on the whole time?"

Sonya nodded—then stopped. Her eyes opened a little wider. "When Caleb got between us, his shoulder brushed my cheek. The mask got pushed sideways. That's when he was yelling in my face. Ricci. He was yelling about Maria."

Haggerty hung his head. His eyes squeezed shut.

"What?" Sonya watched him, seeming confused. "What does—" Her breath caught. Her eyes opened wider. "You think I'm sick? The Dirty Dozen?"

Haggerty raised his head. "I don't know. Most of your symptoms are consistent with internal injuries, including broken ribs. But there are some signs . . ." He listened to the rattle of her breathing. "The bottom line is you were exposed to someone we strongly suspect was carrying the virus. Actually, you were exposed twice counting here in the cave. So . . . I'm worried."

Sonya was quiet a long time. She was working to breathe. Working to manage the pain. Working to process this new possibility—this new source of fear.

Eventually she said, "Okay." Her voice was still weak, but steady. "Thanks for telling me."

Haggerty nodded. "The most likely scenario is that you're busted up inside and you'll need some real medical care once we get out of here." He looked around again at the cave. "But for the long run, you'll be fine."

The ghost of a whisper tickled his mind. *I said you were looking strong. I said I expect you to be okay—and I do.*

"Okay," she said again. "But since we're still here, I'm going to need another story."

He smiled. He started to think through some of the safer memories once again, but she wasn't finished.

"Dad, I'd like to hear what really happened. With Ryan." She paused. "With you and Mom. The whole thing."

Haggerty felt ice water trickle down the back of his neck. It moved slowly and sank deeply. At the same time, his cheeks and his forehead flushed, becoming prickly and warm.

"That's . . ." His mouth was dry. He closed it. Tried to generate some saliva, then started again. "Why?" His voice was a ragged whisper. "Why do you want to know?"

She let her head sink deeper against the backpack, still holding his gaze. "I don't *want* to know. I *need* to know."

Haggerty said nothing. He stayed silent for a long time, waiting for the voice that always harried him whenever he thought about his biggest failure. But the voice never came.

"Please, Dad. I've carried this question inside me for as long as I can remember. I never really knew what happened, but I need to know. I need to understand."

Outwardly, he was nodding as she spoke. Nodding slowly. Hearing without fully listening. Watching without fully seeing. Inwardly, he was focused deep inside his own mind, concentrating on the mental box labeled *Ryan*. He knew what she wanted to hear. He could picture that terrible moment—that terrible day. He could see it in the box like a photograph. He could also see the trip wires attached all around. He felt the explosive potential for pain. For shame. For madness.

"Please, Dad. For me?"

Haggerty felt the trip wires snap as he began to speak.

CHAPTER 9

Sonya was in agony. It hurt to breathe. It hurt to talk. It hurt to move. It hurt to lie still. Her existence in that moment was a whirlwind of pain that radiated from her side and sawed with serrated teeth against every nerve in her body. She wanted so badly to close her eyes and fade away. To stop feeling. Stop thinking. Stop being.

She sensed that option somewhere in the depths of her consciousness. Some vital rip cord she could pull that would allow her to let go of . . . what? Consciousness? Life itself? She didn't know.

Even so, she refused all thoughts and all desires in that direction. Because here was a chance to know. Here was a chance to answer what had been for so long the central question of her life: *What happened? How did everything I thought I knew vanish in a single moment?*

And was it all my fault?

So she remained. If this was the end, whether by injury or illness or any other cause, she was determined to go out knowing the truth. Even if that truth destroyed her more brutally and more efficiently than any virus or chunk of rock ever could.

"Please, Dad." She poured all of herself into the words. All of her yearning and longing and need. "For me?"

She waited through another long moment of silence. An unbearable stretching.

"There was a mixer at the hospital. Walter Reed." He spoke in a monotone, like a robot reciting a script. "It was a Saturday. Lots of soldiers were there. Lots of families with kids. I brought Ryan with me, but your mom stayed home with you. You wanted to come because Ryan said there would be dessert, but you were too young. You cried."

Sonya watched her father as he spoke, the words dropping mechanically from his lips. His head was back and his eyes were closed. Fingers clenched into fists.

"Somehow Ryan got exposed to a deadly bacteria. Neisseria. It was probably one of the hospital water fountains. Maybe he used someone else's cup. I don't know.

"Monday after school, he had a sore throat. Slight fever. Your mom and I both thought it was a regular bug. No big deal. He wanted to go bike riding with his friends, and we said yes. I thought the fresh air would do him good."

He shifted in his place against the railing, one hand rubbing at a spot on his back that seemed to be sore.

"There was a crash. They were riding through the woods, going down a big hill, and Ryan rubbed tires with one of the other boys. They were going fast, and Ryan went down." Dad looked up at her, his eyes opening. "Do you remember the crash?"

"Yeah." Mom had taken a phone call, then rushed out of the house. She'd brought Ryan back in the passenger seat of their minivan, the bike tossed in the back. Sonya remembered how dirty he was when her mom helped him into the house. He was covered in mud and grass and leaves. Also blood. He was smiling like he was enjoying the attention.

"It was bad," she said.

Her dad snorted. An angry, resentful, regretful sound. "Not bad enough. Lots of contusions. Lots of abrasions. He was busted up pretty good, but nothing was broken. I patched him up myself, so there was no need for a visit to the ER. That's what we thought."

A longer moment of silence hovered as he tapped the back of his head against the railing.

"He stayed home from school the next day. Tuesday. His fever was a little higher, but it was the other stuff that kept him home. The scrapes and the bruises. He was very sore. Mari—your mom didn't want him running around at recess and making things worse.

"I left for the hospital after lunch. I was planning to work a double shift, so I . . ." Another long pause ensued. When he spoke again, his voice had lost some of its robotic quality.

"I went into the living room to check on him before I left. He was watching TV. Cartoons. You were with him, curled up on the recliner with your blanket." He looked over at her again, his eyes moist. "Do you remember?"

"Yes." She intentionally kept her response short, not wanting to interrupt him. Not wanting to stem the flow in any way. "I was excited about the cartoons."

Their mom had kept both children home from school that day, which was her usual policy. If she had to stay and take care of Ryan, she wanted the chance to spend time with Sonya as well. Sonya remembered feeling fascinated by the wrappings and bandages on Ryan's hands and arms and face. She also remembered the sandwiches Mom had made for lunch. PB&Js with the crusts on for Ryan and the crusts off for Sonya, plus Star Crunches for dessert. It was like a party.

"Yeah." Dad nodded. "I remember the cartoons. Anyway, before I left, I checked Ryan's bandages. Checked his fever. Checked the bruises I could see. I did it quickly and efficiently, and then I said, 'Try not to be in front of the TV all day, okay? Let's do something productive if you can.' Then I left."

He was weeping now. The glistening trails reflected the emergency light. "Then I left." He said it again, and his voice was choked with emotion.

Oh no. Sonya gasped, involuntarily bringing her hand up to her mouth—a painful motion, but she almost didn't notice. *Oh, dear God.*

"That was the last thing you said to him." Not a question.

He nodded again. "I told him a lot of things while he was in the coma. I told him I loved him. I told him I was proud of him. I told him he was strong and good and brave." He was still weeping as he spoke, but his voice was now edged with anger. And shame. "But the last thing my son heard me say—the last thing I told him when he could still hear me—was to quit watching so much TV and try to do something productive."

He brought his hands to his eyes for a moment, then rubbed at his temples with his thumb and middle finger. When he lowered his hand, he looked at her accusingly. Almost petulantly. As if he were saying, *Why are you making me do this?*

So much of Sonya wanted to end it. She wanted to offer words of grace and peace. *It's okay, Dad. No more. You can stop.* But no. He was so close. *She* was so close. She said nothing.

"It was a long shift. A hard shift. Two amputations below the knee, back-to-back. Both the result of IEDs. I was twelve hours in with four to go when your mother called. It was midnight, so I knew something had to be wrong. She should have been asleep.

"She told me Ryan was worse. His fever was 102. He couldn't rest, couldn't be still. His neck was hurting and he couldn't move it very well. That should have gotten my attention, but . . ." He held his hand out toward her, like an appeal. "I knew he'd hurt his neck when he crashed his bike. I knew it was sore. I . . . I thought that's what she meant."

He dropped his hand. Took a moment to breathe.

"Then she told me about the bruising. I . . ." He rolled his head to the left, then back to the right. "She said there were a lot more bruises than before. That they were all over his body. But again—the bike. He'd rolled down a hill with rocks and tree trunks and everything else. He already had a lot of bruises when I checked him over. I thought it was . . ."

He paused, then again shook his head back and forth, almost as if he was correcting himself. "I *assumed* it was the same thing."

Sonya didn't understand why he seemed stuck on these word choices, but she held her tongue.

"I told your mom that everything she was describing was consistent with his bicycle accident." He paused. "Except the fever. She kept bringing up the fever. She told me she felt like he was burning up, and that he was restless, and that he was rolling back and forth on the bed. I told her he must still be dealing with whatever bug was bothering him over the weekend. The fever and the sore throat.

"She asked me to come home." A terrible thickness choked his voice now, as if the words had to be shoved up his throat and through his mouth. "She wanted me to come home and check on Ryan . . ." He trailed off. He said nothing for a long time.

That's the end, Sonya thought. *That's all he can do—all he can say.*

She was wrong.

"I told her no." He spoke with the same thickness. The same horrible effort. He was still weeping. "I said Ryan would be fine. I told her to give him a strong dose of NyQuil. That he needed sleep more than anything else. That she needed to sleep as well. That I would . . . that I would check him when I got home."

Keep going, Dad. Keep going for both of us. For all of us. Please!

He kept going.

"I went home at the end of the second shift. Five in the morning. Your mom was asleep on the couch. She didn't wake up when I came in. Exhausted. I was exhausted too. I . . . I didn't go into his room. I didn't check on him. I went to bed."

His shoulders heaved in huge, spasmodic jerks. He was sobbing, his head hanging low, his eyes fixed on the ground. But he kept talking.

"Your mother woke me up a few hours later. The sun was up. She was shaking me. She was yelling, 'Something's wrong with Ryan. He's worse! He's worse!' As soon as I went into his room, I knew. He was raving, rolling his head back and forth, but his neck wasn't moving. He was covered in sweat. He was covered in lesions. Purplish lesions, not bruises. I lifted his shirt, and his stomach was one big purple splotch."

She saw the way he looked at her own abdomen, the pain and apprehension clearly redoubling as the twin images connected in his mind.

"I called the ER director on the way to the hospital. Told him Ryan was already septic. Told him I suspected meningitis. *Meningococcemia*. They had him on fluids and antibiotics a minute after we came through the door, but . . ." A long, slow shake of the head. "He never regained consciousness. He was in a coma for a week. Then he was gone."

Neither of them spoke or moved for a long time. Sonya was still struggling with the pain. Trying to stay on top of it. Trying with each breath to pull enough air into her lungs in a way that did not increase her agony. Her dad was now slumped more than seated against the metal railing, head back and eyes closed. Face still glistening with untouched tears.

Eventually he stirred. He raised his head and looked at her in a silent plea. *Let it be enough. Let it end there.*

Sonya saw his movements through half-closed eyelids. She saw the question on his face—the desire to bury this terrible conversation alongside the memory of his son.

She'd known some of what he'd already shared. Her mom told her about the meningitis and the bike crash—the confusion of those jumbled events. In her words, "Ryan caught a rare and terrible disease, and we didn't catch it until it was too late."

Sonya had pieced together other details of her brother's death based on her own memories and other scraps she'd managed to scrounge up. Finding out her dad's part was new, including his failure and negligence. But those were not the details she had coveted for so long.

I want to be done with it, Dad. But we're only halfway through. We can finish it. And then we'll be ready for whatever else happens or doesn't happen inside this cave.

Out loud she said, "I need to hear the rest of it. What happened with you and Mom."

He nodded, then closed his eyes again. Sonya marveled at the way such a large man could appear so small. So deflated. When he spoke, even his voice seemed timid.

"There's not a lot to tell when you boil it down. When I boil it down." He sighed. "Internally, I knew it was my fault. Ryan's death. I failed him at every step. Even if I'd checked on him at five in the morning, like I promised—those precious extra hours could've . . . He might have . . . But I didn't check on him. And he died."

He opened his eyes and looked at her. "Which means I killed him. My own son."

Once again, Sonya felt an overwhelming desire to contradict him. To shout him down. *No, Dad! A terrible thing happened, but that doesn't mean it was your fault! That doesn't mean you have to keep carrying the blame and the pain and the weight of the world on your shoulders!*

She said nothing.

"I knew all that inside," he continued, "but I couldn't admit it. I couldn't face it, even with myself. I was the doctor. The healer. The hero. Ryan's death couldn't be my fault. So . . ." His voice once again became heavy with emotion. "So I blamed Marianna. I blamed my wife. 'You said he had bruises,' I told her. 'You should have said purple spots. If you had said purple spots, I would have known what was going on.' Ridiculous."

He sighed again, rubbing his hands up and down the sides of his face. "I was so filled with anger. With rage. Even when Ryan was still in the coma, I couldn't hold it in. It was eating me from the inside out, and so I dumped it all on . . . on your mother."

He looked over at her, meeting her gaze. "She was terrified for Ryan. She was doing everything she could to figure out a way for it all to be okay. But I couldn't see past my own ego. After the funeral, I . . . I said some terrible things. I kept saying them until she couldn't take it anymore. She left. Took her car and some clothes and you, then drove back to Millersville. Back with her mother."

Sonya remembered that day. Her mother's weeping. Her frantic packing. She had tried to distract Sonya by letting her watch TV, but Sonya kept creeping back to the bedroom because she knew something big was happening. Something momentous was shifting under her feet. She could sense it but did not understand it—had never been able to understand it. But she'd been desperate to find closure ever since.

"I remember when we got to Grandma's house. Everyone was so sad. Every day I asked Mom where Ryan was and when he was coming home. She told me he was in heaven, but . . . I kept thinking he would come back."

She gave herself a moment to rest. Long, slow inhalation. Long, slow exhalation. Limiting the pain.

"Every day I asked Mom where you were." She now stared at the husk of her father slumped on the ground. "She always said you were still at our old house. I'd ask her when you would come to be with us, and she always said the same thing: 'Soon, Sonya Pie. Daddy will come soon.'"

The words struck him, and he shuddered with the force of the blow.

"I kept waiting. For weeks, every day I woke up expecting to see you. Every night, I went to bed believing tomorrow would be the day. *Daddy will come tomorrow.* But you didn't come."

He hadn't been totally absent, of course. There had been phone calls. He'd told her he loved her. That he missed her. But it was more than a year after Ryan's funeral before she physically saw her dad again. By then she'd given up hope of her family being restored.

There in the cave, Sonya realized for the first time that she'd never asked *him* when he was coming to be with her again. She'd chatted with him on the phone about school and Grandma and toys, then pestered her mom about when he'd come back once he hung up the phone.

Maybe I already knew the answer.

Looking at him now, watching him marinate in the pain of memories long buried, Sonya asked the question that had burned in her chest ever since the moment when hope for his return had fizzled and died like a guttering flame.

"Dad . . . I needed you. We needed you. Why didn't you come?"

To her amazement, he rolled himself slightly forward and rose to his knees. He lowered his chin so his eyes were level with her own. When he spoke, his voice was firm. And steady. And sorrowful.

"Because I was a coward, Sonya. Because I was so wrapped up in myself and my failure and my pain that I couldn't see anything else." He was looking at her with tenderness and compassion. "After Ryan's death, I threw myself into my work at the hospital, where people kept praising me for how brave I was. For how dedicated I was. I'm a good doctor, and I worked hard, and I was successful—and all of that allowed me to cocoon myself against what I was doing to you and your mom."

He held out his hands toward her. "I should have taken you both away the day after the funeral. You and your mom. I should have done everything I could possibly do to help you and comfort you and love you. I know you needed me, Sonya Pie, and I should have come." He was crying again, his body shaking with sobs. "I'm a hypocrite, and I made the worst decision of my life when I chose not to come to you, and I am so, so sorry."

He could barely speak. He was drowning in weeping, but he kept trying to offer the same words: "I'm so sorry. I'm so sorry. I'm so sorry."

Something inside Sonya lifted at those words. Something bent was made straight. Something broken was healed. She found herself sliding up from the little pallet he'd made for her, and she half lurched, half crawled into his arms. The pain was incredible. The joy was incredible.

"It's okay." Her hand stroked his cheek, feeling the rough stubble and the warm wetness of his tears. "It's okay."

He was holding her gently. Telling her, "No, no, you'll hurt yourself," as she tried to climb higher in his arms—to pull herself deeper into his embrace. She remembered the feeling of being hugged like this. She remembered the solidity of him. The smell of him. And the wonder of experiencing those things again after so long, after so much wanting, almost dulled the hot wire of agony that was burning its way across her chest.

Almost.

"You're going to be okay," she told him. "You're going to be okay." She still touched his cheek, which was good. She felt the strength of his arms cradling her, carrying her gently back toward the scant warmth of his jacket on the ground, which was good. She felt the wire in her chest rip free and the blackness roll over her and overwhelm the pain—which was very, very good.

Then she felt nothing except the deep knowing that her father was near. Her father was with her. Her father loved her. And that was enough.

CHAPTER 10

K eep it still. As still as possible."

Haggerty was kneeling in front of an older Italian couple, both of whom were sitting down and resting against a smooth section of the cave. The woman's left arm was wrapped in a makeshift sling Haggerty had rigged up the day before from a zippered sweatshirt. He didn't tell anyone that he'd "borrowed" the sweatshirt from one of the bodies pulled out of the rubble.

He pointed to her arm, then shook his head again and signaled "No" with his hands. "Don't move it." He raised his left arm and propped it against the wall railing, then lowered it down near the ground. Shook his head. He raised it back up and nodded slowly and approvingly. "Keep it above the heart."

The old woman nodded at him, smiling wearily. The man did the same, then reached out to shake Haggerty's hand.

"Okay. You're going . . ." Haggerty gestured to the woman again and offered a thumbs-up. "She's going to be okay."

He rose to his feet, wincing at the sharp stab of pain in his lower back. What he wouldn't give for an ice pack or a bottle of ibuprofen or . . .

He winced again as he looked down at the old woman now resting her head atop her shoulder. Her husband was gently smoothing his hand down her leg in small, comforting pats.

Haggerty felt a hot spike of shame burn down the back of his neck. He thought of what this woman must have experienced in the past thirty hours—the physical pain and the emotional weight of not knowing when the pain would end.

Let's get a little perspective, Haggs. Do what you can to make things better.

And he did. He moved down the line of injured survivors, offering aid and playing his own game of medical charades whenever English was hard to come by. All of his "patients" were as stable as could be hoped for—except for Sonya.

Deal with that when you can. Deal with what's in front of you right now.

After several more minutes, he stopped to take out his phone. The battery was at 11 percent in spite of his careful rationing; it wouldn't last much longer.

Might be true of all of us without water.

In Haggerty's opinion, lack of water was the biggest threat for most of the survivors currently huddling in anxious enclaves throughout this chamber of the cave system. Not injuries. Not starvation. Not suffocation. It was the gnawing, burrowing, overwhelming reality of thirst that posed the greatest risk.

There *was* water in the cave, which made the situation especially problematic. Even now, he could hear the sound of droplets free-diving into ancient, shallow pools. It was maddening.

Haggerty had done his best to warn the survivors against those pools. He'd walked up and down with an ad hoc interpreter who told each person in Italian, "There is bacteria in the cave water. If you drink it, you will become very sick. You will probably die."

Even so, he was pretty sure several people had already slipped away to take a sip when their thirst became unbearable. Probably more than a sip. Those who hadn't would surely give in to the temptation in another day at most.

What about you, Haggs? How long can you last? He took a moment to assess himself, smacking his lips and rasping his tongue in a futile effort to drum up a measure of saliva. He felt the sandpaper *swick, swick* of his eyelids when he blinked.

One more day. Maybe.

Perhaps to reassure himself, he touched the half-filled plastic water bottle in his pocket—the few precious sips he was saving for Sonya. She'd lost consciousness for several hours, and he knew she'd certainly be thirsty when she came around once more. The question was how to make her drink after he refused.

Cross that bridge later. Do what you can right now.

With a sigh, he checked the time on his phone: 5:53 a.m. Another sunrise was coming soon somewhere on the other side of the craggy cage all around him—the second since the earthquake. He turned off the phone, replaced it in his pocket, and walked back to his daughter.

She was awake, unfortunately.

He paused for a moment about four or five feet from where she lay, studying what he could see of her. She was lying very still but was flexing her fingers, wrists, and feet every few seconds as he'd encouraged her to do. Good for circulation. The movements were slow and clumsy. Her face looked sunken and stretched too tight, which he knew was from the pain. Her unwashed hair was gathered in a loose, dark pile next to her cheek. She had one hand tucked under that cheek; the other arm was still cradled protectively around her injured side.

"Come on in, Dad," she croaked. "Grab a Coke from the fridge. Turn the game on."

He smiled, then slumped down in his usual place in front of her and leaned back against the railing.

"I need to pee," she said, "but I'm waiting to see if my body changes its mind. Also, I don't want to get up."

Haggerty said nothing. Apparently she was resorting to jokes again. He thought it might be an effort to make it seem as if she were feeling better.

Eventually he laid his hand on the top of her foot. "Whatcha been thinking about?"

"God."

His eyebrows shot upward. "Wow. That's a big one."

"Yeah. Been thinkin' for a while now."

"What started you on that?" He stroked the missing chunk at the top of his ear, trying to keep his surprise from leaking into his voice.

She moved one shoulder a few inches—her best impression of a shrug. "I guess Mom. She started talking with Caleb about it."

"Caleb." Something in Haggerty's stomach flipped, then soured. "Caleb Johnson?"

She nodded, moving her chin slowly and carefully up and down. "After Tess died. Then Mom and I started talking about it some. Here and there."

"How?" He saw the confusion on her face. "How did they talk? Caleb and your mom? How often?"

Another miniature shrug. "Couple times a month. She texts him with questions." She paused. "Questions about spiritual stuff."

Haggerty nodded as his mind ground rustily into gear. *Caleb. Calling Marianna. After Tess died.*

"I started meeting with a group," Sonya said. "We go to a lady's house every week and have dinner. Jan's house. Then we talk about a book or a part of the Bible. And . . ." She hesitated for a moment before adding, "And pray together."

Haggerty was still nodding, but he was distracted by the ringing alarms in his mind. Caleb calling a couple of times a month. Marianna texting Caleb with lots of questions. After Tess died.

"At first I just liked the company. They're nice people, and Jan's a really good cook. But the book we studied was really interesting. And . . . the Bible stuff was interesting. I guess I hadn't, like, heard much about it before."

"Don't like the like." Haggerty spoke automatically. Robotically. He was thinking about his previous conversation with Caleb in Benghazi. About Tess. *"She's gone and you're still here. How are you handling it so well?"*

"Dad . . ."

He pictured Marianna standing alone in her immaculate kitchen. Hearing her phone ring, then picking it up. Seeing Caleb's photo on the screen. Smiling. Tucking a lock of hair behind her ear before answering. The image birthed something slimy in his gut. It made his fingers flex—spreading outward, then collapsing into fists.

It could be. He clenched his teeth. *It could happen if they—*

"Dad!"

He jerked forward. Startled. Sonya was holding her stomach as if the yell had pained her. Probably had.

"Sorry," he said. "Sorry, I . . . I don't know where I went." He rubbed his eyes with his palms, working to push out pictures he didn't want to see.

"I said I wanted to know what you thought about all that." Her voice was smaller now. Weaker. "About the Bible and my group. About God."

There was a long period of silence as Haggerty kept dragging his hands up and down over his face. Sonya watched him, waiting. Eventually she broke the silence again. "I don't think you and I ever talked about . . . about that stuff."

No, we never did. I made sure of that.

Out loud he said, "I think you know what I think. What I believe." He could see the confirmation in her eyes. He was startled to also see disappointment. *What have you been telling them, Cay? What have you been preaching at my girls?*

"I'm still pretty exhausted from yesterday," he continued. "From talking about . . . about Ryan." *Is it easier to say his name now?* He was surprised to find it was. "I'm a little hollowed out, to be honest." He looked around himself again. The walls. The wounded. The empty backpack.

"Yeah. I get it. I just . . ." She seemed uncertain about how to say what she wanted to say, which was rare. She glanced down at her hand, then quickly up again. Looking there, he saw an edge of something sticking out between her thumb and forefinger. Some kind of cloth.

"What?" he asked. "What's going on?"

She raised her head an inch to pull her hand free. As she did, Haggerty noticed the rattle in her breathing. *Is it louder? Yes. A lot louder.* He listened to the dampness of it, feeling concerned. It was almost like he was waking up from a daze—as if critical systems in his brain had been shut down but were now coming back online.

How did I miss this?

She held out her hand, then slowly and carefully unfolded her fingers. Haggerty reached over and plucked a crumpled paper towel from her hand. He unfolded it. Gasped.

"No. Oh no, no, no." He felt a prickling and tingling sensation over the skin of his arms and the back of his neck. As if every pore were opening. As if his body were trying to sweat but couldn't find the main ingredient. He felt a cold vise clamp down on his chest and begin to squeeze. And squeeze. And squeeze.

The paper towel was pocked and spattered with blood.

"I'm trying not to cough," Sonya said. "I have to try very hard.

It hurts and . . ." She nodded toward the paper towel in his hand that used to be white but was now splotched with dull, rusty purple under the harsh blue glare of the emergency lights. "I have to—"

Then, as if in nightmarish confirmation, she wheezed an exhalation that quickly shifted into a series of short, stifled coughs. "Nnnnnnnn," she moaned, holding her side. Then she coughed again. Louder. Harder. Her body spasmed inwardly in sharp little bursts. In the middle of the fit, her eyes widened. Her mouth worked, and she held out her hand toward Haggerty, fingers splayed and urgent.

He handed back the paper towel. She crushed it to her lips, which Haggerty now saw were painted a deep crimson. She was still coughing as she held the cloth to her mouth—coughing and gagging and choking. The sound was horrifying as she worked her lips and tongue. A slick sound. A wet sound.

Haggerty was helpless. He was in the middle of a new kind of earthquake, and the aftershocks were still reverberating back and forth across every aspect of his being.

Eventually the coughing faded, then finished. Sonya lay on her side, eyes glazed with pain. There was blood on her lips. Blood on her chin. Blood on her fingers.

"My mother die?" The memory invaded Haggerty's mind. "My sister die? . . . Dr. America . . . good doctor."

He stared in horror at his daughter as her eyes rolled up, down. He realized his own lips were still moving—still saying, "No, no, no."

"Dad," she said, her voice so small, the voice of his little girl. "I think . . ." Long, shuddering breath. "There's a reason . . . to talk about God."

Later that morning, Haggerty stumbled down an unfamiliar section of the cave system, the thud of his boots ringing out an irregular rhythm on the metal walkway. He'd spent the past hour kneeling next to Sonya and offering what little comfort he could produce. He'd stroked her hair and held her hand. Helped her drink the rest of his water.

More than anything, he'd talked with her. He told her stories of when she was a little girl. He told her more stories about Ryan. He told her about meeting Marianna after a football game during their freshman year of high school. He shared moments during his time in the Army when he'd felt afraid. Or uncertain. Or lost.

He'd made it a point to tell her he loved her. That he was proud of her. That she was one of the most incredible people he had ever met. That she reminded him of her mother, and that he could offer no greater compliment to any woman.

He'd also told her that he would take care of her. That he would help her get out of this cave and that the pain would soon be a distant memory. That she would be okay.

He did not believe those things. Not deep down, where it mattered.

It could be internal injuries, he reminded himself. Which was true. Coughing up blood was consistent with the physical trauma she'd sustained to her side and chest, including her broken ribs. But the image of Sonia back in Crete was prominent in his memory. And not just Sonia, but the dozens of young people—women and men—he'd witnessed coughing up blood hours before they slipped away.

The cold, logical, medical part of his mind kept telling him it would be better if she *had* contracted the Dirty Dozen because the end would come more quickly—and likely with less pain. She would drown in her own blood long before he, Haggerty, died from dehydration. Or, more likely, long before he died of an intense bacterial infection that took root in his digestive system because he could not resist the temptation to drink contaminated water.

As always, the cold, logical, medical part of his mind offered no comfort. Now, head spinning and thoughts whirling, Major General John Haggerty slid to his knees deep in the dark bowels of the earth. He was finished with tears. Finished with tenderness. He had come here to rage. To accuse. To seek some way to strike.

And, if possible, to pray.

Haggerty slumped forward, positioned more like a boxer at the count of seven than a petitioner at any altar in any respectable church. He raised his hands in front of his face, fingertips steepled against fingertips. Then he remembered his father had always prayed that way—palms and fingers held together and raised toward the sky. Immediately, mouth twisted in disgust, Haggerty lowered his hands and rested his knuckles against the cold, textured solidity of the floor.

"You took Ryan from me." He raised his chin to stare up at the ceiling. "You took him from me. So don't You dare take Sonya." His chest rose and fell with great gasps of air. Then a cry: "Don't You dare!"

Haggerty slammed his right fist down against the metal walkway. The clang echoed around the cave. He struck the walkway again, relishing the flares of pain that stabbed him with each blow. Relishing the sight of his own blood on the top of his hand rather than the blood of his children.

Still breathing heavily, he leaned forward and rested his palms against the ground. He was on all fours, his head raised high.

"Please." He spoke more softly now. This was as close to pleading as he could bear. "Please don't take Sonya from me. Please don't take her from Marianna."

As he spoke the words, Haggerty was aware of his awkward position—aware of his own disbelief. His defiance and hypocrisy.

"You know what I've been through. You know what *he* did." He spat the word onto the metal grating as if it were a rotten tooth. "You know I'm better than him. You *owe* me! You—"

He stopped, taking several deep breaths to calm himself and contemplate his situation.

I should bow. The thought floated up from somewhere deep in his mind, or deep in his history. He pictured himself lowering his chin until his forehead came to rest against the ground. He decided to do it. Tried to do it.

Could not do it.

Haggerty leaned forward, seeking again to prostrate himself, but his shoulders would not relax. His neck would not bend. Something inside would not—could not—relent to such a posture of humility. Of submission. No matter how hard he tried, no matter how many ways he tried, he continually refused his own decision. Each time he made an attempt, his neck stiffened instead of softening. His chin pushed higher rather than sinking toward his chest.

This inability to bend his neck recalled an image of Ryan rolling back and forth on his bed, raving, the muscles and sinews tight around his throat. That memory brought the anger back. The rage. Thinking of Ryan again solidified the image of Sonya lying on the ground, her body racked with coughs and her lips smeared with blood. Haggerty felt more anger and rage. More resentment and resistance on every level.

Rising to his feet, Haggerty punched a fist toward the ceiling of the cave. He was shaking with fury.

"You take everything!" he roared. "You demand everything! Here . . ." He bent down and grabbed a chunk of rock that had skittered onto the walkway during the earthquake, then heaved it out into the deep emptiness of the cave. "Take it!" He grabbed another rock and threw it. Another. "Take it all!"

Overcome by a wave of dizziness, Haggerty leaned against the cave wall, exhausted. He listened to the rocks as they bounced and clattered and clanged within the chamber. He listened for a long time.

Too long.

They can't still be bouncing. That's something else.

He turned his ear toward the sound, which was now less clattering and more grinding. It was a constant, regular, rhythmic noise. Haggerty closed his eyes. Concentrating. Straining to hear—

Voices! Rescue!

"Hey!" he called out, hoarse from his recent shouting. He cleared his throat and yelled again. "Hey, over here!"

The sounds were closer now. They were coming toward him, not from the front of the chamber where Lorenzo Ricci still lay, unmoving, but from behind—from the opposite end. There must have been a side tunnel or some kind of emergency shaft accessible through another branch of the cave.

Haggerty looked up at the ceiling once more. The stalactites hung down in their millennial silence like accusing fingers—each one pointing at him.

Do I say thank you? Do I pray now? Beg now?

"No." He shook his head and remained on his feet, waiting for the cavalry to come.

CHAPTER 11

JULY 16
FRASASSI CAVES, ITALY

I will lift up mine eyes unto the hills, from whence cometh my help.'"

Caleb whispered the words of the psalm as he drove a long prybar under a wedge of limestone, gently rocking the blade back and forth to slide it forward.

"'My help cometh from the Lord, which made heaven and earth.'" He felt the edge of the bar jam, and he pulled downward a little to try to create some space, then pressed forward once more. "'He will not suffer thy foot to be moved.'"

When the prybar jammed again, Caleb wrapped his gloved hands around the end and repositioned his feet. "'He that keepeth thee will *not* slumber.'" On the word *not*, he heaved his weight backward and downward, pulling up on the end of the bar and yanking the limestone chunk out of the pile in which it had been buried.

"'The Lord is thy keeper.'" Setting aside his tool, Caleb bent at the knees and gripped the edges of the rock with both hands. "'The Lord is thy shade upon thy right hand.'" He lifted, pivoted, and half tossed, half placed the limestone into the bucket of the little front-end loader beside him.

Lord God, he prayed, leaning briefly on the prybar and wiping sweat from the top of his head, *be the keeper for Haggs and Sonya. Protect them. Preserve them.*

Caleb selected another promising chunk of limestone. He thrust forward again with the prybar's blade. Then he began rocking the end of the bar left and right, left and right, all the while gently moving it forward.

"'The sun shall not smite thee by day, nor the moon by night.'"

He had not seen either of those orbs for many hours. After his phone call with General Burgess the previous morning, Caleb returned to Spoleto to carry out her orders—orders he still could not believe, let alone understand. He'd spent several hours with other senior leaders working to slap together a transition team and reshape mission priorities; then he'd repeated the same steps over at the quarantine center. He'd never seen a group of doctors so angry.

After another hour of supervising the new teams and answering dozens of questions—often the same question phrased in slightly different words—Caleb had called to confirm the rescue operation was still underway at the caves. There was no breakthrough yet. No contact with those who'd been trapped, survivors or otherwise. He'd set his alarm for exactly ninety minutes, hit the rack, and slept hard. Then he'd returned alone to the caves a little after midnight this morning.

This time, Caleb had avoided any frustrating conversations with the leader of the rescue team. He'd simply put on work gloves, grabbed his prybar—both of which he'd brought with him from the base—and joined the crew. When the team leader saw Caleb fulcrum out a large chunk of limestone and heave it into the bucket, he'd given a small nod, said something in Italian to the other members of the team, and left Caleb alone from that point on.

That was almost six hours ago. Despite the gloves, Caleb's palms and fingers were calloused and sore. Despite the back brace one of the men had loaned him, Caleb's spine protested each time he heaved another chunk of rock. Even so, he was strangely grateful for the work. Grateful to be doing something that felt productive rather than presiding over yet another meeting.

Grateful to be a little closer to his friend.

"'The Lord shall preserve thee from all evil,'" Caleb recited, letting the rhythm of the psalm infuse his movements. "'He shall preserve thy soul.'"

"Ay! *Americano,* ay!" The cries came from behind him. Caleb turned and saw several of the crew members waving in his direction. He stepped back and joined them, then watched as the front-end loader slowly pressed forward into the pile of rubble and rock. The plow swung slowly from left to right, then right to left, dislodging whole portions of the pile in a loud, chaotic rumble.

When everything stopped moving and rolling, the team leader gave a shout, and several men fanned out to grab the legs of the portable metal shelter over their heads. Everyone wore hard hats, of course, but the shelter added another layer of protection from falling rocks, which Caleb appreciated. The entire team was well equipped with hydraulic braces, hammer drills, thermal-imaging equipment, and more. A well-run squad.

The team leader shouted again. The men lifted the portable shelter and shuffled forward several steps until it covered the newly bulldozed section of debris. Then the men collected their various tools and stepped forward once more to resume their work.

Caleb stepped up with them, heaving his prybar. He was leveraging himself against another large chunk of stone when he noticed an intense conversation taking place among several rescue workers to his left. One of them held the thermal-imaging sensor and was gesturing to a specific spot on the screen. The team leader stepped over and joined the conversation. Caleb leaned against the prybar, waiting.

After another few moments, the team leader gestured for everyone to step back. Caleb watched as the front-end loader raised its plow and pushed forward against a specific spot on the rock pile—first gently, then with greater force. There was a large crash and clamor as huge boulders were once again displaced. This time, however, those boulders rolled backward, away from the machine.

A series of cries and cheers resounded in the cave. They had broken through!

Caleb smiled and sent up a few cheers of his own. This was the second time they had penetrated an impasse and entered a new chamber of the cave system. The first time had revealed seven survivors huddled together—all with scrapes and bruises, but otherwise no serious injuries. Neither Haggerty nor Sonya had been part of that group, but the sight of actual survivors was an amazing boost to Caleb's spirit. It allowed him to hope more freely.

We're coming, Haggs. He felt impatience rising as various members of the crew stepped in to apply braces within the new opening, securing it against any further shifting of the rock.

Caleb tapped his foot against the stone. Waiting. Wondering. Praying.

You have preserved their lives, heavenly Father. I believe that in faith.

Finally, the team leader gave a signal, and men started picking their way across the pile. Caleb was the third man through the hole—and his mouth immediately gaped at the sight of this new chamber. It was huge! Up to that point, *cavernous* had been only a vocabulary word, but now it made sense. More, the chamber was filled with an incredible array of beautiful stone blobs. He couldn't think of any other word to better describe what he saw: huge towers and rounded piles of limestone in creamy white and pinkish white and other shades of white.

"Glory to God," he said softly to himself.

The two men ahead of him had carefully picked their way back to the metal grating, and Caleb quickly joined them. Then he hurried forward, spurred on by the eerie echoes of his footsteps.

He turned a corner, then a second. The other men were following him, perhaps happy to let the American be the tip of the spear—which was fine with Caleb.

He rounded another corner—and saw Haggerty. Right there, leaning against a rock wall. Big as life.

"Haggs!" Caleb shouted with joy, then turned back to the men following him. "Survivors! *Sopravvissuti! Sopravvissuti!*"

The men nodded excitedly. Several of them rushed forward with Caleb toward Haggerty, who had now stumbled away from the rock wall and was lurching deeper into the cave and waving his arms in a "follow me" gesture.

Quickly they came to an observation deck. Haggerty was kneeling next to what looked like a ragged pile of clothes. Coming closer, Caleb saw Sonya lying in the middle of that pile—and his stomach dropped at the sight. She was in bad shape, with blood on her lips and chin. She was breathing raggedly and obviously in a great deal of pain.

Haggerty was speaking to her. "Gonna be okay, just like I said. You're gonna be okay."

Two of the rescue personnel had already placed a litter down beside her. They were trying to move Haggerty out of the way so they could reach her, but he stopped them for a moment. Gestured to her side, then rocked the litter back and forth, then waved his hands in a gesture that obviously meant "No." *Keep her still*, he was saying. He pointed to her side again and made a twisting, breaking gesture with his fingers. *Broken ribs.*

Oh, Sonya. Poor girl. Hang in there.

With Haggerty's help, the rescue workers maneuvered Sonya onto the litter and began the process of strapping her to the board. Haggerty watched everything with sharp, ever-shifting eyes. He checked the tension of each strap, making sure it was tight enough to keep his daughter stable but not so tight it squeezed her and caused unnecessary pain.

Once she was secure, the two rescue workers counted to each other in Italian: "*Uno, due, tre.*" They lifted her gently on "*tre*," then began making their way carefully back toward the opening in the chamber. Back toward hospitals and pain medication and tests and—Caleb hoped very much—recovery.

All this time, Caleb had remained several yards back from Sonya and the rescue team, watching the proceedings from a distance. Not wanting to be in the way. Now he walked forward to Haggerty, who had slumped back to the ground and was leaning wearily against a section of the metal railing.

He looked terrible. Not as bad as Sonya, but . . . *What happened here?*

"Haggs." Caleb walked forward, extending a hand to help his friend off the ground. "Will Sonya—?"

Haggerty ignored the hand, choosing instead to lever himself up against the railing. Then he punched Caleb in the face. There was no subterfuge to the blow. No deception or feint. Haggerty's right foot braced against the metal walkway and pushed forward. He twisted at the waist, transferring kinetic energy from his lower body into his upper body. Haggerty's left arm swung forward in a short, violent, chopping motion. His right hand let go of the railing and launched, fingers clenched into a fist like a brick, directly at Caleb's nose.

Caleb saw every step of the punch, but his mind refused to accept it. Refused to believe it could be happening. Only at the last possible moment did Caleb's instincts kick in and cause him to swing his head slightly to the right, moving with the punch to minimize some of the force behind it. But it still felt like a hammer when Haggerty's fist belted him square on his left cheek.

Caleb stumbled backward. He grabbed onto his own side of the railing, seeing little flecks of color dancing on the left side of his vision. "Wha . . . ?"

Haggerty wasn't finished. Fists raised and ready for another strike, he charged directly at Caleb. "How long?" the big man roared, swinging again.

This time Caleb dodged inward, ducking under the blow. But Haggerty caught him before he could slip free. Caleb felt his friend's fingers dig into his shirt collar and the flesh of his shoulder like claws.

"How long have you been seeing my wife?" Haggerty swung a third time, holding Caleb with his left and driving forward with his right.

Caleb stepped forward and twisted, taking the blow on his shoulder instead of losing all his teeth. The force of it caused him to stumble, but Haggerty retained his hold and jerked him forward again. This time Caleb swung his arm around Haggerty's neck, using his height to muscle the shorter man into a head-lock.

"What are you talking about?" Caleb cried. "What are you doing?"

Haggerty flung his arms around Caleb's waist and began to heave, trying to lift the taller man off the ground. Caleb planted his feet and quickly twisted his hips to the left. The move sent Haggerty stumbling forward. Then he went down on his back.

"*Arrrgggh!*" The commander cried out in pain. He tried to roll to his feet, but he was clearly exhausted. He managed only to flip over onto his back and look up at Caleb, who stayed out of range of any kicks from Haggerty's heavy boots.

"What are you doing, Haggs?" Caleb rubbed his injured cheek, which was already swelling. It hurt to yell, but he yelled anyway. "What happened to Sonya?"

The name seemed to cut through whatever delirium or delusion had hijacked Haggerty's mind. His eyes sharpened. He looked up at Caleb and saw him—really *saw* him for the first time.

"We got a problem, Cay. Big problem. One of the leaks was in here with us. Lorenzo something."

Ricci? Here? Is that possible?

"He's dead," Haggerty said, "but . . . Sonya. Respiratory symptoms. Coughing up blood. She was exposed, and she . . . Cay, she may have the Dirty Dozen. She'll have to go to the quarantine center. We all have to go to the quarantine center . . . all the survivors. And all the rescuers. I'm sorry. I . . . I'm sorry, Cay."

Now it was Caleb's turn to slump down to the ground, sitting across from Haggerty. He pulled out his phone. "We'll get Sonya to the hospital. But there is no quarantine center. Not anymore. There is no quarantine—either in Italy or in Greece. It's all been shut down."

"Shut down?" Caleb could almost see Haggerty try to stop his mind from spinning. "That's not possible."

Caleb tapped his phone twice, then handed it over. "This is a summary of our new orders from General Burgess. All PPTF operations are suspended—in Italy, in Crete, our holdovers in Spain and Brazil. Everywhere. All personnel are recalled back to Fort Meade. Including you and me."

Haggerty stared for several seconds, mouth working but saying nothing. Eventually he croaked, "How? Why?"

Caleb sighed. "A little less than two days ago—actually, right around the time you were getting stuck in this cave—there was a terrorist attack in Jerusalem. Eight suicide bombers. They were positioned at different points in the courtyard around the Al-Aqsa Mosque, and they detonated their ordnance simultaneously."

"No . . ." Haggerty's face was white.

Caleb nodded. Wearily. "Yeah. Lots of civilians in the courtyard, and a large percentage of them ran *into* the mosque for cover. Which was bad, because about thirty seconds after the initial explosions, a second attack directly targeted the mosque. Heavy explosives. The news reports say it was RPGs, but our intel agencies think it was a Reaper-type drone. Probably multiple drones."

Haggerty gaped. "Not one of ours . . . ?"

Caleb shook his head. "No, but a similar level of tech."

"With the civilians still inside," Haggerty said.

Not a question, but Caleb nodded once more. "Military precision in the timing and coordination. Hundreds are dead. Thousands injured. They hit the Dome of the Rock as well. The Western Wall, the Temple Mount—the whole complex is destroyed."

Haggerty looked up at Caleb with haunted eyes. "Do we know who did it?"

"No."

"But . . ." Haggerty's brain was starting to make connections. Slowly and sluggishly, but they were coming. "The whole compound destroyed. Iran. Lebanon. They're accusing Israel?"

"Yes."

"That's why Burgess recalled the task force," Haggerty said. "She's afraid we're on the brink of World War III."

Caleb sighed and shook his head. "Burgess didn't just recall the PPTF. She's pulled back *all* our task forces. All five. And not because we're on the brink of war." He took a deep breath and looked his friend in the eye. "The president called us back because we're *in the middle* of World War III—it's already begun. We have no idea who started it. We have no idea what's at stake. And we have no idea what comes next."

PART 2

INTERLUDE

APRIL 7, 1988
FORT WAYNE, INDIANA

The man was deeply drunk. And driving. And singing.

"Swing looooooooow, sweet charioooooooot!"

He was a big, flannel-clad bear of a man with a loud voice, and he growled out the song with obvious relish. His flushed, unpleasant face made it all the more surprising to hear the rich baritone of his "looooooooow" and his "charioooooooot."

The man was saddled behind the wheel of an old Chevy C10. The truck had a rust-colored exterior with actual patches of rust starting their slow assault against the sharp angles of the hood and side panels. Three fishing rods rattled in the bed like discarded swords next to a bright red Igloo cooler. The man's hands were vised tightly to the wheel, and his head swung up and down, up and down while he crow-cawed the long-remembered hymn. A startling recital boosted to alarming levels by the uncaring volume of his alcohol-induced daze.

"Coming for to carry me hooooooooome!"

A teenager slumped next to the man on the bench seat. He was young. Thirteen, with a hint of lingering chubbiness around the face and belly, but also broad shoulders and long legs. He had a big mop of brown hair he kept pushing out of his eyes and curling around one ear. He wore faded blue jeans and a navy blue Chicago Bears T-shirt.

A smaller boy sat by the window. Boasting another mop of brown hair and pair of jeans and Bears shirt, he galloped the plastic horse in his hand across the door handle in big, jerky jumps.

No seat belt for the man. Or the teenager. Or the boy. Not on the ruler-straight two lanes of rural Indiana. Not in 1988.

"Swing loooooooow, sweet charioooooooot!"

The teenager released a long sigh as he settled back against the bench. Arms folded across his chest, he looked quickly over at his father, then quickly back. The familiar stirrings of hatred and disgust soured his belly, while the old love and longing filled his chest. He resisted both, setting himself to the task of keeping his head above those waters at any cost.

Twenty more minutes, he thought. *Maybe twenty-five.*

The day had started out normally. The boys gobbled stale cereal and cold milk after tossing their backpacks by the front door. Mom dished out circles of eggs and strips of bacon while packing lunches in brown paper bags. She asked questions while they mumbled answers in between bites.

Then the man had come in from the garage, red Igloo in hand.

"I'm thinking there's some fish ready to bite today, boys," he said, with something rusty in his voice. Something sharp. "Let's go get 'em."

Little Mark whooped in delight. "Yeah! Fishing!"

John and his mother shared a glance. His eyes were wide. Her lips were pursed.

Mom stepped away from the sink where she'd been washing plates, then shuffled closer to her husband. Her reddish-brown hair dangled down her back. Her shoulders drooped and her hands dropped to her sides. When she tilted her slender neck upward to meet her husband's eyes, the fulcrum of it seemed worn out—like the muscles rarely pulled in that direction.

"Steven, it's a school day. The boys—"

"The school's not going anywhere. It's just one day."

"What about work?" She raised her chin a little higher with effort, as if she were pulling against a rubber band. "Mr. Lewis doesn't like it when you don't give notice."

The man exhaled, then rubbed his hands together as if holding something between them. "I need a break. The kids need a break." He gestured toward Mark, who was reeling in an invisible smallmouth from his seat at the breakfast table. "It'll be fine."

"But, Steven . . ." Her voice quivered. She looked back at the table and cleared her throat. "I say no. Not today. I don't think it's—"

"I said it's fine, Emma!"

Both children saw the man step toward his wife. Both saw the hardening in his face. The clenched jaw. The clenched fist. Both saw Mom shy back and step to the right, putting the table between herself and her husband. Both saw the way she lowered her head and rubbed both hands down, down, down her dress to smooth an unseen wrinkle over her waist. Then over her belly.

Both children saw. One child understood.

"Put the poles in the back, boys," said the man. "Let's go."

So they'd gone. There were plenty of lakes and ponds around Fort Wayne, but they'd driven an hour out of town to find the fishing hole the man liked best. They stopped at the local bait shop to grab their night crawlers and ice for the cooler. And bottles for the cooler.

They fished for most of the day, tossing back the catfish and carp but keeping the bigger bass and the only walleye. Mark kept trying for trout, but nothing took his bait.

The man held his own rod for the first couple of hours. Practiced casts. Confident reads on the line. Quiet instructions for his sons. But every time a fish went into the cooler, two bottles came out. Eventually he gave his rod to John and settled in his chair along the shoreline, silent and brooding.

When the last bottle was empty, they all three piled in the truck.

And now they were driving home. And Dad was drunk. And he was singing his church songs and swinging his head up and down, up and down, up and down. And Mark was happy with his horse and his fish in the cooler and no school. And John sat between them and tried not to hate them and tried not to think about what was going to happen later at the house when his dad took the fish out of the cooler and the cooler was empty and there were no more bottles.

Twenty more minutes, he thought again. *Maybe twenty-five.*

Too long.

"Hey." He tapped his brother on the shoulder. "Switch with me."

"Huh?"

The windows were down, making it hard to hear much of anything over the whoosh of the air and the bellow of the man behind the wheel.

John made a swapping motion with his hands, pointing at each of them in turn. "Switch seats!"

"No! I'm playing." Mark galloped his horse up his leg and across the door handle and out through the window into the open air.

"You've been there the whole ride. It's my turn."

"No!"

"Fine!" John pushed his brother against the window. He'd pushed him with that same arm-pistoning precision a thousand times. The motion was calibrated to communicate dissatisfaction without causing injury. John pictured his brother striking the door frame of the truck with his shoulder and bouncing slightly back. A just punishment.

Mark's shoulder did hit the frame of the door—but he didn't

bounce back. Instead, the door opened. It swung wide while the truck rounded a rare bend in the road.

Maybe the door never got closed the right way back at the fishing hole or the plastic horse caught in the latch and popped it open when the boy's shoulder hit the metal. Maybe it was just an old truck with an old door. But it swung open at fifty miles an hour on an empty road outside Fort Wayne, Indiana—and Mark swung with it.

His arm hooked around the open window frame, and he hung on for his life with his feet kicking and dangling and swinging over the asphalt below.

Their father didn't see. Didn't hear. Didn't notice. Couldn't see or hear or notice much of anything outside his buzzing focus on the road and the song still pouring from his lips.

"I looked o'er the Jordan, and what did I see?" He was still cawing loudly like an old crow, the words blending in and out of tune. "Coming for to carry me hooooooooome!"

John sat stunned for a full three seconds, watching the impossible picture of his brother, hair flying in all directions, clinging to the open door of the moving truck. He felt the shift of new wind inside the cab and heard his brother's screams, even as he heard the man still singing beside him.

Then his brain slipped into gear and he scooched himself over on the bench and grabbed his brother's elbow where it was wrapped around the window frame. By this time the wind had pushed the door mostly closed again, but the boy had slid downward and his body was caught between the door and the frame. His waist was squished against the edge of the bench, but his legs dangled and swung outside above the road.

"Aaaahhhhhhhh!" He was screaming, his neck twisted to look with wide eyes back into the cab. Back toward his brother. "Aaaaaahhhhhhhh!"

"Hang on! Hang on!" John tried to brace his legs against the door and pull the boy back inside, but the door only pushed out wider. He tried to brace his legs against the inside of the cab and twist his brother across his lap and onto the bench, but he didn't have the strength. Mark was a deadweight, clinging to the window frame, and would not release his grip.

The horse fell, finally pulled by the wind from the boy's right hand. It struck the road with a *clack!*—struck the road with its head and its pointed plastic ears—then went skittering into the weeds of an old Indiana farm.

The truck drove on. The man sang on. "A band of angels comin' after me! Comin' for to carry me hoooooooome!"

John shifted his weight and prepared to scoot back along the bench and hit his dad until he came to his senses or stopped the truck or did something to help. But as he leaned away from the door, he felt a sharp pain on the top of his head. Mark's hand—now horseless—had buried itself deep in John's mop of hair.

John tugged his head, trying to pull free.

"Noooo! Don't go! Don't go! Pull me in, Johnny!" Mark's fingers, like little hooks still seeking that uncaught trout, sank deeper into his brother's hair and scalp.

"I gotta stop the truck!" cried John. "Let go!"

Mark shook his head furiously. His eyes were wide with terror and watery from the wind.

John craned his neck to look back at the man. "Dad!" he cried. "Daaaad!"

Nothing.

Both boys cried out together, their voices wild and panicked in the still-rushing wind. "Daaaaaaaaad! Daddy! Daddy!"

Their father heard nothing beyond the pouring forth of his own bellows. He thought nothing beyond his own thoughtlessness. At the back of his mind—still way down deep but percolating like the beginnings of strong coffee—he was aware that his wife had disrespected him that morning, and had done so in front of his sons. She had not treated him the way any part of a household should treat the head of that household. Something would need to be done about that.

For now, he drove home.

The boys stopped trying to get their dad's attention. John was once again shouting at his brother. Even pleading. "I gotta stop the truck! You understand? I gotta get to Dad!"

Mark kept shaking his head. Kept squeezing the metal frame of the door. Kept his hand in his brother's hair. Kept his legs dangling over the hard, unforgiving road.

"He's drunk!" shouted John. "He won't stop, so I gotta stop the truck! You gotta let go!"

Mark squeezed his eyes shut.

John tugged his head, then winced at the pain. "You gotta let go!"

He tugged and tugged and tugged, feeling desperate. Feeling the weight of responsibility on his shoulders. "You gotta let—"

Mark let go.

CHAPTER 12

L et go!"

Haggerty jerked awake the same moment he cried out. He was sitting at the little desk in his apartment with his left elbow resting on the wood and his chin cradled in his palm. There was a string of drool on his wrist, and he wiped it off on the leg of his jeans as he blinked his eyes and shook his head.

The dream again. The truck.

Muddy memories ping-ponged around his mind—a red cooler, a toy horse, the old man's bellowing voice—but they slipped away when he tried to recall anything concrete. It had been a long time since he'd had that dream. Years.

It was cold in the apartment, and he wore an old Chicago Bears sweatshirt that was a little too small. The alpaca slippers on his feet were a Christmas gift from Marianna. She'd sent the box with a card and a note that ended, "Thanks for taking care of our little girl." Which had made him feel . . . a whole lot of things. Miserable. Warm. Hopeful. Helpless.

He was thinking about getting up from his desk to grab another cup of coffee when his laptop emitted a soft *beep*—a new email. He clicked the notification and saw a message from Abel Battachya, one of the task force's pointy heads responsible for data analysis. The subject line read, "New Report RE: Global Impact, SARS-CoV-12."

Haggerty opened the report, and there, about a third of the way through the spreadsheet, was the number he had been dreading for more than a week: "Reported Global Deaths: 1,043,666."

A million people had died from the Dirty Dozen. More than a million. In six months.

Because of you. Because you failed.

Haggerty walked over to the living room window and looked outside at the parking lot and the cars and the building façades across the empty street. Snow still covered the ground from earlier in the week, now jaundiced from the streetlights and the lack of a moon.

He wanted very much to smash something. Punch a hole in the drywall maybe, or put on his boots and kick the cramped, constricting desk until it was nothing more than a pile of splinters in his office.

What's the difference between 987,446 and 1,043,666? Almost nothing. Almost everything.

He stepped over to the kitchen and fished a bottle of beer from the refrigerator. He opened it and set it on the granite countertop. Then he crossed his arms and looked at it for a long time. Thinking. Remembering.

His phone rang with an irritating jangle that made him wince. He sighed, then pushed himself away from the counter and snatched the phone from the top of his desk. When he saw Sonya's picture on the screen, something shifted in his chest. Something warm. A smile tugged at the corners of his lips.

"Hey. How are you feeling?"

"It's been six months, Dad." Her voice was packed with faux exasperation. "You don't have to keep asking me how I'm feeling every five minutes. *You* gave me a clean bill of health, remember?"

He did remember. She'd been in the ICU for a week after their rescue from the cave, and Haggerty had stayed with her the whole time. Technically he'd violated orders by doing so, but he cited his own need for medical evaluation. Early blood tests confirmed Sonya had not contracted the Dirty Dozen, which had been a huge relief. But she still worked through four broken ribs and a lacerated kidney, among other internal injuries. They were serious injuries that necessitated a long road back to health. Later he'd flown with her to D.C. and set her up at Walter Reed, where he still maintained a lot of connections. She'd been well cared for.

"Okay," he told her. "Fair enough. How's work?"

A longer-than-usual silence stretched from the other end of the line before she said, "You don't sound so good, Dad. How are *you* feeling?"

Haggerty shook his head. Smiling. Somehow she could always tell. Just like her mother had always been able to tell.

"It's nothing," he said. "Work stuff. Just more bad news."

"I saw your interview on TV last night. That news lady was being really mean. I wanted to smack her!"

"Yeah, me too. But that's what happens when a million people die on your watch."

"Oh, for crying out loud." Now her voice was packed with genuine exasperation. "It wasn't your fault, Dad! Are we gonna have to have this whole conversation again?"

"No, Sonya, I—"

"The government on Crete fought the quarantine the whole time, even though it was there to protect the world. Right?" She kept talking without waiting for an answer. "And by the time we were dealing with the secondary outbreak in Italy, people were already getting sick in other parts of Europe. And Egypt too, which of course you didn't know about. Right?"

Should have known about, he thought but said nothing.

"Oh, and on top of everything else, some idiot decided to blow up the Middle East and start World War III, which meant you guys had to leave the area and come back to America, which wasn't your decision at all. Right?"

He let the silence stretch for a long moment, knowing that answering or arguing would only make her more insistent. Truth be told, bad publicity was the least of his problems. Several members of Congress were already threatening to convene hearings and launch investigations. The sharks were circling, and he could do very little if they decided to bite.

Haggerty glanced at the phone screen. It was 11:17. "You didn't call this late to talk about this stuff. What's on your mind?"

She was quiet again for several seconds. Hopefully regathering her thoughts for a change of direction. "Yeah, well . . . I guess I'm calling to ask a favor."

"Yeah? Please go on."

"Okay, well . . . I just got back from my group. From my Bible study." He clenched his fist at those last two words. "So, we talk about a lot of stuff in the group. About what's on our minds and things. And I guess . . . I guess a lot of us are worried. Like, we're wondering how bad things could get with the fighting and everything."

Huh. Good question. Wish I knew.

There had been a lot of fighting in the six months after the attack on Jerusalem. Of course, a lot of it was centered on Israel. Missile strikes and drone bombardments were a regular threat from all over the region—Iran and Iraq and Syria and Lebanon and Jordan. What was left of Yemen. Even Egypt was funding terrorist

cells again, or so he'd heard. There had been a huge spike in suicide bombers as well.

Israel was holding strong. They'd completely closed off their borders, including Jerusalem, which caused a major stink among the
political class around the world. But the Iron Dome continued to
function, and the Israeli military continued to receive support from
the United States and other allies. Israel remained relatively stable.

The same could not be said of many other nations and regions
across the world, starting in the broader Middle East where the
animosity between Sunnis and Shiites had once again intensified.
There seemed to be a new civil war or state-sponsored terrorist
group erupting each month. Beyond that, the attack on Jerusalem
served as a spark for other conflicts that had been smoldering for
years or even decades. India had launched preemptive attacks
against Pakistan, claiming fears over nuclear weapons; those two
nations were officially snarled in a hot war. Ditto for Turkey and
Greece. And now that Venezuela had finally completed its economic collapse, many nations in South and Central America were
viciously squabbling over the remnants of its oil reserves. Hot war
seemed inevitable there as well.

*That doesn't even take into account Russia and Ukraine. The
whole thing's a mess.*

"Dad?"

"Sorry, Sonya Pie . . . just thinking how to answer. What kind of
fighting are you worried about specifically?"

"I don't know. It's just . . . people keep talking about nuclear
weapons and drone attacks. There's all those private armies
marching around all over the place. And you're sitting there in the
center of the bull's-eye if some crazy dictator decides to push a
button."

She's worried about me, Haggerty realized. *She's scared by all the
chaos, but she's also scared for me.*

"Okay, first things first, I haven't heard anything that suggests we're looking to get more involved. America, I mean. We're trying to calm things down, and I think it's been working. There's been some progress."

Not much, he thought, but that wasn't the point.

"Second thing, if I ever start to think I'm in a bad spot, I'll get out of here. I promise. *And* . . . if I get even a whiff of a hint that you and your mom are in danger, I'll come get you and bring you someplace safe. I'll do whatever it takes, okay? I promise."

"Okay, Dad." He thought he heard reassurance in her voice. Hopefully it wasn't just wishful thinking. "Thanks. I appreciate it. I'm sorry I called so late."

"Don't even mention it."

The silence stretched for a moment, and Haggerty realized with a clenching feeling in his chest that she was winding down the conversation. About to hang up.

"Although," he said, voice artificially chipper, "I do think we need to keep things fair."

"Fair?"

"Yep. You asked me for some insider information. Now it's my turn."

"Oh, I see." She was smiling now. He could tell. "What kind of information are you in the market for, Commander Haggerty, sir?"

He closed his eyes and took a breath. He tried to modulate his voice to sound as normal and as innocent as possible before saying, "It's about your mom. I've been wondering . . . I mean, for a while now . . . Argh."

So much for normal.

She waited, uncharacteristically quiet as he struggled to find the words.

Just say it, you idiot!

He opened his eyes. "Sonya, is your mom happy? Has she been happy?"

There was a long stretch of silence. Too long. Needing something to fill the void, Haggerty snagged the beer off the countertop and poured it down the sink, watching the play of dark liquid and light foam on the stainless steel.

"That's pretty personal, Dad."

"Yeah." He kept waiting.

"I haven't asked her that question, you know—woman to woman. But if you want my opinion . . . ?"

"I do."

Another pause. Then, "I guess I would say she's as happy as you are, Dad."

Oh, I really hope that's not true.

"Okay." He felt like he knew what she meant, what she was trying to communicate. "Thank you. And hey—I miss you, Sonya Pie."

Which certainly *was* true. After her discharge from Walter Reed, she'd stayed with him in this apartment for almost three months. He'd been back to work by then, but they'd continued their Italian routine of dinner together, followed by a long walk through the streets of D.C. It had been a special time. A wonderful season.

When she told him at the beginning of December that she needed to get back to Millersville—"back home," as she'd called it—the news hit him hard. Hit him like a chunk of limestone to the chest, in fact. The weeks since she'd gone had been especially long. And hollow. And lonely.

He was beginning to realize he'd been living in those realities for a long time. He'd experienced only a shell of a life ever since Ryan's death and his divorce. He just never understood the emptiness of that life until Sonya had come and filled it for a time.

"I miss you too, Dad. Thanks again. Good night."

"Hey, one more thing. I might be getting some time off before the end of the month. How would you feel if I came that way for a few days? Would that be okay?"

"Yeah, definitely!" she said. And to Haggerty's immense relief and intense amazement, she sounded excited by the idea. Or at least approving. "I would love that."

"Okay. I'll be in touch. Good night, Sonya Pie."

"Night, Dad."

When she hung up, he remained still for another minute or so, just standing by the sink and thinking. Then he put the glass bottle in the recycling bin, stepped over to close his laptop, and went to bed.

CHAPTER 13

I hate this room."

Haggerty spoke in a whisper, although he wasn't really worried about being overheard. He was talking to Caleb, who had just sat next to him.

"The room?" Caleb whispered back. "What can you hate about a room?"

Haggerty looked around. They were in the same Pentagon conference room that housed all the global task force meetings, including the one six months ago—the one where he'd somehow convinced himself it would be a good idea to bring his daughter to ground zero of a quarantine situation and the seeds of a possible pandemic.

It was the same room, but the massive mahogany table now seemed less impressive. Less imposing. The leather chairs surrounding the table were filled with the same powerful and dedicated people—mostly the same—but now they all looked noticeably haggard and worn down. Fewer staffers and support personnel hovered about the table than in previous meetings.

Even the smell of lemon-scented cleaning products now seemed intended to cover up a lingering sense of staleness and desperation.

Haggerty took a sip of his coffee, still pondering. "It's problems. This room is always filled with problems."

Caleb narrowed his eyes. "You love problems."

Haggerty barked a laugh. Short and bitter. "I like solving problems. This . . ." He gestured around the room and all it represented. "I don't think these problems can actually be solved. Not anymore."

"Well, solve one problem for me." Caleb tried to peer over Haggerty's shoulder. "Where are the donuts?"

Haggerty took another sip of coffee. "No donuts. Budget cuts."

Caleb scowled.

Doesn't that about sum things up? Haggerty thought. *Things are so bad Army executives don't even get donuts. #TheHorrors.*

"About today," said Caleb. "Is the plan still the plan?"

Haggerty nodded. "Everything has been buttoned up. I think you and I should—"

Motion at the corner of his eye caused Haggerty to look to his right as General Burgess walked up to the lectern at the head of the table. The buzz of conversation in the room quickly faded to a murmur, then to silence.

Burgess smiled. Her dress uniform was pressed and polished. She stood in front of her colleagues as strongly and sturdily as ever. Yet there were creases at the sides of her eyes and a sharpness at her cheekbones that had not been present during previous meetings. She looked weary in spite of her strength.

"Ladies and gentlemen, let's get started." She spoke clearly and efficiently. "We have a long day ahead of us and much to talk about, so I will be brief in my opening remarks." She made eye contact with many of those seated at the table.

"Let's start by placing reality at the center of this room: It's been a difficult six months. Not for us, but for the world. For the people we have been charged to serve, beginning with our own citizens and branching outward to all nations. Those people are currently living under the shadow and the terror of war. Many of them are hungry and burdened by food insecurity for their families. Many of them are sick; many have lost family members to new and dangerous diseases." She did not look at Haggerty as she said these words.

"Many of them feel endangered by the too-steep flood of refugees washing across their borders, and many know too well the uncertainty and ignominy of being caught up in that flood. All are under threat from a changing climate, including from storms raging around them and from the ground shaking under their very feet."

Now General Burgess did look at Haggerty. With compassion, he thought.

"Hard times," she continued. "Frightening times. Dangerous times." Another pause. "But these are precisely the times for which our task forces were created. *This* is precisely the time for which all of us in this room have been gathered together and empowered to make a difference. To find solutions."

Haggerty found himself nodding along with the general's words. He felt a familiar stirring of pride in his chest. *Maybe we can still do this. Maybe it's not too late.*

"Before we begin the presentations from our different task forces," Burgess resumed, "I know we're all interested in hearing more about the current military situation. There are a lot of rumors floating around, so I've asked Mr. Cory Jenkins"—she lifted a hand toward a small man wearing a tan suit sitting at the opposite end of the table—"to give us an update from the State Department. Mr. Jenkins."

There was a smattering of claps as Jenkins walked over to the lectern. He was only a little taller than Burgess, but he seemed much less substantial as they passed each other. Much less significant. He had a sparse mop of sand-colored hair, a very little chin, and large black glasses that matched his black belt and black shoes.

Caleb caught Haggerty's eye and raised one eyebrow, looking pointedly over at the seat Jenkins had just vacated—the seat that was typically occupied by the secretary of state during these meetings.

Where's Williams?

Haggerty shrugged his right shoulder and shook his head. *No idea.*

"Thank you, General," said Jenkins. "And thanks to each of you for having me." He spoke in a croaking, wheezy way that made Haggerty lean forward to try to hear more clearly. "A little less than six months ago, an unknown adversary carried out a daring attack against the Al-Aqsa compound in Jerusalem. The result was the complete destruction of that compound in addition to six hundred thirty-six fatalities and more than two thousand individuals injured. From the very first moment, US intelligence operatives have worked diligently to uncover the source of that attack. We have sought to determine who carried it out and why."

He paused. "As of this morning, those two questions remain unanswered."

Haggerty seriously doubted that could be true—doubted the CIA and the FBI and the NSA and the entire US intelligence machine could really be kept in the dark for so long on a matter of such critical importance. And yet, every time Haggerty had tapped one of his contacts in those different intel silos, they'd all returned the same answer: "We don't know."

Jenkins continued, "I'm aware people have been using the term

World War III in recent months to describe current events, but we in the State Department feel such descriptions are largely overblown—at least so far. Certainly there was an eruption of violence in the days following the attack. But those incidents have remained *relatively* contained."

He held up his hands, as if forestalling an imminent wave of objections. "Yes, it's true there have been many outbursts from the Islamic community both regionally and globally. And yes, we are monitoring the active conflicts in Asia and South America and Northern Europe. And the civil wars in Africa. *And* the increasing threat of piracy across global shipping lanes. However, given what *could* be happening in each of those examples and beyond, the State Department has chosen to label our current global political climate as relatively contained."

Haggerty and Caleb exchanged a long look, eyebrows raised.

I'd hate to hear what this guy considers a bad day for the global political climate.

"Now." Jenkins placed his hands on either side of the lectern, apparently just getting warmed up. "We at the State Department have identified two key patterns discernible in the actions of national leaders and militaries over the past few months. The first is *preparation*. A wide swath of nations have responded to the July 14 attacks by securing borders and stockpiling critical resources—including military resources. The United States is a good example. In addition, many governments are taking great pains to equip their proxies in different regions. Russia is actively arming Iran, for example. China is doing the same with North Korea and many separatist groups in Central Asia. There's also South Africa's growing embrace of South Sudanese warlords, and so on.

"Many nations, including many we have long considered our allies, seem to be preparing for a broader escalation of global war. Some are no doubt preparing in order to defend themselves, while others may be preparing for opportunities to strike vulnerable targets."

Jenkins paused and looked around, as if he was expecting questions or reactions. There were none.

"The second key pattern," he continued, "is *hesitation*. State actors we would expect to be aggressors in the current climate are instead holding back. China, for example. Perhaps they are waiting for another shoe to drop. *Or*"—Jenkins pushed himself provocatively up on his tiptoes—"perhaps they are nervous about something that occurred in the past. Perhaps they *think* they know who instigated the Jerusalem attack and that knowledge is causing them to hesitate."

It was very clear from Jenkins's mannerisms that he believed the second possibility was most likely. It was also clear that he really wanted to share who these other nations thought had instigated the attacks.

But Li Fan beat him to the punch. "It's us. They think *we* destroyed the Temple Mount, don't they?"

Jenkins looked like someone had stolen his lunch money. "Yes, that is our private assessment," he said. Grudgingly. "From the beginning, world leaders have been skeptical of our claim that we do not know the identity of the attacking nation or organization on July 14. During those early weeks, the international scuttlebutt was that America knew what happened but wasn't telling."

Oh man, Haggerty thought. *Leave it to this guy to use a word like* scuttlebutt.

"More recently," Jenkins continued, "opinion has shifted. World leaders have begun asking openly—through secure channels, of course—whether it was the United States that carried out the attack. Some of our allies have gone so far as to demand we tell them *why* we did it."

"What sense does that make?" Benjamin Abramowitz sounded

aggrieved. "What could we possibly gain or achieve from launching an attack against Israel? Against Jerusalem?"

Jenkins shifted nervously from one foot to the other. "The short answer is distraction, and perhaps economic stimulation. America has been hit especially hard by the . . . upheaval of recent years. There has been chatter on several channels suggesting we may be seeking to unite the American electorate—and perhaps stimulate the American economy—by dragging the world into an armed conflict we are well equipped to win."

Silence reigned in the room for several seconds. Then Haggerty asked the question he assumed everyone else was thinking. "So, did we do it?"

"No, Commander Haggerty," Jenkins answered. "No, we did not."

"Let's keep things moving for now," said General Burgess, who was still standing near the head of the table. "Mr. Jenkins, is there anything else you feel is pertinent for us to know or understand?"

"Um . . . yes." Jenkins seemed unsure if he'd just been chided, but he decided to move forward as instructed. "We are at a hinge point when it comes to the potential for global war. Right now the world's uncertainty about America's past actions and present goals seems to have created a relatively stable situation—and again I say *relatively*. From our perspective at the State Department, two possible events could tip that stability into global chaos.

"The first would be a Russian invasion of Israel using Iran as a proxy." Several people around the room gasped or muttered in surprise, but Jenkins spoke through them. "We have high confidence that Russia views Israel as a high-value asset. Not necessarily geographically but technologically. Russian leadership is quite covetous of Israel's capabilities when it comes to surveillance, advanced weapons systems, and cybersecurity penetration."

Several hands were raised around the room—despite General Burgess's earlier directive—but Jenkins once again kept going.

"If you're wondering whether Russia attacked the Temple Mount in order to spark a conflict with Israel, we can say with definite certainty the answer is no. We were watching. They did not strike."

The hands dropped.

"The second event that could potentially escalate our current situation would be an invasion of Taiwan at the hands of China, or possibly a Chinese and North Korean coalition. Obviously, China has been circling Taiwan like a shark for decades, but it's our belief they view the current global situation—and subsequent distraction—as an ideal moment to strike. In fact, we strongly believe they *would have* made a play on Taiwan already if they did not fear the possibility that we instigated the Jerusalem attack in an effort to goad them forward into war."

Jenkins paused to see if there were any questions, but nobody stirred or spoke. "In conclusion, we may currently be at the beginning or even near the middle of what laypersons describe as World War III. Our world *is* in conflict. However, that conflict can best be described as a stalemate in this current moment, largely because each player on the national stage is uncertain about America's motives and plans. It is our sincere hope to use this stalemate as an opportunity to de-escalate the global crisis and regain humanity's momentum toward peace and progress. Thank you."

There was a small round of applause as Jenkins returned to his seat; then General Burgess quickly transitioned the meeting back to its regularly scheduled programming.

Haggerty leaned back in his chair and did his best to settle in. Elbows on armrests, fingers steepled in front of his chest, and chin resting on his index fingers. Unlike during the previous meeting, he was not deeply, soul-crushingly tired. In fact, he felt wide awake. Unfortunately, he thought it probable he was about to hear quite a lot of presentations filled with quite a lot of bad news.

In that, at least, he was not disappointed.

First up was the Task Force Tackling Climate Change. Commander Singh and several additional team members spoke with passion and power about the imminent dangers of rising global temperatures and sea-level increases and endangered species counts and fossil-fuel consumption and much, much more.

The one element Haggerty did find interesting, and rather frightening, was a report on the increasing severity of hurricanes and cyclones throughout the world. There had been nineteen named storms throughout the world during the previous year, which was a high number when compared with the historical record. But an incredible eleven of those storms had reached Category 3 or higher on the Saffir-Simpson scale. A typical year would normally produce only three or four storms of that intensity.

As if earthquakes and famines and pandemics aren't bad enough. Now hurricanes are up.

The Seismic Anomalies Task Force presented next. Commander Li Fan opened her remarks on a sad note.

"Please join me in taking a moment to recognize the life and career of Henry Wilson." As she spoke, Henry's face appeared on the screen behind her—a tasteful and dignified headshot. "Henry was a dedicated public servant who contributed to the United States government for more than four decades in various roles. He was a good scientist. A good man. A good colleague. And a good friend. For those of you who may not have heard, Henry passed away two months ago due to complications associated with SARS-CoV-12. He leaves behind his wife, Angela, his two married daughters, and his four grandchildren." Li turned to face the screen and added, "Henry, you will be missed. Thank you for your service."

A familiar flush rose in Haggerty's cheeks. Shame. Guilt. Anger. Sorrow. He'd served as Henry's primary physician at Commander Fan's request, and he'd used everything he'd learned in Crete and

Italy and beyond to help the older man recover. But in the end, Henry had slipped away. Like so many others in the past six months.

Our fault, he thought for the thousandth time. *My fault.*

The rest of Dr. Fan's presentation was relatively brief. There was no progress on her team's attempt to build a predictive model for locating earthquakes before they struck, which was unfortunate but expected. There had also been another sharp increase in the number of severe earthquakes occurring throughout the world even since the previous task force gathering—seventy-seven such quakes in the past six months.

Next was the Global Hunger Task Force. Standing behind the lectern, Ivo Marcello seemed even more out of place and uncomfortable than usual in his ill-fitting, rumpled uniform. He seemed especially exhausted, and his normally resonant voice was raspy and hoarse.

Less than a month after the attack against the Temple Mount in Jerusalem, China had officially implemented a policy forbidding the export of foodstuffs and many other raw materials. Most other high-producing nations had followed suit. The ramifications of those policies were still being finalized throughout the world. Food insecurity had improved in several nations whose exporters were now forced to sell domestically—including China, Germany, Mexico, Brazil, Vietnam, France, Russia, and more. But for people and countries largely dependent on imports, the situation was dire. Whole regions had become food insecure. All around the world, individuals and families were starving.

Two other members of Ivo's team offered presentations on specific proposals for stemming the tide of famine and hunger given the realities of what they called the "new world." Neither proposal seemed promising. Not when a significant number of nations refused to offer aid or support beyond their own borders. Not in a political climate constantly sharpened by the reality of war and the threat of further violence.

The depressed mood of the day showed on Benjamin Abramowitz's face when he took his place behind the lectern to represent the Refugee Resettlement Task Force. He seemed vulnerable even as his tall frame towered over General Burgess. He looked forlorn. Beaten down.

"I'm afraid I need to start with some rather distressing news," he said, sounding as dejected as he looked. "Three weeks ago, we lost contact with the administrators of our refugee camp in South Sudan. All of our administrators. All staff. We sent additional personnel to investigate, and they discovered the entire camp had been overrun by its residents. Staff and security officers had been attacked—brutally attacked. Some were killed, others forced to flee. The secondary personnel we sent to investigate barely escaped with their lives."

Haggerty remembered his own horrific experiences at that same camp. He tried to picture what it would be like in that place with no security—no authority. He shuddered.

"A month ago," Abramowitz continued, "we had eleven RRTF refugee camps around the world. As of this morning, eight of those camps have been overrun by insurgents. No doubt a coordinated effort, and we have been forced to consider shuttering the final three camps as a precautionary measure for our staff."

He paused for a moment, overcome by emotion. "I thought we were making a difference. But . . ." He shook his head slowly from side to side. Seemingly out of things to say.

"Ben." General Burgess spoke softly from the head of the table. "Let's move forward with the presentations."

Just like that, it was Haggerty's turn. Before rising, he felt Caleb's hand on his shoulder. A gentle squeeze. Caleb was looking at him with eyebrows raised and his head tilted slightly to the left. *You going through with it?*

Haggerty nodded. *We'll be okay.*

Standing behind the lectern, Haggerty took a moment to study the faces of his colleagues across the table. His peers. In many cases, his friends. These were some of the brightest women and men in the world. They were passionate, fearless, and dedicated to improving the health, wellness, and security of all people in all nations across the world.

And yet, after two years of all five task forces working together and leveraging their many resources to make a difference in the world, the world had gotten worse. Everything had gotten worse.

It is too late. We can't do this. We've failed.

"Good afternoon, everyone. I'll be brief. I'd like to thank everyone in this room who reached out with condolences and offers of assistance after the earthquake in Italy. I'm grateful to say that my daughter, Sonya, is doing as well as can be hoped given her injuries. In the long run, she's going to be okay."

He paused, looking over at General Burgess, who offered a short, quick nod. Then a sad, knowing smile.

"Unfortunately, the same cannot be said for the 1.1 million people who have lost their lives over the past six months after contracting SARS-CoV-12. Otherwise known as the Dirty Dozen. Including"—he looked over at Li Fan—"my friend Henry."

He waited a moment in respectful silence. "There were reasons to believe we could contain the Dirty Dozen in Crete. It's my personal conviction that if I had acted more decisively in implementing a broader quarantine—if I had made the call more quickly and expanded the reach of that quarantine—the novel epidemic would have starved itself out. However, I did not. Therefore, it did not. Even as I was chasing a possible expansion of the disease into Italy, new patients were already being hospitalized in Turkey and Cyprus without our knowledge, and even as far as Cairo. By that time, there was no possible way of nipping it in the bud.

"And so, a mere six months later, hundreds of millions of people have contracted the disease, and more than a million have died. Our best estimates indicate that another million may be killed before the virus runs its course. It is my opinion that this outcome represents a singular failure on the part of the Potential Pandemic Task Force to complete its critical mission. To each of you who has been affected by this new and terrible disease, I offer you my deepest and most heartfelt apology. The blame is mine, and I am sorry."

Haggerty glanced again at Burgess. He received another nod.

"It is also my opinion that the current political climate in our world—including but not limited to the constant threat of war—makes it impossible for the Potential Pandemic Task Force to fulfill its charter mission in the present and for the future. For that reason . . ." A deep breath. A final look at Caleb for support. "I am officially requesting that the PPTF be dissolved, and its resources redistributed to other task forces."

Haggerty half expected a round of gasps or confused conversation from those around the table, and there were a few murmurs of surprise. But the major players had already been briefed about this development, including the other commanders. He and Burgess had worked through the details yesterday, including new locations for the majority of his staff.

When silence returned, Commander Abramowitz rose to his feet. "General Burgess, I would like to enter my own request into this official record. I request that the Refugee Resettlement Task Force likewise be shuttered and its resources reallocated to areas of greater need."

This, too, had been planned out in the days before the joint meeting. Most of the financial resources and personnel from the

Refugee Resettlement Task Force and the Potential Pandemic Task Force would be merged into the Task Force Tackling Climate Change. Most of the personnel with scientific backgrounds would be reassigned to the Seismic Anomalies Task Force.

"Commander Abramowitz, Commander Haggerty . . ." Burgess spoke formally, still standing at her usual place at the head of the table. "I will consider your requests and work with each of you to determine the best possible outcomes for yourselves and for your teams moving forward. I want to thank both of you for your faithful and commendable service."

Several people around the table clapped—a smattering that grew after a few seconds into a genuine appreciative round of applause. A little awkward maybe, but heartfelt.

And that, Haggerty thought with a rueful and bitter smile, *is that.*

CHAPTER 14

There's another of those camps, Cay." Haggerty was peering through the passenger window of Caleb's electric pickup truck. It was the morning after their final task force gathering at the Pentagon, and they'd left D.C. several hours ago. "What are they called again?"

"Hoovervilles."

"Hoovervilles," Haggerty repeated. "That's a big one."

Caleb glanced across the shoulder to see a large highway rest area just coming into view. It was packed with tents. Hundreds of camping tents in all shapes and sizes were scattered across the grass—lots of nylon in greens and browns and shades of blue. Some of the tents were arranged in rows matching the landscaped contours around the facilities, but most had been erected haphazardly. A few RVs were mixed in among the personal vehicles jamming up the parking lot.

People filled the camp. Some were walking, while others were cooking or warming themselves over low fires. Still others just stood together in small clumps, talking or looking lost. They all had coats and hats. They all breathed smoke like lesser dragons in the January air.

Caleb returned his attention to the road. Folks had been gathering in similar tent cities and other semipermanent homeless camps around the country for a few months. The first ones had appeared at highway rest areas because bathroom facilities were accessible for free. Once people realized the Feds weren't shutting the encampments down, they'd spread like wildfire.

"Does something like that make you rethink anything?" Haggerty asked. "About your future?"

"You mean retiring?" Caleb chuckled. "No. That's all settled. The house is paid for. Got solar panels for this thing"—he patted the steering wheel—"so gas can hit ten bucks a gallon and I'll still be able to get around."

It might just do that, Caleb added to himself, *the way things are going.*

"What about your kids?" Haggerty asked. "They doing okay?"

Caleb tilted his head from side to side. "For the most part. Michael has eight years left in the Air Force. At least eight. Abby's in Millersville, so she'll be close to me if she needs anything. She's due a month from now—did I tell you that?"

Haggerty nodded. "Your fourth grandchild?"

"Right. Our first granddaughter, though."

Caleb expected a twinge of pain at his use of the word *our,* but it never came. There had been fewer of those stings and stabs in recent months. Fewer emotional hangnails to tear on this or that. *Maybe I am doing okay, Tess. What do you think about that?*

"Simon is still Simon," he continued, eyes on the road.

Haggerty laughed. "You mean still a globe-trotting YouTube sensation?"

Caleb nodded. "He says it pays the bills. I take him at his word.

But if any of my kids ever get in a bad way, we've got Pappy's farm in the country. Farmhouse too. There should always be food and a place to stay."

"Well, that's good."

Silence simmered in the cab for a few minutes. On the radio, Hootie & the Blowfish sang about a girl sitting alone by a lamppost, trying to find a thought that escaped her mind.

"What about you?" Caleb asked. "Are you staying in for the money?"

Haggerty had agreed to join the Seismic Anomalies Task Force as the executive officer, replacing Henry Wilson. But General Burgess made it a condition that he take at least a week of vacation to clear his head. Which was why he was riding back to Millersville in the passenger seat of Caleb's truck.

One of the reasons why.

"I don't need money for me," Haggerty said. Which Caleb knew was true. Like himself, Haggs had been in the Army for almost thirty years. His housing had been covered, plus most meals. Much of their salary went directly into savings or investment accounts. Or, in Haggerty's case, was diverted to others who could use it.

"You're staying in for Sonya and Marianna."

Haggerty nodded. "That's a big part. Yeah." He paused. "Also, I don't know what I would do if I got out. Probably drive myself crazy."

"You're excited to see Sonya." Not a question.

Haggerty smiled. "Yeah."

"Maybe excited to see other folks as well?" Caleb kept his eyes forward as he asked the question, fingers tapping on the wheel.

"Maybe," Haggerty admitted. "If it happens."

"Well, Abby tells me lots of ladies shop at the Miller Mart on Thursday mornings. Something about fresh inventory."

There was another long stretch of silence as the pickup rolled along. The subject of Marianna was still a little tender between the two of them. Haggs had told him he was sorry—that he'd cracked under the various issues pressing down on him in that cave. Caleb believed him, but the tenderness remained. A soft spot in a solid friendship.

Tess always told him men were terrible at resolving conflicts, which Caleb guessed was true in many ways. But she was short on practical suggestions.

How do we finish fixing it? What does that look like?

He had no idea.

Traffic was sparse on the highway. Most traffic was down these days. The price of gas made commuting more of a luxury than a necessity—not to mention the ever-increasing cost of cars. And insurance. And maintenance. And everything else. Even those with electric vehicles often had trouble justifying car trips because of the significant rise in the price of electricity.

Caleb didn't blame Haggerty for wanting to maintain his financial security. But for his own part, he was ready for some peace and quiet. Ready for some grandchildren. Ready to figure out how to become a whole person when he still felt like half of himself was missing—if that were even possible.

Do you really think you're prepared for the future, old man? It was a question he'd been asking himself a lot lately. *Do you really think there's much of a future left?* That was a bigger question. A more frightening question.

Caleb thought of his children and the lives they were working to build—had been working hard to build for years. He thought of his grandchildren and the future they were likely to inherit. What was the world going to be like a year from now? Ten years? Twenty-five years? What were the chances that those who came behind him would find something worth cherishing?

What were the chances they would find anything left at all?

"'For nation shall rise against nation,'" he whispered to himself. Haggerty glanced his way. "What was that?"

Caleb sighed. "Nothing, Haggs. Just . . . just thinking."

The cab rocked a little bit as Haggerty shifted his weight to face him more directly. "Seems like there's been something on your mind for a while now. More than a week, I'd say. What is it?"

Uh-oh. Here we go. Over the past couple of weeks, Caleb had been looking for an opportunity to speak with Haggerty about something important but also sensitive. He wanted to hear his friend's thoughts, and he wanted to share his own opinions and beliefs. But this particular topic had been a sticky one between them in the past. He was hesitant to pry open a can of worms.

"I don't know, Haggs. It's spiritual stuff. So . . ."

Your will be done, Father. If this talk is going to happen, please season it with salt. Please give me wisdom and an open door.

"Spiritual stuff," said Haggerty.

"Yep."

"Well, we've still got"—he checked his watch—"at least three hours to go on this drive, and I'm still officially your CO until the paperwork gets processed. So out with it."

Caleb chuckled to himself. *I guess I won't get any door more open than that.*

"Well, what I'm thinking about right now, and really what I've been thinking about for weeks—what I can't stop thinking about—is the end of the world."

"Oh." Haggerty leaned back in his seat. He seemed genuinely surprised, which made Caleb smile.

Didn't see that one coming, did you, Commander?

"You're talking about the Apocalypse and Armageddon and the four horsemen and all that? Book of Revelation stuff?"

Caleb shook his head. "Not quite. At least, not yet. The Bible says a lot about the final days of human history—what some people call the end times. Revelation is the most famous example, but I'm actually thinking of what Jesus said in His last sermon."

"Matthew 24," said Haggerty. "The Olivet Discourse."

Caleb's mouth dropped open. His eyebrows shot skyward as he looked at his friend. *You sly dog.* Haggerty's understanding of the Bible and spiritual concepts was frustratingly difficult to pin down. He rarely allowed himself to be drawn into these types of conversations. When he did, he often seemed remarkably ignorant about spiritual concepts. Yet other times he could pull up surprisingly specific information seemingly on command.

"How do you know that?"

Haggerty chuckled. "Just something I picked up along the way."

Caleb grunted. *Probably from one of your dad's sermons, but you won't talk about any of those.*

"Well . . ." Caleb tried to regain his train of thought. "Can I set the scene a little bit?"

Haggerty extended a hand, palm outward. "By all means."

"Okay. What we call the Olivet Discourse was really a conversation between Jesus and a few of His disciples. It was a private conversation, and it happened after a big fight between Jesus and the religious leaders of the day."

"The Pharisees."

Caleb nodded. "And the scribes and some other groups. They were trying to put Jesus in His place, and He tore them up. Verbally. Called them 'blind guides' and 'whitewashed tombs' and a 'brood of vipers.'" Caleb couldn't help smiling. "They were big-time hypocrites, and He let them have it."

Haggerty nodded. He seemed to be listening.

"Anyway, after that big show, Jesus led His people up a hill right outside Jerusalem. The Mount of Olives. They could see the city, and they had a good view of the Jewish temple. Some of the disciples were admiring the structure of the temple, which was a beautiful building, but Jesus told them the whole thing was going to be torn down—not even one stone left on another. Which did happen forty years later when the Romans sacked Jerusalem."

He paused to look over at Haggerty. "You following me?"

Haggerty nodded. He made a twirling gesture with his finger. *Keep going.*

"Anyway, the four disciples sitting with Jesus started peppering Him with questions about the future. They wanted to know when the temple would be torn down, but they also wanted to know about the end of the world. And"—Caleb shrugged—"Jesus told them."

"In the interest of avoiding a full sermon," Haggerty said, "what part of Jesus' answer has been stuck on your mind for the past few weeks?"

Caleb made a pretense of appearing offended. "I thought we had three hours."

Haggerty said nothing.

"Okay. What's bothering me is that Jesus listed several specific signs that would take place right before the end of the world."

"What kind of signs?"

"The first one is wars and rumors of wars," Caleb answered. "Nations will rise against nations. Jesus also mentioned famines and earthquakes and pestilences all over the world. Those are signs as well."

For the first time Haggerty's face looked confused. He shook his head. "Doesn't make sense, Cay. Those things have always been part of the world. Every year has wars and famines and earthquakes and plagues."

"That's true. But Jesus also gave us a key for interpreting the signs. He said all these are the beginning of the birth pains. Like the pain a woman experiences in labor."

Haggerty still looked confused. "You're gonna have to connect those dots for me, Cay."

"Okay, labor pains start out relatively mild and infrequent. Right?"

He wiggled his hand back and forth. "I can't speak from experience, but that's the medical understanding. By the time us doctors get involved, things are usually pretty lively."

"Right! That's *exactly* the point Jesus was making. Labor pains start out mild and far apart, but then they become more intense and more frequent. And the pain becomes most intense and most frequent right before the baby is born."

"So . . ." Haggerty was tapping a finger on his knee, which meant his mind was engaged. Which was good. "So you're saying there have always been wars and famines and earthquakes and plagues. But as we get closer to the end of the world, those things will become more intense and more frequent."

"Correct. Specifically, Jesus was telling us there will be a sharp increase in the signs—not just one sign, but all of them together— when the end is near."

"And you feel like that's happening now?"

"I feel like it's on my mind," Caleb corrected. "But wouldn't you say that's happening now? Think of the charts we saw from the SATF. There's been a huge increase in earthquakes over the past eighteen months. Right?"

Haggerty nodded. "A big increase in *big* earthquakes too. So, more frequency and intensity."

"Right." Caleb was in a rhythm now, feeling excited. "And what would you say about pestilences—or should we call them pandemics?"

Haggerty grunted.

"Too soon?" Caleb asked.

Haggerty ignored him. "There have been lots of epidemics and pandemics throughout history. The bubonic plague. The Plague of Galen. Spanish flu."

"But have they gotten more frequent in recent decades? And more intense?" Caleb was genuinely curious to hear the answer.

Despite his place on the Potential Pandemic Task Force, he had not researched the history of global disease—but he was sure Haggerty had done so. Probably quite a bit.

Haggerty wiggled his hand again. "Black Plague was pretty intense. But a bit of an outlier. In the twentieth century we had the Spanish flu, Asian flu, and Hong Kong flu. Also HIV/AIDs. Ebola." He was quiet for a moment. Thinking. "So far this century we've had Ebola and AIDS again, plus H1N1, SARS, MERS, COVID-19—"

"A big one," Caleb interjected.

"Right. Plus the RSV eruption, duck flu, and now the Dirty Dozen."

"Another big one."

"Yeah. Another big one." Haggerty sighed. He rubbed his hands up and down over his face. "So . . . yeah, I guess you could say pandemics have increased in frequency and intensity in recent decades. But I think that's linked to the increase in human population. There's a lot more people, which means a lot more disease."

"Okay, but the point still stands. What about famines?"

Another several seconds of silence passed before Haggerty answered. "Not really my field."

"Not mine either. But don't you think it's interesting that the problem is so severe right now that it has its own task force?"

Haggerty nodded. "It's interesting that we have task forces for three of the four . . . What did you call them?"

"Signs," said Caleb. *The signs of the times.* "And the only reason we don't have a task force for 'wars and rumors of war' is because the DOD beat us to it by several decades." He took his eyes off the road to look at his friend. "Speaking of which, would you say war is on the upswing? More frequent and more intense?"

"They keep telling us the twentieth century was the bloodiest on record. Definitely doesn't look like things are about to calm down anytime soon."

"Right," Caleb agreed. "Yeah. And it's important that Israel is involved."

"Why?"

"Two reasons. First, Israel became a nation thousands of years ago with Moses and Joshua and David and Solomon and those guys. They were in the promised land. You've heard of that?"

Haggerty nodded. He twirled his finger again. *Keep going.*

"When the ancient Israelites rebelled against God, they lost the promised land. They were conquered by the Assyrians and then the Babylonians. Even in Jesus' day, it was the Romans who controlled the promised land. But the Bible is filled with promises that one day the Jews would return to the promised land—that they would have their own nation again." He glanced at Haggerty. "You remember when that promise came true?"

"In 1948," he answered. "After World War II."

"Yep," said Caleb. "And did you know Israel is the *only* nation to lose its identity and its geographical borders and then *regain* them after thousands of years?"

"I hear ya." Haggerty made the twirling motion with his finger again. "What's the second reason Israel is important for the end of the world?"

"Right." Caleb's thoughts were spinning in several directions, but he tried to focus on speaking calmly and clearly. *Just talk about the basics.* "Right. The second reason is that Israel plays a big role in all the events connected with the end of the world. It *will* play a big role, I mean. The rebuilding of the temple. The Antichrist. The—"

Something that had been nagging at the back of Caleb's mind finally clicked into place. He looked over at Haggerty—really *looked* at him for the first time in several minutes. The big man had turned himself in Caleb's direction and was leaning slightly forward. He had his foot crossed over his left knee. His hands were folded neatly in his lap. His face was alert and attentive. One side of his mouth was raised in a polite half smile.

The whole thing was a textbook example from the active listening seminars all senior staff had to attend in the Army. A perfect picture of polite interest.

"You're humoring me," Caleb said. Not a question.

Haggerty seemed surprised. "I'm listening to you."

"You are listening. But you're not tracking with me. You think it's baloney."

Haggerty sighed. "I'm not saying anything is baloney, Cay. But no . . . I'm not gonna sell my condo and go live in the woods because the world is about to end."

Caleb clenched his teeth. His fingers squeezed the steering wheel in front of him. He took a deep breath and held it for a moment, feeling the subtle hum and vibration of the road coming up through the tires. As he exhaled, he forced his fingers to stop squeezing, then allowed his jaw to release.

He glanced again at Haggerty's face and saw the confidence in it. The arrogance. Even defiance. Haggerty met his eyes and held them. Nothing angry or accusatory in his gaze, but nothing apologetic either. The two men stared at each other for what felt like several seconds.

Then Caleb smiled. "Hey." He turned his eyes back to the road. "Remember that time in Italy when you punched me in the face?"

Haggerty raised his eyebrows. "I do. I also remember apologizing. A lot."

Caleb waved it away. "You did. I understand you weren't yourself. Still." He rubbed his jaw. "It hurt like hell. So I need a little something in return. A little remuneration."

"Okaaaay." Haggerty looked more amused than concerned. "You want the condo?"

"No. I want to have one conversation on a spiritual topic with you, my best friend, that does not include you deflecting or waffling or passively listening without getting involved. I just want one conversation where I hear what you honestly believe—and why." After a moment he added, "Commander."

Haggerty looked at him for several seconds, then nodded. Then he shifted his gaze forward, out across the road. He said nothing. The radio was still playing softly. Counting Crows singing about Mr. Jones and never being lonely.

I pushed it too hard, Caleb scolded himself. *Pushed it because I felt embarrassed by his polite disinterest.* Still, he waited.

"I remember one time Dad took us on a fishing trip. Me and Mark. This was back when we lived in Fort Wayne, when I was a freshman."

Caleb felt a rise of excitement flow through him. A rush of curiosity. Haggerty almost never talked about his father, even all the way back to high school.

"'Course, it wasn't really about fishing. Dad wanted to spend the day drinking, so he got off work and pulled us out of school and we drove an hour out of town. We were at the lake five hours, I think. Maybe four. However long it takes to drink two six-packs. We did get to catch a lot of fish, me and Mark." Haggerty sighed. His right hand massaged the side of his head, as if rubbing something tender. Something painful.

"Dad was drunk as a skunk driving home. I mean, completely out of it. Hunched over the wheel and singing at the top of his lungs. Me and Mark got into some kind of horseplay on the bench—this was an old Chevy pickup—and somehow the passenger door opened and Mark fell out."

Caleb gawked in surprise. "He fell out of the truck?"

"Kind of. He fell out of the cab but held on to the door. He was screaming. So was I. Dad didn't even notice. Didn't even stop singing." Haggerty paused. "I was able to drag Mark back inside and get the door closed again—and then we rode the rest of the way home like nothing had happened. Mark cried for a long time but stopped before we got to our driveway. That night, when the buzz wore off, Dad beat up Mom again. I tried to stop him, and he put me on the ground a couple times. The next day I went to school. Like normal."

From the corner of his eye, Caleb could see Haggerty's right hand probing along the right side of his head. Probably touching the missing piece from his ear—a gesture that was as familiar as it was mysterious.

Caleb reached down to turn off the radio, saying nothing. He waited.

"So here's what I honestly believe, Sergeant Major. I believe this world is a lot like that Chevy. There's bad stuff going on. A lot of suffering. There may be Someone or something behind the wheel—I truly don't know. But everything I've seen tells me we're on our own. We gotta fix our own problems, and we gotta do everything we can to take care of those who can't."

Oh, Father, Caleb thought, *please have mercy. Please help me be helpful in this moment.*

Haggerty leaned his head deeper against the headrest and closed his eyes. "Is that what you wanted to hear?"

Caleb reached over and placed a hand on his shoulder. "Yes. Thank you." Then another thought struck him. "What about the rest of your family? Did they feel the same way?"

"Mom believed all the way to the end," Haggerty said. "Even with all of Dad's . . . stuff. Even after the police got involved, she kept going to church and all that. I had a hard time when the cancer came back—I felt like I'd let her down somehow. But she was smiling and talking about going home right before her last breath."

"Going home, Cay." He heard the echo of Tess's words in his mind again. *"Going home today."*

"What about Mark?"

Haggerty shrugged. "He learned how to talk the talk when he had to, but mostly he stayed out of Dad's way. None of it stuck for him either."

They drove on for a long time.

Eventually Haggerty said, "What about you, Cay? Same topic. What's your take?"

"You know what I think. You've always known."

"Yeah, but let's both get it out on the table. I'd like to hear it in your words."

"Okay." Caleb thought for a moment. He wanted to be as clear as possible. "I agree the world is filled with suffering, but I believe that's something we've chosen for ourselves by rejecting our Creator. I believe that suffering is going to get worse, not better. Much worse. I believe God is very much behind the wheel." He flexed his fingers on top of his own steering wheel. "And I believe God has a plan to steer us through the mess we've made and bring us to something better."

"Let's flesh that out." Haggerty sat up and turned toward Caleb. He seemed to be engaged in the conversation once again. "Let's say you're right about these signs and the end of the world and all that. What does that mean practically?"

"Practically?" Caleb frowned. "I don't get you."

Haggerty shrugged. "I guess I'm interested in hearing more about the plan. If you're right about the birth pains thing, what's next? What's the next step in the plan?"

The answer was fixed firmly in Caleb's mind. "The Rapture."

"The Rapture," Haggerty echoed. "Tell me about it."

"It's a rescue mission. God's rescue mission. When the current age of history comes to an end, Jesus will reach down into this world and physically remove every person who is a child of God." He glanced at Haggerty. "You know what that means?"

"Saved," he answered. "Washed in the blood. A Christian."

Caleb nodded. "Everyone who is connected to Jesus will be rescued. Taken out of this world and taken up to heaven. The Bible says it will happen in a moment—in the twinkling of an eye."

"Rescued," Haggerty repeated. "From what?"

Caleb took a moment to try to phrase things correctly. "From judgment. God promised to punish evil, but He will rescue His children first."

"Every Christian in the world . . ." Haggerty tapped his finger on his knee. Thinking. Calculating. "How many people would that be?"

Caleb shrugged. "Hundreds of millions. Maybe billions."

Haggerty flashed a smile. "That'll be an exciting day. I bet even us pagans will notice something like that."

"Yeah." Caleb laughed, glad to see his friend smile. Glad to be having this conversation.

"I'll tell you what." Haggerty reached over to jiggle the steering wheel. Lighthearted for a moment. "If I ever wake up one day and there are billions of people missing without any explanation, I'll sprint over to the first church I can find. Deal?" He stuck out his hand.

Caleb looked at it. He wanted to say, "That will be too late, Haggs." He wanted to say, "Today is the day of salvation." He wanted to say, "Seek ye the Lord while he may be found, call ye upon him while he is near."

But no. Haggerty had come a long way in this conversation—shared things Caleb had long believed would never be shared.

Don't push it. There's time.

With a grin, he shook the hand offered to him and hoped he was right. Hoped there was still time for so many things.

CHAPTER 15

No, no, no. Don't start all that, Cay." With an effort, Haggerty took a breath and tried to lower the volume of his voice. "You are completely misconstruing what I said."

"I'm not misconstruing anything, Haggs. You're backpedaling faster than a figure skater."

They were in the enclosed back porch of Caleb's house in Millersville. Both men were sitting comfortably in reclining chairs. Both wore jeans and sweatshirts with slippers on their feet. Both were holding mugs of steaming coffee. It was a little before noon, and sunlight filled the room through several wide windows.

Haggerty took a tentative sip of his coffee, but it was still too hot. "Look, the Bulls were great. They were dominant. I think they're the best dynasty in NBA history. But if the Bears become the first team to three-peat in the NFL, I think that's more impressive. That's all I'm saying."

"That's all you're saying." Caleb put his coffee on a side table before throwing up his hands in mock indignation. "You like cake, Haggs. I've seen you eat cake all over the world. So tell me what's better: two cakes or one cake?"

Oh, not this again.

"Yes," Haggerty said. "I know the Bulls had two three-peats. But these are totally different leagues, Cay. It's—"

They sat up and turned their heads at the sound of the front door opening.

"Dad?" a woman's voice rang out. "You home?"

"On the porch, Abi-girl."

Haggerty and Caleb glanced at each other with raised eyebrows. *We'll talk about this later.* Then they heaved themselves out of their recliners as Caleb's daughter walked into the room.

"Hey!" She held her arms out and shuffled between the two chairs toward her father, and he wrapped his long arms around her in a tight embrace. "Welcome back!"

She was tall, like her father—her head rested just below Caleb's chin as they hugged. She had the same angular slenderness as her father; long limbs and sharp cheekbones and a pointed chin. She was also very obviously pregnant, and she wore a navy blue dress that draped gracefully over her belly and hung loosely over black boots.

Now she turned toward Haggerty, a smile on her face. "And hello to you." She stepped gingerly forward to squeeze his shoulder. "So good to see you, Uncle John."

Haggerty grinned at the old nickname. She'd started calling him that as a little girl, and the name had stuck through birthday parties and sports games and graduations and weddings. And funerals.

"It's good to see you, Abigail." He looked over at Caleb. "Hey, I've got some work to jump on. I'll catch up with you in a bit."

"No, no." Abigail was shaking her index finger. "I'm just stopping by for a few minutes on my lunch break. Please stay."

Haggerty considered for a moment. "I'll stick around if you sit in the recliner."

She smiled. "Deal."

He said little over the next fifteen minutes, happy to sip his coffee as father and daughter reconnected. Caleb wanted to know about what her doctor was saying and what all the latest tests had to say. She showed them both a picture of her most recent sonogram. For her part Abigail wanted to know more about why Caleb was retiring and what kind of plans he'd made for the future.

Haggerty soaked it in, just enjoying the simple pleasure of observing a normal conversation without needing to be part of it.

Truth be told, he still felt a little on edge from his talk with Caleb during yesterday's drive. It wasn't the first time someone had shoehorned him into talking about a sensitive subject—Sonya had become a master of that process in recent months. But Haggerty and Caleb had always maintained what felt like a comfortable separation between church and state. Between belief and . . . whatever Haggerty believed or didn't believe. Yesterday felt like a shift.

You asked him what he was thinking. You basically ordered him to tell you, and he did.

Which was true. More than that, Haggerty had shared his own experiences and his honest opinions—and Caleb had heard them. He had thanked him and then moved on.

You're worried things will change now that he's retired. No more buffer of professionalism. You don't want to start thinking of him the same way you think of used-vacuum salesmen.

Maybe that was it. In any case, his interactions with Caleb so far today had been normal. Just like old times.

"What was that, Abigail?" Haggerty asked. Something she'd said a moment ago had raised a flag at the back of his mind. "What's happening that's sinister?"

She turned toward him. "Oh, there's a problem at work that's been driving me crazy." She had short brown hair gathered into a tangle of springy coils, and she took a moment to slide one back from her forehead with a slender finger. "I'm having trouble getting anyone on the phone."

"Yeah, but you said *sinister*." The word had piqued his interest. Not something he heard every day.

"Well, I'm trying to finish an audit for companies that had billable hours with us last year. Which isn't that many, really." She was a financial analyst for the local electrical co-op. "But this particular company has a huge gap between their work hours and the actual billed hours."

"They overcharged you?"

"No." She shook her head. "That's just it. They billed us for far fewer hours than I know they were on our premises based on key card data. Which means they had access to our facilities for a large chunk of time that was not accounted for on the invoices. The discrepancy there felt . . . sinister."

Haggerty and Caleb exchanged a glance.

"Let me get this straight." Haggerty grinned. "Somebody put in a bunch of work without charging you, and now you want to track them down and . . . what? Make them send more invoices?"

She smiled back at him, but Haggerty heard the steel in her voice when she answered. "These technicians were given access to critical infrastructure. They had to receive special clearance. So when I see a difference between how long they spent at our facilities and how many hours they billed us for—something doesn't add up." She raised her chin half an inch. "I don't like it when things don't add up."

Haggerty inclined his head. "Spoken like a true accountant."

Caleb met Haggerty's eyes and offered a slow wink. *Be careful, big fella.* Then he turned to his daughter. "What does this company do, anyway?"

She sighed. "We hired them to assist with hardening the power grid throughout the county."

"Hardening?" Haggerty asked. "What's that?"

"It's a specific term for electrical systems. It means adding protection to make those systems less vulnerable to disruption or attack."

"Physical attack?" Caleb sounded surprised. "You mean bombs or drones?"

Abigail shook her head. "The biggest problem for power grids is always weather events. Which . . . doesn't it seem like there's a lot more of those happening these days? Earthquakes and storms and that kind of thing?"

Caleb made a point of raising both eyebrows toward Haggerty, but he ignored it, keeping his focus on Abigail. "What does hardening a grid actually mean? What happens?"

"It can be several things. A lot of it is replacing older infrastructure with new equipment that's more robust. Sometimes there are critical power lines that need to be moved underground so they're not exposed to danger. There are also automated systems that can be installed to detect faults or other problems in microseconds and shut things down before they spread to the rest of the grid."

"Yeah, but you said *attack*." Caleb seemed to have fixated on that word—perhaps because his daughter was involved. "What kind of attack would target a power grid?"

"Oh." Abigail thought for a moment. "The biggest concern would be an EMP attack, but that's very unlikely."

"Huh." Haggerty felt a familiar tickle at the back of his mind. His brain wanted to make a connection with something she'd just said, but . . . it wasn't coming. *Electromagnetic pulse attack. Why is that important?*

"I know that look," Caleb said. "What are you thinking, Haggs?"

"I think I'm starting to come around to Abigail's point of view on this. I don't like the idea of anything fishy being connected with the power grid."

Abigail looked pleased as she pushed another rebellious lock of hair away from her eyes. "I'm sure the company is legitimate, and I haven't heard anyone complain about the actual work. It's just frustrating that I can't get in touch with anyone. I send emails, I leave messages, I call at different times of the day. Nothing."

"Well." Haggerty leaned back and took a long, slow slurp of his coffee. "It's too bad you don't know anyone with government connections who could dig a little bit and find some answers for you."

Abigail sat forward. She glanced between Haggerty and her dad.

"Not me," said Caleb. "Haggs is the one who knows everybody."

"Do you think you could help?" She spoke to Haggerty. "Do you think you could find better contact info?"

"I think I can try," Haggerty said. His face warmed as he had an idea. "Hey, I'm meeting Sonya at Mac's this evening when she gets off work. Wanna join us and I'll tell you what I find?"

"That quick?" She looked surprised. "Yes, that would be great. Thank you!"

"My pleasure. What's the company called?"

"RediCert. I think they're based in Pennsylvania. Or maybe Illinois."

"Okay. When you get back to the office, text me whatever information you've got on them and I'll see what I can do."

A little more than five hours later, Haggerty stuck a fork into the final bite of his latest mega-donut from Mike MacIntosh's

Magnificent Café. He'd ordered another plain version, while Sonya was once again working through about a thousand calories of whipped cream and caramel sauce and chocolate chunks and sugar-sprinkled fried dough. She was sipping coffee from a mug, while Haggerty—who'd reached his caffeine limit back at Caleb's porch—opted for sparkling water.

Six dollars for water with bubbles in it. Tell me that's not a sign of the end of the world.

"I think the hardest part has been having to learn so much on the fly." Sonya was telling him about her new job. "Dr. Keen expects everything to keep rolling along like it did six months ago, but he lost two of his main staff to the . . . to illness." She offered an apologetic smile.

Haggerty said nothing.

"Anyway, there weren't any training manuals written up or instructions to follow. We didn't even have any of Gladys's passwords for any of the systems we use. So the first few weeks were pretty tough. But I'm more in the swing of things now."

Don't ask how much money she's making, Haggerty reminded himself for the third time. *Don't ask if any young men are part of the staff.*

"Do you enjoy it?"

She shrugged. "It's managing a doctor's office, not scouring luxurious Italian villas to catalog fine art collections. But the people are nice. Most of our patients are nice. And really, considering the way things are right now, most people think of any reliable job as a privilege." She nibbled on her donut for a moment. "There were more than seventy-five applications for my position, I think. Just from people here in Millersville."

"Wow. That is surprising."

Under the guise of finishing the last few swigs of his sparkling water, Haggerty examined Sonya's face as she continued eating. In most ways she looked similar to when he'd seen her in this same café six months ago. She'd let her hair grow out a bit. He still saw some gauntness around her cheeks and under her eyes that most other people wouldn't notice—evidence of her time in the hospital and in rehab.

But she also had a presence about her that was different from before. There was something new and something engaging in the way she carried herself.

Some of it's confidence. Assurance. But there's something else as well.

Without thinking, he reached across the table and took her hand. "It's so good to see you doing well. I'm proud of you."

She smiled. "Let's not get *too* cheesy, Dad. We don't want to end up on the Hallmark Channel. But I do—"

Her smile broadened as she looked up at something over his shoulder. "Abby!"

Haggerty turned in his chair and saw Abigail carefully negotiating her way through the maze of tables. Sonya ran over to offer a hug, and the two women stood together for several minutes, chatting and catching up on each other's news.

Feeling content where he was, Haggerty surveyed the café. Most of the tables were empty. The same had been true when he first came in almost an hour ago. He'd always remembered Mac's as a busy, bustling place—especially during the morning and evening rushes. But not tonight.

Maybe it's a fluke. Or maybe there aren't many people left in this town with enough disposable income for ten-dollar donuts.

Eventually Abigail came over and gingerly took the seat next to Haggerty at their square table. She placed a manila folder on the table in front of her. When Sonya gathered up her hat and coat from the other chair, Abigail seemed surprised. "You're leaving?"

"Yeah, I've got Bible study tonight," Sonya answered. "I have a little more reading to do, and it's my turn to bring a dessert." She bent down to kiss Haggerty on the cheek. "Bye, Dad."

He squeezed her hand. "Dinner tomorrow?"

"Sure thing. I'll text you."

When she left, Abigail and Haggerty stared at each other for a moment. He was trying to figure out what sort of niceties needed to be satisfied before they moved on to the business with RediCert, but apparently she was one step ahead of him.

With a look of anticipation, Abigail clapped her hands together. "Did you get anything?"

"I sure did." Haggerty pulled a small notebook out of his pocket and flipped through a few pages. "First things first . . ." He ripped out one of the pages and slid it across the table to Abigail. "This is contact information for the RediCert employee who interfaces with the federal government. Name, email, and phone number. All confirmed as active."

"That's wonderful." Abigail folded the paper and tucked it in her purse. Then she looked back up at him. Waiting. Expectant.

Okay. Further down the rabbit hole it is.

"I also did a little digging on the company itself." He flipped to another page. "RediCert was incorporated twelve years ago. C-Corp, but they only had about twenty employees when they first started. Now they have a little more than forty. Kind of small for the type of contracts they deal with, but . . ." He shrugged. "Their work is pretty specialized. What's interesting is they've done work all over the country, but they can't have a regional workforce with so few employees. So their people must travel from job to job."

Abigail pursed her lips. "Is that important?"

"No idea. I guess it makes sense given the work they do. Again, highly specialized. They must have found a team that doesn't mind moving wherever the work takes them."

A waitress arrived and set a coffee mug in front of Abigail. Then a cookie on a plate. Haggerty dug in his pocket for his wallet. "Did you . . . Can I—?"

She waved a hand in front of her chest. "You'll get it next time. What else did you find out?"

A slow grin stretched across Haggerty's face. He couldn't help shaking his head.

"What?"

"I don't know. Just . . ." He tried to think of a way to phrase it that wouldn't be offensive. "You remind me a lot of your father."

"Oh. That's nice." Then she clapped her hands twice and asked again, "What did you find?"

"The strangest thing is what I didn't find, which is the actual owner of the company. Or ownership group." He flipped to another page in his notebook. "RediCert is part of a holding company called COMM NRG."

"Communications and energy. Sounds right."

"Yeah, COMM NRG manages several companies in the utilities industry. They're mostly pretty small and very specialized. Just like RediCert. But when I tried to figure out who owns COMM NRG, I came up against a wall. It's a subsidiary of a European corporation I can't identify."

Abigail still looked expectant. "Is that bad? Does that mean anything?"

Haggerty shrugged. "No idea. It just feels funny that a company doing work in Millersville has such massive connections."

"Okay. We'll file that away."

Incredibly, Haggerty actually saw the moment when she mentally stored what he'd told her and transitioned to what she wanted to tell him. Her facial expression switched from "receiving" to "transmitting."

"I found something too," she said. Clearly keen to share. "I talked with Jimmy this afternoon. He's in charge of security access and key cards for any nonemployees who need access to physical structures on the power grid. He said the RediCert people were here for about two months, and it was mostly the same people coming and going each day. *Mostly.*"

Haggerty twirled his finger. "And?"

"Jimmy said the advisory crew were very nice. That's what he called the RediCert techs: the advisory crew. They were up and down our transmission lines and in and out of substations. No problems. No issues. *But*"—Abigail brushed a coil of hair off her forehead—"another group of techs came for about a week, and Jimmy said they were super rude. He called them the install crew. *Install.*"

"Install," Haggerty repeated. "Why is that important?"

"Because . . ." She opened the manila folder on the table in front of her. "I've been through every invoice we received from RediCert, and *none* of them include any charges for materials or equipment."

"So if they installed something, they didn't bill you for it."

"Right. But it's more than that. All of our systems require high clearance to access, for obvious reasons. Our own technicians normally wouldn't let anyone breathe on the equipment on our critical substations, let alone install something without direct, active supervision."

Haggerty frowned. Confused. "I thought that's what RediCert did—all the hardening stuff. Isn't that what you said?"

She shook her head. "John, RediCert is an advisory company. They're consultants. They're supposed to show us which parts of the grid are vulnerable, and then they offer specific recommendations for improvement. But . . ." She closed the folder. "It will take our technicians two years to implement all those suggestions. We have to buy equipment and physically dig trenches and work through installations. Two years at least."

"Huh." Haggerty's mind was spinning fast, flagging questions and logging inconsistencies and making jumps. Problem-solving mode.

Curiouser and curiouser.

"So we've got a semi-mysterious company who spent two months evaluating your systems and exploring every part of the local power grid throughout the county."

She nodded.

"This same company brought in a secondary crew for a short period of time. That crew apparently installed something connected to the grid—and did it secretly. Maybe even to the point of not billing for their work so it wouldn't be discovered."

She nodded again.

"To me that sounds . . ." Haggerty trailed off and raised his eyebrows.

She grinned and finished for him. "Sinister."

CHAPTER 16

O h, you have got to be kidding me."
Haggerty meant to mumble the words under his breath, but frustration had turned up his volume more than he realized. An old woman standing in front of him turned around and craned her neck to look up at his face. She frowned. Then scowled. Then said, "Humph."

Right back at you.

He'd come to the Miller Mart exactly when it opened, hoping to get quickly in and quickly out. Alas, no plan survived first contact with the enemy—not even grocery runs. The line at the door wrapped around the side of the building, which meant he'd waited fifteen minutes before he could even grab a cart and begin shopping. Once inside, he found the shelves half empty in most places. There was no organic produce, and the prices for the regular stuff were eye-popping. When he was finally ready to check out, he had to choose between a long line at one register and a very long line at another.

He chose the long line.

Now he was listening to an older gentleman try to explain to the young woman at the register why he couldn't download the app on his phone to get the latest Miller Mart coupons because he never used any apps on his phone. He only used his phone to call his three daughters. And did the young lady go to school with any of his daughters? Or did the young lady have any children who might have gone to school with any of his grandchildren?

"You," Haggerty growled. "Have. Got. To. Be. Kidding."

There was motion at the corner of his eye, and Haggerty glanced left toward the store entrance. A woman and two small children were walking through the door. Nobody he recognized.

Needing some distraction, Haggerty took out his own phone and opened the News app. Which ended up being a mistake. The headlines had been pretty much the same for weeks:

OFFICIALS OFFER NO HOPE FOR LATEST DIRTY
DOZEN STATS:
"JUST HAVE TO GET THROUGH IT"

OPINION: THE WORLD DESERVES "RESULTS
FORCES" NOT "TASK FORCES"

DEATH TOLL FOR MOST RECENT SAN JOSÉ QUAKE
REACHES 1,500

HISTORIC CYCLONE BATTERS COAST OF INDIA;
THOUSANDS WITHOUT HOMES

He put his phone back in his pocket. The old man had finally checked out, but six people were still in front him.

Just take a breath, John. You don't have anywhere you need to be

today, so forget about the line. You can afford twelve dollars for a
carton of eggs, so drop—

There was a burst of voices behind him from the entry door—
voices and laughter. Women's voices. Haggerty heard snippets of
their conversations as they picked out carts and baskets: "... never
would have told her that if I'd known ..."; "... didn't have it last
time, so I really hope it's back in stock ..."; "... working at the same
doctor's office, but it's a different job."

One voice rang in his ears like a bell. It was earnest, musical,
and hypnotic. A voice he would have recognized and responded to
anytime and at any place in the world.

He turned slowly, uncertain if he felt excited or afraid of what
he might find. She was already there, and already looking at him
with a warm, sad smile.

"Hello, John."

He tried to think of something smart to say. Or mysterious. Or
creative. A hundred different options were considered and rejected in the space of a second.

"Hello, Marianna."

He'd seen her several times since the divorce was finalized, but
always at official functions of one kind or another. Sonya's sports
games or honors or graduations. Wedding ceremonies of mutual
friends. (Although Haggerty never stayed for receptions.) The
last time he'd seen her had been two years ago at Tess's funeral.

As always, encountering her in person made him feel stunned
and clumsy. Physically, she was the opposite of Haggerty: slender
and petite, with delicate features, bright eyes, and a wide smile.
She had warm, golden skin and long, thick hair the color of coal.
With a start he realized streaks of gray marked her hair.

"Yeah," she said, following his eyes. "I thought about coloring
it. Even made an appointment, but—I decided I don't have the
energy."

"You look wonderful, Marianna." He meant it. He hoped she could tell he meant it.

They stared at each other for several seconds before Haggerty realized the silence was stretching toward awkwardness. Before he could think of anything to say, Marianna stepped forward and reached into the grocery cart.

"Let's see what we've got here. Two bags of carrots. Celery. Peppers. Apples." She met his eyes and patted her fingers together. A golf clap. "Very healthy. But . . ." More rummaging. "Potatoes. Potatoes. Sweet potatoes. Ground beef. Ground beef. Ground beef. Hamburger buns." She looked back up at his face. "I'm sensing a theme here, Captain."

Haven't been a captain for a long time. It's major general now. He realized with a sense of grief that he wanted her to know about his rank. He wanted her to know what he'd achieved.

You hoped she'd been keeping track of your career. That's what you wanted her to say.

"Uh-oh." She was still fiddling in the cart, and now she held up two chocolate bars, her face a picture of triumph. "I knew it!"

Haggerty shrugged. "Can't win 'em all."

"No, you can't." She dropped the candy back in the cart. "What's with all the burgers, though?"

He shrugged again. "Caleb and I haven't done much cooking in the last"—he made a show of checking his watch—"thirty years. Army food isn't the best, but it does the job."

"Ah . . ." She made a show of restoring the carrots and potatoes and other groceries to their original arrangement in the cart. "You had a different cook for some of those years, though." She looked up to catch his eyes. "Fifteen, if you don't remember."

Haggerty felt a flush prickle over his arms and up his cheeks. A familiar wave of awkwardness and embarrassment. She'd always run circles around him in these types of conversations. Always. At every level of their relationship.

Don't try for a clever comeback, John. Not even five minutes and she's already stuck a sword through your liver.

"I remember," he said.

She was wearing what Haggerty assumed were fashionable jeans and a thick black turtleneck that was snug. He plucked one of her sleeves at the wrist. "Cold outside. No coat?"

It's in the car, he thought.

"I left it in the car," she said. "As I'm sure you remember."

He laughed. It was one of the things he used to tease her about. The whole point of a coat was to be warm outside, he'd tell her. Why leave it in the car? Why bring it at all? She always told him she brought it so she'd have it when she needed it.

"You have it if you need it," he told her, smiling.

She smiled back and spread her arms. "Exactly."

Something made her turn around slightly, and Haggerty followed her gaze. The group of women she'd come in with were standing about twenty feet away. Heads gathered. Whispering. One of them seemed to be giggling.

Marianna looked back at him again. "I should go. And . . ." She pointed toward the register. "Looks like it's almost your turn."

After a brief burst of confusion, Haggerty swiveled toward the line of people in front of him—except the line was mostly gone. There was a large gap between himself and the old lady.

He looked back at the only woman he'd ever loved. "It's good to see you, Marianna." She'd never been Mary or Mare or any other nickname. Not to him. He liked the elegant and exotic flow of "Marianna" from his lips.

"You too, John." She seemed to hesitate for a moment, then she stepped swiftly forward and kissed him on the cheek. "Thank you for taking care of our Sonya Pie," she whispered. Then she turned and walked back to her friends. The group strolled up the produce aisle all the way to the back of the store, then turned left. Out of sight.

Haggerty watched Marianna the whole way, his eyes wide and mouth open. He still felt stupefied by their brief encounter. Their quick closeness.

She did not turn back.

CHAPTER 17

D ecisions, decisions."

Haggerty was sitting at a table in Mac's again, alone for the moment. He was staring at his phone, which was ringing. General Burgess's picture was on the screen. It was the same picture he'd always seen when she called, but somehow she seemed sterner than he remembered. Or more disappointed.

With a flick of his thumb, Haggerty sent the call to voicemail. This was the second time she'd called in the past couple of days. He didn't know why he'd ignored both calls. Not in his conscious mind, anyway. For one thing, he was still officially on vacation. This was Saturday, and he wasn't due to fly back to Washington until Monday morning. But there was something else. He perceived it without understanding it.

He let out a deep sigh as he continued to watch his phone. If there was an emergency of some kind—if Burgess needed to contact him urgently—she'd call back a second time. Immediately after the first. She'd leave a message as well, so he watched and waited.

Nothing. He put the phone in his pocket.

Two minutes later, Abigail walked through the door. This time he jumped up and escorted her to the counter to place—and pay for—both of their orders. When they returned to the table with their food, Haggerty skipped the preliminaries and jumped right to business.

"You said something happened at work yesterday that freaked you out." He tried not to sound either skeptical or conspiratorial. "What's up?"

"I talked with the contact you gave me for RediCert. At first she was very closed and suspicious. Like, she asked several times where I'd found this contact number." She held out a placating hand, as if Haggerty were about to object. "I just told her I used the company Rolodex. Nothing else."

Haggerty grinned. "Appreciate it."

"I told her about the discrepancy in billable hours. That there was a deficit on our side that needed to be resolved." She paused a moment, struck by a thought. "Even that was weird. It took me a long time to get her to understand the issue—that RediCert's technicians had worked more hours than they'd billed us for. I kept asking if there were additional invoices we hadn't received yet, but she said she didn't know. She kept asking what I thought was the best way to resolve the issue. She used that phrase several times: 'How do you feel we can best resolve this issue?'"

"Like she just wanted to get you off the phone."

"Yes! That's exactly what it felt like." She took another bite before adding, "This is good, by the way."

He nodded. "Is that what freaked you out?" He wasn't picking up any hint of a threat or danger from what she'd said so far.

Abigail shook her head. "No. Melody told me she would check up on the invoices and get back to me. So . . . I guess that's the best I could hope for."

Haggerty waited. He'd already finished his toast.

"The reason I called you," Abigail continued, "is because half an hour after I got off the phone, my boss came over to my cubicle. He asked me what I'd been working on, and I told him a few of the items on my agenda—including the RediCert invoices."

"Let me guess. He wanted to talk about those invoices."

She nodded. "As soon as I mentioned them, he sat on my desk and settled in. Like he was gearing up for a big conversation. He asked me what the problem was, even though I hadn't mentioned any problem. I gave him all the details, and he listened. But then he got a real serious look on his face—which is rare for him."

"He's not a disciplinarian?"

"No. More of a puppy dog. But today he told me very sternly, 'You've spent enough company time chasing these rabbits.' That's how he put it. He told me to finish the rest of the audit and move on. 'Just forget the RediCert thing. It's not worth the risk for any of us.'"

"The risk. Huh." Haggerty had both elbows on the table and was leaning toward Abigail. What she'd said threw up red flags left and right. It was a genuine mystery. A problem that begged to be solved. But there were risks involved—and not for Haggerty. He had to keep that in mind.

"You think someone talked to your boss. Leaned on him." Not a question.

"Yeah, I do." She was finishing up her last bite of toast. "It's so strange."

"Okay." Haggerty clapped his hands together and leaned back in his chair. "So what's next?"

She frowned at him and tilted her head to one side. "What do you mean?"

"I mean, what are you going to do about it?"

She looked at him for several seconds, absently pulling one of her curls straight and then letting it spring back into place. Then she slumped down in her chair and let her whole head rest against the back. "I was hoping you'd tell me what to do next."

Haggerty shook his head. "I'm on a plane Monday morning. Back to D.C. I'll be spending the next few months hopping all over the globe, trying to figure out how to predict earthquakes—if such a thing is possible. I can mention all this to one of my contacts in the FBI, if you want, and see if they decide to dig any deeper, but . . ." He shrugged.

"You don't think anything would come of it."

"I don't. Somebody has to drive the bus."

As they sat together, Haggerty saw the struggle written on her face. The desire to *know* pushing and pulling against the practical reality of time. And effort. And limited resources. And fear.

"Abigail." He spoke gently. "What happened with your boss proves there's at least some risk involved here." He glanced down toward her belly, then back up to her face. "If you want my opinion, I think it makes the most sense to let this go. There's not much to gain if you keep pushing—maybe nothing at all. But there's a very real chance you could be sticking your hand in a hornets' nest."

She shook her head. Slowly at first, then with firmness. "No, Uncle John, I . . . I need all this to add up. I need to keep going."

He smiled and thumped a hand on top of the table. "I was hoping you'd say that! And I was hoping I'd get to tell you this . . ." He pulled his little notebook out of his pocket and flipped through a few pages. "That FBI contact I mentioned? He owes me a favor, so I asked him to dig a little more on COMM NRG—you remember the holding company from Europe?"

"I do, yes." Now she was the one leaning forward on the table, eyes sparkling with interest.

"There's a third company that's owned COMM NRG for several decades now—almost thirty years. Um . . ." He tapped his notebook. "URC Life. Huge corporation. And *that* company is part of the Vilks empire. Have you heard of them?"

Abigail shook her head.

"They keep a low profile. Especially internationally. But I've dealt with enough stuff in Europe to bump up against one of their operations every now and again. Very old family from the Baltics with businesses that go back centuries. Three hundred years ago they had a network of trading ships that financed a huge network of mineral mines and timber and other commodities. All that income has funded more businesses than probably even the government can keep track of."

"And this family—this . . . empire"—Abigail looked mystified— "has some kind of interest in Millersville? How can that be?"

"Well, it's not just Millersville. RediCert has done work all over the country, which . . ." He took out a pen and made a few notes on a blank page. "I'll see if I can check how extensive that work has been. Plus, RediCert is separated from the Vilks family by at least three layers of corporate bureaucracy. So the actual higher-ups may have no idea what's going on over here."

She nodded. Thinking. "But someone knows."

"Yes. Someone knows. So let's keep digging." He rose from the table and started to put on his coat—then stopped. "Hey, when you talked with the lady from RediCert. Uh . . ."

"Melody."

"Thank you. When you talked with Melody, did you ask her about the installation thing? About what their secondary team was installing and why?"

"I . . . no. I was going to, but once I got on the phone, it felt like a bad idea. I don't really know why."

Haggerty was bundled up and ready for the cold. "That was wise. Best not to give too much. In fact, until we really understand what we're dealing with, let's keep all this in the family. Sound okay?"

"Okay. Thank you, Uncle John."

He squeezed her shoulder. "I'll see what I can find out."

Later that evening, Haggerty eased himself into a worryingly small chair at the local Italian restaurant. He had a healthy mistrust of dining chairs in general, having broken several of them during his decades of adulthood. But restaurant chairs were the worst culprits. Most of them seemed overused and broken down.

In this case, though, after a few exploratory shifts of his weight from one side to another, Haggerty decided he was stable. For now.

"Solid as a rock?" Sonya had been watching his ritual testing.

"It'll do." He pointed at the glass of wine in front of her. "I didn't think you were a fan of red."

"Oh." She looked at the glass and shrugged. "Just trying something new."

Haggerty took up the menu with some hesitation. He was hungry, but he wasn't especially looking forward to the food. Getting spoiled by culinary delights was one of the few negative consequences of spending time in Italy.

"I know." Sonya seemed to be reading his mind. Or probably his face. "Frozen-entrée Italian should be outlawed. No strangozzi, either."

He closed the menu. Confused. "Then why'd you pick this place? Especially on a Saturday night?"

She was starting to answer when her eyes flicked upward and focused on something behind him. She smiled and waved, still looking over his head.

A party of three, Haggerty realized. They hadn't discussed this.

Someone from the Bible study? he wondered. *Or a boyfriend? Could it—?*

He turned in his seat and saw Marianna walking toward them. She was smiling at Sonya, but Haggerty could see the confusion on her face. The distress.

She didn't know, either. He saw a brief mental picture of Admiral Ackbar from *Star Wars* yelling out, "It's a trap!"

Haggerty was on his feet now, facing Marianna. He reached out an arm to give her a side hug, but right at that moment she lifted a hand to pat his opposite shoulder. They ended up circling each other for two seconds like wrestlers at the beginning of a match until, mercifully, Marianna managed to squeeze him on the forearm and step back.

"Oh, that was terrible," Sonya said. "The judges award no style points."

Both Haggerty and Marianna turned toward their daughter with the same motion. Marianna spoke first. "Sonya, what are you—?"

"Yes! Yes! I confess." She draped her arm over her forehead in dramatic fashion. "I inadvertently scheduled dinner with both of my divorced parents on the same night, at the same time. But did I have the courage to admit my mistake?" She glanced between them. "Did I have the moral fortitude? Alas. No."

"Sonya." Haggerty was doing his best not to smile. "This is all—"

"No, no, my *pater*. There is no place for weakness of character in a functional society." She'd taken her coat off the chair and was now putting it on. "Off to bed with no supper. It's the only way I'll learn."

Now Haggerty felt alarmed. He'd assumed Sonya intended for the three of them to have dinner together—just like old times. But if she really was planning to leave . . .

"Whoa, whoa." He reached out both hands in a calming-down gesture. "You can't just—"

But she could. She did.

"Think better of me, Father," she trilled, kissing him once on the cheek and stepping over to give Marianna a hug. "Good night, Ma!" She whispered something into Marianna's ear, then walked briskly toward the exit—and through the door.

Haggerty glanced around. The restaurant was about half filled. Mostly older couples chatting across small tables in the dim lighting. A few families.

He turned to face Marianna, who hadn't moved. Haggerty felt heat on his cheeks and the back of his neck. His heart pounded more and more rapidly in his chest even as his arms and legs felt paralyzed. He had absolutely no idea what to say or what to do.

Oh, you'd better say something, Haggs. You'd better say something right now!

But it was Marianna who broke the silence. "I blame *you* for this."

Haggerty leaned back, startled. "Me? How? Why?"

She shook her head. "This never would have happened if you didn't save her life in those caves."

He barked out a laugh and closed his eyes, feeling some of the tension begin to ease out of his joints and limbs. Not trusting himself to actually say anything, he stepped around the table to where Sonya had been sitting and pulled out the chair. Then he looked at Marianna and waited, eyebrows raised. A smile on his lips.

She stayed where she was, saying nothing. She stared at him for what felt like a long time. A very long time.

Maybe she won't. Maybe she can't. He had no idea what would happen next.

Then, with the same smooth grace that had always been her birthright, Marianna stepped lightly over to the empty chair and turned, standing with her back toward him.

Haggerty reached over the chair and held her coat while she stepped out of it. Then she sat. She was wearing jeans again, plus a cream-colored button-down that must have been tailored given the way it . . . well. He was very pleased with her choice of attire.

What happened next was extraordinary because it felt so ordinary. To Haggerty for certain, but he thought—or maybe he hoped—the same was true for her as well. They opened their menus and considered their options. When the waitress came, they ordered. Lasagna and potato gnocchi, with salad and minestrone to start.

While they waited for the food, they talked. She asked several questions, and he answered. He asked several questions, and she answered. By unspoken agreement they stayed in safe territory— work, the weather, the strange turn of global events, and memories of their daughter.

At one point Marianna held out her glass and said, "This is a good red. Good job remembering."

Haggerty just smiled and shook his head. "Sonya."

When the meals were finished, Marianna ordered tiramisu for dessert. When that was finished, Haggerty ordered coffee. When coffee was finished, they looked at each other for a minute. Not saying anything. Then Marianna rose, and Haggerty helped her into her coat.

"Thank you for dinner." She was looking at him with the same warm, sad smile as in the grocery store.

"I . . ." He was trying to interpret that smile. "We should do this again sometime."

She said nothing. She was standing on the opposite side of the table from him.

"I'd like to do this again," he corrected. "To see you again. Are you free for dinner tomorrow night?"

She stepped forward until she was standing directly in front of him, right in the middle of his personal space. She looked up at him, still saying nothing.

Having her so close set off all of Haggerty's internal alarms. Red alert. Sirens blaring. A lock of black hair had spilled out across her cheek, and he thought about reaching out his hand and tucking it behind her ear. His fingers twitched with the anticipation of that touch.

"I can be free for coffee, John. On Wednesday."

Wednesday. The word was a drop of ice water down Haggerty's back. He was scheduled to fly back to Washington on Monday morning. Sonya knew that. Which meant Marianna knew that. Which meant she was laying a gauntlet at his feet. A challenge.

A choice.

She tilted her head slightly to the left, looking from one of his eyes to the other. "I'm too old to play games, John." She said it warmly but firmly.

Haggerty thought of General Burgess and Commander Fan and increased seismic activity across the globe. He thought of Sonya—the weeks they'd spent together in Italy and the months they'd spent together in D.C. He thought of how different it had been to share his life with another person for that sweet, swift season. He also thought of Abigail and the mysterious problem of an unknown company doing unknown things on critical systems in Marianna's hometown.

You're not ready to make any big decisions right now, Haggs. You're definitely not ready to make any promises you can't keep. His mind was doing the thinking, but his heart spoke first.

"Coffee," he said. "Wednesday morning around ten."

She smiled. The way her eyes lit up made him feel like he could leap through years and never feel the sting of time.

"Wednesday at ten," she said. "I'll see you."

CHAPTER 18

Y ou haven't spoken with Burgess at all?"

It was Wednesday morning. Caleb and Haggerty were standing at the end of the driveway outside Caleb's house. The temperature was below freezing, but at least the sun was out. Both men wore coats, but Caleb had his arms wrapped around himself and was hopping from foot to foot. His voice sounded strained from the cold.

"Nope." Haggerty was unbothered by the weather. "I sent an email on Monday."

"You explained everything?"

Haggerty looked at his friend. "Explained everything? I can't even explain this to myself. I just told her something had come up and I would contact her later in the week." Which was true. And which was extremely unusual for an incurable rule follower like Haggerty.

"That's a bold move, Haggs." They both knew General Burgess didn't tolerate being jerked around. "So . . . what is your plan?"

Haggerty shook his head. "I really don't know, Cay. I'm wingin' it. I need to see how things go this morning, and then . . . then I guess I'll have to make a choice."

Now Caleb was blowing into both of his hands, first the right and then the left. The white fog of his breath curled around his fingers with each attempt to warm himself. Suddenly he looked sharply over at Haggerty. "You haven't talked with Burgess? She had to have called you at least a few times. Right?"

Haggerty said nothing.

"Oh, don't tell me. You're not ignoring her phone calls, are you? Tell me you're not ignoring the general's phone calls, Haggs!"

"There she is." Haggerty gestured with his chin toward a gray SUV as it came around the corner and rolled up to the end of the driveway. Abigail was driving.

Caleb waved, then opened the passenger door. Looking sternly at Haggerty, he said, "Don't you get my baby girl in any trouble, now."

"Will do, Cay. I'll talk with you later."

The drive took about thirty minutes. Neither Abigail nor Haggerty said much along the way. He could tell she was feeling a little nervous. He understood.

When they parked, Haggerty studied a large, flat, open area across the street surrounded by a chain-link fence. The ground of the enclosure was entirely covered in a thick layer of gravel. Metal beams rose out of the gravel in several places. The vertical beams were crisscrossed with a larger number of horizontal beams. The result looked as if someone had built metal frames for cube-shaped houses that were never finished.

In the middle of the enclosure were two additional structures unlike anything Haggerty had ever seen. Each structure had four huge metal coils pointing upward at odd angles from a central concrete base. They seemed like something he'd expect to see on a starship from a TV show.

"Okay, just to confirm: This is the central substation for the Miller County electrical grid. Correct?"

"That's right." Abigail's voice was steady. "This is the big line. It goes all the way up into Columbus."

"And you're certain this is the place where RediCert's install team added something to the system, whatever it was?"

She nodded. "This is where they worked. I confirmed that. And"—she leaned over the steering wheel and squinted across the street—"I can see what they installed. Jimmy described it for me and where they put it."

"Okay. That's good." *Jimmy is quite a helpful young man*, he thought. "And to the best of your knowledge, the station is un-manned? Nobody is in there?"

"There shouldn't be anybody. I'll need to check in when I scan my key card, but that's through a phone line."

"Good. Then take a couple deep breaths, and let's get this done."

He was about to open his door when she put a hand on his shoulder. "You're not wearing any metal, right? No belt buckle? No keys in your pocket? No jewelry?"

"None of that." He patted his shirt and pockets. "What about my phone?"

"Be on the safe side," she said. "Leave it."

They climbed out of the car and walked across the street. The sun was bright in Haggerty's eyes, but it offered little warmth. Patches of woods extended beyond the fenced area on two sides. He also noticed three cameras mounted at different locations along the street.

Abigail stopped in front of a small kiosk close to the fence. She took an ID card out of her pocket and scanned it, then pressed a red button on the kiosk. Haggerty heard a whirring, beeping sound for a few seconds—a dial tone. Then a click.

"MCECO control, this is Turner."

"This is Abigail Hart. I'm about to enter Substation Number One."

A pause dragged out on the other end of the line. "Hello, Abigail. You're not on the schedule for today."

"Hi, Frank." Her voice was calm. At ease. "I just need visual confirmation of some new hardware before I authorize an invoice. It'll be quick."

"Roger that. Stay safe."

A louder click sounded, then Abigail pushed through a gate in the fence. Haggerty stepped through after her but left the gate open slightly. He didn't relish the thought of being locked in.

Getting stuck here would be . . . shocking. He smiled to himself, wishing Caleb were here so he could say it out loud.

"Over here." Abigail was walking toward the far corner of the enclosure, away from the street and away from the main gate. She stopped in front of a large metal cube about four feet tall and four feet wide. It was painted a dull green. The gravel around the base of the cube was a slightly different color than the stuff in the rest of the enclosure.

Next to the cube was a thin metal pole about eight feet high. A solar panel was bolted to the pole right below the level of Haggerty's head.

Abigail was looking at the cube. "It doesn't seem like much. A metal box."

Haggerty walked around the box in a circle, keeping one hand on the metal top and his eyes on the ground. A metal conduit ran from the bottom of the pole to the box, but nothing else. No other connections that he could see.

"It's interesting," he said. "Whatever this is doesn't seem to be tied into the actual power grid in any way. No wires or pipes, unless they're underground. But it seems unlikely they would dig trenches in a place like this."

"I talked with a couple other guys who maintain these substations." Haggerty looked sharply over at her, but she held up her hands. "Unofficially. Just office gossip. They were told RediCert installed this as some kind of monitoring equipment."

Haggerty grunted. "I guess that's possible." He gently kicked the pole. "Solar panels to power whatever's inside here . . ." He kicked the box—and stopped. Surprised. He had expected a metallic clang when his steel-toed boot hit the panel, but there was only a dull thump. He kicked it again. Same sound.

Stepping closer, Haggerty saw where two of the box's metal panels were joined together by a vertical row of bolts. He knelt beside the box and checked each of the heads with his fingers. All tight. He moved to the other side of the box and worked his way down the row of bolts. One at the bottom was loose. With a grimace he pinched it with his fingertips and started twisting it to the left.

"John?" Abigail sounded nervous.

"One minute." He finished working the bolt loose, then realized it was actually a self-tapping screw. He rubbed his fingertips against his shirt for a moment. They were sore.

Abigail stepped around to see what he was doing.

"Just checking something." With his left hand Haggerty pulled the metal panel away from the box. He slid two fingers of his right hand underneath the panel and felt around for a few seconds. "Huh. It's concrete."

"Concrete? Why would they make a cube out of concrete?"

"I'm not sure. Could be a protective thing. They're trying to keep the instruments in there safe."

Abigail frowned. "Wouldn't that interfere with whatever those instruments are supposed to be measuring?"

He nodded. "I would think so, yes. But the only other reason to use this much concrete would be . . ." Haggerty's voice trailed off.

He was still kneeling next to the box, working the screw back into place. Now he stopped and looked up. Looked around the enclosure at the various types of equipment looming above him and beside him. Looked beyond the enclosure in the direction where Millersville was located.

Abigail watched him with a curious expression.

"Hey. Come over here for a second." He led Abigail about fifteen feet away from the box. "Warmer here in the sunlight. I'll be right back."

Not waiting for a response, Haggerty returned to the box and stood still for a moment. Thinking. Then he lifted his foot and kicked downward into the gravel at the base of the metal panel. He struck with his heel pointing down, and then he dragged it backward away from the box so it scraped up a small pile of gravel—like his heel was a small shovel. He did it again: Kick, drag. Kick, drag. Kick, drag.

After a minute, he knelt again and scooped more gravel out of the way with his hands. He glanced over at Abigail while he worked. She was watching, but she didn't say anything.

Good girl. He appreciated her trust.

Haggerty bent down a little farther to examine his work. As he expected, the metal panel stopped just below ground level—but not the concrete. He'd excavated about ten inches of gravel, but he couldn't see the end of the slab. It kept going down.

"These aren't blocks." He looked back at Abigail. "They either used whole slabs, or they set up forms and poured the concrete around each side."

"John." The strain in her voice made him look up. She was facing back across the street to where they'd parked. "I think someone's here."

"Okay. Not a big deal." He kept his voice calm as he quickly scraped the gravel back in place. "Let's walk out. If you have to say anything, be confident. You belong here."

She nodded. He stood. They made their way toward the gate at a normal pace, with Abigail walking in front. Haggerty saw a white SUV parked next to their own vehicle. The letters *MCECO* were stenciled on the side. Miller County Electrical Co-Op.

"Hey, Jimmy. What are you doing out here?" Abigail sounded cheerful as she walked through the gate and addressed a short, thin, young-looking guy who had just stepped down from the SUV. Haggerty followed her and closed the gate behind him.

"Mr. Pace sent me." Jimmy's voice was high and a bit reedy. He shielded his eyes with his hand as he gazed up into Abigail's face.

"Hi, Jimmy." Haggerty stepped forward and extended his hand to shake. "John Haggerty."

The young man scowled at him. He shook, but with a noticeable lack of enthusiasm. Then he turned back to Abigail, and the look on his face instantly changed back to a dopey smile.

Ah. Haggerty suddenly had a better understanding of why Jimmy had been so helpful.

"I don't think you're supposed to be out here," Jimmy said to Abigail.

Haggerty's mind was already sprinting toward a plan. He took a half step forward, digging a hand in his pocket to pull out his military common access card. *I can say I asked Abigail to show me the station,* he thought, mind whirring. *Something about national security, or maybe—*

Abigail put a hand on Haggerty's shoulder. "You're right, Jimmy. I just needed to check something. We're leaving now, but . . ." She took her hand off Haggerty's shoulder and rested a few fingers lightly on top of Jimmy's arm. "Do you think you could tell Matt nobody was around when you got here? That would save me a whole lot of paperwork."

Jimmy looked down and actually kicked the gravel with his shoe. *He may as well rub the back of his neck and say, "Aw . . . shucks,"* Haggerty thought. *Poor kid.*

"Sure thing, Abigail. I'm just gonna take a walk around. I'll see you later." He gave her a final wave, then started off along the outside of the fence. Haggerty might as well have been a ghost.

Abigail watched him go, then turned back to Haggerty. She shrugged.

"You forgot to bat your eyelashes," he said.

"Oh, shut up." She grinned. "Let's get out of here."

————————————

Two hours later, Haggerty felt himself on the verge of doing something stupid—something he wanted to do but was sure he'd regret.

He'd met Marianna at Mac's right at ten o'clock. They'd both ordered coffee and a donut, then sat at an isolated table off in a corner of the café. They'd resumed the conversation from the other night. Just picked it back up as if they'd kept talking without stopping for the past four days.

She had a lot of questions about the countries he'd visited in recent years, which gave him a chance to share several of his favorite stories. He was interested to hear about the hobbies she'd picked up over the past decade. She was excited to tell him about her progress as an amateur photographer—and about the side business she kept promising herself she would start.

They stayed on safe ground again, but the opportunity to learn so many new things about each other was refreshing. And pleasant. And sweet.

When Marianna said she needed to walk off some of the "sugar calories," Haggerty asked if he could join her. Which was why they were strolling side by side down Third Street. Which was where Haggerty began to feel an internal pressure to say something he was pretty sure was a bad idea. He dismissed it—or tried to dismiss it. But the pressure kept building. In fact, he realized it had been building for years.

He stopped walking. She kept going for a few steps, then turned around and looked back at him. Waiting.

What have you done, Haggs? He felt sick. His mouth was dry and his stomach was churning.

"Marianna, I . . ." He cleared his throat. "There's something I need to tell you. Something I should have told you a long time ago."

She seemed worried now but said nothing.

"When everything happened with Ryan." He paused. He shook his head and started again. "When Ryan died, I was overwhelmed by guilt. By failure. And I . . . I said some terrible things to you. Horrible things."

Her face softened. She took a step in his direction.

"It's . . . I can't . . ." With a growing sense of horror, Haggerty realized he was stuck. The words he wanted to say were jammed in his throat somehow. He wasn't able to speak. He was going to stand here in front of his ex-wife and choke on his attempted apology until she walked away in disgust.

Come on, Haggs. Win this fight!

He thought back to the moment with Sonya in the cave, when she'd asked him to talk about Ryan. And the divorce. And his failure to be a father. He'd felt the same way in that cave—stuck. But he'd been able to push through because Sonya *needed* him to do it.

Marianna was still staring at him. *With pity*, he thought. *Maybe even compassion?*

"There's no way I can fix what I said back then. The damage it caused you. I know that. And there's no way I can help with the heaviness you've had to carry all those years because of my words. But I . . ." He paused, taking his own step toward Marianna. "But there are things I need to tell you now just because they're true.

Because you need to hear them and . . . and because I need to say them. So here goes."

He cleared his throat. "Ryan's death was not your fault. None of it was your fault." He waved a hand in front of his chest. "The sickness, the bruises. The separation." Haggerty again felt stuck, but he pushed through. "The divorce. None of it."

She took a final step toward him and set her hand on the top of his arm. Her face was still filled with compassion. "Thank you, John. I appreciate that." Then she nodded down the road. "Shall we keep moving?"

They took another first step together. Moving forward. Moving on.

After a minute, Marianna said, "I didn't think I'd ever hear you say that, John. Honestly, I didn't think you'd ever be *able* to say it."

He blew out a sigh and nodded his head. "Pretty pathetic, huh?"

"Maybe." She grinned at him. They walked on. "There does seem to be something different about you. Something that's changed. Do you feel that?"

He nodded. "I think spending time with Sonya knocked something loose inside me. Not just the time in the cave, but . . . but all of it." He looked over at Marianna's face. "I never understood how calcified I'd become. I still don't understand it, but . . . but I feel a change. Yeah."

"I almost want to test it." A mischievous quality laced her voice that made Haggerty's eyebrows rise. "You know," she said, "see how far this new John actually goes. How deep."

He stopped walking again and turned to face her. He bowed theatrically, sweeping his right arm down across his legs and then out to the side. "You may ask anything you desire, and I shall grant it. Up to half my kingdom."

He expected her to laugh, but she didn't laugh. She looked thoughtful.

Uh-oh. She's serious about this. The thought sent a cold wave cascading through his guts.

"Okay. Then tell me about this." She reached up and lightly touched the top of his right ear. Set her slender finger inside the missing chunk. Haggerty had to concentrate very hard to avoid wincing and drawing back, but he managed.

"Tell me what happened, and tell me why you've never been able to talk about it."

You can do this, Haggs. You can win this one. For her.

And to his amazement, he realized it was true. He could. So he did.

"It happened when I was a freshman in high school. Back in Fort Wayne. Before we moved here. I think it was a Thursday. We didn't go to school that day because Dad took us fishing—or took himself drinking, more accurately. About an hour after we got back, I heard him yelling, and then I heard Mom wailing. Then she was screaming. A horrible sound.

"I ran to the bedroom, and they were both there. Mom and . . . and Dad. She was on the ground. Her dress was covered in blood. She'd been pregnant. I don't know how far along, but she was showing a little. Five months, probably. But I knew from the way she was wailing and sobbing that she wasn't pregnant anymore. Miscarriage."

Haggerty wasn't speaking robotically this time. He could hear the bitterness in his words. The hatred.

"He was kneeling down beside her. Comforting her." Haggerty shook his head and felt like spitting on the sidewalk. "He looked around at me when I came through the door, and right away I knew he'd done it. I could see it right there in his face. He'd hit her too hard or one too many times. Or maybe he'd kicked her this time. I don't know if it was on purpose—if he meant to kill the baby. But I knew he'd done it. And I could see by the way he was looking at me that he knew I knew."

Haggerty and Marianna had started walking again. She was closer to him than she'd been before. Not touching, but close.

"I waited until late that evening. I knew he'd be out in the garage, working on his sermon." He glanced at Marianna. "I told you he was a deacon at the church back then, right? They let him preach every couple months?"

She nodded.

"Anyway. I took a baseball bat with me when I went to the garage. My Louisville Slugger. He was at his workbench, with his Bible spread open on the edge. I don't know why, but he always had to be fiddling with something when he practiced preaching. Doing something with his hands. This time he was holding a pair of vise grips—kind of like needle-nose pliers, but they can lock in place. I think he was trying to fix a dining room chair." Haggerty chuckled. "I probably broke it."

Marianna stayed close.

Does she really want to hear this?

"He was still taller than me back then, but I was bigger. Heavier. Stronger—or so I thought. He turned around when I closed the door, and we just stood there staring at each other for a while. It was probably ten seconds, but it felt like ten minutes. I showed him the bat. I told him to get out or else I'd make it so they took him in an ambulance. I told him I meant it.

"He took a couple steps away from the workbench. Then he did the last thing I ever expected. He slid down to his knees, and he raised his left hand above his head, and he yelled out, 'Oh, Johnny, I've sinned. Oh, Johnny, I've sinned.' He was wailing as loud as my mom had wailed earlier. And he was crying."

Haggerty squinted in silence for a moment, as if rewatching his father kneeling on that oil-stained concrete.

"I don't know why I did it. Something about seeing him crying there . . . It was like my legs started moving automatically. I went over to him and bent down. I don't know if I was going to hug him or help him up or something like that, but . . ." He shook his head. "Then I felt the most pain I've ever experienced in my life.

"He still had the vise grips in his right hand. When I bent down, he reached up and grabbed my ear with the pliers. He clamped 'em on right here." Haggerty touched the spot as he walked. "He locked 'em in place. I tried to pull away—instinct, you know, but . . . that was worse."

Marianna covered her mouth with her fingers. She looked horrified.

"I dropped the bat when he first grabbed me. Surprised. But as soon as I realized what had happened, I balled up my fist and swung my arm back and got ready to punch. I was going to knock him into next week." Haggerty sighed. "He just sneered at me and twisted the clamp." Haggerty made a rotating motion with his wrist and hand.

Marianna was still covering her mouth, but he could hear her saying, "No, no, no," under her breath.

"The twisting took most of the fight out of me. I slid down, and then he stood up. So now I was on my knees and he was standing over me. He still had hold of the pliers. He bent his face down and he snarled at me like a dog and said, 'You think you're better than me, Johnny? I know it. You think you're better than Jesus, don't you? Say it!'

"I was looking right into his eyes, and I saw how crazy he was. I mean, I saw the absolute lunacy there. And I felt terrified. But I made up my mind I would *not* yell or cry out or ask for help or anything like that. I poured everything I had into not letting him win."

He looked over at Marianna. He could feel tears in his eyes. Wetness on his cheek.

She took hold of his arm for a moment, stopping him. Then she sat on a bench next to the road and motioned for him to join her. He did. Then he kept going.

"He kept talking the whole time. 'You think you're better than Jesus, don't you, Johnny? Tell me you think you're better than Jesus!' I wouldn't say it. I refused to say it. But then he started twisting again. Twisting and pulling." Haggerty leaned forward on the bench, his elbows on his knees. He watched the vapor of his breath rise in small, fleeting puffs.

"I said it. I yelled it out. 'I think I'm better than Jesus!' But he kept squeezing. So I yelled it again. And again. Then I started crying. And then I started begging him to stop. Begging him to let me go."

Marianna's eyes kept growing wider and wider. Her hand still covered her mouth.

"I don't know how long it lasted. Eventually he raised his foot and put the bottom of his boot against my chest." Haggerty raised his own boot as an example. "He grabbed the clamp with both hands, and then he kicked out with his leg and pulled with his arms. I think he meant to take the whole ear off, but . . ." Haggerty tapped the missing chunk. "He only got a piece. Then he left. I was too scared to go back in the house, so I stayed in the garage the whole night. And that's the story."

He lifted his arm to put it around Marianna's shoulders, trying to offer some kind of comfort. Some kind of connection.

"That's what happened. As far as why I don't talk about it—"

"No, John!" She sounded almost panicked. "You don't have to—"

"It's okay, Marianna." He relished the feeling of saying her name while she sat next to him and his arm was draped protectively over her shoulders. "It's okay."

He took another deep breath. "The reason I haven't been able to talk about it is because he won. He beat me. *Defeated* me—and not just that night. He broke something in me that I never got back.

Branded me. I kept growing, but I never tried to run him out again. Even when he was drunk and I outweighed him by fifty pounds, I never could get up the nerve to do anything. Because of the pain.

"Even when the police got involved. Even when he went to prison, he and I both knew it had nothing to do with me. I never tried to fight him again. I never tried to challenge him again." Haggerty was quiet for several seconds. "That's the part of myself I hate most."

Having finished the story, he felt spent. Physically and emotionally drained. Yet he also felt cleaner somehow. Stronger.

The two of them stayed on the bench a long time. Eventually Haggerty realized they were only a few feet away from Marianna's car. They'd made a circuit around town and come all the way back to the café.

"Why did he want you to say you're better than Jesus?" she asked. "What was that about?"

"Oh." Haggerty sighed. "I wasn't buying what he was selling, that's all. The faith stuff. I guess I was pretty vocal about my unbelief back then. Although, honestly . . ." His voice trailed off as he noticed somebody walking down the sidewalk toward them. Somebody short and stocky and strolling with a deep-seated confidence. Somebody wearing an Army service uniform?

Haggerty jolted upright on the bench. Marianna looked around to see what was the matter, then noticed the visitor. They both stood as the woman stopped in front of them.

"Hello, John," said General Burgess. "I haven't been able to reach you."

"General." Haggerty felt dumbfounded by the way she'd seemingly materialized out of the mist.

How in the world did she find me? Then he realized the answer was in his pocket. All task force phones were easily traceable for security and rescue purposes.

"General," Haggerty said again. He looked at Marianna. "This is my . . . I mean, this is . . ."

She stepped forward and said, "Marianna Rodriguez."

Comprehension dawned in Burgess's eyes. "Ah." She looked between the two of them. "I see."

"Is something wrong, General?" Haggerty asked. "Is there some kind of emergency?"

"No, nothing like that. Nothing new, anyway. But I don't like losing track of senior personnel. I view that as a major problem, so I decided to solve that problem as quickly as possible." Haggerty saw the disappointment in her face. He heard it in her tone. "Which begs the question: When can I expect you to report for duty back in Washington, Major General?"

Oh, man. The million-dollar question.

Marianna was looking up at him, and he realized with another jolt of surprise that she seemed afraid.

Is she more afraid of me going or me staying? Then a new thought struck him. *What am I afraid of losing?*

But he already knew the answer. Knew it down to the marrow of his bones. Knew it without doubt in the recently rediscovered chambers of his heart.

He put his arm around Marianna's waist and looked down at Burgess. "I won't be reporting back, General. I'm sorry for being tardy in my paperwork, and I apologize for wasting your time and expenses on this trip. But I won't be returning to Washington at all."

He felt the impact of his words through Marianna's body, but he didn't have the courage to look in her eyes and see how she felt about it. Not yet. Instead, he watched as Burgess processed the news.

The general frowned and narrowed her eyes. "I see," she said, voice clipped. "Then I look forward to seeing that paperwork on my desk as soon as possible." Without another word, she turned and walked away.

No turning back now, Haggerty thought. The door to the Seismic Anomalies Task Force had been slammed shut. The door to any kind of meaningful work in the Army had been slammed shut. Which, Haggerty realized, was okay.

Marianna slipped out from under his arm, then turned to face him. Her wide, serious eyes were filled with questions. He hoped very much they could find the answers together.

"Marianna, would you have dinner with me Friday night?"

She smiled. She nodded. "Yes, John. I would like that very much."

CHAPTER 19

Quit grumbling, Cay. Or do it quieter."

It was 3:37 in the morning. Friday morning. Haggerty and Caleb were carefully picking their way through the little woods to the side of Miller County Substation Number One. The sky was overcast, which meant there was very little ambient light from the moon or stars. The night was also deeply cold. Each time Caleb spoke, his breath poured out of his mouth and nostrils in long, silvery streams.

Caleb was speaking a lot.

"Don't tell me to quit grumbling," he grumbled. Although he did speak a little more softly. "Not even retired two weeks and I'm getting dragged out here at three in the morning in the freezing cold to look at some godforsaken chunk of concrete."

"Would you rather I asked Abigail to come with me?"

"I would rather you never dragged my baby girl into this whole bunch of nonsense in the first place. That's what I'd rather."

Haggerty smiled. They both knew Abigail had asked for *his* help, but it was fun to hear Caleb become so unintentionally entertaining.

They walked on. The ground was covered with a soft loam, so their steps were largely silent—broken only by the occasional crackle of a twig or a fallen branch. No bird chirps. No ominous hootings from owls or nocturnal critters. No traffic on the nearby road.

Haggerty thought of Marianna. He'd called her briefly the night before just to say hello. She told him she'd bought a new dress for their date this evening.

Don't get ahead of yourself, Haggs. She never called it a date.

Which was true, but it felt like a date. In fact, for Haggerty the whole thing felt like a strange combination of first date and long-awaited reunion. He tried to picture what kind of dress she'd bought.

I hope it's red. He liked it when she wore red.

"... probably a whole mess of raccoons out here, and some nasty little thing is about to drop out of a tree and bite my hand, and then I'll have rabies." Caleb was still muttering. "Or else pneumonia, 'cause it is freez—"

Haggerty stopped and held up his right hand. Instantly Caleb's grumbling ceased, which was one of the benefits of training.

They'd reached the edge of the woods, and Haggerty signaled for Caleb to lie down. He did the same. He could barely make out the dark shape of the mystery box just behind the chain-link fence. He knew there were surveillance cameras at the compound's gate, which was why they'd approached from the trees.

As quietly as possible, Haggerty belly-crawled out of the woods and up to the fence. He pulled a pair of reinforced cutters from his pocket and began snipping the metal in front of him. *Click. Click. Click. Click.* Creating just enough space to squeeze through without producing an actual hole visible from a distance.

He felt Caleb crawl up beside him. "What's the plan?"

"I go through the fence. I need a few minutes to breach the box.

Then you hand me the case through the fence." Haggerty looked back. "You still have the case?"

"Yes." Caleb pulled it up to his chest—a dull yellow case about the size of a laptop but much thicker.

"Okay. Hang tight." Still on his stomach, Haggerty pushed both of his arms through the cut in the fence, then wriggled forward. He felt the metal edges snag and pull on the thick material of his coat. Not a big deal. There was one moment when he thought he might be stuck, but Caleb tugged the fence back a little farther and Haggerty was able to work his way through.

He kept crawling until he was directly behind the box. Caleb was about six feet behind him, still on the other side of the fence.

Working calmly, Haggerty pulled the cutters from his pocket again and snipped through the metal conduit that ran from the bottom of the pole and into the box. He cut a V, then used his gloved thumb to peel back the exposed triangle. With any luck, he should be able to push the metal back in place and crimp it so nobody would see the cut unless they got down on their hands and knees to search for it.

Haggerty assumed the conduit carried electrical wires from the solar panel into the cube, which meant it would be hollow and it would have some extra space around the wires. He set the cutters on the gravel, then pulled out a roll of metal wire and unspooled about fifteen feet. The end of the spool had already been wrapped with electrical tape to limit chafing.

Haggerty looked back and saw Caleb on his knees, scanning the surroundings from left to right. Keeping watch.

He nodded. Then he slipped the taped end of the metal wire through the slice in the conduit. There was room. Slowly, carefully, he fed the wire farther in. Whenever he hit a snag, he stopped immediately—it would be a bad idea to jostle or damage anything in there—then repositioned the wire before moving it forward again. Still slowly. Still carefully.

Eventually he could not push the wire forward any farther. End of the road.

I sure hope this isn't stupid. Then he checked himself. *Actually, it would be great if this whole thing is stupid. Stupid would be wonderful.*

The gravel crunched as Haggerty rolled to his side, then inchwormed back to the fence.

"You ready to tell me what this is all about?" Caleb's teeth were chattering.

"I guess so." Haggerty leaned up on one elbow. "I think there's a bomb in that box."

"What?" Caleb leaned forward until his forehead was pressed against the fence. "Why in the world would you think that?"

"Because RediCert—the company Abigail was telling us about— had a crew here for a week installing something they weren't authorized to install. They tried to hide it by not charging for their hours. When the MCECO techs asked about it, RediCert said it was monitoring equipment. But why would anyone build a concrete cube around monitoring equipment?"

Caleb shrugged. "To protect it?"

Haggerty shook his head. "To me, the concrete only makes sense if they're trying to hide what's in the box. To make it harder to identify—harder to find."

"Explosives, you mean? Or chemicals?"

Haggerty nodded. "I guess the cement could also protect the explosives from triggering accidentally. The way they have it set up now, the solar panels provide power for the trigger mechanism. There's probably some kind of cell signal wired in as well."

Caleb thought for a moment. "What's with the wire?"

"Well . . ." Haggerty hesitated to say it out loud. He felt a little silly, to be honest. "It's my attempt to eliminate a worst-case scenario."

"Worst case? What could be worse than a bomb in the middle of an electrical substation?"

"Depends on the bomb."

"Depends on the . . ." Caleb was starting to sound frustrated again. "C'mon, Haggs. You already know what kind of bomb could fit in that box just based on the size. The only thing that could make any real difference is if it . . . were . . ."

There it is. Haggerty wished he could see the look on his friend's face.

"What's in the case?" Caleb sounded on edge. "What's in the case, Haggs?"

"A Geiger counter."

"A Geiger counter!" Caleb shouted.

"Shhhhhhhh," Haggerty hissed. "Keep it quiet, Sergeant."

"Oh, heck no, Haggs. Heck no!" He was equal parts angry and terrified. "You think there's a nuclear bomb in that box—*and you were poking it*?"

Haggerty made a "calm down" motion with both of his hands, although he doubted Caleb could see it. "Take it easy, Cay. First of all, you know how tough they make the casing around pocket nukes. They're designed to be carried around a battlefield. I could hit it with a baseball bat and nothing would happen."

"Not helping me take it easy, Haggs."

"Second, I *don't* think there's a nuclear bomb in that box. Like I said, I just want to eliminate the worst-case scenario."

Caleb was shaking his head. Haggerty could see a patch of moonlight glinting off the top as it swung back and forth. "And how are we doing that?"

"Okay, the electrical conduit has to go through the concrete and all the way to the device. Actually, if there *were* a pocket nuke in the concrete, there would probably be an additional layer of lead. But . . . anyway. I pushed the metal wire through the concrete, so now it's in close contact with the bomb. Or whatever's in there. If there *is* anything nuclear in that cube, the wire will soak up some of the radioactive particles and then trigger the Geiger counter when I pull it back out."

"But you don't think that will happen." Not a question.

"Nope. Most likely scenario is I scan the wire and nothing happens. Then we pack everything up and go home. I use my military credentials to throw my weight around and get a meeting with whoever is in charge of this place. We bring Abigail to the meeting. She explains about the cover-up. We have the bomb squad come out here and defuse the bomb. And—*bang*—Abigail is a national hero."

"Well, I do like the sound of that." Caleb's voice was calmer. "Why a national hero?"

"Because RediCert goes way beyond Miller County, remember? They've done work all over the country. All fifty states."

"You think there's more bombs?"

Haggerty nodded. "If there's one here, there will be others."

The quiet stretched between them for several seconds. There was still no sound from birds or animals or cars in the early morning. Just the muffled crunch of gravel as Haggerty shifted his position.

"What if the bomb squad comes out and finds nothing but monitoring equipment, just like that company said?"

Haggerty thought for a moment. "Then I guess Major General John Haggerty will apologize profusely, make sure everyone knows the whole debacle was his idea, and then announce his retirement due to diminished cognitive function."

Caleb grunted. "But again—you don't think that will happen."

"Let's find out."

Caleb pushed the yellow case through the fence, then Haggerty rolled over and crawled back to the box. He opened the case and pulled out a black rectangular device, which he held in his left hand. He'd spent most of the day yesterday tracking it down from an old contact at a local university. The professor had shown him how to use the device, but it was relatively simple. There were four buttons below a small LED screen. Between the buttons and the screen was the symbol for radiation—a circle divided into six wedges of alternating color. The middle of that circle was an LED light.

Haggerty turned on the Geiger counter and waited until it emitted a soft beep. The LED window glowed a dull, ominous green. As a control, he leaned back and held the device in the air for a few seconds. Nothing happened.

Satisfied, Haggerty placed it gingerly on top of the box, then waited. Nothing happened.

He moved it down to the base of the metal conduit near the pole with the solar panels, then waited. Nothing happened.

He shifted the Geiger counter over to the base of the cube where the metal conduit passed through the concrete. Nothing happened.

Once again satisfied, Haggerty placed the device on the gravel, then carefully withdrew the metal wire from the conduit, pulling softly with two fingers to prevent any snags. When the wire was all the way out, he took the end wrapped with electrical tape and set it on the gravel. Then he set the Geiger counter directly on top of the wire.

Something happened.

The device emitted a rapid series of beeps and clicks, as if it had suddenly come alive. The LED eye in the middle of the radiation symbol glowed a vivid, dangerous red.

Oh no. Oh, please no. Please no.

He pulled the Geiger counter up and away from the ground, and it died. He placed it back on the wire, and it came alive again with the same eruption of beeps and clicks. Numbers appeared on the green LED window, but Haggerty had no idea what they meant. Only that this whole situation had transformed into a horrible mess.

"It's radioactive." Caleb spoke calmly. Somehow.

Haggerty just stared at him. His mouth open wide. His eyes wider. He pulled the device away from the wire again, and the ensuing silence was deafening. Suffocating.

This can't be happening. This can't be real. This is . . . This is . . .

Caleb finished the thought out loud: "This is bad, Haggs."

"Yeah." His own voice was shaky. "It's real bad, Cay. Let me think a minute."

But thinking was hard. He tried to grind his brain into gear, but everything was sluggish and slow, as if his synapses were jammed by worry. And fear. And memories.

It was Caleb who made the next connection. "Remember what Abby told us about hardening? She said one of the things they're trying to protect the power grid *against* is EMPs. Electromagnetic pulses."

"And?"

"Don't nukes create an EMP when they detonate?"

Haggerty nodded to himself. A picture was starting to form in his mind. A shadow of the threat now looming up around him— threatening to envelop him, but not just him. Marianna. Sonya. Caleb and Abigail. Burgess and Li Fan and Hardeep Singh. Millersville and Washington and California. All of America.

RediCert's been in business more than ten years. They have trust in the industry. They come as consultants to show counties and cities how to protect the power grid, but they leave behind a nuke. Ten years. All fifty states. What are they planning?

"If this nuke goes off, Cay . . ." Haggerty paused. "*When* this nuke goes off, it will completely destroy the power grid for all of Miller County. Maybe for most of Ohio. Beyond whatever gets vaporized in the blast, the EMP will fry every electrical system on the grid. The whole thing."

"And people will die."

"Yeah. Lots of people. But, Cay . . ." He paused again to gather his thoughts. "If there are nukes planted like this throughout the country, then all of *those* grids would be fried as well. Which means someone—RediCert or whoever's behind that shell company—can take out the entire US power supply with the push of a button."

"We don't know if there are other nukes, Haggs."

"We don't. But we do know RediCert has contracts in every state, and they've been doing this for ten years. Which means they *could* have planted more nukes. Lots of nukes. Even if they only had a handful in each state—even just *one* in each state at strategic positions—they could take us out. Completely."

"Us?"

"The United States. There would be no power for houses. No power for businesses or hospitals. No cellular network. No computers. No credit card transactions. No bank records—survivors would have to rely completely on cash. We'd have to tear out the entire electrical grid and rebuild it from the ground up. We'd be helpless for years."

Caleb's eyes glowed white in the scant light of the moon.

"This is the endgame, Cay. This is the destruction of the United States of America as we know it."

"Please answer. Please answer . . . come on."

It was 6:47 a.m. Still Friday morning. Haggerty was standing next to Caleb's breakfast table. A mug of coffee sat untouched on the table. Next to it was a large backpack stuffed with clothing and supplies.

"Come *on*," Haggerty repeated. He was staring at the phone and tapping his foot, the picture of impatient frustration.

"Dad?" An answer! "Kind of early, don't you think?"

"Sonya! Yeah, I'm sorry it's early, but is your mom still at home? She's not answering her phone."

"She turns it off at night." Haggerty heard what sounded like a huge yawn from the other end of the line.

"Can you get her for me? It's . . . it's important."

"Okay, okay. Keep your pants on." Haggerty heard a rustling sound—probably his daughter getting out of bed. "Incidentally, Mom tried on her new dress last night. I know it's weird for me to say this, but"—another yawn—"I think you're going to be one happy puppy when you see it."

Oh, Marianna. Please understand. I know you can understand. Please . . .

"Morning, Mom . . ." Sonya's voice sounded far away. "It's Dad."

Then Marianna was on the line. "Good morning, John. This is a fun surprise." She sounded happy. Lively and carefree.

Please forgive me.

"Hey, Marianna. Good morning. I . . ." Despite his impatience, something inside wanted to stretch out this moment of normalcy for just another few seconds. "How are . . . ? I mean, how'd you sleep?"

"Fine. Normal." He could hear the hesitation in her voice. "You sound like something's wrong, John. What's up?"

Haggerty shook his head. She could always tell.

"Yeah, well . . . something's happened. An emergency. It's . . . honestly, Marianna, it's really hard to explain, but millions of lives are at stake."

He paused for a moment to allow her to react—to say, "Oh my goodness," or "That's terrible," or something. Anything.

She said nothing.

"I've booked a flight to D.C., and it leaves in about ninety minutes. I just wanted to tell you that I will get this figured out, and then I will be back as quickly as I can. I promise."

"You told me you were out, John." The pain in her voice was devastating. "You told *her*—that general. You said you were finished."

"I know, and I am." He tried to keep the desperation out of his voice. "This doesn't have anything to do with the Army or the task forces or any of that. Caleb and I just . . . we kind of stumbled on this emergency. But, Marianna, here's the important thing, and this is going to be really hard, okay?"

"Yes, please tell me the important thing, John." So much bitterness. "I'd really love to hear what you consider important."

"Marianna, there's a bomb about half an hour outside the city. It's a nuclear bomb. So I need you to go someplace else. Take Sonya. Tell everyone you can, but . . . but go somewhere else. Except don't go near any big cities. Find somewhere in the country."

He was rambling. He forced himself to stop and listen.

"Why are you doing this, John?"

"I'm not doing this, Marianna. It's not what you . . ." He tried to regroup. "Please hear me. If you ever loved me, please take Sonya and find someplace safe. I will—"

"*If I ever loved you?*" There was rage now, seething. "How dare you say that to me, John Haggerty? How do you question *me* after everything you put our family through?"

"Okay, you're right, that was the wrong thing to say." He felt panic burning in his chest. "Please just get Sonya and find someplace safe. I will figure this out in D.C., and I will come join you. I promise."

"No, John. I don't know what's really going on, but I told you I was too old to play games. So don't come back." He could hear in her voice that she was crying.

"Marianna—"

"Just shut up! Just leave me alone!" She spat the words between sobs. "Don't send any more money, John. We don't need it. We don't need you! So don't come back and don't call me. I never want to hear from you again!"

The line went dead. Haggerty stared at the phone for a long time. *This can't be happening.*

He felt Caleb's hand on his shoulder. "Take the truck." He held out a key card. "I'll have Abby come get me, and we'll pick it up later."

Haggerty nodded. "Talk to Marianna for me, okay? Make sure she and Sonya get out. See if you can help her understand"—he made a circle with his hand—"this whole mess."

"I will." The two men embraced, and then Caleb added, "Go get 'em, Haggs. Go save the world."

Haggerty grabbed his backpack and hustled outside to Caleb's truck. His mind kept replaying Marianna's words as he backed out of the driveway and started down the road. *"We don't need you. Leave me alone. Don't come back."*

Two minutes later, he saw Marianna's house in front of him on the right side of the road. It was on the way out of town—on the way to the airport. *Please be outside,* he thought, slowing down to look more closely. But she wasn't outside. She wasn't in the driveway or in her garden, which still looked lovely. "Mary, Mary, quite contrary," he whispered, "how does your garden—?"

He was staring so intently at the garden as the truck rolled along that he almost didn't see the little white SUV back out of the driveway and jerk to a stop in the middle of the road—directly in front of him.

He slammed on the brakes, and the electric pickup skidded to a stop not even two feet away from the white car. Sonya's car.

She was already in the street. Already running around the front of the SUV toward him, wearing gray sweatpants and a baggy gray sweatshirt. Haggerty hopped down and held out his arms, ready to catch her in an embrace. But she slammed into his chest with both arms raised.

He staggered back a step, startled. Sonya continued forward. She struck him with her fists on his chest. His arms. His shoulders.

"How could you do this?" she cried. "How could you do this to Mom? How could you do this to me?" Each question was delivered with another blow.

Haggerty didn't feel her fists, but the words struck home. Each one hit hard and sank deep. Little thorns stuck in and ripped out.

She was still crying, "How could you? How could you?" when he finally corralled her in his arms.

"Sonya, it's not what you think." He tried to hold her. Calm her. "Shhhhhh. Stop, please! I'm coming back!"

"Don't say that!" She forced her way out of his arms and stepped back. She looked up at him, her face a grimace of pain smeared with tears. "Don't make any more promises!"

"Hey, Sonya. Hey . . ." He put his hands on both of her arms. She didn't shake him off. "I need you to hear me, Sonya Pie. Will you hear me?"

She didn't answer, but she was staring at him, her eyes wide and searching.

"Something terrible is about to happen. I know that sounds crazy, but it's true. You can talk to Caleb when . . ." He almost said *when I go* but stopped himself. "You can talk to Caleb. I don't know if I can stop what's happening, but I have to try. Okay? Millions of people will die if I don't stop it. They'll *die*, Sonya!"

"Then make some phone calls, Dad. I'll help you. We'll spend the whole day calling everyone who needs to hear."

He shook his head.

"Why not? Why can't you stay here and send out the alert or whatever? Why do you have to go?"

"For one thing, I'm not sure the people I need to talk to would even take my calls right now. I'm . . . It's a long story. More importantly, Sonya, I don't know who I can trust. Somebody's been plotting an attack for a long time, and they've got their finger on the button. If they find out I know about their plans, they'll strike. That's why I have to go. I have to talk with the right people and make them understand."

"No!" She pulled away from his touch. "*You* don't understand, Dad! Things were just starting to get better after years and years and years." She gestured to Marianna's house. "We were just starting to heal. To be a family again. And now you're going to rip everything open just to go be some hero?"

Haggerty had no idea what to say. He thought furiously for something—some way to make her understand.

"You've spent your whole life out there saving the world, Dad. But we needed you. *I needed you!*"

"Sonya—"

"No, listen!" She stepped a little closer. Her voice was choked with emotion. "When I was a little girl, if I had understood what was happening the day Mom took me away, I would have run back to the house and grabbed your leg and begged you to come with us. I would have begged you, Dad. And I would have been right, wouldn't I? Wouldn't I?"

He nodded. "You would have been right. I never should have left you, Sonya."

She slid to her knees. She grabbed hold of his leg.

"Sonya! Don't—"

"Listen to me now, Dad. Please!" She was looking up at him from the ground. "I'm begging you right now. Don't go. Don't go! I feel something in here"—she beat a hand against her chest—"telling me you shouldn't go. I feel it, Dad!"

He felt the manic strength of her arms as she squeezed him. The desperation. "Sonya, I will make things right with your mom. There will be time once I get back. Lots of time for—"

"No." She was shaking her head, still crying. "There won't be time, Dad. Not if you go. I don't know how I know that, but . . . but I feel it."

Haggerty felt the tremendous pull of time ticking away—the wrenching finality of his duty and his family tugging from either side. Something broke loose inside him. A deep well of sadness filled him. It was drowning him. He couldn't make her understand.

"I'll come back." He pulled his leg free and stepped back. Stepped away from his daughter. "I'll come back, and I'll explain everything. You'll understand then. Your mom will understand. We *will* be a family, Sonya, but I have to go."

He opened the door of the truck.

"Fine!" she yelled, still on her knees. "That's fine, Dad! Me and Mom will try not to watch too much TV while you're gone, okay? We'll do something productive!"

"Hey!" Haggerty whirled around. "That's not fair!"

"Tell me why, Dad. Let's hear some of your fatherly wisdom before you leave again for the next decade or so." She put a hand to her ear. "Whaddya got, Pop?"

In his anger Haggerty discovered there were many things he wanted to say—verbal ammunition that snapped up behind his teeth like bullets in a magazine. He wanted to tell her to grow up. That being an adult meant making hard choices. That he was tired of hearing about all the ways he'd failed to meet her needs and her expectations. The resentment had been building inside him for so long. The frustration and bitterness and humiliation and shame.

He opened his mouth to speak—to fire.

Then a picture blossomed in his mind's eye. A memory. He'd been the one to put Sonya in the car the day Marianna left—the day her little world had been ripped in two. He'd opened the door, and she'd hopped in the back seat. Unknowing. Unafraid. He'd buckled her seat belt and handed over her favorite teddy bear. He smiled at her and winked. She smiled back. And then he told her the lie that he knew had tormented her for the rest of her life: "I'll see you soon, Sonya Pie."

Haggerty looked down at his daughter. His little girl on her knees in the middle of the street. He went to her. He knelt and held her face in both his hands. He kissed her forehead.

"I love you, Sonya."

Then he climbed in the truck and closed the door. He drove around the SUV and continued down the road. When he checked the rearview mirror for the last time, he saw Marianna and Sonya standing together in the middle of the street. Hugging. Comforting. Still giving each other what they should have received from him.

He drove on.

CHAPTER 20

THE DAY: UNKNOWN
THE HOUR: UNKNOWN
THE PENTAGON

J ohn Haggerty. How are you still here?"

He was sitting on a wooden bench in the middle of a dark hallway deep in the bowels of the Pentagon. He'd been staring at the patterns in the reflective tile on the floor when he heard footsteps coming down the hall. General Burgess stood about fifteen feet away, glaring down at him with cold exasperation.

"Because it's urgent, General. I've been trying to tell you—"

"No," she said, cutting him off. "I mean *how* are you still here? I had your key card revoked. Security clearances too."

Haggerty shrugged. "Something this important, I find a way. I'll keep finding a way."

It had been several days since he'd left Ohio. He wasn't sure how many. He didn't even know the day of the week. From the moment he landed at Dulles, he'd been singularly focused on raising the alarm about RediCert and the nuclear threat against America. He'd sent hundreds of emails. He'd made dozens of calls each day. The first two days—back when his key card still worked—he'd haunted the halls of the Pentagon and other government buildings in an effort to set up meetings or pounce on spontaneous conversations.

It all amounted to nothing. He'd achieved nothing.

It was obvious from the start that Burgess had blackballed him in some way. She didn't answer his calls or his emails, and neither did any senior staff member from any of the task forces. Not Li Fan. Not Ivo Marcello. Not Hardeep Singh. Haggerty had pivoted to lower-ranking officers both in the task forces and in different divisions of the Army. He'd been able to force a few conversations, but the result was always some variation of "I'll have one of my people look into it."

Haggerty had been ignored, humored, and hung out to dry.

Now he watched as General Burgess—one of the few people in the world who possessed the authority to act swiftly on this crisis—shifted her pile of paperwork to one arm and pulled out her phone to check the time.

"I've got five minutes, John." She walked past him and down the hall to her office.

Haggerty followed. He'd been wearing the same clothes since the day he arrived, and he knew he looked terrible. Probably didn't smell too great, either. He was exhausted and weighed down by frustration and disappointment. And he knew this was almost certainly his last chance to get someone to hear him and take him seriously.

Gotta win this one, John. He willed himself toward alertness and clarity. *You must win this fight!*

Burgess set her paperwork on the desk and motioned for Haggerty to sit. She kept standing, as always. "Five minutes," she repeated. "Tell me what's so urgent that you've been making a fool of yourself all over D.C."

"There's a credible nuclear threat against the United States."

She sighed. "I read your emails, John. I've got the basics." When he started to protest, she held up a finger. "I *skimmed* your emails. Tell me why you think this threat is credible." There was a strong hint of scare quotes around the word *threat*.

Willing himself to be calm and clear, he told her everything. He started with Abigail and the accounting red flags that had brought RediCert to their attention. He walked her through his own research and the breadth of RediCert's contracts throughout the country. He described the "install crew" and the box and the concrete and the solar panels. He ended with the metal wire and the Geiger counter and the reality that, if RediCert had planted one pocket nuke in Miller County, chances were good they had planted similar bombs all over the nation's power grid.

"General . . ." He was losing his voice, but he cleared his throat and kept going. Kept pushing. "Unless we do something quickly, this is an extinction-level event for the United States of America."

He leaned back in his chair and waited. *I really should have taken video of that Geiger counter*, he thought, berating himself for the thousandth time.

Burgess picked up her phone and tapped it a few times. "I made some inquiries after I read your first email. I talked with top-level people from the Army and from every three-letter intelligence agency. They all told me there is no possible way any nation or organization could smuggle fissionable material into this country at the level you're describing. None."

Haggerty shook his head. "They're wrong, General. It's there. You can come see it for yourself if you just—"

She cut him off with the wave of a hand. "I've already made one wasted trip to Ohio on your behalf, John. No thanks." She glanced at her phone again. "Five minutes are up. I have actual issues to deal with, so I won't walk you to the exit. Goodbye."

"Actual issues!" He fought against exasperation and disbelief.

"What could possibly be more important than a nuclear attack against this nation?"

Burgess's expression shifted for a moment as she looked at the papers and folders on her desk. Her mask of calm disregard slipped for a second, then returned.

"What?" asked Haggerty. "What's happening?"

She sighed. "China is happening, John. They've got an unprecedented naval presence heading toward Taiwan, including aircraft carriers. They're calling it an exercise, but we don't think so. We think it's finally the real thing." She pointed a finger at him. "That's classified."

That *did* cause Haggerty to hesitate. *If China attacks, we'd have to declare war. We've already drawn that line in the sand a dozen times.*

He shook his head. *Not relevant right now, John!*

"Okay, you're staring down a war. I get that. But I'm talking *hundreds of millions* of American citizens under threat *right now*. Millions of lives are at stake!"

"No, John." There was anger in her voice now. Anger and . . . something else. "Millions of lives have already been lost—or will be lost in the coming months. That's what this is about." She was speaking with an exaggerated patience—as if she were talking to a child. "I understand what you must be feeling, but I don't have the time to massage your failures right now. It's over."

My failures . . . With a start Haggerty realized she was trying to generate compassion for him. Pity.

"My failures? You think this is about Italy? You think this is about the Dirty Dozen?"

"I do." She was still speaking with that same tone of exasperated benevolence, and Haggerty's blood began to boil. "I think you're having a hard time handling the loss of so many people on your watch. Millions will die, but now you've invented a situation where you get to *save* millions of lives."

Invented. The word bounced around Haggerty's brain like a crazed hornet.

"It's pathetic, John, and you need to snap out of it before— Oh!"

With a huge *boom!* Haggerty had slammed his fist onto the metal top of Burgess's desk. The rage had been building and building until he couldn't contain it anymore.

"You have to listen to me!" he roared. He slammed his fist again, making a dent in the metal. "Stop with this nonsense and listen to me!"

Burgess had actually jumped back the first time his fist hit the desk, but now she stepped quickly forward and picked up the receiver on her desk phone. She dialed a number. "Security. My office. Now."

Haggerty was on his feet. He loomed over his former boss, but she did not shrink back. "Go home!" She was yelling. "Go back to Ohio!"

"You're making a mistake, General. You're putting this country at risk—"

"*You* made the mistake, John. When you quit."

"Is that what this is about?" Haggerty tried to lower his voice in spite of his rage. "You're mad because I walked away from the task force?"

"No, John. I'm mad because I vouched for you. I *fought* for you! Just six months ago the president pegged me for deputy secretary of defense, and she wanted me to pick my replacement. Now we've got a million people dead and we're in the middle of World War III, but all you care about is your girlfriend or your wife or whatever you call her. Well, that's fine. You made your choice, so go back to Ohio. I'm done with you."

Well, that at least solved one mystery. His team's failure to contain the virus had cost Burgess a promotion. Evidently it had cost Haggerty one, too, although he hadn't been aware of it.

"General, I know you—"

Two security officers hustled into the room. Without any instruction from Burgess, they each grabbed one of Haggerty's arms. He pulled against them for a moment, then relaxed. They had Tasers, and they wouldn't hesitate to put him on the ground and drag him down the hall.

"Take him to the exit." Burgess spoke to one of the guards. "Make sure he goes out and stays out."

"Don't do this!" The two men had already dragged Haggerty halfway into the hall. "General!"

"Goodbye, John. Good riddance." She was standing at the office door. "If you come near me again, I will have you arrested on sight."

She turned around and slammed the door on Haggerty's last, best, and only hope.

———————

A little while later, Haggerty stepped off a concrete path and set his foot on loosely packed gravel. He stumbled for a second— surprised. He hadn't been watching where he was going. Just wandering around the grounds outside the Pentagon, trying to wrap his mind around everything that had happened. Trying to come up with some way to make everything all right.

He stopped walking and looked around. It only took him a moment to realize where he was: the Pentagon Memorial. A park designed to commemorate the 184 people who'd been killed when American Airlines Flight 77 was hijacked on September 11, 2001. Haggerty had been here a few times before. It was a peaceful oasis in the middle of Arlington's congestion and clamor.

Funny that I came here without thinking about it.

He walked farther along the gravel path. The memorial contained 184 benches—one for each person who died during the attack. The benches were constructed in an interesting way. One side rose out of the ground at a graceful angle, then straightened for about four feet. Then each seat cut off abruptly, with no second side returning to the ground. The shape and the angles always reminded Haggerty of wings. Each bench also had a small trough of water flowing underneath the seating area.

Wasn't it somewhere along this row? Each bench had a name engraved on its edge. Haggerty was searching for a particular name—one he'd found a few times before.

There it is. He stopped in front of the name Todd M. Beamer.

That's a hero. Someone who actually accomplished something.

Moving slowly and painfully, he turned and lowered himself to sit on the bench, exhaling softly. He was so, so tired.

The park was next to Washington Boulevard, but the sounds of traffic were muffled by a concrete wall at the park's perimeter. Instead of the rumble of tires, Haggerty heard birds chirping in the trees above him and water gurgling in the trough below him. It was nice. A respite.

He reached to pull his phone out, then winced and flexed his fingers. Apparently he'd damaged something other than Burgess's desk when he pounded on it. He tried again more gingerly and brought out the phone. He dialed Marianna's number . . . one ring, then straight to voicemail.

Still blocked.

He dialed Sonya's number. Same result.

The shame washed over him once more. The guilt. He'd caused tremendous damage to the two people he cared about most in the world because he thought it was up to him to save the world. Because he thought he was *able* to save it—or that he was obligated to try.

What had come of those obligations? Nothing. Just more pain.

He'd spoken to Caleb a few times since he arrived in D.C. His friend had tried to connect with both women—had offered to corroborate Haggerty's story. But they didn't want to hear from him, either. Haggerty assumed they were shutting out everything to do with him, including his best friend.

There's time. Now that I'm really and truly out of the game, there's time to rebuild. Time to reconnect.

He hoped that was true. Hoped it was possible.

"Excuse me. Sir?"

Haggerty looked around, startled out of his thoughts. A woman was standing on the concrete path a few feet away. She was older, and her eyes seemed magnified behind big, black-framed glasses with pointed corners at each side. She was bundled in a huge sheepskin coat. The material was tan, and there were white, curly patches at the cuffs and across the shoulders. There was also an alarmingly fluffy hood.

Is that actually wool? he thought. Then he remembered she was talking to him. "Yes?"

"This is a stupid question because you're already doing it, but . . . is it okay to sit on the benches?" She had a strong New York accent.

"Yeah, it's okay." Haggerty looked around for other corroborating examples, but they were the only two people in the park. "They want you to sit."

"Thank you." She gave him a little wave. "Didn't want to offend. God bless."

He watched her walk down the next row, maybe searching for a specific bench.

God bless, Haggerty thought. *Not today, lady.*

A sound caught Haggerty's attention. A far-off, droning buzz that stood out from the regular background noise of city life. It was an airplane. Private. Probably a turboprop. Probably a good size if he could hear it from this distance. He searched the sky and spotted it out to the west. It seemed like it was heading his way.

Maybe gonna land at Reagan.

He kept his eyes on the plane as his thoughts wandered back to Millersville. Back to Marianna and Sonya. He'd done everything he could do here, which meant it was time for him to return. He would need to make sure they were safe, first and foremost. Make sure they relocated somewhere far from the bomb once he could properly explain the situation.

Assuming they believe me.

Once the women were safe, Haggerty and Caleb could return to the box and gather solid proof there was something radioactive inside. If he went to the local authorities, they'd have to investigate the specific threat to Miller County. Once that was exposed, he could try again to do something at the national level.

But how do I keep it quiet? If the locals find a nuke in the middle of Ohio, the news will get out. Whoever's been planning all this will just press the button for the rest of the bombs, and then all hell will break loose. So how can I—

Haggerty's concentration returned to the present situation with a jolt. He focused on the incoming airplane once again. It sounded noticeably louder and looked much closer. It was still heading in his direction—looked like it was coming right at him, actually.

"What in the world?"

This was wrong. The Pentagon sat in the middle of a wide circle of restricted airspace. Nothing should be flying toward it like this. The plane should have turned south minutes ago and approached the Reagan airfields from that direction. Even if the pilot wasn't bound for Reagan, he had to be receiving warnings right now over the radio that he was violating airspace restrictions.

But no. The plane kept coming.

Turn around, buddy. Turn around or they'll—

Sure enough, the unmistakable growl of pursuit aircraft quickly overwhelmed all other sounds. Fighter jets. Probably F-16s from

Andrews Air Force Base. NORAD wouldn't let any unauthorized aircraft get close to the Pentagon, especially given the level of tension General Burgess had described with China.

Still watching the turboprop, Haggerty physically jumped back when one of the F-16s streaked directly across its flight path. Haggerty tried to follow the jet with his eyes, but it was too fast.

Turn around! He willed the pilot of the turboprop to understand what was happening. *That's the only warning you'll get!*

The back of Haggerty's mind registered the sound of honking behind him. Honking and . . . alarms? Yells? But his ears and his attention were quickly overwhelmed by the whooshing scream of a second F-16 tearing into the area. There was a mechanical coughing sound, then a series of bright flashes.

The turboprop exploded into a ball of flames.

"No!" Haggerty stepped forward, his arm raised to shield his eyes against the explosion. But the fireball was already collapsing into a column of black smoke. He could see one large piece of what had been the turboprop spiraling down, down, and then disappearing behind the silhouette of buildings beyond the freeway.

What just happened? Haggerty's mind was racing through possible scenarios. *An attack? A mistake? Something medical?*

The F-16s must have continued to circle the area, because the roar of their engines was deafening. Haggerty put his hands over his ears and searched the sky, but he was unable to locate either jet against the clouds. He looked for any other rogue airplanes that could potentially be new targets—new threats. He looked for any other signs of danger.

Nothing. The roar continued for another minute, and then with surprising speed it dissipated and was gone.

Instead of an eerie silence, however, Haggerty was assaulted by another wall of sound—except this one was even more chaotic. He heard the relentless whoop and bray of car alarms. The staccato honk of horns. The less loud but somehow more urgent pitch of human voices yelling and crying out in unpredictable patterns. Screaming voices and screeching tires.

It sounded like a hundred cars had crashed at the same time.

Maybe the jets caused a sonic boom? Broke some windows? Haggerty started jogging toward the road to investigate—then stopped in his tracks.

A coat lay on the gravel next to one of the memorial benches—the sheepskin coat with the patches of white wool. The old woman's coat. Haggerty looked around, but he didn't see her anywhere. He was alone in the park. He reached down to pick up the coat and set it on the bench—then froze again.

The woman's glasses were lying next to the coat. Large black frames with pointed corners. Unmistakable.

"What the . . . ?" Haggerty picked up the glasses. He picked up the coat—then he felt another wave of shock roll through him as he uncovered a complete set of clothing underneath.

He set the coat aside and lifted an expensive-looking blouse. Then a pair of slacks with ladies' underwear still tucked inside. Tennis shoes were on the ground as well. Skechers. A complete outfit lying right in the middle of the park.

Did she change her clothes? Is she naked? Haggerty was dumbfounded.

He started walking deeper into the park to search for the woman when a huge crash erupted behind him, sending him stumbling forward in surprise. He whirled around, the old woman and her coat quickly forgotten.

A city bus had crashed through the concrete barrier between the memorial park and Washington Boulevard. The front corner of the bus poked through the wall. Several chunks of concrete had spilled onto the ground, and one was still rolling down the dividing berm in short, spasmodic hops.

Haggerty gaped at the bus. It was huge and silver with an orange stripe under the windshield. The scrolling banner at the top read, "4B . . . PERSHING AVE."

Shaking off his paralysis, Haggerty ran forward, hopped a low fence, then scrambled up the berm toward Washington Boulevard. He used the broken sections of concrete to lever himself over the wall, edging past the corner of the bus as he did so. The engine was still running.

Now standing on street level, Haggerty was once again over-whelmed by chaos and cacophony. The highway was a war zone. Several cars sat crunched and smoking in the middle of the street. Others were crushed against concrete barriers on the shoulders. Alarms blared. He could still hear the honking of horns, although that had mainly died down. Several people were milling around in dazed groups, talking together or just staring blankly at one or more crash scenes. Most appeared as confused as Haggerty felt.

"Aayanah!" A short woman on Haggerty's left cried out at the top of her lungs. "Aayanah! Where are you, sweetie?" She was standing next to the open rear door of a cream-colored SUV. She kept ducking her head into the car and then pulling it back out again to yell down the street once more. "Aayanah! Aayanah!"

She was holding a winter coat in one hand. Bubble-gum pink. A little girl's coat. She had a sparkly pink boot in the other hand.

Haggerty scanned the street from left to right. He didn't see any little girls wandering alone—didn't see any children at all.

Motion flashed in Haggerty's peripheral vision. He turned to see a black Toyota Camry rolling slowly down the street. A large dent creased the driver's side of the hood and front bumper, as if the car had struck something and then kept going. The Camry glided past the short woman holding the pink coat, who didn't no-tice at all; she was still calling out for Aayanah. Without pausing, the car bumped softly against the rear tires of the bus and came to rest.

Haggerty stepped forward to check on the driver, but there was no driver. When he bent down to peer through the passenger window, he saw an empty car. He tried the handle but the door was locked. Looking through the window again, he noticed a pair of deflated jeans lying across the driver's seat. The legs of the jeans trailed down toward the pedals. A crumpled sweatshirt lay on the seat as well.

Probably a pair of shoes on the floorboard, he thought. He had no idea what was going on, but he was starting to recognize several patterns.

Haggerty stepped back and looked down at the car. He put a hand on the roof and felt the vibration. The car was still running.

This thing didn't start itself. It didn't drive here itself. It's empty save for a bundle of clothes, but it's locked from the inside.

Impossible. The whole situation was impossible. Everything about the past five minutes was impossible. Haggerty felt something in his mind begin to uncouple—to try to disconnect from reality. Or what seemed like reality. He felt an internal urge to walk away from this entire scene and to keep walking until he ended up in a place where things made sense again.

"Take a breath, Haggs." Talking seemed to help. Seemed to ground him somehow. "You don't know what's happening, but you can figure it out. You can do something."

He heard a knocking sound from behind him. A thumping. It was coming from the bus. Stepping closer, Haggerty saw a young woman standing on the other side of the bus door, pounding her fist against the plastic window. She was stuck. She was trying to get his attention.

Haggerty waved to her and stepped closer. He curled the fingers of his left hand underneath the rubber seal in the middle of the door, then used his right hand to make a pushing motion toward the woman. He repeated the motion twice more while showing an exaggerated series of tugs with his left hand.

You push. I'll pull.

The woman nodded. Haggerty raised three fingers and counted down: *Three, two, one . . .*

He pulled. She pushed. The door resisted for two or three seconds, then split down in the middle. Both halves opened outward with an automated smoothness.

The woman stumbled forward off the elevated stair but caught herself on Haggerty's arm and shoulder.

"Thanks," she said, straightening up. "I ain't about to be stuck on no bus."

"What happened?"

The woman shrugged. She was young, with ebony skin and long charcoal braids. She was wearing a backpack, which meant she might be a local student. Or a tourist.

"Didn't see much." She started to walk away, which made Haggerty feel alarmed. He was desperate for answers.

"Hey! Wait . . ."

The way she flinched made him realize he was speaking far too loudly. *Too much adrenaline. Get a grip, Haggs.*

"Sorry." He held up his hands. Placating. Nonthreatening. "I'm a doctor. Are you hurt?"

She shook her head. Based on what Haggerty could see, she didn't appear physically injured, but she'd crossed her arms over her chest and was leaning forward with her head low and knees flexed. The posture was hunched and protective. Almost like she was ready to run if necessary. She was staring off into space, which could be evidence of shock.

He took a step closer, still keeping his hands up. "What's your name?"

She looked at him, though her eyes remained unfocused. "Sheneya."

"Sheneya," he repeated. "Did you see what happened with the bus? Why it crashed?"

Another shrug. "She up and vanished."

"Vanished? Who vanished?" He thought he already knew the answer, but his mind demanded solid information in one form or another. It craved confirmation.

"The driver. She disappeared. I was watching out the front. The bus was turning, then . . . she was gone. The bus kept going for a little while. I didn't want it to hit nobody, so I got the wheel." She blinked rapidly several times, trying to hold back tears.

"You steered into the wall so the bus wouldn't hit any other cars?"

She nodded, wiping the corner of one eye.

"Okay." Haggerty was thinking fast. "I'll see if anyone's hurt. Sheneya"—he touched her on the shoulder to make sure she was seeing him—"don't stay in the street, okay? Move off the road, and I'll come check on you in a few minutes."

She nodded again and turned away. Haggerty spun around and climbed into the bus. Sure enough, he found a deflated WMATA uniform instead of a driver behind the wheel. A dark blue vest over a light blue shirt rested on the chair. A pair of dark blue pants had puddled in front of the pedals next to dark blue flats. Bending down, Haggerty read the gold name tag pinned to the vest: *Wanda Davis*.

"Where did you go, Wanda?" he whispered. "Where did they all go?"

Haggerty looked down the bus's main aisle. Twenty or so people were sitting, most of them talking on their phones. One older man was standing near the middle of the bus. He held his hand against his forehead, where Haggerty could see a red smear. He must have knocked against something during the crash. Several of the passengers had gathered their belongings and were shuffling toward him, apparently ready to follow Sheneya out into the street. He didn't stop them.

Walking forward, Haggerty noticed a few more piles of empty clothes. Blue jeans and a Washington Commanders jacket lay on one seat, with white sneakers on the floor. Gray slacks and a gray sport coat and black oxfords. A floral dress with a soft white sweater and matching flats.

One aisle seat held a baby carrier with straps buckled in place around a green crocheted blanket. Haggerty could see the sleeves of a little winter coat poking out of the blanket in two places. The sleeves warmed no chubby arms and framed no fragile fingers, but a long, black, puffy jacket lay crumpled on the adjoining seat. A pair of black ankle-high boots rested on the floor next to a folded-up stroller tucked at an angle below the window.

Haggerty stared at the stroller for several seconds. Trying to think. Trying to remember how to think. Part of his mind kept shuffling through possible scenarios or probable explanations for everything he'd seen and heard in recent minutes—shuffled them like cards in a deck. But another part of his mind rejected each attempt as logically impossible.

Am I insane?

He was still standing and staring at the stroller when someone tapped him on the shoulder. The old man with blood on his forehead.

"I can't find Emmaline." He spoke in a calm, dispassionate voice, as if he were ordering breakfast. "She lost her coat."

Haggerty touched the old man on the arm, confirming he was there; he was solid. "Where were you sitting when it happened?" He wasn't sure what he meant by *it*.

The old man half turned and gestured to a pair of seats. One of them was empty. The other was covered by a large fur coat that had slid most of the way down the backrest. Haggerty leaned forward and saw black pants poking out from under the coat. He couldn't lean far enough to see whatever shoes had been abandoned on the ground.

He pointed. "This is Emmaline's seat?"

"Yeah," said the old man. "She lost her coat. She'll be cold."

Now in the middle of the bus, Haggerty could hear some of what people were saying into their phones. A woman's voice: ". . . waiting for the police to come. I don't know what the driver was thinking." A man: ". . . has to be in the house if the child locks are on. She can't open any of the doors, can she?" An older woman: ". . . hard to hear you with all this racket. Who disappeared?"

Haggerty's legs felt numb. He sat down. The old man was forgotten. The noises and conversations around him were forgotten.

He pulled out his phone and checked the News app. Nothing. Just regular stories. He opened his socials, and the hashtags stabbed up at him from the screen. #VANISHED. #DISAPPEARED. #MISSING. #RAPTURE.

He clicked and skimmed through post after post from Florida. From Michigan. From Texas. From Brazil. From Ireland. From Nigeria. Whatever was happening wasn't happening only in this area. It was all over the country. All over the world.

Haggerty heard Caleb's voice in his head: *"Everyone who is connected to Jesus will be rescued. Taken out of this world and taken up to heaven."* Then his own voice: *"If I ever wake up one day and there are billions of people missing without any explanation, I'll sprint over to the first church I can find. Deal?"*

Haggerty thought of Sonya and her weekly Bible study. He thought of Marianna texting Caleb with spiritual questions—questions about salvation.

He pulled out his phone and called Caleb. It took two attempts because of his shaking, fumbling fingers. There were seven rings—

Haggerty counted each one—then the connection clicked over to voicemail. Haggerty called a second time. He listened again to all seven rings, then hung up.

In some dim corner of his brain, Haggerty noted that his palms and his forehead had broken out in sweat. His heart was racing; he could feel it in his neck and his temple. His head was swimming. Dizzy. Disoriented. Calmly, clinically, he diagnosed himself as suffering from the beginning stages of a panic attack.

I need to lie back. I need to breathe. I need to focus on something calming.

Instead, he stood. He shambled forward, barely noticing when he knocked against a woman. He stumbled off the bus. Then he walked down the street, his legs pressing forward in quick, erratic jerks. He lurched past Sheneya, still standing at the edge of the road, perhaps waiting for him to come back. He didn't stop. He didn't speak.

He just kept walking. Then jogging. Then sprinting forward, spurred on and on by the unending dread of an uncertain future.

CHAPTER 21

THE DAY: UNKNOWN
THE HOUR: UNKNOWN
MILLER COUNTY HOSPITAL

Ladies and gentlemen, it's your boy Hart-X broadcasting live from the maternity ward over at the fabulous Miller County Hospital. We got a great show for you this morning!"

Abigail was aware of her husband's voice as she rolled along the long hallway, but she didn't really hear it. Just like she was aware of the dirty, enamel-colored linoleum and the textured eggshell walls but didn't really see them. For Abigail, all external sensation had been collected and compressed and downgraded in comparison to the overwhelming awareness of internal satisfaction.

Because it was over. She'd done it. She'd brought her baby into the world.

My Booker. My sweet child.

"First up is our award for the most outstanding mother on the planet. Let's give it up for all the moms out there, y'all!"

Abigail felt a subtle change in momentum as Xavier let go of her wheelchair so he could mock-clap his hands and make little whistling, cheering sounds with his mouth. She heard the giddiness in his voice. The joy and the delight. The knowledge of her husband's happiness made her smile.

"And now for the results. The world's most outstanding mother, winning by a unanimous landslide of epic proportions, is Millersville's very own Abigail Hart!"

Abigail felt the change in momentum again as Xavier clapped and whooped behind her. She heard the squeak of his sneakers as he jumped and danced and scooted back in place to guide the wheelchair once more.

A small voice chimed up in her mind to say that Xavier was being too loud—that he would disturb the other moms currently occupying the ward. And what about the babies? The voice sounded like her mother's voice. But Abigail didn't have the energy to express those concerns. Instead, she let her body relax even deeper into the soft padding of the chair as it rolled along.

Wish you were here, Mom. Wish you could see what we did today. Your grandson is so beautiful.

They'd come to the hospital only as a precaution. She'd felt something in the early hours of the morning—a series of stirrings that she'd been certain were only Braxton Hicks contractions or something similar. They couldn't be the real thing, not when she was only thirty-six weeks along. But Xavier told her, "Better safe than sorry." He helped her to their little SUV and drove with one hand tightly on the wheel and the other gently stroking her left arm.

Her water broke while they were in the observation room, and that had been the end of any questions about whether this was the real thing. Her medical team swung into action with practiced efficiency.

She didn't know how long ago that had been. More than a day, since this was another morning. Which meant she'd endured at least twenty-four hours of sweating into pillows and sheets. A full day of nurses poking and jabbing and whispering with Miranda, the midwife, and then asking Abigail to rate her pain. A full day of Xavier's cheerful smiles and cheerful slogans.

The pain had increased throughout those twenty-four hours and more. The pressure too—the squeezing, crushing compression that marched up and down between her belly and her back. She wanted a natural birth, and she'd been able to bear the squeezing and unsqueezing for what seemed like a long, long time. She breathed with her husband in short little gasps: *Shhhhh. Shhhhh. Whooooooooosh. Shhhhh. Shhhhh. Whooooooooosh.* She took sips of water and shifted positions to stretch her back whenever possible. She pushed when Miranda said to push and relaxed when Miranda said to relax.

She was going to be okay. Everything was going to be okay.

Then it all changed. The entire experience intensified in ways Abigail never would have dreamed possible. The pain and the pressure exploded throughout every inch of her body, and she knew she wasn't going to be okay. She wasn't going to make it.

Even when Xavier squeezed her hand and kissed the back of her head, she knew it was all going wrong. Even when Miranda had called out in a clear, confident voice, "That's exactly right, Abigail. You're doing great!" Abigail had been overwhelmed by utter hopelessness and despair. She'd never make it. She'd never see her boy.

Then the door to her delivery room burst open and her daddy was there. He wasn't supposed to be there. She'd told him in no uncertain terms to stay in the waiting room because she didn't want him to see anything that either of them would find difficult to forget. But somehow he'd sensed what she was feeling; somehow he'd known that she needed him. And now he was here.

He strode into the room with his long, measured steps. His smiling face was filled with confident assurance, and his eyes stayed on her eyes until he lowered himself to kiss her forehead. Then he held a cup of crushed ice to her lips, and she felt the delicious coolness run across her tongue and down the back of her throat.

"You're doing so good, Abi-girl." His voice was packed with emotion as he took her hand and whispered in her ear. "I'm so proud! Your momma is so proud!"

The pain and the pressure were worse. Somehow they kept intensifying. But she felt her daddy's hand holding her fingers. And she felt her husband's hand holding her shoulder. She heard them telling her she could do it—she was doing it. She heard Miranda say, "I see the head, Abigail! I see Booker's head!" And the name was a balm that washed over her like a river of cool, clear water. Then he was crying. Her Booker was crying, and she was crying because she couldn't contain so much joy. She couldn't see much through the tears and the sweat still stinging her eyes, but she felt the baby pressed against her chest—felt the radiant warmth of the little body still connected to her own body through deep and vital ties.

How long ago was that? An hour? Thirty minutes?

She didn't know.

Her daddy's voice pulled her out of her reverie and back to the present. "Xavier, what do you say we keep things down to a dull roar?"

"Sure thing, Pops."

Abigail rolled her head up in the chair and looked at both men from the corner of her eye. They were smiling at each other. Grinning, actually. Then, as if acting on some cue, they both turned and beamed down at her with expressions of such tenderness and affection that she almost felt a little afraid of the intensity of their love for her.

Not just for me, she realized. *They love my Booker as well. He's a gift to them as much as to me—a little boy to be molded and mentored and shaped and taught by the good men who love him until he becomes a good man in his own right. A gift to the world.*

Abigail realized in that moment that she would never be alone. No matter how scared she might feel about raising a child, no matter how insecure she felt in her own wisdom or her own instincts, and no matter how much she missed her mom and longed for her guidance, she would always have these two men standing next to her. Supporting her. Protecting her.

The knowledge was wonderful.

What could be better than this feeling? All I need is my Booker, and everything will be perfect. Everything will be right.

She could see the long windows of the nursery up ahead, and her body began to ache with anticipation. She rose up in her seat, trying to see into the room ahead. Trying to spot her boy. Two nurses moved about the nursery like birds, flitting from bassinet to bassinet and bending this way and that. Abigail could see the head of another woman down low—probably another mother in a wheelchair like herself.

"We're so close."

"Almost there, baby." Xavier spoke warmly and squeezed her shoulder again. "But I get dibs on holding him first, okay?"

The smile in his voice was evident without seeing his face. She wanted to say something back—something clever to spar with him and make him laugh. But her brain was so sluggish. She was so tired. "No deal, Hart-X," was all she could manage.

She felt the change of momentum again—the feeling of gliding along the hallway as he let go of the wheelchair.

He's about to run out in front of me, like he's racing me to Booker. Like he's going to get there first and leave me here all by myself.

She waited to see him burst into view in front of her with graceful strides on long, athletic legs. Waited to see him turn around with that goofy, giddy grin. "Gotcha!" She was already wearing a

"Don't mess with me" expression on her face—already prepared to break into a grin or laugh at whatever antics he pulled next.

Nothing happened.

Abigail's smile faltered as her wheelchair slowed, slowed, then stopped. She turned back and to the left to see what Xavier was up to, but she saw nothing. She turned to the right to see what her daddy thought about Xavier's antics, but she didn't see her daddy. She saw no one.

"What in the world are you—"

Her eyes rested on a pile of clothes on the ground. They were her daddy's clothes—his jeans and a Chicago Bulls sweatshirt. It was his favorite sweatshirt, and she'd seen him wear it hundreds of times. She knew it, just like she knew the little black pair of reading glasses that had been resting on his forehead and were now lying haphazardly on the floor. The whole outfit was crumpled in a pile right where she expected her daddy to be.

"Daddy?"

She swiveled in the opposite direction, swinging her arms to look back over the edge of her chair. Xavier's clothes were on the ground behind her. His light blue scrubs lay on the linoleum like he'd thrown them toward a hamper and missed. Leaning back, Abigail saw the white rectangle of his surgical mask poking out from the top of the pile—and then the cream-colored tips of his lucky Air Jordans poking out from underneath the scrubs. She recognized the scuffs and the stains on top of those shoes; she knew them like a fingerprint.

"What's going on?" She felt angry now. Angry and afraid. "What are you two doing? This isn't funny, Xa—"

Someone screamed from inside the nursery. The sound was huge and harsh, cutting through the prior silence like an out-of-tune trumpet. Abigail whipped around as the screech stretched and stretched, seeming to grow louder and more terrified with each passing moment. She quickly spotted the screamer through the window—one of the nurses. She was standing alone and looking down with horror at something on the ground.

Booker! My baby!

The knowledge that her son was in that room ripped through Abigail's mind. She took one last look behind her—still no one there. Xavier and her daddy were missing. They were gone, somehow, but she couldn't think about that now. Not when her baby needed her.

Reaching out wide, Abigail grasped the wheels of her chair and pistoned her arms outward. The chair jolted and lurched forward. She was about ten feet from the nursery wall. The nurse was still screaming.

Abigail launched herself forward again. Then again. She was six feet away. Four feet. She was at the wall, pushing up from the chair and scrabbling her fingers against the window sills in search of purchase.

"Oh. *Ohh!*" The pain in her abdomen awoke with a fiery intensity—a sleeping dragon suddenly enraged.

It didn't matter. Abigail was on her feet. She was shuffling forward.

Suddenly the nursery door burst open a few feet in front of her, and the nurse came out—the one who'd been screaming. Only now did Abigail realize the screaming had stopped.

"We have an emergency in the maternity ward nursery!" The nurse was mashing her fingers against an intercom button next to the door, pressing it again and again. "We have an emergency in the nursery! Cynthia's gone. She disappeared. And the babies! All the babies! I . . . I don't know what to do!"

Abigail had reached the door, which caught the nurse's attention. The woman held up her hands to prevent Abigail from moving into the room but ended up catching her as she tumbled forward.

"Ma'am, no. No!" The nurse tried to guide Abigail back toward the wheelchair. "There's been an emergency. You can't go in right now. You have to—"

Abigail shoved the woman away from her, then staggered toward the open door.

"My boy! My Booker!" Her words were both explanation and repudiation tossed back toward the nurse, who had tripped and fallen to the ground.

"Booker!"

Abigail stepped into the nursery—and froze. It was deserted. She saw a set of nurse's scrubs on the ground that were the same color and style as those worn by the woman she'd just pushed down. She saw an empty wheelchair about fifteen feet from the door. It was the same type of chair she'd just left in the hall. She saw three rows of clear plastic bassinets lined up in the center of the nursery. Each one had a crisp sheet over a thin mattress. Some had little piles of clothing and blankets puddled near the center of that sheet.

None of the bassinets had babies in them. Every single one was empty.

"No, no, no." Abigail started moving down the first row, using the bassinets to support her weight as she pitched from bed to bed, reading the little placards attached to the front. The dragon was roaring now. Pain flared from her midsection as she moved back and forth between the beds. She ignored it.

"No, no, no, n—"

The name was a thunderbolt through her mind: *Booker Caleb Hart*. Her Booker. Her baby's name.

But there was no baby in the middle of the bed. She saw the little blanket Miranda had wrapped him in. She saw the little hat Abigail herself had placed over his sweet, soft head. She saw the plastic hospital bracelet and picked it up, holding it directly in front of her weeping eyes: *Booker Caleb Hart*.

In that moment, she knew. She understood it all. Her missing husband. Her missing father. Her missing baby—and herself not missing. She *knew*. And in that knowing, she believed.

"Oh, God!" She cried out the prayer as comprehension crushed down on her mind and her heart. "Oh, God, please no! Please have mercy!" She cried out the prayer as her own body cried out for her son—cried out to see and hold the sweet child who was only just born yet had already been born again and borne away.

Abigail slumped to the ground, still holding the little plastic bracelet. Still wailing and weeping. Still hoping to wake up from this nightmare that she knew was not a nightmare because the Sun of righteousness had risen with healing in His wings—but not for her.

CHAPTER 22

O h, that's crazy talk, Tim. You're embarrassin' yourself."

"Me crazy?" Tim seemed genuinely offended. "*Me* crazy? You're the one talkin' 'bout aliens, Jerry."

"'Course I'm talkin' about aliens! We got people disappearin' all over the place in broad daylight. If that ain't aliens, what is?"

Haggerty sat between the two men at the Farmhouse Diner as they bickered back and forth in their own affable, cantankerous style. He could tell their current conversation was only the latest foray in a larger verbal confrontation that stretched from roadside diner to roadside diner and greasy spoon to greasy spoon across rural Pennsylvania over the course of years. Or decades.

". . . tell me where the ships are. Huh?" Tim was a short, thin man with small eyes, a long nose, and wavy white wisps of hair. His voice was high and reedy but confident. "There's ten million folks missin' at least. So where's all the spaceships to hold that many people? We'd a seen 'em, Jerry."

Jerry was already shaking his head, equally confident. He was as short as Tim but twice as heavy. He had a bushy gray beard under his generous chin and a mop of bushy gray hair tucked under a faded red baseball cap. His voice was low and gravelly.

"These is aliens, Tim." He still wagged his head with benevolent patience. "You think they come from a zillion miles away in outer space, but they cain't fool our little satellites?"

"We'd see 'em in the sky," Tim countered. "We'd see 'em with our own eyes, same way as you see the moon at night—if you ever opened your eyes, that is."

"Well, it ain't been night yet, has it?" said Jerry. "Chances are we *will* see 'em tonight. Chances are we been seein' their scouts for decades now, with all them UFO sightin's."

Ain't been night yet, Haggerty thought. *That's the crazy part.*

It was hard to believe he'd been sitting in Burgess's office in the Pentagon less than eight hours ago. Not even a full workday. It was hard to believe he'd eaten breakfast in one world—a world where crises needed to be solved, but at least the fundamental principles of life made sense—and was now eating dinner in a completely new world. A completely new reality.

Images flashed through Haggerty's mind. The turboprop exploding in midair. The woman holding an empty jacket and calling for her daughter. The bus driver's uniform abandoned like an empty shell on the seat. The old man searching for his wife and pointing to her jacket. *"She'll be cold."*

After the bus, Haggerty had run all the way to Reagan International Airport—or tried to. He'd been blocked by guards at the entrance. Military. He later learned that *all* flights had been grounded at every airport in the U.S., a precaution the FAA was taking due to the "unprecedented nature of the day's events and the potential for security breakdowns." Which was perhaps the understatement of the century.

Unable to fly or rent a car, Haggerty made his way up Route 1 until he hit Interstate 395, intending to hitch a ride. But when he passed an idling SUV with three-quarters of a tank of gas and only one pile of clothes in the driver's seat, he bit the bullet and hopped in. The roads were in terrible shape, and Haggerty witnessed the aftermath of hundreds of accidents. A few crews were attempting to clear the streets, but they were few and far between. Progress was slow.

Haggerty met up with Jerry on 270 west of Rockville, Maryland. They'd compared notes on the unprecedented nature of the day's events while waiting in line to pay for gas. When Jerry found out Haggerty was heading west, he'd offered a ride in his faded green box truck. "Little comp'ny might be nice on a day like this." Haggerty had accepted based on instinct—a gut feeling that had been confirmed as wisdom by the confident way Jerry maneuvered through shoulders and over medians and around blockages as if he'd been doing so his entire life.

Now Haggerty was sitting next to Jerry at the Farmhouse Diner somewhere south and west of Pittsburgh, listening to his new friend argue with an old friend about what the news media had already dubbed the "Great Disappearance."

"What would be the point?" asked Tim. "If these aliens is so sophisticated, what would they want with millions of people anyway?"

Jerry had ordered a burger and french fries. Now he grabbed two fries between pudgy fingers and raised them to his mouth with exaggerated slowness. He chomped on the fries and waggled his eyebrows up and down.

"Oh, phaw," said Tim. "Gross."

Jerry shrugged. "Aliens gotta eat. Same as you an' me."

"Nope." Tim cut off a piece of his country-fried steak but just looked at it. Perhaps affected more than he wanted to admit by Jerry's theory. "Nope, I say it's the government." He pronounced it as "gover-ment," without any hint of an *n*. "The government done it."

"Which government?" asked Jerry.

"Ours, a'course. Who else'd have the resources to pull off somethin' like this?"

Who has the resources? Haggerty thought. *That's the million-dollar question, old-timer.*

"Okay, then same question you asked me: Why would the government disappear so many people? What for?"

"Well." Tim was chewing now, slowly. "I figure it's connected to the whole global warmin' thing. Too many people. Too much pollution. Not enough food."

Jerry abandoned his burger in shock. "You think the government *killed* all them people? On *purpose*?"

"Well . . . I don't think they done it by accident." Tim touched a finger to the tip of his long nose, then raised his narrow white eyebrows as high as they would go.

Haggerty contemplated his own half-eaten hamburger for a moment, then continued to tackle the mountain of fries piled next to it. He ate mechanically. Efficiently. He wasn't hungry, but his Army training told him to put fuel in the tank whenever fuel was available. Especially during uncertain situations.

He looked up at the TV monitor, which had the news from one of the major networks. The chyron near the bottom read, *The Great Disappearance: Devastation and Catastrophe.* The video footage cycled between several dozen chaotic scenes that had been captured after the initial moment of vanishing earlier this morning: Cars smashing into each other in massive pileups. Fire crews spraying down burning vehicles. A conveyor belt in a shipping warehouse throwing dozens of cardboard boxes on the ground. Dogs wandering down city streets with leashes trailing behind them. An airplane skidding down a long runway and then erupting into flames. Mobs of looters smashing store windows or running with hoods pulled over their faces and arms hugging mounds of merchandise. A distraught young woman standing in a vacant elementary school classroom, then the camera panning out to reveal piles of clothing on the ground. Kids' clothing. More piles of clothing on street corners and sidewalks, on couches, in the middle of office cubicles, on park benches, on beaches.

On and on. The cumulative effect was horrible. Inconceivable.

The network avoided showing videos of people actually disappearing into thin air. Those videos existed, of course. Haggerty had scrolled through dozens of them while riding in Jerry's truck. He'd seen footage from CCTV and security cameras, from people's phones, and even professional shots from Hollywood production companies.

There were hundreds of clips. Probably thousands. They all showed the same thing: people vanishing in an instant. No warning. No flash of light. No bolt of energy striking down from the sky. Every video showed a person or people solidly *there* in one frame and then instantly *not there* in the next frame. They were gone. Disappeared without a trace, save for a pile of clothing on the ground.

Haggerty had watched one particular clip on X over and over. It was professional quality, probably a marketing company shooting a commercial or maybe a TV show. The video showed a young woman riding a skateboard up the side of an empty pool and performing some type of trick—Haggerty had no idea about the lingo of that particular subculture.

The clip was unique because it started at normal speed, with the young woman zooming down one side of the pool and up the other side. Then, right before the trick, the video kicked into slow motion. You could see the exhilaration on her face as she rose into the air inch by inch and frame by frame, her board and her shoulders perpendicular to the camera. She wore baggy jeans and a loose, flowing button-up over a black undershirt. Plus a black skullcap pressed over long, dirty-blonde hair.

Right at the zenith of her jump, she broke into a slow-motion smile. Lips parting. Teeth gleaming. Eyes widening. A picture of unbridled joy.

Then she vanished.

Even with the slow-motion recording, it happened instantly from one frame to the next. She was there, elated, and then she was gone. Completely. The clip did capture her clothes and her board continuing forward for several seconds—empty but still holding the relative shape of a person—before the footage returned to full speed and everything crashed to the ground in a formless mound.

That was the most striking example Haggerty had seen of video footage from the Great Disappearance, but there were already many other equally memorable moments captured on X and Reddit and other online spaces. So why weren't they featured on the news?

Something to that, Haggerty thought. *There's something behind that, but . . .* He tried briefly to grapple with the problem—to engage with hypotheses and probabilities and possible solutions. But the effort tripped an unseen breaker in the internal wiring of his brain, and he felt his mind go blank. He didn't have the capacity for problem-solving. Not right now. Not after everything he'd seen and heard and wondered.

Now the news showed huge crowds of people lined up outside of banks and other financial institutions. One of the anchors was saying, ". . . thousands expressing their frustration with today's FDIC decision to freeze withdrawals from all bank accounts for at least the next three days, citing the impact of the Great Disappearance on regulatory agencies. One moment . . ."

The anchor touched a finger to her ear and tilted her head to one side for several seconds. "We have a breaking news alert. I'm being told the president will address the nation at 8:00 p.m. Eastern Standard Time, which is about seventy minutes from now. Her address will come from the Oval Office rather than the Situation Room, as previously speculated."

Good. Took you long enough.

He felt a tap on his shoulder. Jerry. "Hey," Haggerty said, looking over at the driver. "What's up?"

"I was just tellin' this guy"—a knowing nod tipped in Tim's direction—"about the real reason for this vanishing thing."

Haggerty raised his eyebrows. "Not aliens?"

Jerry raised and lowered opposite hands in a gesture that said, *Maybe yes, maybe no.* "If it wasn't aliens, then it would have to be . . ." He glanced around the diner, first to the left and then to the right. "It would have to be . . . those Israeli fellas." He put a heavy emphasis on the second syllable: "Is-*ray*-li."

Haggerty said nothing.

"I read about it a couple times, see?" Jerry was talking to Tim again. He held his hands above his head, palms down so his fingers dangled downward. "Space lasers."

Tim looked impressed in spite of himself.

Haggerty threw the last few fries into his mouth, then asked, "How long until we roll, Jerry?"

"Oh, a little longer." The little man picked up his soda and took a swig. "Need to let the bubbles settle."

Haggerty grunted. He'd offered to pick up the tab for both men out of gratitude for the ride. Jerry, it seemed, was determined to take full advantage of the opportunity. Hamburgers were a luxury for many these days.

Leaning back, Haggerty tried to ignore the feeling of panic that had been buzzing and building at the back of his mind for hours. He was desperate to hear something from Marianna and Sonya. Or from Caleb. But none of them had answered his calls, and he didn't have contact information for anyone else in town.

He pulled out his phone and looked at the screen. No calls. No messages. No texts.

He clicked a few buttons and scrolled through his contacts.

Despite the warnings from General Burgess, Haggerty had again spent much of the day attempting to call different associates in the Army and on the remaining task forces, with no luck. Everyone either was too busy or had blocked him because of his earlier demands for attention.

I have to be going crazy. That's what's happening. That's the only possible solution that makes any se—

His phone rang. It was an unfamiliar number, but he answered anyway, desperate for information from any possible source. "Haggerty."

"John?" The voice at the other end of the line was high and girlish. "This is Li."

"Dr. Fan! Hello!" He stood and hustled over to an empty corner, checking the phone screen again as he walked. This wasn't Li Fan's usual number, which meant she was taking precautions while speaking to him. Which meant he probably owed her a big favor.

"John, I know you must be going crazy." Her voice was a little out of breath, and he could hear the sounds of traffic in the background. She was walking down a city street. Probably D.C. "I'm not supposed to speak with you, but if our positions were reversed, I . . . I would want to know. And I consider you a friend."

"I'm grateful, Li," he said, and meant it. "What's happening? Who did this?"

She sighed, sounding as exhausted as he felt. "We don't know. I know you probably won't believe me, but it's true. We don't know who did this. We don't know how they did it. We don't even have a full understanding yet on what's been done—on how many people are . . . how many have disappeared."

Rats. Haggerty did believe her. Which was terrifying.

"Are we considering extraterrestrials as a legitimate option?"

"Everything is a legitimate option, John. Yes, including ET. In a lot of ways that would make the most sense given the technology gap that seems to be in play."

"What do you mean? What technology gap?"

"We don't have any actual readings or data to evaluate when it comes to the disappearances," she said. "But we have lots of video evidence."

"Yeah, I've seen some of those."

"Did you watch the skateboard one? The girl?"

"Yes." He thought again of the young woman's face right before she vanished—the freedom and the joy.

"Well, we authenticated that specific video from every angle. Nothing fake. No special effects. So it's a real recording. And all of our technicians tell us it's impossible."

"What's impossible?"

"That kind of disappearance. Instant evaporation or transportation of matter without any subsequent production of detectable energy. It violates everything we know about the law of conservation of mass. Or everything we thought we knew . . ."

If it doesn't fit our understanding of natural, it really could be extraterrestrial. Or supernatural.

Once again he heard Caleb talking in his head. *"Everyone who is connected to Jesus will be rescued. Taken out of this world and taken up to heaven. The Bible says it will happen in a moment—in the twinkling of an eye."*

Haggerty heard the echo of his own voice in response. *"If I ever wake up one day and there are billions of people missing without any explanation, I'll sprint over to the first church I can find. Deal?"*

He pushed those thoughts aside. He also pushed the implications of those thoughts aside. Or at least tried to.

"Li, what can we learn from the people who vanished? Are there any patterns? Is it true what they're saying about children?"

"Yes, that is true, John. We don't have anywhere close to a total count of the people who disappeared, but we can confirm that they include almost all children under the age of seven, and most of the children between the ages of seven and ten."

A bitter ball began to roil inside his belly. Every kid under the age of seven just . . . gone. Vanished. He thought again of the woman holding the little pink coat and calling out, "Aayanah! Aayanah!" He thought of the empty baby carrier on the bus and the folded-up stroller.

He thought of Ryan. He thought of Sonya.

"Are there any other patterns, Li? Anything spiritual or religious?"

The silence from the other end of the line stretched for several seconds. Then, "What do you mean, John?"

He heard Caleb's voice in his head once more. *"You know what that means?"*

He heard his own voice: *"Saved. Washed in the blood. A Christian."*

"Have the disappearances been connected to a specific set of religious beliefs? To Christians?"

"How do you know that?"

Haggerty closed his eyes. He remembered Sonya talking about the people in her Bible study, and how nice they were, and how they were helping her work through some difficult questions. He remembered the rage he felt at the idea of Marianna seeking out spiritual advice from Caleb, one of her oldest friends.

Could it be true? Could you be up there while I'm stuck down here?

He shook his head, more in an attempt to refuse the direction of those thoughts than to evaluate them in any meaningful way. *We don't know anything. That whole idea is just happenstance as far as I know—nothing but a series of coincidences all tied together. Or I'm just hallucinating . . . That makes as much sense as—*

"John, are you there?" Li sounded a bit flustered. Maybe even panicked. "It's true that those who self-identify as Christians were among the vanished at significantly higher rates. In fact, at statistically improbable rates, given everything else we've learned. But that's information we were very intentionally holding back. I'd really like to know how you—"

The line went dead. Li Fan's voice was cut off in an instant.

At almost exactly the same moment, the news feed on the television went fuzzy, then black. Haggerty had been staring at it while he spoke to Li, and he saw the signal wane, then die.

Less than a second later, the lights of the Farmhouse Diner cut out, leaving the patrons in darkness. Exclamations of surprise rang out and several murmurs from the customers. Then a generator kicked in, and the interior of the restaurant was bathed in a weak, yellowish glow.

In that moment, Haggerty knew what had happened. He didn't guess. He wasn't speculating. He *knew*. He was certain.

The bombs. In his mind, he pictured the little concrete cube outside of Millersville disappearing in a blinding flash, transformed instantly into a hideously churning cloud that boiled its way up, up, up. He imagined that same thing happening all over the country at the same time. Perhaps all over the world.

The part of him that was still a military man appreciated the cold efficiency of the dual attack. *Whoever planted the bombs was responsible for the Great Disappearance. Either they were responsible or they knew about it ahead of time . . . like Caleb did.*

Moving on unstable legs, Haggerty hurried over to Jerry and Tim, who were both staring dumbly up at the emergency lights. He slapped Jerry on the shoulder, partly to get his attention and partly to knock him out of whatever haze he'd slipped into.

"Time to go. We need to move. Now."

CHAPTER 23

NEW ERA—DAY 3
MILLERSVILLE, OHIO

ttention, citizens . . . This area has been placed under quarantine by the office of the governor of Ohio. There is no current threat from radioactive fallout. Repeat: There is no current threat from radioactive fallout. For your safety, all residents are required to remain in their homes until a full threat assessment has been completed by the Ohio National Guard."

Haggerty watched the tactical vehicle roll down the middle of the road just inside the Millersville town limit. It was a big, blocky green-and-brown truck with a loudspeaker bolted to the top. He'd seen it a few times already this morning—it or another truck just like it. He knelt in a copse of trees just off the road as it passed him by.

No current threat. Wouldn't that be nice.

The claim about low radiation levels could be true, depending on how many kilotons had been packed into the tactical nuke at the Miller County substation. Haggerty had seen a few dead bodies on the road in the past two days, but they were all from auto accidents. He had not seen any charred corpses or piles of bodies— no evidence of the death toll he'd expected to find after a nuclear attack. Not yet.

He'd stayed with Jerry for another full day after the detonations—what he was already starting to think of as D-Day. Death Day for the United States of America. They left the diner and moved away from Pittsburgh as quickly as was manageable given the condition of the roads, then spent the night in the truck in the middle of nowhere. They didn't sleep, and their ears itched for the distant boom of ordnance, but they heard nothing. Their eyes constantly flinched against any hint of a faraway flash, but they saw nothing.

Yesterday they'd ventured back to Interstate 70 and continued west into Ohio for several hours. There was no electricity, which meant no operating gas stations. When the truck hit empty, Haggerty shook the old man's hand and thanked him. Then moved on.

Haggerty snagged a few other rides going west. The longest and most helpful was courtesy of a patrol unit in an older model Humvee when the driver responded to Haggerty's military ID.

He'd avoided Columbus by detouring south toward Dayton. But the woman who gave him a lift on Highway 71 near Jeffersonville—a middle-aged lady named Bonnie who drove an old farm truck—told him she'd been near the city when all the power went out. According to Bonnie, there hadn't been any explosion inside Columbus itself, but she'd seen something like a mushroom cloud far away to the northeast.

"Terrible sight," she told him. "Terrible colors. Just like on TV."

After leaving Bonnie, Haggerty had walked most of the night, sleeping on the ground in spurts of fifteen or thirty minutes at a time. The National Guard patrols had started by then, and he mostly avoided them—although he doubted those driving the trucks had any actual authority to detain anyone. He guessed they were rolling message boards and nothing more.

"There is no current threat from radioactive fallout. Repeat: There is no current threat from radioactive fallout. For your safety, all residents are required to remain in their homes . . ."

This particular rolling message board came to a brief stop about a block beyond Haggerty's position, then turned right. Soon it was out of sight.

Haggerty's joints popped and cracked as he rose to his feet. His back was very sore, and he tried to stretch and twist himself into some semblance of fighting shape. It didn't do much good.

He moved forward, walking on the grass just outside the tree line. As he walked, he thought again about what Bonnie had told him. No explosion inside the city of Columbus but likely a nuclear strike to the northeast. Millersville was roughly southwest of Columbus, and the Miller County substation would be a major supplier of power to that city.

Did they structure it that way on purpose? Bracketing the city would destroy all the infrastructure but limit human casualties. Is that what they wanted?

Haggerty had no idea, and the reality of his ignorance galled him. He didn't know who "they" were. He didn't know their motives or their goals. He didn't know the extent of the damage they had caused, although he suspected a complete failure of the nationwide power grid and other critical systems.

No idea who or how or why. I am completely in the dark.

But no, that wasn't right. He wasn't completely in the dark. He knew his own personal "who" and "how" and "why." He'd traveled hundreds of miles in less than forty-eight hours with a singular goal in mind. He'd sustained himself through stress and strain and uncertainty by focusing on that specific mission—that single destination.

And now he could see it up ahead on the left side of the road. A little redbrick house with big bay windows and a colorful garden off to the side.

They'll be in the house, he told himself for the hundredth time that morning. *They'll obey the quarantine, which means they'll be in the house. I'll find them, I'll gather our supplies, and I'll take them somewhere safe. We'll find a way to make a life together.*

Still moving forward, he reached the spot in the road where he'd looked back through his rearview mirror all those days ago— looked back to see his wife and daughter hugging each other. Comforting each other because he was leaving. Again.

"No more." He said the words out loud, then began to jog toward Marianna's house. "No more leaving. I promise."

As he ran up to the gate, a memory flashed through his mind. He saw himself and Marianna pulling up to this same curb in their old tan minivan, with Ryan and Sonya strapped in their car seats. Marianna's mom had stepped through the door and was waving to them on top of the little concrete staircase.

That's when Ryan had called out, "Aboolah! Aboolah!"

Sonya echoed him in her little girl's singsong. "Aboolah! Aboolah!"

Haggerty and Marianna had locked eyes for a long moment. Faces serious. Both trying not to be the first to smile at the mispronunciation of *Aboolah* instead of *Abuela*. They'd kept staring at each other. Holding that moment.

Then Haggerty had shrugged and said, "Close enough." He winked and grinned.

She'd thrown her head back and howled with joy and mirth and happiness. That moment had become a sparkling memory of his old life, but back then it was just a regular day. Just a normal part of their family rhythms and routines.

Now Haggerty pushed through the same little iron gate. He ran up the same concrete stairs. He twisted the same knob on the same door—locked. He thought about knocking but he couldn't wait—couldn't contain his excitement and his terror long enough to stand patiently in front of this door and hope the people inside would hear him and come to him and open the latch.

So he took a half step back, then lurched forward and rammed his shoulder against the wooden door right above the knob. It swung inward with a crash, then banged against the interior wall.

That's okay. We can't stay here anyway.

"Marianna! Sonya!" He stepped through the entrance and caught the door, swinging lazily back toward him. "Marianna? It's John!"

No answer.

Haggerty stepped farther into the home. There was a small living room with a hallway running down to the left toward the bedrooms. He'd never seen most of the furniture in the living room, but he recognized Marianna's style in the matching wing-back chairs across from a comfortable-looking couch, all cream colored. There was a black coffee table and tasteful accent tables. Classical and elegant.

"Marianna? Girls? It's okay!"

He took another step forward to look down the hall, which was when he saw the pictures on the wall. Lots of them. Pictures of the children when they were young. Pictures of Sonya in high school. In college. Pictures of Marianna with her mom and her sister and other family members.

There were also pictures of him. Haggerty's own face stared back at him from several places on the wall: him holding up the children during a trip to Cedar Point, big smiles on all three faces. Him standing with Sonya at her college graduation. Him standing stiffly in his dress uniform at one of his promotion ceremonies.

And there, right in the middle of the hallway, was their wedding picture. John and Marianna. The photographer had captured the moment right after Haggerty said "I do" when she'd jumped forward into his arms and smooched him long before the priest could say anything close to, "You may kiss the bride."

Haggerty felt stunned. He stood there for several seconds, shaking his head. *I thought she threw that away. Years ago.*

"Marianna?" He peeked into the kitchen before starting his way down the hall. "Son—"

Two piles of clothes lay on the kitchen floor.

"Oh no." Ice filled Haggerty's belly and chest. His pulse pounded in his ears and his breath caught in his throat. "No, no, no."

He stepped forward and knelt in front of the first pile. Sonya's sweater had crumpled on top of blue jeans. He recognized the sweater because he'd bought it for her in Spoleto. Cashmere. Turquoise. A bit of a flare in the fabric at the end of each sleeve. She'd stopped to admire it in a shop window during one of their walks after dinner, and he'd gone back to purchase it later that evening. When he gave it to her, she told him the color reminded her of the ocean.

"Oh no. Please no." He touched the fabric gently, feeling the softness between his thumb and forefinger.

A ceramic mug had shattered on the tile floor close to Sonya's clothes. Haggerty could see a dried-up teabag in the midst of the shards.

She was standing here drinking tea. Standing right here when . . . when it happened.

Haggerty pivoted, still on his knees. The second pile of clothes was deeper in the kitchen, close to the modest bar on the front side of the island. He saw a pair of fuzzy black slippers on the tile, with some kind of pink-and-black leggings or yoga pants spilled around them.

But it was the shirt that caught his attention. His shirt.

Three chairs were tucked up under the bar, each with a high back made from wrought-iron leaves and vines painted black. A fourth chair was pulled out slightly. The chair Marianna had been using two mornings ago. She must have been perched on the edge of the seat—not standing, but not really sitting either.

When she vanished, her shirt had collapsed downward and

would have fallen to the floor to join the leggings, but one corner of the sleeve caught on an edge of the metal vine. The shirt was dangling from the chair as if hung on a clothesline. It looked deflated. Empty. Lifeless.

Haggerty raised himself to his feet. Held the shirt in his hands. It was navy blue with faded orange lettering across the front. *Chicago Bears*. He turned it over and saw the equally faded name on the back. *Payton*. His favorite player.

Another memory bloomed in Haggerty's mind with vivid clarity. He saw himself and Marianna standing in their kitchen outside of D.C. He'd come out of their room already dressed in his uniform. She was cooking breakfast and wearing his favorite shirt. When she saw him, she smiled and brought him a cup of coffee, steaming and fragrant.

"I see you've been raiding my closet again."

She smiled, then raised her arms and twirled in a circle. "Do you like my pj's?"

"Your pj's look an awful lot like my favorite shirt."

She stepped close to him then. Dangerously close. She cut right through all of his defenses and asked, "Do you mind?"

He didn't mind, but he was enjoying the moment. He pulled the material away from her waist, then let it settle back in place. "It's huge on you. It's all baggy."

"I know." She smiled up at him with a victorious grin. "But it's so comfortable. And . . ." She gathered more of the material from around her neck and held it up to her nose. Inhaled. "It reminds me of you."

He grunted. "That's something, I guess."

"It can still be your favorite shirt, you know."

He shook his head. "Nope." He pulled her to him and kissed her. "Now it's my lucky shirt."

My lucky shirt, Haggerty thought as the memory faded. *Still here. She kept it all these years. She kept wearing it after everything I did . . . after everything I failed to do.*

Feeling like he was in a dream, or maybe still stuck in memory, Haggerty lifted the shirt to his own face and inhaled deeply through his nose. The fragrances filled him. Slight scent of perfume. A familiar shampoo or conditioner. Lingering aroma that was intensely feminine and acutely familiar.

Her. The shirt smelled like her.

Haggerty sagged to his knees once more, the fabric still pressed to his face. He felt things unlocking inside him. Uncoupling. Something about the smell of his wife—his Marianna—brought home the finality of his current reality with the sharpness of a blade.

She was gone.

Sonya was gone.

They'd been taken somewhere or sent somewhere or obliterated in some unknown way, and he was still here.

Questions overwhelmed him as he began to weep. *Can I follow? Can I find them? Have I lost them forever?*

They're gone; that's all that matters. He recognized the soft hiss of that voice—one he hadn't heard for a long time. *They were taken from you.*

"Why?" He threw the word into the empty room like an accusation. "Marianna! Sonya! Where are you?"

But the questions brought no answers, which meant he had no hope. No outlet for the love still inside him that was tearing him apart.

CHAPTER 24

Lord God, please give me the strength to do this. Please give me strength to see this house and whatever is inside this house. Please lift me up right now."

Abigail spoke softly as she walked down the street toward her parents' house. It still felt strange to be praying. *Really* praying. Talking to a God she now understood was really there. Who really heard what she said—and responded.

She'd said prayers her whole life, of course. Praying had been an unquestioned ingredient in her family life for as long as she could remember, and she'd joined willingly in the ritual of recitation. "Dear God, thank You for this food." "Dear God, please bless our day." "Dear God, please protect me while I sleep."

What she was experiencing today—what she'd been experiencing for several days now—was new. It was an awareness of God's reality not as a divine presence floating somewhere in the universe, but as a divine person who was close by. As near as a whisper. A divine person who had a name, *and who knew her name*.

The sensation was more than a bit frightening but also wonderful. It felt mysterious and familiar at the same time.

"I believe in You," she said, now approaching the house. "Please help me keep believing."

And there it was: an answer. Not in words, necessarily. Not a disembodied voice speaking from the clouds. Instead, she felt an affirmation inside her own self—an echo in her heart and mind. It was an inner voice that spoke to her through emotion and through an unnamed sensation and said, *Yes. I will help you.*

"Thank You," she said, still whispering in spite of her solitary status on the street. "Thank You."

This is faith. This is what they always talked about. The pastors. The teachers. Mom and Da—

Just like that, her good feelings vanished. The warmth that had flared up in her heart at the sensation of an answered prayer flickered, then sputtered, then died. Because Mom and Dad were gone. Xavier was gone. Her little Booker was gone. Probably her siblings too. Everyone she loved had been swept up in God's glorious embrace. They were celebrating in paradise, while she slunk down this old familiar street in Millersville. Alone.

She tried to summon her father's voice: *Come on, Abi-girl, stay focused.* But the truth was, she'd been swinging back and forth between two extremes for the past two days. Sometimes it seemed like she was being torn apart by everything she'd lost. Other times it felt like she was being transformed by the faith she'd gained. Often she was stretched between both sensations at the same time.

She was aware of that stretching now as she stood in the driveway of her parents' home, a rolling suitcase by her side. It was a light suitcase, because the dragon was still slumbering in her midsection. The doctors had patched her up at the hospital before the power went out—before the attack—and they'd sent someone to drive her home the next day once the roads had been partially cleared. But she was still weak.

Am I strong enough to go inside? Can I bear it?

She shook her head to clear it, then stepped forward. Only one way to find out. Walking up to the front door, she fit her key in the lock, then stepped inside.

A man was sitting at the breakfast table. A big man.

Abigail froze midstep. Her body tensed and coiled like a spring. She gasped, her hand flying involuntarily to her chest. Then she relaxed as recognition took hold.

"Uncle John!"

"Abigail?"

He rose from the chair he'd been sitting in, and she thought he looked much slower than he had just a week earlier. Much older. He walked around the table and stood in front of her, holding out both hands.

"How . . . ? When did . . . ?" He seemed unable to comprehend her appearance out of nowhere.

For her part Abigail felt a flood of emotions as she took his hands in her own. Relief was first among them. Happiness not to be alone—to find someone she knew in this strange new world. Guilt over being glad to see this man who likely did not understand what had happened and what it meant.

"I'm glad to see you, John. Even if . . . I mean . . ." Now it was her turn to stammer.

He looked her up and down—quick and clinical. A doctor's scan. Then the shock registered on his face. He glanced down at her stomach, then stared into her eyes, mouth widening into a smile. "The baby! You've already—"

She didn't say anything. She didn't shake her head. But she saw the comprehension dawn on his face as he put two and two together. She saw the moment his expression changed from delight to confusion, then from confusion to sorrow. Then to grief.

"Oh, Abigail. I am so, so sorry."

Don't cry, she told herself. *Don't you cry*. But she already felt the tears trailing down her cheeks.

"Caleb?" He looked slightly hopeful asking the question, but she shook her head.

"Daddy and Xavier were both with me, but they both . . . they're both gone." And there it was again—the pulling in two directions. Joy and grief. Fear and gratitude.

Haggerty wrapped his arms around her, hugging her tightly. Abigail let go of the suitcase and leaned into the embrace. She didn't know this man. Not really. But his lifelong connection to her daddy lent him a paternal air that felt comforting. And familiar. And safe.

She let her head fall down to rest on his chest and felt his arms holding her close. There was something basic about this personal contact—maybe the simple humanity of being held and cared for in this way—that helped her feel like a person again. She felt reconnected to herself somehow. Reconnected to her body and her thoughts and her emotions.

Abigail's tears became sobs as the memories of four days ago overwhelmed her: the sensation of birth and new life replaced by the hollow ache of loss. Of nothingness. *Oh, my boy! Oh, my Booker.* The name was a valve that turned sobs into rivers, and she poured herself out in the arms of this man who was a stranger but not a stranger, weeping and shaking. Lamenting the loss and clinging to her only source of hope. *Take care of him, Lord Jesus. Take care of my boy.*

Haggerty didn't speak. He didn't move. He just held her tightly and let her grieve.

She didn't know how long it lasted, whether one minute or five. But eventually the river ebbed, then ran dry. She breathed in and out, finding a rhythm that was almost like sleep. Still held tightly in the protective power of kindness.

When she finally raised her head, he opened his arms to let her step back. "Here." He pulled out a chair. "Let's sit, okay? It's okay."

She sat, and he joined her at the table. She noticed a bottle of beer on the tabletop. It was open but seemed full.

"Thank you," She wiped her eyes. "Oh, I'm sorry." There was a large wet spot on the front of his button-up shirt. "I think I got you there."

He looked down and touched the wet spot, then smiled. "I think that's gonna be the least of our problems today." He looked down at the ground and gestured with his chin. "Why the suitcase?"

"Oh, just clothes and stuff from ho—from my house. Too many pictures there. Too many memories." She stared steadily into his eyes as she spoke, willing him to understand.

It seemed he did, because he patted her hand and said no more.

"Do you understand what's happened, John?" There was still a quaver in her voice as she changed the subject, and she cleared her throat. "Not the explosions and the blackout and . . . and all that, but when people vanished four days ago? The Great Disappearance. Do you know what that was?"

He was already shaking his head. "No. I don't know anything." He was looking over her shoulder, not meeting her eyes. "Do you know what it was?"

She braced herself to push through any embarrassment as she prepared to answer, but . . . there was none. She felt confident in what she believed, and she was pleased when that confidence infused her words.

"It was the Rapture."

"The Rapture." He repeated the word with a surprising level of disdain. "Your dad was telling me about that. Oh, man . . . I guess it was only a couple weeks ago." He rubbed his eyes for a moment, then turned back to her. "So you feel like God is responsible for all these people being taken. Marianna and Sonya. Children. Everyone."

"He didn't take people, John. The Rapture isn't about God stealing people from our world. It's a rescue mission."

"Rescue." Such bitterness hardened his voice. She understood. She carried it as well, but the feeling was gilded with hope in a way that made it bearable. At least for now. "Rescue from what, Abigail?"

"From what's coming. From the next seven years. From . . . argh." She sighed. There was so much to tell—so much she'd been told over the years or read about or heard from different sermons or messages. How could she boil everything down to a single conversation?

"Stick to the basics, Abi-girl." Now she did hear her father's voice in her head. It was comforting. *"Stick to the basics and tell the truth."*

"Honestly, do you want to talk about this right now?"

He grasped the bottle in his fingers and tapped it on the table a couple of times. Then a couple more times. "Yeah, I want to hear what you believe."

She heard the subtle stress in "you," and she was surprised to feel compassion for someone so much older and more experienced than herself.

"The Bible says God's already planned out all the pages of history—past, present, and future. You know about Jesus, right? He became a person, He died on the cross to save us, and then He rose from the grave. You're familiar with all that?"

He nodded. "The gospel. Yes."

"Okay." She'd heard from her dad on a couple of occasions that Haggerty was hostile to Christianity, but he seemed to have at least a working knowledge of biblical claims. She pressed forward. "Ever since the resurrection, we've been living in the age of grace. That's the period of history where the church spread throughout the world. God was giving all people a chance to hear the gospel and be saved—to accept His gift of forgiveness." She paused a moment. "Does that . . . ?"

He twirled a finger in front of his chest. *Keep going.*

"Right . . . well, the Bible says at some point God is going to turn the page of human history. That we would move from the age of grace to the age of judgment. That's the time God set aside to punish the evil and sin in our world. All the corruption and violence and greed. All the ways people have rebelled against Him and harmed one another. That's all going to be dealt with in the age of judgment."

"Judgment," said Haggerty. "Punishment. But I keep hearing that God is love. How does that square?"

"Wouldn't you say confronting evil is a loving act? Wouldn't you say justice is connected with love?"

He didn't answer, but he kept looking at her. He seemed to be paying attention.

"The Rapture is the turning point between those two ages. It's the last second in the age of grace and the first second in the age of judgment. That's what we experienced four days ago, John. That's what happened to my dad. And my husband. And my . . . and my son."

Oh, Booker. Oh, my Xavier. The grief of her separation was still real—still suffocating on so many levels. *But it's not forever! I have to remember that. I will see them again.* The knowledge was an anchor not only for their futures but also for her own.

Suddenly she remembered something Haggerty had said earlier. "Did you say Marianna and Sonya are gone?"

"Yeah, I found their clothes, but they . . . vanished."

She smiled. "That's wonderful! I had no idea they—"

He was on his feet in an instant, his hands twisting and pulling in his hair. "Wonderful?" he cried out with grief and pain. *"Wonderful?"*

His intensity made her feel abashed and ashamed at her lack of consideration. Her lack of compassion. This man had lost as much as she had—his child, his wife, and his best friend. But there had been no corresponding gain. There had been no baptism into belief, no anchor to hold him steady in the chaotic waters threatening to pull him under.

"I'm sorry, John. That was a stupid thing to say. I just mean there's a lot of bad stuff that's about to happen, and the people who vanished get to be spared from all that. They've been rescued."

Haggerty folded his arms across his chest, looking down at her. His head was tilted to the side, as if he was considering her. Studying her. He seemed like he wanted to say something but was holding back.

"What?" she asked. "What are you thinking?"

He pointed a finger at her. "If you know all this stuff . . . if you believe all this stuff . . . the Rapture and everything else . . . then why are you still here?"

Ouch. It was a painful question but fair. One she'd been thinking about quite a lot over the past few days.

"There's a difference between knowing and believing. A big difference." She sighed. "My mom and dad were always so serious about their faith. It was a huge part of our lives. I learned how to say all the right things, and after Simon I never really wanted to do any of the rebellious stuff, so . . . I don't know."

She felt silly trying to explain it, but Haggerty surprised her.

"You learned how to pretend." He spoke more softly now. More gently. "How to fit in."

She nodded. "It was like being part of a culture. I went along. And parts of it were nice, really. A lot of it was nice. The stories, making friends at church, knowing what was right and wrong. I liked all that, but . . . but I never took it seriously. I never made it real for myself, you know?"

"Yeah, I know." He sat again and put his head in his hands.

Abigail picked up the bottle. "I thought you didn't drink? I always thought that was because of your dad getting arrested and all that."

Haggerty raised his head, focusing on the bottle. "I don't drink. Never had a sip of alcohol because of my dad. Because of everything he said he was and everything I saw him do." He reached out and picked up the bottle. It looked almost comically small in his hand.

"I guess I started this habit five or six years ago," he said. "Maybe a little longer. Whenever I went to a nice restaurant, I'd buy a beer. Let the waiter pour it out in a glass, but never take a sip. Or if I was home by myself, I'd take a bottle out of the fridge and open it. Let it sit there for a while. Then pour it out."

Abigail felt confused. "You open it just to pour it out?"

He nodded. "I did it when I felt something I knew would have made him want a drink." He looked at her. "My dad, I mean. If I felt lonely. Or stressed out. Or angry. Or proud because I accomplished something important. Then I'd open a bottle, just like he always opened a bottle. But I never took the step that destroyed his life. That destroyed all our lives, really."

"So, you were proving what—that you were different from him?"

"That I was better than him. That's what I always believed."

Abigail realized he was crying, which shocked her. This huge man, this indomitable force, was weeping right in front of her. Silently and openly.

"I don't believe that anymore. My dad was a drunk and a hypocrite. He caused a lot of harm to his family because he couldn't beat his addiction, and it made him mean. It made him crazy. But look at me." He wiped his palm down both cheeks to brush away the tears. "I'm a hypocrite. I've made it my life's mission to help people, but I let my own son die because I didn't listen to my wife. Then I abandoned my wife and daughter because I couldn't deal with my own failure. I threw myself at promotion after promotion. I let everybody clap their hands and tell me how great I was because I was saving lives. But when my wife and daughter needed me most, I left them again to save the world. And I failed. And they're gone. And I have nothing."

He held Abigail's eyes for several seconds, then looked back at the bottle. "And I did it all without taking a single drink."

Abigail had no idea what to say, so she didn't say anything. She just waited.

"I was sitting here all morning before you came through that door. Hours and hours. Sitting here and staring at this bottle. This is the first time I ever really wanted to take a drink. To see what it's like." He looked at her. "I still don't know what I'm gonna do."

To her great surprise, Abigail felt her previous compassion drain away, even in spite of his brokenness. Even in spite of everything they'd both experienced over the past few days. Now she felt angry.

"I know what you're going to do, John Haggerty." She noted the way his eyebrows rose toward his scalp. *Good. Be surprised. And pay attention.*

"You're going to pour out that beer in that kitchen sink." She pointed over his shoulder. "Then you're going to sit down here with me, and we're going to make a plan. I know that because you're a soldier, and there's a war coming. Not a war between America and China or anything like that. This is a war between good and evil, and we've all got to pick a side."

She leaned forward. She felt the intensity of the truth boiling up from inside, rushing to get out. To be revealed.

"The people we love are gone because they made the right choice. They're in a wonderful place right now, while you and I and billions of other people are left behind—left here in the middle of hell. But that doesn't mean we're hopeless. That doesn't mean we can't see them again. You have to understand that!"

"See who?" His voice was rough. Hoarse.

"See them all. My dad. My mom. My husband and my . . . my boy. But also Marianna and Sonya and Ryan." She knew what had happened to his son, and she saw the pain written on his face. "They're still out there, John. They've been rescued, but they're coming back. And they're coming soon."

"Back?" She heard the agony in that word. The confusion. "What are you talking about?"

There's so much to say, she thought. Whole books had been written about these topics. Entire libraries. How could she make him understand?

Then she had an idea. She got up without saying anything and walked over to the study. Her dad's study. His Bible was on the desk—exactly where he always left it when he finished reading. It was big, black, and worn out, with rumpled pages and scuffs all up and down the leather cover. She knew he'd written notes on most of the pages inside, and she was eager to read them. But for now she walked back to Haggerty and placed the book gently in the middle of the table.

"I told you, John. It's all laid out in the Bible. Everything that's about to happen. The age of judgment will last for seven years. It's called the Tribulation. There's going to be a ruler who takes over the world. The Antichrist. You've heard about him, right?"

"I . . . Abigail, I don't . . ." He seemed stunned again. Stuck.

"Doesn't matter. The point is, the whole world—everyone who's been left behind—is going to get divided into two groups. Most people will follow the Antichrist. He'll consolidate power and try to lead a rebellion against God. But there will be lots of people . . . millions of us who resist. Millions who choose good over evil. And if we can stay strong until the end, we'll be reunited with those we love when they come back at the end of the seven years. The end of the Tribulation."

Arrrgggh! She yelled at herself internally. *You're making this sound so complicated!*

"Seven years," he said. "Seven years . . . and then they come back? Back to earth?"

Abigail nodded. "Seven years. I don't want to lie to you, because it's going to be terrible. The Antichrist will take over, and he will be ruthless. There will be wars. And famines. And plagues. And natural disasters at a level you've never even imagined. It's going to be hell on earth, but we have hope. We have a secret that can bring us through."

"What hope? What secret?"

The look of longing on his face brought back her compassion. He was devastated by loss and grief and pain—just like she was. He needed the hope she had found if he were to have any chance of staying afloat.

"That we win. That's the secret. Everything that's about to happen has already been described in the Bible. I know exactly what's going to come, and I can teach it to you. We can make it through together. But you have to make a choice." She looked at the bottle still clutched in his hand. "You can drink it, John. You can drink every bottle you find, and you can become a sheep that gets led to slaughter two years from now or five years or seven at the most. Or you can pour that out and fight for what's good. Fight for what's right. Fight for the people we love."

She watched him, studying his face as it worked and writhed. She could see the battle tearing at him from the inside.

After a long moment, he stood and walked to the sink. She heard a *clink* as he set the bottle down. Then she heard the *glub glub* and *fizz* as the beer went down the drain.

Haggerty sat back down. His face was sober. Stern. "Tell me what you know." He gestured with his chin to the old Bible. "Tell me the truth. I'm listening."

DISCUSSION QUESTIONS

1. How is hope portrayed as a driving force in the novel, and what role does it play in character motivation and narrative progression? If you are familiar with Dr. Jeremiah's other works, do you see any correlation between his insights on resilience and looking toward a divine plan?

2. What significance does faith hold in the narrative? Discuss how characters like Caleb Johnson incorporate spirituality into their coping mechanisms. Did you resonate with a specific character and their relationship to faith?

3. How does the novel show the theme of redemption, especially in John Haggerty's character arc and his search for personal reconciliation?

4. Which characters in this story did you most resonate with? Why?

5. In what ways is John Haggerty successful? What are the areas you see in which he could grow?

6. How do the environmental and natural disasters described in the novel correlate with Dr. Jeremiah's references to signs of the times in his nonfiction work?

7. What themes in the book resonated most with you, and why?

8. Were there any moments in the book that surprised or shocked you? How did they shift your perspective?

9. Which relationships in the book did you find most compelling, and why?

10. What moral dilemmas presented in the book stood out to you, and how would you have handled them?

11. What events in the story did you notice as having drawn inspiration from biblical prophecy? How did you feel about the way they played out?

12. What do you anticipate happening in the next book—based on what you might already know of Dr. Jeremiah's work, what you know of the Bible, or what you predict from the story in general?

13. If you could ask the author one question about the book, what would it be?

From the Publisher

GREAT BOOKS

ARE EVEN BETTER WHEN THEY'RE SHARED!

Help other readers find this one:

- Post a review at your favorite online bookseller

- Post a picture on a social media account and share why you enjoyed it

- Send a note to a friend who would also love it—or better yet, give them a copy

Thanks for reading!

LOOKING FOR MORE GREAT READS? LOOK NO FURTHER!

THOMAS NELSON
Since 1798

Visit us online to learn more:
tnzfiction.com

Or scan the below code and sign up to receive email updates
on new releases, giveaways, book deals, and more:

@tnzfiction

WANT TO LEARN MORE?

Check out the following excerpt from
Dr. David Jeremiah's nonfiction!

Available in print, e-book, and audio

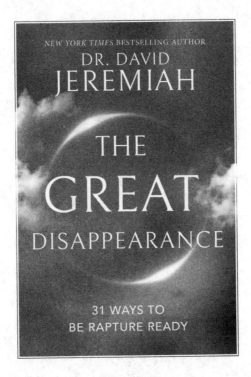

W Publishing Group

An Imprint of Thomas Nelson

Chapter 1

Chaos on Earth

Imagine a Moment coming soon to our planet that will change everything and everyone forever. Imagine ambivalent, unaware people conducting their business, scurrying around, trying to make sense of their lives. Depending on where you look on our globe, the scene may be very different, yet in many ways it's the same.

In the United States, in China, in Argentina, in Indonesia, in Kazakhstan.

People loving, laboring, longing.

All over the world that day, billions will be eating and drinking, marrying and giving in marriage, celebrating birthdays, battling sickness, digging graves. People will be getting up or going to bed, working or playing, enjoying their pleasures or indulging their vices.

I try to imagine these things happening all over the world, from the rising of the sun to the place where it sets. What will people think when the Moment comes?

I wonder what the headlines will be on the morning of that day. Wars and rumors of war. Earthquakes. Famines. Loud voices deceiving many. New laws. Old lies. New dilemmas. Nation rising against nation, kingdom against kingdom. Parts of the world may report an earthquake, a famine, or a plague.

Will the news be written by artificial intelligence? Will people be able to tell truth from fiction?

I wonder what the weather will be that day. Sunny in one place, cloudy in another? Something is about to happen in the skies—if only people would look up in expectation! In the unseen realms, the glory of the Lord is gathering, the angels are assembling, and the skies are preparing to part. But most people will be looking down at their phones, addicted to the newest messages or oldest sins.

I wonder what Christians will be doing that day. Will they be as surprised as everyone else when the Rapture occurs? Will they be eager, ready, and waiting?

Can't you see the masses moving about as usual? Millions of people walking around all day on the streets of New York, Tokyo, Mumbai, worried about their money, wondering about their relationships, anxious about their images, following the world stock markets, the latest music, the latest sports scores.

It will be an ordinary day on this globe—until, suddenly, it isn't.

One day soon, the world will face the Great Disappearance!

Billions of people. Gone in a flash more powerful than an atomic burst, yet silent. Invisible! Sudden! Inexplicable!

Try to imagine this extraordinary Moment on planet Earth. Every single follower of Jesus Christ, as well as all those under the age of accountability—all the babies, young children, and mentally disabled—gone in a flash, along with all those who have died in Christ.

Bodies will disappear from their coffins at funeral homes all over the world. Patients will vanish from hospital beds. Babies from their cribs. Children from their classrooms.

Imagine cars flying down the freeway with missing drivers, planes with missing pilots, nuclear submarines with missing commanders, nations with missing leaders, parents with missing children.

In various parts of the world, Christian congregations will be meeting for worship. Suddenly the buildings will be empty—or nearly so—as the churches resume their services in the sky! Soldiers will be missing in action. Emergency responders will find their numbers depleted. Prisons will be partially depopulated, especially those filled with Christians under persecution.

News reports will spread like wildfire, but the Christian press will be strangely silent. There'll be no believers to report the news.

People will frantically search for their loved ones, but phone calls will go to voicemail and texts will be unanswered.

In today's world, just one missing-person case can grip the nation. What about a billion? What will people think? What panic will they feel? What theories will they embrace?

The FBI has been tracking missing-person cases for years. The bureau has a website devoted to it with picture after picture of those whose whereabouts are unknown. These people seemingly just vanished. Many times foul play is involved. In virtually every case families are torn apart with grief, community life is disrupted, and law enforcement is focused on solving the mystery.

The oldest active missing-person case in America involves Marvin Clark, who vanished October 30, 1926, while on his way to visit his daughter in Portland, Oregon. He traveled by bus. He boarded the bus in Tigard, Oregon, but failed to get off at his destination. He simply disappeared. He was in his early seventies at the time, and his case is still open. Authorities are still looking for his remains—if there are any.[1]

One of the strangest missing-person cases in Canada involved thirty-two-year-old Granger Taylor of British Columbia. On November 29, 1980, he left a note to his parents saying: "Dear Mother and Father, I have gone away to walk aboard an alien spaceship, as reoccurring dreams assured a 42 month interstellar voyage to explore the vast universe, then return. I am leaving behind all my possessions to you as I will no longer . . . require the use of any."[2]

No one has seen Granger since.

For the record, I don't believe he was abducted by aliens, but I can see how the world will be gripped by a thousand conspiracy theories in the aftermath of the coming Rapture. Global panic will help prepare the way for a one-world government, the emergence of an ironfisted ruler, and the onset of the Tribulation.

It will be utter chaos on an unimaginable scale for those left behind.

For most of my life I've been thinking about this very day: the predicted Moment when Jesus will reenter earth's atmosphere for His church. The reason I'm asking you to imagine it is because I've been doing the same for decades. It's hard to get your head around the pandemonium that will engulf our planet when Jesus fulfills His promise to come for His people.

I think it helps us to visualize that day as best we can.

After I graduated from seminary, I became the youth director of a large New Jersey church. It takes special skill to work with teenagers, and I don't mind telling you I was nervous about relating to them and them to me.

It didn't help when the senior pastor told me that my first contact with the group would be at a summer conference where I was to teach them a weeklong study on Bible prophecy. I've never had a more challenging assignment!

Thankfully, someone had given me a copy of a fictitious newspaper designed to show the events and headlines on the day of the Rapture. The headlines said:

Millions of People Disappear! Airplanes Crash!
Children Vanish! Panic in the Streets!

On the first night of the conference, I asked a few kids to play the historic role of newsboys and go throughout the group, hollering "Extra! Extra! Read all about it!" Soon, the teenagers were devouring the paper.

The lead article began: "At 12:05 this morning a telephone operator reported three frantic calls regarding missing relatives. Within fifteen minutes all communications were jammed with similar inquiries. A spot check from around the nation found the same situation in every city. Sobbing husbands sought information about the mysterious disappearance of their wives. One husband reported, 'I turned the light on to ask my wife if she remembered to set the clock, but she was gone. Her bedclothes were there. Her watch was on the floor, but she vanished.'"

Another headline read:

Throngs in the Nation Die of Heart Attacks

I can tell you those teenagers didn't just sit idly through my talks about prophecy. They wanted to know the details!

This wasn't hypothetical, I told them, but prophetic. The same Bible that describes our Lord Jesus ascending into the sky and disappearing into the clouds also tells us of His imminent, impending return for His people. For reasons I'll explain in this book, we call it the Rapture. It's the resurrection of those who are dead in Christ, immediately followed by the "snatching up" of the final generation of Christians on earth.

Dr. Tim LaHaye pondered this approaching day at length. He said that at the Moment of the Rapture "a million conversations will end midsentence. A million phones will suddenly go dead. A woman will reach for her husband's hand in the dark, and no one will be there. A man will turn with a laugh to slap a colleague on the back and his hand will move through empty air. A basketball player will make a length-of-floor pass to a teammate streaking downcourt and find there is no one there to receive it."[3]

This isn't science fiction, conspiracy theory, or mindless speculation. When Christ comes for His people, it will be in the twinkling of an eye. The trumpet will sound, the Lord will shout with the voice of authority, the dead will rise, and we who are alive will be caught up in the air to meet the Lord in the sky.

Between the resurrected and the raptured, billions of people will exit this planet in an instant. But billions more will be left behind. It will be chaos on our globe but incredible, glorious joy in the skies.

This is the Rapture—the Great Disappearance. I've been studying this in Scripture all my adult life, and now I want to write about it as fully as I can. It's vital to know what the Bible says about this coming day, the next event on God's prophetic agenda for the earth.

I think you'll be fascinated, motivated, and highly encouraged as you study the pages to come. Most of all I hope you'll be well prepared for that day.

It's one thing to try to imagine that day and another to see what the Bible truly says about its who, why, when, where, and how. I believe the Scriptures are clear on this subject, and I want to show you the pertinent passages in God's Word that discuss it. That's because we're not just to imagine it but to anticipate it with all our hearts and look forward to it with all our souls.

Don't put this book down yet. Just turn the page, and let's get started. After all, time is short. I can't wait for you to see what's just ahead. The Moment can come at any moment.

Even now!

Chapter 2

A Great Day

In all of his mansions, there's not a room big enough for all his awards. Sir Paul McCartney may go down in history as the greatest musician of all time—a founding member of the Beatles and a man who became, as the *Guinness Book of World Records* puts it, the planet's "most successful musician and composer in popular music history."[1]

His fans know it's been a rough ride. Some of McCartney's hardest days were after the Beatles broke up. McCartney tumbled into a dark place. He stayed in his Scottish home smoking pot and getting drunk. He lost hope. After all, how do you follow the Beatles? Is there life after that kind of ride?

McCartney's turnaround started when the chords of a song came to him, one he'd worked on from time to time. The music made him feel optimistic, and he crafted it into a song for his children. He didn't record it until years later, but for him it was a personal song of hope.

He called the song "Great Day." The lyrics talked about a future day that was coming. And it was going to be a "Great Day"! And it wouldn't be long in coming, so it was something to look forward to . . . something to celebrate.

McCartney explained, "I liked the idea of a song saying that help is coming and there's a bright light on the horizon. I've got absolutely no evidence for this, but I like to believe it. It helps to lift my spirits."[2]

Paul McCartney doesn't realize how close he is to the truth. There is a Great Day coming—and it won't be long. There's a bright light on the horizon, and we have plenty of evidence for it. We have biblical evidence, and, boy, does it lift our spirits!

Jesus Christ is coming back for us—and soon!

If only McCartney realized that. If only the whole world—this world filled with hopelessness and despair—realized this truth of Scripture: "The great day of the LORD is near; it is near and hastens quickly" (Zeph. 1:14).

The apostle Paul talked excitedly about the heavenly crown awaiting him, "which the Lord, the righteous Judge, will give me on that great day of his return. And not just to me but to all those whose lives show that they are eagerly looking forward to his coming back again" (2 Tim. 4:8 TLB).

This is a book about a Great Day that's coming—the day of the Rapture. The exact date is already circled on God's calendar. We aren't privy to those records, but the year, month, day, hour, minute, and second are locked into God's program for our planet.

The Rapture is an event in the impending future when all of us, living or deceased, who have put our trust in Jesus Christ for salvation and eternal life will be suddenly caught up from this earth into the heavens. We'll be reunited with loved ones who have preceded us in death. We'll be met by the Lord Himself, who will usher us into heaven to live forever in perfect fellowship with God.

John Walvoord considered the Rapture a central event in biblical prophecy, writing, "The Rapture of the church is one of the most important practical prophecies in Scripture for believers today. It is an essential part of the many other prophecies in

Scriptures. Though the Rapture is only a small fraction of the large body of prophetic Scripture, it stands out as one of the most important."[3]

Why is this day so great?

I'll deal with that question throughout this book, but let me give you some previews.

IT'S A GREAT DAY OF HOPE

The Bible uses the word *hope* repeatedly to describe the feelings we should currently have because of this imminent event. Peter called it a "living hope" (1 Pet. 1:3), and he said we could rest fully on that hope as we await the coming of Jesus (v. 13). The writer of the book of Hebrews called it "the hope set before us" (6:18) and "an anchor of the soul" (v. 19). The apostle Paul called it "the blessed hope" (Titus 2:13); he said this hope will never disappoint us (Rom. 5:5).

When the Bible uses the word *hope* in this sense, it doesn't simply mean a desire that may or may not occur. It means the "eager expectation" for something that will certainly happen, that is impending and swiftly coming.

Biblical hope is the excitement we feel today about what Jesus will do tomorrow.

In other words, when we grasp the reality of the approaching Rapture, it brings today's events into a happy perspective. There is an end to evil. There is an expiration date on suffering. There's coming a Great Day when we'll realize the sufferings of this present world aren't worth comparing to the glory that's about to be revealed (Rom. 8:18).

The energy that surges through us as we ponder this reality—well, that's what the Bible calls *hope*.

It's a Great Day of Homecoming

The Rapture will also be a day of homecoming when we'll be reunited with the entire family of Jesus Christ and we'll meet those who have gone before. In his primary passage about the Rapture in 1 Thessalonians 4, Paul made a point to emphasize this aspect of the Great Day so that bereaved Christians will not "sorrow as others who have no hope" (v. 13).

Mark Hitchcock wrote, "The truth of the Rapture is a source of supernatural comfort and hope to all of God's people when a believing loved one or friend goes home to be with the Lord. These words [in 1 Thessalonians 4] have certainly been read at thousands of funerals throughout the centuries."[4]

Seeing that statement gave me a jolt! I've often read 1 Thessalonians 4:13–18 at funerals and graveside services, but I'd never thought another pastor was doing the same 100 years ago, and 1,000 years ago, and 1,500 years ago, and 1,900 years ago. All of us standing by open graves, reading the same passage, literally from the days of Paul till now. And undoubtedly on this very day around the world, godly pastors are reading this text at the homegoing of faithful Christians!

Perhaps no words have ever given more hope to more people in more places during moments of raw grief.

It's a Great Day of Healing

As we'll see, the moment of the Rapture is going to be the greatest healing event in human history. Talk about a healing service! During His ministry on earth, Jesus healed quite a few people; but on this day He is going to heal all His believers instantly and totally and eternally, whether they are still alive or have passed away, of any and all ailments of body, mind, or soul.

Imagine a dreaded case like cancer. (Many of us don't have to imagine; we've experienced it.) We're at the hospital receiving doses of medication that seem, at the moment, to make us ever sicker. Suddenly, in the twinkling of an eye, we're totally healed. Old age will be reversed, and physical deformities will be corrected—all in an instant. The total healing of every follower of Christ, immediately.

The dead will be raised imperishable, and all of us who remain will be caught up to heaven with new, glorified bodies. I can't wait to get to the chapter that deals with that promise in detail.

It's a Great Day of Happiness

The very word *rapture* has become a term describing unbridled happiness. People talk about a rapturous event, and this will be the ultimate one. In fact, thinking about the Rapture brings me happiness right now, which is why I'm writing this book—to share the same wonderful information with you.

But our happiness now can't compare to the rapture of the actual Rapture!

And think of this: it's not just a happiness for you and me. Imagine how elated the resurrected saints will feel, how delighted the angels will be, and think of the joy that will flood over the face of our Lord Jesus as He gathers His children home.

Psychologists often talk about "mental triggers." Sometimes these are negative. A certain sound, smell, or memory can trigger a negative emotion, such as for those suffering post-traumatic issues. But there are positive triggers also. A favorite Scripture framed on the wall. A midmorning pause to breathe deeply. A slogan to get the day started. An uplifting hymn.

During the course of this book, I'm going to quote many, many verses of the Bible. Some will be from three major passages in John 14, 1 Corinthians 15, and 1 Thessalonians 4. But there will be many others—too many for me to count right now. I encourage you to select one or more of those verses. Be looking for them. When we get to a verse that especially speaks to you and brings you a ray of cheer, underline or highlight it. Then pick two or three of your favorite ones, memorize them, turn them into little songs, post them where you can see them daily, share them, and let them serve as positive mental triggers for the rest of your life.

The Rapture brings us happiness as we ponder it now, followed by unspeakable joy when it occurs.

It's a Great Day of Holiness

The Great Rapture Day will also be characterized by total and all-encompassing holiness. When we're caught up into the sky, we'll leave behind all our faults and failures, our shame and embarrassment, our weaknesses and woes. We'll be transformed not just physically but spiritually. Made holy in every way!

When we receive Christ as Savior, we're declared holy in God's sight. But our condition doesn't always match our position. Every day we're striving to live up to the supreme example of Christ. But on that future day we'll become holy in every thought, word, deed, and attitude.

The apostle Paul said, "Being confident of this, that he who began a good work in you will carry it on to completion until the day of Christ Jesus" (Phil. 1:6 NIV).

Galatians 5:5 says, "But we who live by the Spirit eagerly wait to receive by faith the righteousness God has promised to us" (NLT). I don't know about you, but I'm ready to get beyond the reach of the devil and his temptations.

So there's a bright light on the horizon, and we have plenty of evidence. It's going to be the greatest of all great days—the best day of your life. A Great Day of hope, homecoming, healing, happiness, and holiness. It's going to be a Great Day with Him who is preparing at this very moment to return in the skies *above* us and *for* us.

For the first time ever, the whole family of Christ will be together. No one will be left behind. If you don't think that's important, ask Van Ho.

One day during the Vietnam War, this little Vietnamese girl woke up as usual when the rooster crowed at five. But something was wrong. Her mother, sisters, and brother were gone. She went around the house, but her family had vanished. During the night, they had escaped from the invading Communists. Van Ho was too young for the rigorous trip, and her grandmother was too old, so they were left behind together to care for each other temporarily. When the rest of the family made it to America, they began desperately trying to find a way for the two who were left behind to join them.

In time, Van Ho was reunited with her family in Canada, and her first day there was unbelievable. For the first time, she saw modern conveniences like a bathroom with running water, a television with moving pictures, and cold milk from the refrigerator.

She later wrote, "I was still scared about leaving everything behind that was familiar. I was not sure about Canadian food or the snow. It bothered me that I couldn't understand everything my family talked about. . . . But I didn't care. For the first time since

I was three years old, my whole family was together again. Nobody was left behind."[5]

That's what Jesus and Paul want us to know. For those of us who are followers of Christ, the Lord has gone ahead of us, but we're not forgotten. The whole family of God will be together again on that great and coming day.

None of His children will be left behind.

Certainly not you!

ABOUT THE AUTHOR

Dr. David Jeremiah is the founder of Turning Point, an international ministry committed to providing Christians with sound Bible teaching through radio and television, the internet, live events, and resource materials and books. He is the author of more than fifty books, including *The Book of Signs, The Great Disappearance, Where Do We Go from Here?* and *The Coming Golden Age.*

Dr. Jeremiah serves as the senior pastor of Shadow Mountain Community Church in El Cajon, California. He and his wife, Donna, have four children and twelve grandchildren.

Sam O'Neal is Senior Writer for Write Great Stories, Inc., where he helps produce great stories that advance the kingdom of God.

www.WriteGreatStories.com